Les Misérables

Volume IV: The Idyll in the Rue Plumet and the Epic in the Rue St. Denis

Les Misérables

Volume IV: The Idyll in the Rue Plumet and the Epic in the Rue St. Denis

Victor Hugo

MINT EDITIONS

Les Misérables was first published in 1862.

This edition published by Mint Editions 2020.

ISBN 9781513279794 | E-ISBN 9781513284811

Published by Mint Editions®

MINT EDITIONS

minteditionbooks.com

Publishing Director: Jennifer Newens
Design & Production: Rachel Lopez Metzger
Project Manager: Micaela Clark
Translated by: Isabel F. Hapgood
Typesetting: Westchester Publishing Services

More in this Series
Les Misérables Volume I: Fantine P|9781513267449
E|9781513272443
Les Misérables Volume II: Cosette P|9781513263465
E|9781513264011
Les Misérables Volume III: Marius P|9781513279787
E|9781513284804
Les Misérables Volume V: Jean Valjean P|9781513279800
E|9781513284828

Contents

BOOK FIRST
A FEW PAGES OF HISTORY

I

Well Cut

1831 and 1832, the two years which are immediately connected with the Revolution of July, form one of the most peculiar and striking moments of history. These two years rise like two mountains midway between those which precede and those which follow them. They have a revolutionary grandeur. Precipices are to be distinguished there. The social masses, the very assizes of civilization, the solid group of superposed and adhering interests, the century-old profiles of the ancient French formation, appear and disappear in them every instant, athwart the storm clouds of systems, of passions, and of theories. These appearances and disappearances have been designated as movement and resistance. At intervals, truth, that daylight of the human soul, can be descried shining there.

This remarkable epoch is decidedly circumscribed and is beginning to be sufficiently distant from us to allow of our grasping the principal lines even at the present day.

We shall make the attempt.

The Restoration had been one of those intermediate phases, hard to define, in which there is fatigue, buzzing, murmurs, sleep, tumult, and which are nothing else than the arrival of a great nation at a halting-place.

These epochs are peculiar and mislead the politicians who desire to convert them to profit. In the beginning, the nation asks nothing but repose; it thirsts for but one thing, peace; it has but one ambition, to be small. Which is the translation of remaining tranquil. Of great events, great hazards, great adventures, great men, thank God, we have seen enough, we have them heaped higher than our heads. We would exchange Cæsar for Prusias, and Napoleon for the King of Yvetot. "What a good little king was he!" We have marched since daybreak, we have reached the evening of a long and toilsome day; we have made our first change with Mirabeau, the second with Robespierre, the third with Bonaparte; we are worn out. Each one demands a bed.

Devotion which is weary, heroism which has grown old, ambitions which are sated, fortunes which are made, seek, demand, implore, solicit, what? A shelter. They have it. They take possession of peace, of tranquillity, of leisure; behold, they are content. But, at the same time certain facts arise, compel recognition, and knock at the door in their turn. These facts are the products of revolutions and wars, they are, they exist, they have the right to install themselves in society, and they do install themselves therein; and most of the time, facts are the stewards of the household and fouriers who do nothing but prepare lodgings for principles.

This, then, is what appears to philosophical politicians:—

At the same time that weary men demand repose, accomplished facts demand guarantees. Guarantees are the same to facts that repose is to men.

This is what England demanded of the Stuarts after the Protector; this is what France demanded of the Bourbons after the Empire.

These guarantees are a necessity of the times. They must be accorded. Princes "grant" them, but in reality, it is the force of things which gives them. A profound truth, and one useful to know, which the Stuarts did not suspect in 1662 and which the Bourbons did not even obtain a glimpse of in 1814.

The predestined family, which returned to France when Napoleon fell, had the fatal simplicity to believe that it was itself which bestowed, and that what it had bestowed it could take back again; that the House of Bourbon possessed the right divine, that France possessed nothing, and that the political right conceded in the charter of Louis XVIII was merely a branch of the right divine, was detached by the House of Bourbon and graciously given to the people until such day as it should please the King to reassume it. Still, the House of Bourbon should have felt, from the displeasure created by the gift, that it did not come from it.

This house was churlish to the nineteenth century. It put on an ill-tempered look at every development of the nation. To make use of a trivial word, that is to say, of a popular and a true word, it looked glum. The people saw this.

It thought it possessed strength because the Empire had been carried away before it like a theatrical stage-setting. It did not perceive that it had, itself, been brought in in the same fashion. It did not perceive that it also lay in that hand which had removed Napoleon.

It thought that it had roots, because it was the past. It was mistaken; it formed a part of the past, but the whole past was France. The roots of French society were not fixed in the Bourbons, but in the nations. These obscure and lively roots constituted, not the right of a family, but the history of a people. They were everywhere, except under the throne.

The House of Bourbon was to France the illustrious and bleeding knot in her history, but was no longer the principal element of her destiny, and the necessary base of her politics. She could get along without the Bourbons; she had done without them for two and twenty years; there had been a break of continuity; they did not suspect the fact. And how should they have suspected it, they who fancied that Louis XVII reigned on the 9th of Thermidor, and that Louis XVIII was reigning at the battle of Marengo? Never, since the origin of history, had princes been so blind in the presence of facts and the portion of divine authority which facts contain and promulgate. Never had that pretension here below which is called the right of kings denied to such a point the right from on high.

A capital error which led this family to lay its hand once more on the guarantees "granted" in 1814, on the concessions, as it termed them. Sad. A sad thing! What it termed its concessions were our conquests; what it termed our encroachments were our rights.

When the hour seemed to it to have come, the Restoration, supposing itself victorious over Bonaparte and well-rooted in the country, that is to say, believing itself to be strong and deep, abruptly decided on its plan of action, and risked its stroke. One morning it drew itself up before the face of France, and, elevating its voice, it contested the collective title and the individual right of the nation to sovereignty, of the citizen to liberty. In other words, it denied to the nation that which made it a nation, and to the citizen that which made him a citizen.

This is the foundation of those famous acts which are called the ordinances of July. The Restoration fell.

It fell justly. But, we admit, it had not been absolutely hostile to all forms of progress. Great things had been accomplished, with it alongside.

Under the Restoration, the nation had grown accustomed to calm discussion, which had been lacking under the Republic, and to grandeur in peace, which had been wanting under the Empire. France free and strong had offered an encouraging spectacle to the other peoples of Europe. The Revolution had had the word under Robespierre; the cannon had had the word under Bonaparte; it was under Louis XVIII and Charles X that it was the turn of intelligence to have the word. The wind ceased, the torch was lighted once more. On the lofty heights, the pure light of mind could be seen flickering. A magnificent, useful, and charming spectacle. For a space of fifteen years, those great principles which are so old for the thinker, so new for the statesman, could be seen at work in perfect peace, on the public square; equality before the law, liberty of conscience, liberty of speech, liberty of the press, the accessibility of all aptitudes to all functions. Thus it proceeded until 1830. The Bourbons were an instrument of civilization which broke in the hands of Providence.

The fall of the Bourbons was full of grandeur, not on their side, but on the side of the nation. They quitted the throne with gravity, but without authority; their descent into the night was not one of those solemn disappearances which leave a sombre emotion in history; it was neither the spectral calm of Charles I, nor the eagle scream of Napoleon. They departed, that is all. They laid down the crown, and retained no aureole. They were worthy, but they were not august. They lacked, in a certain measure, the majesty of their misfortune. Charles X during the voyage from Cherbourg, causing a round table to be cut over into a square table, appeared to be more anxious about imperilled etiquette than about the crumbling monarchy. This diminution saddened devoted men who loved their persons, and serious men who honored their race. The populace was admirable. The nation, attacked one morning with weapons, by a sort of royal insurrection, felt itself in the possession of so much force that it did not go into a rage. It defended itself, restrained itself, restored things to their places, the government to law, the Bourbons to exile, alas! and then halted! It took the old king Charles X from beneath that dais which had sheltered Louis XIV and set him gently on the ground. It touched the royal personages only with sadness and precaution. It was not one man, it was not a few men, it was France, France entire, France victorious and intoxicated with her victory, who seemed to be coming to herself, and who put into practice, before the eyes of the whole world, these grave words of Guillaume du Vair after the day of the Barricades:—

"It is easy for those who are accustomed to skim the favors of the great, and to spring, like a bird from bough to bough, from an afflicted fortune to a flourishing one, to show themselves harsh towards their Prince in his adversity; but as for me, the fortune of my Kings and especially of my afflicted Kings, will always be venerable to me."

The Bourbons carried away with them respect, but not regret. As we have just stated, their misfortune was greater than they were. They faded out in the horizon.

The Revolution of July instantly had friends and enemies throughout the entire world. The first rushed toward her with joy and enthusiasm, the others turned away, each according to his nature. At the first blush, the princes of Europe, the owls of this dawn, shut their eyes, wounded and stupefied, and only opened them to threaten. A fright which can be comprehended, a wrath which can be pardoned. This strange revolution had hardly produced a shock; it had not even paid to vanquished royalty the honor of treating it as an enemy, and of shedding its blood. In the eyes of despotic governments, who are always interested in having liberty calumniate itself, the Revolution of July committed the fault of being formidable and of remaining gentle. Nothing, however, was attempted or plotted against it. The most discontented, the most irritated, the most trembling, saluted it; whatever our egotism and our rancor may be, a mysterious respect springs from events in which we are sensible of the collaboration of some one who is working above man.

The Revolution of July is the triumph of right overthrowing the fact. A thing which is full of splendor.

Right overthrowing the fact. Hence the brilliancy of the Revolution of 1830, hence, also, its mildness. Right triumphant has no need of being violent.

Right is the just and the true.

The property of right is to remain eternally beautiful and pure. The fact, even when most necessary to all appearances, even when most thoroughly accepted by contemporaries, if it exist only as a fact, and if it contain only too little of right, or none at all, is infallibly destined to become, in the course of time, deformed, impure, perhaps, even monstrous. If one desires to learn at one blow, to what degree of hideousness the fact can attain, viewed at the distance of centuries, let him look at Machiavelli. Machiavelli is not an evil genius, nor a demon, nor a miserable and cowardly writer; he is nothing but the fact. And he is not only the Italian fact; he is the European fact, the fact of the sixteenth century. He seems hideous, and so he is, in the presence of the moral idea of the nineteenth.

This conflict of right and fact has been going on ever since the origin of society. To terminate this duel, to amalgamate the pure idea with the humane reality, to cause right to penetrate pacifically into the fact and the fact into right, that is the task of sages.

II

Badly Sewed

B ut the task of sages is one thing, the task of clever men is another. The Revolution of 1830 came to a sudden halt.

As soon as a revolution has made the coast, the skilful make haste to prepare the shipwreck.

The skilful in our century have conferred on themselves the title of Statesmen; so that this word, *statesmen*, has ended by becoming somewhat of a slang word. It must be borne in mind, in fact, that wherever there is nothing but skill, there is necessarily pettiness. To say "the skilful" amounts to saying "the mediocre."

In the same way, to say "statesmen" is sometimes equivalent to saying "traitors." If, then, we are to believe the skilful, revolutions like the Revolution of July are severed arteries; a prompt ligature is indispensable. The right, too grandly proclaimed, is shaken. Also, right once firmly fixed, the state must be strengthened. Liberty once assured, attention must be directed to power.

Here the sages are not, as yet, separated from the skilful, but they begin to be distrustful. Power, very good. But, in the first place, what is power? In the second, whence comes it? The skilful do not seem to hear the murmured objection, and they continue their manœuvres.

According to the politicians, who are ingenious in putting the mask of necessity on profitable fictions, the first requirement of a people after a revolution, when this people forms part of a monarchical continent, is to procure for itself a dynasty. In this way, say they, peace, that is to say, time to dress our wounds, and to repair the house, can be had after a revolution. The dynasty conceals the scaffolding and covers the ambulance. Now, it is not always easy to procure a dynasty.

If it is absolutely necessary, the first man of genius or even the first man of fortune who comes to hand suffices for the manufacturing of a king. You have, in the first case, Napoleon; in the second, Iturbide.

But the first family that comes to hand does not suffice to make a dynasty. There is necessarily required a certain modicum of antiquity in a race, and the wrinkle of the centuries cannot be improvised.

If we place ourselves at the point of view of the "statesmen," after making all allowances, of course, after a revolution, what are the qualities of the king which result from it? He may be and it is useful for him to be a revolutionary; that is to say, a participant in his own person in that revolution, that he should have lent a hand to it, that he should have either compromised or distinguished himself therein, that he should have touched the axe or wielded the sword in it.

What are the qualities of a dynasty? It should be national; that is to say, revolutionary at a distance, not through acts committed, but by reason of ideas accepted. It should be composed of past and be historic; be composed of future and be sympathetic.

All this explains why the early revolutions contented themselves with finding a man, Cromwell or Napoleon; and why the second absolutely insisted on finding a family, the House of Brunswick or the House of Orleans.

Royal houses resemble those Indian fig-trees, each branch of which, bending over to the earth, takes root and becomes a fig-tree itself. Each branch may become a dynasty. On the sole condition that it shall bend down to the people.

Such is the theory of the skilful.

Here, then, lies the great art: to make a little render to success the sound of a catastrophe in order that those who profit by it may tremble from it also, to season with fear every step that is taken, to augment the curve of the transition to the point of retarding progress, to dull that aurora, to denounce and retrench the harshness of enthusiasm, to cut all angles and nails, to wad triumph, to muffle up right, to envelop the giant-people in flannel, and to put it to bed very speedily, to impose a diet on that excess of health, to put Hercules on the treatment of a convalescent, to dilute the event with the expedient, to offer to spirits thirsting for the ideal that nectar thinned out with a potion, to take one's precautions against too much success, to garnish the revolution with a shade.

1830 practised this theory, already applied to England by 1688.

1830 is a revolution arrested midway. Half of progress, quasi-right. Now, logic knows not the "almost," absolutely as the sun knows not the candle.

Who arrests revolutions half-way? The bourgeoisie?

Why?

Because the bourgeoisie is interest which has reached satisfaction. Yesterday it was appetite, to-day it is plenitude, to-morrow it will be satiety.

The phenomenon of 1814 after Napoleon was reproduced in 1830 after Charles X.

The attempt has been made, and wrongly, to make a class of the bourgeoisie. The bourgeoisie is simply the contented portion of the people. The bourgeois is the man who now has time to sit down. A chair is not a caste.

But through a desire to sit down too soon, one may arrest the very march of the human race. This has often been the fault of the bourgeoisie.

One is not a class because one has committed a fault. Selfishness is not one of the divisions of the social order.

Moreover, we must be just to selfishness. The state to which that part of the nation which is called the bourgeoisie aspired after the shock of 1830 was not the inertia which is complicated with indifference and laziness, and which contains a little shame; it was not the slumber which presupposes a momentary forgetfulness accessible to dreams; it was the halt.

The halt is a word formed of a singular double and almost contradictory sense: a troop on the march, that is to say, movement; a stand, that is to say, repose.

The halt is the restoration of forces; it is repose armed and on the alert; it is the accomplished fact which posts sentinels and holds itself on its guard.

The halt presupposes the combat of yesterday and the combat of to-morrow.

It is the partition between 1830 and 1848.

What we here call combat may also be designated as progress.

The bourgeoisie then, as well as the statesmen, required a man who should express this word Halt. An Although-Because. A composite individuality, signifying revolution and signifying stability, in other terms, strengthening the present by the evident compatibility of the past with the future.

This man was "already found." His name was Louis Philippe d'Orleans.

The 221 made Louis Philippe King. Lafayette undertook the coronation.

He called it *the best of republics*. The town-hall of Paris took the place of the Cathedral of Rheims.

This substitution of a half-throne for a whole throne was "the work of 1830."

When the skilful had finished, the immense vice of their solution became apparent. All this had been accomplished outside the bounds of absolute right. Absolute right cried: "I protest!" then, terrible to say, it retired into the darkness.

III

LOUIS PHILIPPE

Revolutions have a terrible arm and a happy hand, they strike firmly and choose well. Even incomplete, even debased and abused and reduced to the state of a junior revolution like the Revolution of 1830, they nearly always retain sufficient providential lucidity to prevent them from falling amiss. Their eclipse is never an abdication.

Nevertheless, let us not boast too loudly; revolutions also may be deceived, and grave errors have been seen.

Let us return to 1830. 1830, in its deviation, had good luck. In the establishment which entitled itself order after the revolution had been cut short, the King amounted to more than royalty. Louis Philippe was a rare man.

The son of a father to whom history will accord certain attenuating circumstances, but also as worthy of esteem as that father had been of blame; possessing all private virtues and many public virtues; careful of his health, of his fortune, of his person, of his affairs, knowing the value of a minute and not always the value of a year; sober, serene, peaceable, patient; a good man and a good prince; sleeping with his wife, and having in his palace lackeys charged with the duty of showing the conjugal bed to the bourgeois, an ostentation of the regular sleeping-apartment which had become useful after the former illegitimate displays of the elder branch; knowing all the languages of Europe, and, what is more rare, all the languages of all interests, and speaking them; an admirable representative of the "middle class," but outstripping it, and in every way greater than it; possessing excellent sense, while appreciating the blood from which he had sprung, counting most of all on his intrinsic worth, and, on the question of his race, very particular, declaring himself Orleans and not Bourbon; thoroughly the first Prince of the Blood Royal while he was still only a Serene Highness, but a frank bourgeois from the day he became king; diffuse in public, concise in private; reputed, but not proved to be a miser; at bottom, one of those economists who are readily prodigal at their own fancy or duty; lettered, but not very sensitive to letters; a gentleman, but not a chevalier; simple, calm, and strong; adored by his family and his household; a fascinating talker, an undeceived statesman, inwardly cold, dominated by immediate interest, always governing at the shortest range, incapable of rancor and of gratitude, making use without mercy of superiority on mediocrity, clever in getting parliamentary majorities to put in the wrong those mysterious unanimities which mutter dully under thrones; unreserved, sometimes imprudent in his lack of reserve, but with marvellous address in that imprudence; fertile in expedients, in countenances, in masks; making France fear Europe and Europe France! Incontestably fond of his country, but preferring his family; assuming more domination than authority and more authority than dignity, a disposition which has this unfortunate property, that as it turns everything to success, it admits of ruse and does not absolutely repudiate baseness, but which has this valuable side, that it preserves politics from violent shocks, the state from fractures, and society from catastrophes; minute, correct, vigilant, attentive, sagacious, indefatigable; contradicting himself at times and giving himself the lie; bold against Austria at Ancona, obstinate against England in Spain, bombarding Antwerp, and paying off Pritchard; singing the Marseillaise with conviction, inaccessible to despondency, to lassitude, to the taste for the beautiful and the ideal, to daring generosity, to Utopia, to chimæras, to wrath, to vanity, to fear; possessing all the forms of personal intrepidity; a general at Valmy; a soldier at Jemappes; attacked eight times by regicides and always smiling. Brave as a grenadier, courageous as a thinker; uneasy only in the face of the chances of a European shaking up, and unfitted for great political adventures; always ready to risk his life, never his work; disguising his will in influence, in order that he might be obeyed as an intelligence rather than as a king; endowed with observation and not with divination; not very attentive to minds, but knowing men, that is to say requiring to see in order to judge; prompt and penetrating good sense, practical wisdom, easy speech, prodigious memory; drawing incessantly on this memory, his only point of resemblance with Cæsar, Alexander, and Napoleon; knowing deeds, facts, details, dates, proper names, ignorant of tendencies, passions, the diverse geniuses of the crowd, the interior aspirations, the hidden and obscure uprisings of souls, in a word, all that can be designated as the invisible currents of consciences; accepted by the surface, but little in accord with France lower down; extricating himself by dint of tact; governing too much and not enough; his own first minister; excellent at creating out of the pettiness of realities an obstacle to the immensity of ideas; mingling a genuine creative faculty of civilization, of order and organization, an indescribable spirit of proceedings and chicanery, the founder and lawyer of a dynasty; having something of Charlemagne and something of an attorney; in short, a lofty and original figure, a prince who understood how to create authority in spite of the uneasiness of France, and power in spite of the jealousy of Europe. Louis Philippe will be classed among the eminent men of his century, and would be ranked among the most illustrious governors of history had he loved glory but a little, and if he had had the sentiment of what is great to the same degree as the feeling for what is useful.

Louis Philippe had been handsome, and in his old age he remained graceful; not always approved by the nation, he always was so by the masses; he pleased. He had that gift of charming. He lacked majesty; he wore no crown, although a king, and no white hair, although an old man; his manners belonged to the old regime and his habits to the new; a mixture of the noble and the bourgeois which suited 1830; Louis Philippe was transition reigning; he had preserved the ancient pronunciation and the ancient orthography which he placed at the service of opinions modern; he loved Poland and Hungary, but he wrote *les Polonois*, and he pronounced *les Hongrais*. He wore the uniform of the national guard, like Charles X, and the ribbon of the Legion of Honor, like Napoleon.

He went a little to chapel, not at all to the chase, never to the opera. Incorruptible by sacristans, by whippers-in, by ballet-dancers; this made a part of his bourgeois popularity. He had no heart. He went out with his umbrella under his arm, and this umbrella long formed a part of his aureole. He was a bit of a mason, a bit of a gardener, something of a doctor; he bled a postilion who had tumbled from his horse; Louis Philippe no more went about without his lancet, than did Henri IV without his poniard. The Royalists jeered at this ridiculous king, the first who had ever shed blood with the object of healing.

For the grievances against Louis Philippe, there is one deduction to be made; there is that which accuses royalty, that which accuses the reign, that which accuses the King; three columns which all give different totals. Democratic right confiscated, progress becomes a matter of secondary interest, the protests of the street violently repressed, military execution of insurrections, the rising passed over by arms, the Rue Transnonain, the counsels of war, the absorption of the real country by the legal country, on half shares with three hundred thousand privileged persons,—these are the deeds of royalty; Belgium refused, Algeria too harshly conquered, and, as in the case of India by the English, with more barbarism than civilization, the breach of faith, to Abd-el-Kader, Blaye, Deutz bought, Pritchard paid,—these are the doings of the reign; the policy which was more domestic than national was the doing of the King.

As will be seen, the proper deduction having been made, the King's charge is decreased.

This is his great fault; he was modest in the name of France.

Whence arises this fault?

We will state it.

Louis Philippe was rather too much of a paternal king; that incubation of a family with the object of founding a dynasty is afraid of everything and does not like to be disturbed; hence excessive timidity, which is displeasing to the people, who have the 14th of July in their civil and Austerlitz in their military tradition.

Moreover, if we deduct the public duties which require to be fulfilled first of all, that deep tenderness of Louis Philippe towards his family was deserved by the family. That domestic group was worthy of admiration. Virtues there dwelt side by side with talents. One of Louis Philippe's daughters, Marie d'Orleans, placed the name of her race among artists, as Charles d'Orleans had placed it among poets. She made of her soul a marble which she named Jeanne d'Arc. Two of Louis Philippe's daughters elicited from Metternich this eulogium: "They are young people such as are rarely seen, and princes such as are never seen."

This, without any dissimulation, and also without any exaggeration, is the truth about Louis Philippe.

To be Prince Equality, to bear in his own person the contradiction of the Restoration and the Revolution, to have that disquieting side of the revolutionary which becomes reassuring in governing power, therein lay the fortune of Louis Philippe in 1830; never was there a more complete adaptation of a man to an event; the one entered into the other, and the incarnation took place. Louis Philippe is 1830 made man. Moreover, he had in his favor that great recommendation to the throne, exile. He had been proscribed, a wanderer, poor. He had lived by his own labor. In Switzerland, this heir to the richest princely domains in France had sold an old horse in order to obtain bread. At Reichenau, he gave lessons in mathematics, while his sister Adelaide did wool work and sewed. These souvenirs connected with a king rendered the bourgeoisie enthusiastic. He had, with his own hands, demolished the iron cage of Mont-Saint-Michel, built by Louis XI, and used by Louis XV. He was the companion of Dumouriez, he was the friend of Lafayette; he had belonged to the Jacobins' club; Mirabeau had slapped him on the shoulder; Danton had said to him: "Young man!" At the age of four and twenty, in '93, being then M. de Chartres, he had witnessed, from the depth of a box, the trial of Louis XVI, so well named *that poor tyrant*. The blind clairvoyance of the Revolution, breaking royalty in the King and the King with royalty, did so almost without noticing the man in the fierce crushing of the idea, the vast storm of the Assembly-Tribunal, the public wrath interrogating, Capet not knowing what to reply, the alarming, stupefied vacillation by that royal head beneath that sombre breath, the relative innocence of all in that catastrophe, of those who condemned as well as of the man condemned,—he had looked on those things, he had contemplated that giddiness; he had seen the centuries appear before the bar of the Assembly-Convention; he had beheld, behind Louis XVI, that unfortunate passer-by who was made responsible, the terrible culprit, the monarchy, rise through the shadows; and there had lingered in his soul the respectful fear of these immense justices of the populace, which are almost as impersonal as the justice of God.

The trace left in him by the Revolution was prodigious. Its memory was like a living imprint of those great years, minute by minute. One day, in the presence of a witness whom we are not permitted to doubt, he rectified from memory the whole of the letter A in the alphabetical list of the Constituent Assembly.

Louis Philippe was a king of the broad daylight. While he reigned the press was free, the tribune was free, conscience and speech were free. The laws of September are open to sight. Although fully aware of the gnawing power of light on privileges, he left his throne exposed to the light. History will do justice to him for this loyalty.

Louis Philippe, like all historical men who have passed from the scene, is to-day put on his trial by the human conscience. His case is, as yet, only in the lower court.

The hour when history speaks with its free and venerable accent, has not yet sounded for him; the moment has not come to pronounce a definite judgment on this king; the austere and illustrious historian Louis Blanc has himself recently softened his first verdict; Louis Philippe was elected by those two *almosts* which are called the 221 and

1830, that is to say, by a half-Parliament, and a half-revolution; and in any case, from the superior point of view where philosophy must place itself, we cannot judge him here, as the reader has seen above, except with certain reservations in the name of the absolute democratic principle; in the eyes of the absolute, outside these two rights, the right of man in the first place, the right of the people in the second, all is usurpation; but what we can say, even at the present day, that after making these reserves is, that to sum up the whole, and in whatever manner he is considered, Louis Philippe, taken in himself, and from the point of view of human goodness, will remain, to use the antique language of ancient history, one of the best princes who ever sat on a throne.

What is there against him? That throne. Take away Louis Philippe the king, there remains the man. And the man is good. He is good at times even to the point of being admirable. Often, in the midst of his gravest souvenirs, after a day of conflict with the whole diplomacy of the continent, he returned at night to his apartments, and there, exhausted with fatigue, overwhelmed with sleep, what did he do? He took a death sentence and passed the night in revising a criminal suit, considering it something to hold his own against Europe, but that it was a still greater matter to rescue a man from the executioner. He obstinately maintained his opinion against his keeper of the seals; he disputed the ground with the guillotine foot by foot against the crown attorneys, those *chatterers of the law*, as he called them. Sometimes the pile of sentences covered his table; he examined them all; it was anguish to him to abandon these miserable, condemned heads. One day, he said to the same witness to whom we have recently referred: "I won seven last night." During the early years of his reign, the death penalty was as good as abolished, and the erection of a scaffold was a violence committed against the King. The Grève having disappeared with the elder branch, a bourgeois place of execution was instituted under the name of the Barrière-Saint-Jacques; "practical men" felt the necessity of a quasi-legitimate guillotine; and this was one of the victories of Casimir Périer, who represented the narrow sides of the bourgeoisie, over Louis Philippe, who represented its liberal sides. Louis Philippe annotated Beccaria with his own hand. After the Fieschi machine, he exclaimed: "What a pity that I was not wounded! Then I might have pardoned!" On another occasion, alluding to the resistance offered by his ministry, he wrote in connection with a political criminal, who is one of the most generous figures of our day: "His pardon is granted; it only remains for me to obtain it." Louis Philippe was as gentle as Louis IX and as kindly as Henri IV.

Now, to our mind, in history, where kindness is the rarest of pearls, the man who is kindly almost takes precedence of the man who is great.

Louis Philippe having been severely judged by some, harshly, perhaps, by others, it is quite natural that a man, himself a phantom at the present day, who knew that king, should come and testify in his favor before history; this deposition, whatever else it may be, is evidently and above all things, entirely disinterested; an epitaph penned by a dead man is sincere; one shade may console another shade; the sharing of the same shadows confers the right to praise it; it is not greatly to be feared that it will ever be said of two tombs in exile: "This one flattered the other."

IV

Cracks Beneath the Foundation

At the moment when the drama which we are narrating is on the point of penetrating into the depths of one of the tragic clouds which envelop the beginning of Louis Philippe's reign, it was necessary that there should be no equivoque, and it became requisite that this book should offer some explanation with regard to this king.

Louis Philippe had entered into possession of his royal authority without violence, without any direct action on his part, by virtue of a revolutionary change, evidently quite distinct from the real aim of the Revolution, but in which he, the Duc d'Orléans, exercised no personal initiative. He had been born a Prince, and he believed himself to have been elected King. He had not served this mandate on himself; he had not taken it; it had been offered to him, and he had accepted it; convinced, wrongly, to be sure, but convinced nevertheless, that the offer was in accordance with right and that the acceptance of it was in accordance with duty. Hence his possession was in good faith. Now, we say it in good conscience, Louis Philippe being in possession in perfect good faith, and the democracy being in good faith in its attack, the amount of terror discharged by the social conflicts weighs neither on the King nor on the democracy. A clash of principles resembles a clash of elements. The ocean defends the water, the hurricane defends the air, the King defends Royalty, the democracy defends the people; the relative, which is the monarchy, resists the absolute, which is the republic; society bleeds in this conflict, but that which constitutes its suffering to-day will constitute its safety later on; and, in any case, those who combat are not to be blamed; one of the two parties is evidently mistaken; the right is not, like the Colossus of Rhodes, on two shores at once, with one foot on the republic, and one in Royalty; it is indivisible, and all on one side; but those who are in error are so sincerely; a blind man is no more a criminal than a Vendean is a ruffian. Let us, then, impute to the fatality of things alone these formidable collisions. Whatever the nature of these tempests may be, human irresponsibility is mingled with them.

Let us complete this exposition.

The government of 1840 led a hard life immediately. Born yesterday, it was obliged to fight to-day.

Hardly installed, it was already everywhere conscious of vague movements of traction on the apparatus of July so recently laid, and so lacking in solidity.

Resistance was born on the morrow; perhaps even, it was born on the preceding evening. From month to month the hostility increased, and from being concealed it became patent.

The Revolution of July, which gained but little acceptance outside of France by kings, had been diversely interpreted in France, as we have said.

God delivers over to men his visible will in events, an obscure text written in a mysterious tongue. Men immediately make translations of it; translations hasty, incorrect, full of errors, of gaps, and of nonsense. Very few minds comprehend the divine language. The most sagacious, the calmest, the most profound, decipher slowly, and when they arrive with their text, the task has long been completed; there are already twenty translations on the public place. From each remaining springs a party, and from each misinterpretation a faction; and each party thinks that it alone has the true text, and each faction thinks that it possesses the light.

Power itself is often a faction.

There are, in revolutions, swimmers who go against the current; they are the old parties.

For the old parties who clung to heredity by the grace of God, think that revolutions, having sprung from the right to revolt, one has the right to revolt against them. Error. For in these revolutions, the one who revolts is not the people; it is the king. Revolution is precisely the contrary of revolt. Every revolution, being a normal outcome, contains within itself its legitimacy, which false revolutionists sometimes dishonor, but which remains even when soiled, which survives even when stained with blood.

Revolutions spring not from an accident, but from necessity. A revolution is a return from the fictitious to the real. It is because it must be that it is.

Nonetheless did the old legitimist parties assail the Revolution of 1830 with all the vehemence which arises from false reasoning. Errors make excellent projectiles. They strike it cleverly in its vulnerable spot, in default of a cuirass, in its lack of logic; they attacked this revolution in its royalty. They shouted to it: "Revolution, why this king?" Factions are blind men who aim correctly.

This cry was uttered equally by the republicans. But coming from them, this cry was logical. What was blindness in the legitimists was clearness of vision in the democrats. 1830 had bankrupted the people. The enraged democracy reproached it with this.

Between the attack of the past and the attack of the future, the establishment of July struggled. It represented the minute at loggerheads on the one hand with the monarchical centuries, on the other hand with eternal right.

In addition, and beside all this, as it was no longer revolution and had become a monarchy, 1830 was obliged to take precedence of all Europe. To keep the peace, was an increase of complication. A harmony established contrary to sense is often more onerous than a war. From this secret conflict, always muzzled, but always growling, was born armed peace, that ruinous expedient of civilization which in the harness of the European cabinets is suspicious in itself. The Royalty of July reared up, in spite of the fact that it caught it in the harness of European cabinets. Metternich would gladly have put it in kicking-straps. Pushed on in France by progress, it pushed on the monarchies, those loiterers in Europe. After having been towed, it undertook to tow.

Meanwhile, within her, pauperism, the proletariat, salary, education, penal servitude, prostitution, the fate of the woman, wealth, misery, production, consumption, division, exchange, coin, credit, the rights of capital, the rights of labor,—all these questions were multiplied above society, a terrible slope.

Outside of political parties properly so called, another movement became manifest. Philosophical fermentation replied to democratic fermentation. The elect felt troubled as well as the masses; in another manner, but quite as much.

Thinkers meditated, while the soil, that is to say, the people, traversed by revolutionary currents, trembled under them with indescribably vague epileptic shocks. These dreamers, some isolated, others united in families and almost in communion, turned over social questions in a pacific but profound manner; impassive miners, who tranquilly pushed their galleries into the depths of a volcano, hardly disturbed by the dull commotion and the furnaces of which they caught glimpses.

This tranquillity was not the least beautiful spectacle of this agitated epoch.

These men left to political parties the question of rights, they occupied themselves with the question of happiness.

The well-being of man, that was what they wanted to extract from society.

They raised material questions, questions of agriculture, of industry, of commerce, almost to the dignity of a religion. In civilization, such as it has formed itself, a little by the command of God, a great deal by the agency of man, interests combine, unite, and amalgamate in a manner to form a veritable hard rock, in accordance with a dynamic law, patiently studied by economists, those geologists of politics. These men who grouped themselves under different appellations, but who may all be designated by the generic title of socialists, endeavored to pierce that rock and to cause it to spout forth the living waters of human felicity.

From the question of the scaffold to the question of war, their works embraced everything. To the rights of man, as proclaimed by the French Revolution, they added the rights of woman and the rights of the child.

The reader will not be surprised if, for various reasons, we do not here treat in a thorough manner, from the theoretical point of view, the questions raised by socialism. We confine ourselves to indicating them.

All the problems that the socialists proposed to themselves, cosmogonic visions, reverie and mysticism being cast aside, can be reduced to two principal problems.

First problem: To produce wealth.

Second problem: To share it.

The first problem contains the question of work.

The second contains the question of salary.

In the first problem the employment of forces is in question.

In the second, the distribution of enjoyment.

From the proper employment of forces results public power.

From a good distribution of enjoyments results individual happiness.

By a good distribution, not an equal but an equitable distribution must be understood.

From these two things combined, the public power without, individual happiness within, results social prosperity.

Social prosperity means the man happy, the citizen free, the nation great.

England solves the first of these two problems. She creates wealth admirably, she divides it badly. This solution which is complete on one side only leads her fatally to two extremes: monstrous opulence, monstrous wretchedness. All enjoyments for some, all privations for the rest, that is to say, for the people; privilege, exception, monopoly, feudalism, born from toil itself. A false and dangerous situation, which sates public power or private misery, which sets the roots of the State in the sufferings of the individual. A badly constituted grandeur in which are combined all the material elements and into which no moral element enters.

Communism and agrarian law think that they solve the second problem. They are mistaken. Their division kills production. Equal partition abolishes emulation; and consequently labor. It is a partition made by the butcher, which kills that which it divides. It is therefore impossible to pause over these pretended solutions. Slaying wealth is not the same thing as dividing it.

The two problems require to be solved together, to be well solved. The two problems must be combined and made but one.

Solve only the first of the two problems; you will be Venice, you will be England. You will have, like Venice, an artificial power, or, like England, a material power; you will be the wicked rich man. You will die by an act of violence, as Venice died, or by bankruptcy, as England will fall. And the world will allow to die and fall all that is merely selfishness, all that does not represent for the human race either a virtue or an idea.

It is well understood here, that by the words Venice, England, we designate not the peoples, but social structures; the oligarchies superposed on nations, and not the nations themselves. The nations always have our respect and our sympathy. Venice, as a people, will live again; England, the aristocracy, will fall, but England, the nation, is immortal. That said, we continue.

Solve the two problems, encourage the wealthy, and protect the poor, suppress misery, put an end to the unjust farming out of the feeble by the strong, put a bridle on the iniquitous jealousy of the man who is making his way against the man who has reached the goal, adjust, mathematically and fraternally, salary to labor, mingle gratuitous and compulsory education with the growth of childhood, and make of science the base of manliness, develop minds while keeping arms busy, be at one and the same time a powerful people and a family of happy men, render property democratic, not by abolishing it, but by making it universal, so that every citizen, without exception, may be a proprietor, an easier matter than is generally supposed; in two words, learn how to produce wealth and how to distribute it, and you will have at once moral and material greatness; and you will be worthy to call yourself France.

This is what socialism said outside and above a few sects which have gone astray; that is what it sought in facts, that is what it sketched out in minds.

Efforts worthy of admiration! Sacred attempts!

These doctrines, these theories, these resistances, the unforeseen necessity for the statesman to take philosophers into account, confused evidences of which we catch a glimpse, a new system of politics to be created, which shall be in accord with the old world without too much disaccord with the new revolutionary ideal, a situation in which it became necessary to use Lafayette to defend Polignac, the intuition of progress transparent beneath the revolt, the chambers and streets, the competitions to be brought into equilibrium around him, his faith in the Revolution, perhaps an eventual indefinable resignation born of the vague acceptance of a superior definitive right, his desire to remain of his race, his domestic spirit, his sincere respect for the people, his own honesty, preoccupied Louis Philippe almost painfully, and there were moments when strong and courageous as he was, he was overwhelmed by the difficulties of being a king.

He felt under his feet a formidable disaggregation, which was not, nevertheless, a reduction to dust, France being more France than ever.

Piles of shadows covered the horizon. A strange shade, gradually drawing nearer, extended little by little over men, over things, over ideas; a shade which came from wraths and systems. Everything which had been hastily stifled was moving and fermenting. At times the conscience of the honest man resumed its breathing, so great was the discomfort of that air in which sophisms were intermingled with truths. Spirits trembled in the social anxiety like leaves at the approach of a storm. The electric tension was such that at certain instants, the first comer, a stranger, brought light. Then the twilight obscurity closed in again. At intervals, deep and dull mutterings allowed a judgment to be formed as to the quantity of thunder contained by the cloud.

Twenty months had barely elapsed since the Revolution of July, the year 1832 had opened with an aspect of something impending and threatening.

The distress of the people, the laborers without bread, the last Prince de Condé engulfed in the shadows, Brussels expelling the Nassaus as Paris did the Bourbons, Belgium offering herself to a French Prince and giving herself to an English Prince, the Russian hatred of Nicolas, behind us the demons of the South, Ferdinand in Spain, Miguel in Portugal, the earth quaking in Italy, Metternich extending his hand over Bologna, France treating Austria sharply at Ancona, at the North no one knew what sinister sound of the hammer nailing up Poland in her coffin, irritated glances watching France narrowly all over Europe, England, a suspected ally, ready to give a push to that which was tottering and to hurl herself on that which should fall, the peerage sheltering itself behind Beccaria to refuse four heads to the law, the fleurs-de-lys erased from the King's carriage, the cross torn from Notre Dame, Lafayette lessened, Laffitte ruined, Benjamin Constant dead in indigence, Casimir Périer dead in the exhaustion of his power; political and social malady breaking out simultaneously in the two capitals of the kingdom, the one in the city of thought, the other in the city of toil; at Paris civil war, at Lyons servile war; in the two cities, the same glare of the furnace; a crater-like crimson on the brow of the people; the South rendered fanatic, the West troubled, the Duchesse de Berry in la Vendée, plots, conspiracies, risings, cholera, added the sombre roar of tumult of events to the sombre roar of ideas.

V

Facts Whence History Springs and Which History Ignores

Towards the end of April, everything had become aggravated. The fermentation entered the boiling state. Ever since 1830, petty partial revolts had been going on here and there, which were quickly suppressed, but ever bursting forth afresh, the sign of a vast underlying conflagration. Something terrible was in preparation. Glimpses could be caught of the features still indistinct and imperfectly lighted, of a possible revolution. France kept an eye on Paris; Paris kept an eye on the Faubourg Saint-Antoine.

The Faubourg Saint-Antoine, which was in a dull glow, was beginning its ebullition.

The wine-shops of the Rue de Charonne were, although the union of the two epithets seems singular when applied to wine-shops, grave and stormy.

The government was there purely and simply called in question. There people publicly discussed the *question of fighting or of keeping quiet*. There were back shops where workingmen were made to swear that they would hasten into the street at the first cry of alarm, and "that they would fight without counting the number of the enemy." This engagement once entered into, a man seated in the corner of the wine-shop "assumed a sonorous tone," and said, "You understand! You have sworn!"

Sometimes they went upstairs, to a private room on the first floor, and there scenes that were almost masonic were enacted. They made the initiated take oaths *to render service to himself as well as to the fathers of families*. That was the formula.

In the tap-rooms, "subversive" pamphlets were read. *They treated the government with contempt*, says a secret report of that time.

Words like the following could be heard there:—

"I don't know the names of the leaders. We folks shall not know the day until two hours beforehand." One workman said: "There are three hundred of us, let each contribute ten sous, that will make one hundred and fifty francs with which to procure powder and shot."

Another said: "I don't ask for six months, I don't ask for even two. In less than a fortnight we shall be parallel with the government. With twenty-five thousand men we can face them." Another said: "I don't sleep at night, because I make cartridges all night." From time to time, men "of bourgeois appearance, and in good coats" came and "caused embarrassment," and with the air of "command," shook hands with *the most important*, and then went away. They never stayed more than ten minutes. Significant remarks were exchanged in a low tone: "The plot is ripe, the matter is arranged." "It was murmured by all who were there," to borrow the very expression of one of those who were present. The exaltation was such that one day, a workingman exclaimed, before the whole wine-shop: "We have no arms!" One of his comrades replied: "The soldiers have!" thus parodying without being aware of the fact, Bonaparte's proclamation to the army in Italy: "When they had anything of a more secret nature on hand," adds one report, "they did not communicate it to each other." It is not easy to understand what they could conceal after what they said.

These reunions were sometimes periodical. At certain ones of them, there were never more than eight or ten persons present, and they were always the same. In others, any one entered who wished, and the room was so full that they were forced to stand. Some went thither through enthusiasm and passion; others because it *was on their way to their work*. As during the Revolution, there were patriotic women in some of these wine-shops who embraced newcomers.

Other expressive facts came to light.

A man would enter a shop, drink, and go his way with the remark: "Wine-merchant, the revolution will pay what is due to you."

Revolutionary agents were appointed in a wine-shop facing the Rue de Charonne. The balloting was carried on in their caps.

Workingmen met at the house of a fencing-master who gave lessons in the Rue de Cotte. There there was a trophy of arms formed of wooden broadswords, canes, clubs, and foils. One day, the buttons were removed from the foils.

A workman said: "There are twenty-five of us, but they don't count on me, because I am looked upon as a machine." Later on, that machine became Quenisset.

The indefinite things which were brewing gradually acquired a strange and indescribable notoriety. A woman sweeping off her doorsteps said to another woman: "For a long time, there has been a strong force busy making cartridges." In the open street, proclamation could be seen addressed to the National Guard in the departments. One of these proclamations was signed: *Burtot, wine-merchant.*

One day a man with his beard worn like a collar and with an Italian accent mounted a stone post at the door of a liquor-seller in the Marché Lenoir, and read aloud a singular document, which seemed to emanate from an occult power. Groups formed around him, and applauded.

The passages which touched the crowd most deeply were collected and noted down. "—Our doctrines are trammelled, our proclamations torn, our bill-stickers are spied upon and thrown into prison."—"The breakdown which has recently taken place in cottons has converted to us many mediums."—"The future of nations is being worked out in our obscure ranks."—"Here are the fixed terms: action or reaction, revolution or counter-revolution. For, at our epoch, we no longer believe either in inertia or in immobility. For the people against the people, that is the question. There is no other."—"On the day when we cease to suit you, break us, but up to that day, help us to march on." All this in broad daylight.

Other deeds, more audacious still, were suspicious in the eyes of the people by reason of their very audacity. On the 4th of April, 1832, a passer-by mounted the post on the corner which forms the angle of the Rue Sainte-Marguerite and shouted: "I am a Babouvist!" But beneath Babeuf, the people scented Gisquet.

Among other things, this man said:—

"Down with property! The opposition of the left is cowardly and treacherous. When it wants to be on the right side, it preaches revolution, it is democratic in order to escape being beaten, and royalist so that it may not have to fight. The republicans are beasts with feathers. Distrust the republicans, citizens of the laboring classes."

"Silence, citizen spy!" cried an artisan.

This shout put an end to the discourse.

Mysterious incidents occurred.

At nightfall, a workingman encountered near the canal a "very well dressed man," who said to him: "Whither are you bound, citizen?" "Sir," replied the workingman, "I have not the honor of your acquaintance." "I know you very well, however." And the man added: "Don't be alarmed, I am an agent of the committee. You are suspected of not being quite faithful. You know that if you reveal anything, there is an eye fixed on you." Then he shook hands with the workingman and went away, saying: "We shall meet again soon."

The police, who were on the alert, collected singular dialogues, not only in the wine-shops, but in the street.

"Get yourself received very soon," said a weaver to a cabinet-maker.

"Why?"

"There is going to be a shot to fire."

Two ragged pedestrians exchanged these remarkable replies, fraught with evident Jacquerie:—

"Who governs us?"

"M. Philippe."

"No, it is the bourgeoisie."

The reader is mistaken if he thinks that we take the word *Jacquerie* in a bad sense. The Jacques were the poor.

On another occasion two men were heard to say to each other as they passed by: "We have a good plan of attack."

Only the following was caught of a private conversation between four men who were crouching in a ditch of the circle of the Barrière du Trône:—

"Everything possible will be done to prevent his walking about Paris any more."

Who was the *he?* Menacing obscurity.

"The principal leaders," as they said in the faubourg, held themselves apart. It was supposed that they met for consultation in a wine-shop near the point Saint-Eustache. A certain Aug—, chief of the Society aid for tailors, Rue Mondétour, had the reputation of serving as intermediary central between the leaders and the Faubourg Saint-Antoine.

Nevertheless, there was always a great deal of mystery about these leaders, and no certain fact can invalidate the singular arrogance of this reply made later on by a man accused before the Court of Peers:—

"Who was your leader?"

"I knew of none and I recognized none."

There was nothing but words, transparent but vague; sometimes idle reports, rumors, hearsay. Other indications cropped up.

A carpenter, occupied in nailing boards to a fence around the ground on which a house was in process of construction, in the Rue de Reuilly found on that plot the torn fragment of a letter on which were still legible the following lines:—

The committee must take measures to prevent recruiting in the sections for the different societies.

And, as a postscript:—

We have learned that there are guns in the Rue du Faubourg-Poissonnière, No. 5 (bis), to the number of five or six thousand, in the house of a gunsmith in that court. The section owns no arms.

What excited the carpenter and caused him to show this thing to his neighbors was the fact, that a few paces further on he picked up another paper, torn like the first, and still more significant, of which we reproduce a facsimile, because of the historical interest attaching to these strange documents:—

Q	C	D	E	Learn this list by heart. After so doing you will tear it up. The men admitted will do the same when you have transmitted their orders to them. Health and Fraternity, u og a' fe L.

It was only later on that the persons who were in the secret of this find at the time, learned the significance of those four capital letters: *quinturions, centurions, decurions, éclaireurs* (scouts), and the sense of the letters: *u og a' fe*, which was a date, and meant April 15th, 1832. Under each capital letter were inscribed names followed by very characteristic notes. Thus: Q. *Bannerel*. 8 guns, 83 cartridges. A safe man.—C. *Boubière*. 1 pistol, 40 cartridges.—D. *Rollet*. 1 foil, 1 pistol, 1 pound of powder.—E. *Tessier*. 1 sword, 1 cartridge-box. Exact.—*Terreur*. 8 guns. Brave, etc.

Finally, this carpenter found, still in the same enclosure, a third paper on which was written in pencil, but very legibly, this sort of enigmatical list:—

Unité: Blanchard: Arbre-Sec. 6.

Barra. Soize. Salle-au-Comte.

Kosciusko. Aubry the Butcher?

J. J. R.

Caius Gracchus.

Right of revision. Dufond. Four.

Fall of the Girondists. Derbac. Maubuée.
Washington. Pinson. 1 pistol, 86 cartridges.
Marseillaise.
Sovereignty of the people. Michel. Quincampoix. Sword.
Hoche.
Marceau. Plato. Arbre-Sec.
Warsaw. Tilly, crier of the *Populaire*.

The honest bourgeois into whose hands this list fell knew its significance. It appears that this list was the complete nomenclature of the sections of the fourth arondissement of the Society of the Rights of Man, with the names and dwellings of the chiefs of sections. To-day, when all these facts which were obscure are nothing more than history, we may publish them. It should be added, that the foundation of the Society of the Rights of Man seems to have been posterior to the date when this paper was found. Perhaps this was only a rough draft.

Still, according to all the remarks and the words, according to written notes, material facts begin to make their appearance.

In the Rue Popincourt, in the house of a dealer in bric-à-brac, there were seized seven sheets of gray paper, all folded alike lengthwise and in four; these sheets enclosed twenty-six squares of this same gray paper folded in the form of a cartridge, and a card, on which was written the following:—

Saltpetre	. . . .	12 ounces.
Sulphur	. . . .	2 ounces.
Charcoal	. . . .	2 ounces and a half.
Water	. . . .	2 ounces.

The report of the seizure stated that the drawer exhaled a strong smell of powder.

A mason returning from his day's work, left behind him a little package on a bench near the bridge of Austerlitz. This package was taken to the police station. It was opened, and in it were found two printed dialogues, signed *Lahautière*, a song entitled: "Workmen, band together," and a tin box full of cartridges.

One artisan drinking with a comrade made the latter feel him to see how warm he was; the other man felt a pistol under his waistcoat.

In a ditch on the boulevard, between Père-Lachaise and the Barrière du Trône, at the most deserted spot, some children, while playing, discovered beneath a mass of shavings and refuse bits of wood, a bag containing a bullet-mould, a wooden punch for the preparation of cartridges, a wooden bowl, in which there were grains of hunting-powder, and a little cast-iron pot whose interior presented evident traces of melted lead.

Police agents, making their way suddenly and unexpectedly at five o'clock in the morning, into the dwelling of a certain Pardon, who was afterwards a member of the Barricade-Merry section and got himself killed in the insurrection of April, 1834, found him standing near his bed, and holding in his hand some cartridges which he was in the act of preparing.

Towards the hour when workingmen repose, two men were seen to meet between the Barrière Picpus and the Barrière Charenton in a little lane between two walls, near a wine-shop, in front of which there was a "Jeu de Siam." One drew a pistol from beneath his blouse and handed it to the other. As he was handing it to him, he noticed that the perspiration of his chest had made the powder damp. He primed the pistol and added more powder to what was already in the pan. Then the two men parted.

A certain Gallais, afterwards killed in the Rue Beaubourg in the affair of April, boasted of having in his house seven hundred cartridges and twenty-four flints.

The government one day received a warning that arms and two hundred thousand cartridges had just been distributed in the faubourg. On the following week thirty thousand cartridges were distributed. The remarkable point about it was, that the police were not able to seize a single one.

An intercepted letter read: "The day is not far distant when, within four hours by the clock, eighty thousand patriots will be under arms."

All this fermentation was public, one might almost say tranquil. The approaching insurrection was preparing its storm calmly in the face of the government. No singularity was lacking to this still subterranean crisis, which was already perceptible. The bourgeois talked peaceably to the working-classes of what was in preparation. They said: "How is the rising coming along?" in the same tone in which they would have said: "How is your wife?"

A furniture-dealer, of the Rue Moreau, inquired: "Well, when are you going to make the attack?"

Another shop-keeper said:—

"The attack will be made soon."

"I know it. A month ago, there were fifteen thousand of you, now there are twenty-five thousand." He offered his gun, and a neighbor offered a small pistol which he was willing to sell for seven francs.

Moreover, the revolutionary fever was growing. Not a point in Paris nor in France was exempt from it. The artery was beating everywhere. Like those membranes which arise from certain inflammations and form in the human body, the network of secret societies began to spread all over the country. From the associations of the Friends of the People, which was at the same time public and secret, sprang the Society of the Rights of Man, which also dated from one of the orders of the day: *Pluviôse, Year of the republican era*, which was destined to survive even the mandate of the Court of Assizes which pronounced its dissolution, and which did not hesitate to bestow on its sections significant names like the following:—

Pikes.
Tocsin.
Signal cannon.
Phrygian cap.
January 21.
The beggars.
The vagabonds.
Forward march.
Robespierre.
Level.
Ça Ira.

The Society of the Rights of Man engendered the Society of Action. These were impatient individuals who broke away and hastened ahead. Other associations sought to recruit themselves from the great mother societies. The members of sections complained that they were torn asunder. Thus, the Gallic Society, and the committee of organization of the Municipalities. Thus the associations for the liberty of the press, for individual liberty, for the instruction of the people against indirect taxes. Then the Society of Equal Workingmen which was divided into three fractions, the levellers, the communists, the reformers. Then the Army of the Bastilles, a sort of cohort organized on a military footing, four men commanded by a corporal, ten by a sergeant, twenty by a sub-lieutenant, forty by a lieutenant; there were never more than five men who knew each other. Creation where precaution is combined with audacity and which seemed stamped with the genius of Venice.

The central committee, which was at the head, had two arms, the Society of Action, and the Army of the Bastilles.

A legitimist association, the Chevaliers of Fidelity, stirred about among these the republican affiliations. It was denounced and repudiated there.

The Parisian societies had ramifications in the principal cities, Lyons, Nantes, Lille, Marseilles, and each had its Society of the Rights of Man, the Charbonnière, and The Free Men. All had a revolutionary society which was called the Cougourde. We have already mentioned this word.

In Paris, the Faubourg Saint-Marceau kept up an equal buzzing with the Faubourg Saint-Antoine, and the schools were no less moved than the faubourgs. A café in the Rue Saint-Hyacinthe and the wine-shop of the *Seven Billiards*, Rue des Mathurins-Saint-Jacques, served as rallying points for the students. The Society of the Friends of the A B C affiliated to the Mutualists of Angers, and to the Cougourde of Aix, met, as we have seen, in the Café Musain. These same young men assembled also, as we have stated already, in a restaurant wine-shop of the Rue Mondétour which was called Corinthe. These meetings were secret. Others were as public as possible, and the reader can judge of their boldness from these fragments of an interrogatory undergone in one of the ulterior prosecutions: "Where was this meeting held?" "In the Rue de la Paix." "At whose house?" "In the street." "What sections were there?" "Only one." "Which?" "The Manuel section." "Who was its leader?" "I." "You are too young to have decided alone upon the bold course of attacking the government. Where did your instructions come from?" "From the central committee."

The army was mined at the same time as the population, as was proved subsequently by the operations of Béford, Luneville, and Épinard. They counted on the fifty-second regiment, on the fifth, on the eighth, on the thirty-seventh, and on the twentieth light cavalry. In Burgundy and in the southern towns they planted the liberty tree; that is to say, a pole surmounted by a red cap.

Such was the situation.

The Faubourg Saint-Antoine, more than any other group of the population, as we stated in the beginning, accentuated this situation and made it felt. That was the sore point. This old faubourg, peopled like an ant-hill, laborious, courageous, and angry as a hive of bees, was quivering with expectation and with the desire for a tumult. Everything was in a state of agitation there, without any interruption, however, of the regular work. It is impossible to convey an idea of this lively yet sombre physiognomy. In this faubourg exists poignant distress hidden under attic roofs; there also exist rare and ardent minds. It is particularly in the matter of distress and intelligence that it is dangerous to have extremes meet.

The Faubourg Saint-Antoine had also other causes to tremble; for it received the counter-shock of commercial crises, of failures, strikes, slack seasons, all inherent to great political disturbances. In times of revolution misery is both cause and effect. The blow which it deals rebounds upon it. This population full of proud virtue, capable to the highest degree of latent heat, always ready to fly to arms, prompt to explode, irritated, deep, undermined, seemed to be only awaiting the fall of a spark. Whenever certain sparks float on the horizon chased by the wind of events, it is impossible not to think of the Faubourg Saint-Antoine and of the formidable chance which has placed at the very gates of Paris that powder-house of suffering and ideas.

The wine-shops of the *Faubourg Antoine*, which have been more than once drawn in the sketches which the reader has just perused, possess historical notoriety. In troublous times people grow intoxicated there more on words than on wine. A sort of prophetic spirit and an afflatus of the future circulates there, swelling hearts and enlarging souls. The cabarets of the Faubourg Saint-Antoine resemble those taverns of Mont Aventine erected on the cave of the Sibyl and communicating with the profound and sacred breath; taverns where the tables were almost tripods, and where was drunk what Ennius calls the *sibylline wine*.

The Faubourg Saint-Antoine is a reservoir of people. Revolutionary agitations create fissures there, through which trickles the popular sovereignty. This sovereignty may do evil; it can be mistaken like any other; but, even when led astray, it remains great. We may say of it as of the blind cyclops, *Ingens*.

In '93, according as the idea which was floating about was good or evil, according as it was the day of fanaticism or of enthusiasm, there leaped forth from the Faubourg Saint-Antoine now savage legions, now heroic bands.

Savage. Let us explain this word. When these bristling men, who in the early days of the revolutionary chaos, tattered, howling, wild, with uplifted bludgeon, pike on high, hurled themselves upon ancient Paris in an uproar, what did they want? They wanted an end to oppression, an end to tyranny, an end to the sword, work for men, instruction for the child, social sweetness for the woman, liberty, equality, fraternity, bread for all, the idea for all, the Edenizing of the world. Progress; and that holy, sweet, and good thing, progress, they claimed in terrible wise, driven to extremities as they were, half naked, club in fist, a roar in their mouths. They were savages, yes; but the savages of civilization.

They proclaimed right furiously; they were desirous, if only with fear and trembling, to force the human race to paradise. They seemed barbarians, and they were saviours. They demanded light with the mask of night.

Facing these men, who were ferocious, we admit, and terrifying, but ferocious and terrifying for good ends, there are other men, smiling, embroidered, gilded, beribboned, starred, in silk stockings, in white plumes, in yellow gloves, in varnished shoes, who, with their elbows on a velvet table, beside a marble chimney-piece, insist gently on demeanor and the preservation of the past, of the Middle Ages, of divine right, of fanaticism, of innocence, of slavery, of the death penalty, of war, glorifying in low tones and with politeness, the sword, the stake, and the scaffold. For our part, if we were forced to make a choice between the barbarians of civilization and the civilized men of barbarism, we should choose the barbarians.

But, thank Heaven, still another choice is possible. No perpendicular fall is necessary, in front any more than in the rear.

Neither despotism nor terrorism. We desire progress with a gentle slope.

God takes care of that. God's whole policy consists in rendering slopes less steep.

VI

Enjolras and His Lieutenants

It was about this epoch that Enjolras, in view of a possible catastrophe, instituted a kind of mysterious census.

All were present at a secret meeting at the Café Musain.

Enjolras said, mixing his words with a few half-enigmatical but significant metaphors:—

"It is proper that we should know where we stand and on whom we may count. If combatants are required, they must be provided. It can do no harm to have something with which to strike. Passers-by always have more chance of being gored when there are bulls on the road than when there are none. Let us, therefore, reckon a little on the herd. How many of us are there? There is no question of postponing this task until to-morrow. Revolutionists should always be hurried; progress has no time to lose. Let us mistrust the unexpected. Let us not be caught unprepared. We must go over all the seams that we have made and see whether they hold fast. This business ought to be concluded to-day. Courfeyrac, you will see the polytechnic students. It is their day to go out. To-day is Wednesday. Feuilly, you will see those of the Glacière, will you not? Combeferre has promised me to go to Picpus. There is a perfect swarm and an excellent one there. Bahorel will visit the Estrapade. Prouvaire, the masons are growing lukewarm; you will bring us news from the lodge of the Rue de Grenelle-Saint-Honoré. Joly will go to Dupuytren's clinical lecture, and feel the pulse of the medical school. Bossuet will take a little turn in the court and talk with the young law licentiates. I will take charge of the Cougourde myself."

"That arranges everything," said Courfeyrac.

"No."

"What else is there?"

"A very important thing."

"What is that?" asked Courfeyrac.

"The Barrière du Maine," replied Enjolras.

Enjolras remained for a moment as though absorbed in reflection, then he resumed:—

"At the Barrière du Maine there are marble-workers, painters, and journeymen in the studios of sculptors. They are an enthusiastic family, but liable to cool off. I don't know what has been the matter with them for some time past. They are thinking of something else. They are becoming extinguished. They pass their time playing dominoes. There is urgent need that some one should go and talk with them a little, but with firmness. They meet at Richefeu's. They are to be found there between twelve and one o'clock. Those ashes must be fanned into a glow. For that errand I had counted on that abstracted Marius, who is a good fellow on the whole, but he no longer comes to us. I need some one for the Barrière du Maine. I have no one."

"What about me?" said Grantaire. "Here am I."

"You?"

"I."

"You indoctrinate republicans! you warm up hearts that have grown cold in the name of principle!"

"Why not?"

"Are you good for anything?"

"I have a vague ambition in that direction," said Grantaire.

"You do not believe in everything."

"I believe in you."

"Grantaire will you do me a service?"

"Anything. I'll black your boots."

"Well, don't meddle with our affairs. Sleep yourself sober from your absinthe."

"You are an ingrate, Enjolras."

"You the man to go to the Barrière du Maine! You capable of it!"

"I am capable of descending the Rue de Grès, of crossing the Place Saint-Michel, of sloping through the Rue Monsieur-le-Prince, of taking the Rue de Vaugirard, of passing the Carmelites, of turning into the Rue d'Assas, of reaching the Rue du Cherche-Midi, of leaving behind me the Conseil de Guerre, of pacing the Rue des Vieilles-Tuileries, of striding across the boulevard, of following the Chaussée du Maine, of passing the barrier, and entering Richefeu's. I am capable of that. My shoes are capable of that."

"Do you know anything of those comrades who meet at Richefeu's?"

"Not much. We only address each other as *thou*."

"What will you say to them?"

"I will speak to them of Robespierre, pardi! Of Danton. Of principles."

"You?"

"I. But I don't receive justice. When I set about it, I am terrible. I have read Prudhomme, I know the Social Contract, I know my constitution of the year Two by heart. 'The liberty of one citizen ends where the liberty of another citizen begins.' Do you take me for a brute? I have an old bank-bill of the Republic in my drawer. The Rights of Man, the sovereignty of the people, sapristi! I am even a bit of a Hébertist. I can talk the most superb twaddle for six hours by the clock, watch in hand."

"Be serious," said Enjolras.

"I am wild," replied Grantaire.

Enjolras meditated for a few moments, and made the gesture of a man who has taken a resolution.

"Grantaire," he said gravely, "I consent to try you. You shall go to the Barrière du Maine."

Grantaire lived in furnished lodgings very near the Café Musain. He went out, and five minutes later he returned. He had gone home to put on a Robespierre waistcoat.

"Red," said he as he entered, and he looked intently at Enjolras. Then, with the palm of his energetic hand, he laid the two scarlet points of the waistcoat across his breast.

And stepping up to Enjolras, he whispered in his ear:—

"Be easy."

He jammed his hat on resolutely and departed.

A quarter of an hour later, the back room of the Café Musain was deserted. All the friends of the A B C were gone, each in his own direction, each to his own task. Enjolras, who had reserved the Cougourde of Aix for himself, was the last to leave.

Those members of the Cougourde of Aix who were in Paris then met on the plain of Issy, in one of the abandoned quarries which are so numerous in that side of Paris.

As Enjolras walked towards this place, he passed the whole situation in review in his own mind. The gravity of events was self-evident. When facts, the premonitory symptoms of latent social malady, move heavily, the slightest complication stops and entangles them. A phenomenon whence arises ruin and new births. Enjolras descried a luminous uplifting beneath the gloomy skirts of the future. Who knows? Perhaps the moment was at hand. The people were again taking possession of right, and what a fine spectacle! The revolution was again majestically taking possession of France and saying to the world: "The sequel to-morrow!" Enjolras was content. The furnace was being heated. He had at that moment a powder train of friends scattered all over Paris. He composed, in his own mind, with Combeferre's philosophical and penetrating eloquence, Feuilly's cosmopolitan enthusiasm, Courfeyrac's dash, Bahorel's smile, Jean Prouvaire's melancholy, Joly's science, Bossuet's sarcasms, a sort of electric spark which took fire nearly everywhere at once. All hands to work. Surely, the result would answer to the effort. This was well. This made him think of Grantaire.

"Hold," said he to himself, "the Barrière du Maine will not take me far out of my way. What if I were to go on as far as Richefeu's? Let us have a look at what Grantaire is about, and see how he is getting on."

One o'clock was striking from the Vaugirard steeple when Enjolras reached the Richefeu smoking-room.

He pushed open the door, entered, folded his arms, letting the door fall to and strike his shoulders, and gazed at that room filled with tables, men, and smoke.

A voice broke forth from the mist of smoke, interrupted by another voice. It was Grantaire holding a dialogue with an adversary.

Grantaire was sitting opposite another figure, at a marble Saint-Anne table, strewn with grains of bran and dotted with dominos. He was hammering the table with his fist, and this is what Enjolras heard:—

"Double-six."

"Fours."

"The pig! I have no more."

"You are dead. A two."

"Six."

"Three."

"One."

"It's my move."

"Four points."

"Not much."

"It's your turn."

"I have made an enormous mistake."

"You are doing well."

"Fifteen."

"Seven more."

"That makes me twenty-two." (Thoughtfully, "Twenty-two!")

"You weren't expecting that double-six. If I had placed it at the beginning, the whole play would have been changed."

VICTOR HUGO

"A two again."

"One."

"One! Well, five."

"I haven't any."

"It was your play, I believe?"

"Yes."

"Blank."

"What luck he has! Ah! You are lucky! (Long reverie.) Two."

"One."

"Neither five nor one. That's bad for you."

"Domino."

"Plague take it!"

BOOK SECOND
ÉPONINE

I

The Lark's Meadow

Marius had witnessed the unexpected termination of the ambush upon whose track he had set Javert; but Javert had no sooner quitted the building, bearing off his prisoners in three hackney-coaches, than Marius also glided out of the house. It was only nine o'clock in the evening. Marius betook himself to Courfeyrac. Courfeyrac was no longer the imperturbable inhabitant of the Latin Quarter, he had gone to live in the Rue de la Verrerie "for political reasons"; this quarter was one where, at that epoch, insurrection liked to install itself. Marius said to Courfeyrac: "I have come to sleep with you." Courfeyrac dragged a mattress off his bed, which was furnished with two, spread it out on the floor, and said: "There."

At seven o'clock on the following morning, Marius returned to the hovel, paid the quarter's rent which he owed to Ma'am Bougon, had his books, his bed, his table, his commode, and his two chairs loaded on a hand-cart and went off without leaving his address, so that when Javert returned in the course of the morning, for the purpose of questioning Marius as to the events of the preceding evening, he found only Ma'am Bougon, who answered: "Moved away!"

Ma'am Bougon was convinced that Marius was to some extent an accomplice of the robbers who had been seized the night before. "Who would ever have said it?" she exclaimed to the portresses of the quarter, "a young man like that, who had the air of a girl!"

Marius had two reasons for this prompt change of residence. The first was, that he now had a horror of that house, where he had beheld, so close at hand, and in its most repulsive and most ferocious development, a social deformity which is, perhaps, even more terrible than the wicked rich man, the wicked poor man. The second was, that he did not wish to figure in the lawsuit which would insue in all probability, and be brought in to testify against Thénardier.

Javert thought that the young man, whose name he had forgotten, was afraid, and had fled, or perhaps, had not even returned home at the time of the ambush; he made some efforts to find him, however, but without success.

A month passed, then another. Marius was still with Courfeyrac. He had learned from a young licentiate in law, an habitual frequenter of the courts, that Thénardier was in close confinement. Every Monday, Marius had five francs handed in to the clerk's office of La Force for Thénardier.

As Marius had no longer any money, he borrowed the five francs from Courfeyrac. It was the first time in his life that he had ever borrowed money. These periodical five francs were a double riddle to Courfeyrac who lent and to Thénardier who received them. "To whom can they go?" thought Courfeyrac. "Whence can this come to me?" Thénardier asked himself.

Moreover, Marius was heart-broken. Everything had plunged through a trap-door once more. He no longer saw anything before him; his life was again buried in mystery where he wandered fumblingly. He had for a moment beheld very close at hand, in that obscurity, the young girl whom he loved, the old man who seemed to be her father, those unknown beings, who were his only interest and his only hope in this world; and, at the very moment when he thought himself on the point of grasping them, a gust had swept all these shadows away. Not a spark of certainty and truth had been emitted even in the most terrible of collisions. No conjecture was possible. He no longer knew even the name that he thought he knew. It certainly was not Ursule. And the Lark was a nickname. And what was he to think of the old man? Was he actually in hiding from the police? The white-haired workman whom Marius had encountered in the vicinity of the Invalides recurred to his mind. It now seemed probable that that workingman and M. Leblanc were one and the same person. So he disguised himself? That man had his heroic and his equivocal sides. Why had he not called for help? Why had he fled? Was he, or was he not, the father of the young girl? Was he, in short, the man whom Thénardier thought that he recognized? Thénardier might have been mistaken. These formed so many insoluble problems. All this, it is true, detracted nothing from the angelic charms of the young girl of the Luxembourg. Heart-rending distress; Marius bore a passion in his heart, and night over his eyes. He was thrust onward, he was drawn, and he could not stir. All had vanished, save love. Of love itself he had lost the instincts and the sudden illuminations. Ordinarily, this flame which burns us lights us also a little, and casts some useful gleams without. But Marius no longer even heard these mute counsels of passion. He never said to himself: "What if I were to go to such a place? What if I were to try such and such a thing?" The girl whom he could no longer call Ursule was evidently somewhere; nothing warned Marius in what direction he should seek her. His whole life was now summed up in two words; absolute uncertainty within an impenetrable fog. To see her once again; he still aspired to this, but he no longer expected it.

To crown all, his poverty had returned. He felt that icy breath close to him, on his heels. In the midst of his torments, and long before this, he had discontinued his work, and nothing is more dangerous than discontinued work; it is a habit which vanishes. A habit which is easy to get rid of, and difficult to take up again.

A certain amount of dreaming is good, like a narcotic in discreet doses. It lulls to sleep the fevers of the mind at labor, which are sometimes severe, and produces in the spirit a soft and fresh vapor which corrects the over-harsh contours of pure thought, fills in gaps here and there, binds together and rounds off the angles of the ideas. But too much dreaming sinks and drowns. Woe to the brain-worker who allows himself to fall entirely from thought into reverie! He thinks that he can re-ascend with equal ease, and he tells himself that, after all, it is the same thing. Error!

Thought is the toil of the intelligence, reverie its voluptuousness. To replace thought with reverie is to confound a poison with a food.

Marius had begun in that way, as the reader will remember. Passion had supervened and had finished the work of precipitating him into chimæras without object or bottom. One no longer emerges from one's self except for the purpose of going off to dream. Idle production. Tumultuous and stagnant gulf. And, in proportion as labor diminishes, needs increase. This is a law. Man, in a state of reverie, is generally prodigal and slack; the unstrung mind cannot hold life within close bounds.

There is, in that mode of life, good mingled with evil, for if enervation is baleful, generosity is good and healthful. But the poor man who is generous and noble, and who does not work, is lost. Resources are exhausted, needs crop up.

Fatal declivity down which the most honest and the firmest as well as the most feeble and most vicious are drawn, and which ends in one of two holds, suicide or crime.

By dint of going outdoors to think, the day comes when one goes out to throw one's self in the water.

Excess of reverie breeds men like Escousse and Lebras.

Marius was descending this declivity at a slow pace, with his eyes fixed on the girl whom he no longer saw. What we have just written seems strange, and yet it is true. The memory of an absent being kindles in the darkness of the heart; the more it has disappeared, the more it beams; the gloomy and despairing soul sees this light on its horizon; the star of the inner night. She—that was Marius' whole thought. He meditated of nothing else; he was confusedly conscious that his old coat was becoming an impossible coat, and that his new coat was growing old, that his shirts were wearing out, that his hat was wearing out, that his boots were giving out, and he said to himself: "If I could but see her once again before I die!"

One sweet idea alone was left to him, that she had loved him, that her glance had told him so, that she did not know his name, but that she did know his soul, and that, wherever she was, however mysterious the place, she still loved him perhaps. Who knows whether she were not thinking of him as he was thinking of her? Sometimes, in those inexplicable hours such as are experienced by every heart that loves, though he had no reasons for anything but sadness and yet felt an obscure quiver of joy, he said to himself: "It is her thoughts that are coming to me!" Then he added: "Perhaps my thoughts reach her also."

This illusion, at which he shook his head a moment later, was sufficient, nevertheless, to throw beams, which at times resembled hope, into his soul. From time to time, especially at that evening hour which is the most depressing to even the dreamy, he allowed the purest, the most impersonal, the most ideal of the reveries which filled his brain, to fall upon a notebook which contained nothing else. He called this "writing to her."

It must not be supposed that his reason was deranged. Quite the contrary. He had lost the faculty of working and of moving firmly towards any fixed goal, but he was endowed with more clear-sightedness and rectitude than ever. Marius surveyed by a calm and real, although peculiar light, what passed before his eyes, even the most indifferent deeds and men; he pronounced a just criticism on everything with a sort of honest dejection and candid disinterestedness. His judgment, which was almost wholly disassociated from hope, held itself aloof and soared on high.

In this state of mind nothing escaped him, nothing deceived him, and every moment he was discovering the foundation of life, of humanity, and of destiny. Happy, even in the midst of anguish, is he to whom God has given a soul worthy of love and of unhappiness! He who has not viewed the things of this world and the heart of man under this double light has seen nothing and knows nothing of the true.

The soul which loves and suffers is in a state of sublimity.

However, day followed day, and nothing new presented itself. It merely seemed to him, that the sombre space which still remained to be traversed by him was growing shorter with every instant. He thought that he already distinctly perceived the brink of the bottomless abyss.

"What!" he repeated to himself, "shall I not see her again before then!"

When you have ascended the Rue Saint-Jacques, left the barrier on one side and followed the old inner boulevard for some distance, you reach the Rue de la Santé, then the Glacière, and, a little while before arriving at the little river of the Gobelins, you come to a sort of field which is the only spot in the long and monotonous chain of the boulevards of Paris, where Ruysdael would be tempted to sit down.

There is something indescribable there which exhales grace, a green meadow traversed by tightly stretched lines, from which flutter rags drying in the wind, and an old market-gardener's house, built in the time of Louis XIII, with its great roof oddly pierced with dormer windows, dilapidated palisades, a little water amid poplar-trees, women, voices, laughter; on the horizon the Panthéon, the pole of the Deaf-Mutes, the Val-de-Grâce, black, squat, fantastic, amusing, magnificent, and in the background, the severe square crests of the towers of Notre Dame.

As the place is worth looking at, no one goes thither. Hardly one cart or wagoner passes in a quarter of an hour.

It chanced that Marius' solitary strolls led him to this plot of ground, near the water. That day, there was a rarity on the boulevard, a passer-by. Marius, vaguely impressed with the almost savage beauty of the place, asked this passer-by:—"What is the name of this spot?"

The person replied: "It is the Lark's meadow."

And he added: "It was here that Ulbach killed the shepherdess of Ivry."

But after the word "Lark" Marius heard nothing more. These sudden congealments in the state of reverie, which a single word suffices to evoke, do occur. The entire thought is abruptly condensed around an idea, and it is no longer capable of perceiving anything else.

The Lark was the appellation which had replaced Ursule in the depths of Marius' melancholy.—"Stop," said he with a sort of unreasoning stupor peculiar to these mysterious asides, "this is her meadow. I shall know where she lives now."

It was absurd, but irresistible.

And every day he returned to that meadow of the Lark.

II

EMBRYONIC FORMATION OF CRIMES IN THE INCUBATION OF PRISONS

Javert's triumph in the Gorbeau hovel seemed complete, but had not been so.

In the first place, and this constituted the principal anxiety, Javert had not taken the prisoner prisoner. The assassinated man who flees is more suspicious than the assassin, and it is probable that this personage, who had been so precious a capture for the ruffians, would be no less fine a prize for the authorities.

And then, Montparnasse had escaped Javert.

Another opportunity of laying hands on that "devil's dandy" must be waited for. Montparnasse had, in fact, encountered Éponine as she stood on the watch under the trees of the boulevard, and had led her off, preferring to play Nemorin with the daughter rather than Schinderhannes with the father. It was well that he did so. He was free. As for Éponine, Javert had caused her to be seized; a mediocre consolation. Éponine had joined Azelma at Les Madelonettes.

And finally, on the way from the Gorbeau house to La Force, one of the principal prisoners, Claquesous, had been lost. It was not known how this had been effected, the police agents and the sergeants "could not understand it at all." He had converted himself into vapor, he had slipped through the handcuffs, he had trickled through the crevices of the carriage, the fiacre was cracked, and he had fled; all that they were able to say was, that on arriving at the prison, there was no Claquesous. Either the fairies or the police had had a hand in it. Had Claquesous melted into the shadows like a snow-flake in water? Had there been unavowed connivance of the police agents? Did this man belong to the double enigma of order and disorder? Was he concentric with infraction and repression? Had this sphinx his fore paws in crime and his hind paws in authority? Javert did not accept such comminations, and would have bristled up against such compromises; but his squad included other inspectors besides himself, who were more initiated than he, perhaps, although they were his subordinates in the secrets of the Prefecture, and Claquesous had been such a villain that he might make a very good agent. It is an excellent thing for ruffianism and an admirable thing for the police to be on such intimate juggling terms with the night. These double-edged rascals do exist. However that may be, Claquesous had gone astray and was not found again. Javert appeared to be more irritated than amazed at this.

As for Marius, "that booby of a lawyer," who had probably become frightened, and whose name Javert had forgotten, Javert attached very little importance to him. Moreover, a lawyer can be hunted up at any time. But was he a lawyer after all?

The investigation had begun.

The magistrate had thought it advisable not to put one of these men of the band of Patron Minette in close confinement, in the hope that he would chatter. This man was Brujon, the long-haired man of the Rue du Petit-Banquier. He had been let loose in the Charlemagne courtyard, and the eyes of the watchers were fixed on him.

This name of Brujon is one of the souvenirs of La Force. In that hideous courtyard, called the court of the Bâtiment-Neuf (New Building), which the administration called the court Saint-Bernard, and which the robbers called the Fosse-aux-Lions (The Lion's Ditch), on that wall covered with scales and leprosy, which rose on the left to a level with the roofs, near an old door of rusty iron which led to the ancient chapel of the ducal residence of La Force, then turned in a dormitory for ruffians, there could still be seen, twelve years ago, a sort of fortress roughly carved in the stone with a nail, and beneath it this signature:—

BRUJON, 1811.

The Brujon of 1811 was the father of the Brujon of 1832.

The latter, of whom the reader caught but a glimpse at the Gorbeau house, was a very cunning and very adroit young spark, with a bewildered and plaintive air. It was in consequence of this plaintive air that the magistrate had released him, thinking him more useful in the Charlemagne yard than in close confinement.

Robbers do not interrupt their profession because they are in the hands of justice. They do not let themselves be put out by such a trifle as that. To be in prison for one crime is no reason for not beginning on another crime. They are artists, who have one picture in the salon, and who toil, nonetheless, on a new work in their studios.

Brujon seemed to be stupefied by prison. He could sometimes be seen standing by the hour together in front of the sutler's window in the Charlemagne yard, staring like an idiot at the sordid list of prices which began with: *garlic, 62 centimes*, and ended with: *cigar, 5 centimes*. Or he passed his time in trembling, chattering his teeth, saying that he had a fever, and inquiring whether one of the eight and twenty beds in the fever ward was vacant.

All at once, towards the end of February, 1832, it was discovered that Brujon, that somnolent fellow, had had three different commissions executed by the errand-men of the establishment, not under his own name, but in the name of three of his comrades; and they had cost him in all fifty sous, an exorbitant outlay which attracted the attention of the prison corporal.

Inquiries were instituted, and on consulting the tariff of commissions posted in the convict's parlor, it was learned that the fifty sous could be analyzed as follows: three commissions; one to the Panthéon, ten sous; one to Val-de-Grâce, fifteen sous; and one to the Barrière de Grenelle, twenty-five sous. This last was the dearest of the whole tariff. Now, at the Panthéon, at the Val-de-Grâce, and at the Barrière de Grenelle were situated the domiciles of the three very redoubtable prowlers of the barriers, Kruideniers, alias Bizarro, Glorieux, an ex-convict, and Barre-Carosse, upon whom the attention of the police was directed by this incident. It was thought that these men were members of Patron Minette; two of those leaders, Babet and Gueulemer, had been captured. It was supposed that the messages, which had been addressed, not to houses, but to people who were waiting for them in the street, must have contained information with regard to some crime that had been plotted. They were in possession of other indications; they laid hand on the three prowlers, and supposed that they had circumvented some one or other of Brujon's machinations.

About a week after these measures had been taken, one night, as the superintendent of the watch, who had been inspecting the lower dormitory in the Bâtiment-Neuf, was about to drop his chestnut in the box—this was the means adopted to make sure that the watchmen performed their duties punctually; every hour a chestnut must be dropped into all the boxes nailed to the doors of the dormitories—a watchman looked through the peep-hole of the dormitory and beheld Brujon sitting on his bed and writing something by the light of the hall-lamp. The guardian entered, Brujon was put in a solitary cell for a month, but they were not able to seize what he had written. The police learned nothing further about it.

What is certain is, that on the following morning, a "postilion" was flung from the Charlemagne yard into the Lions' Ditch, over the five-story building which separated the two court-yards.

What prisoners call a "postilion" is a pallet of bread artistically moulded, which is sent *into Ireland*, that is to say, over the roofs of a prison, from one courtyard to another. Etymology: over England; from one land to another; *into Ireland*. This little pellet falls in the yard. The man who picks it up opens it and finds in it a note addressed to some prisoner in that yard. If it is a prisoner who finds the treasure, he forwards the note to its destination; if it is a keeper, or one of the prisoners secretly sold who are called *sheep* in prisons and *foxes* in the galleys, the note is taken to the office and handed over to the police.

On this occasion, the postilion reached its address, although the person to whom it was addressed was, at that moment, in solitary confinement. This person was no other than Babet, one of the four heads of Patron Minette.

The postilion contained a roll of paper on which only these two lines were written:—

"Babet. There is an affair in the Rue Plumet. A gate on a garden."

This is what Brujon had written the night before.

In spite of male and female searchers, Babet managed to pass the note from La Force to the Salpêtrière, to a "good friend" whom he had and who was shut up there. This woman in turn transmitted the note to another woman of her acquaintance, a certain Magnon, who was strongly suspected by the police, though not yet arrested. This Magnon, whose name the reader has already seen, had relations with the Thénardier, which will be described in detail later on, and she could, by going to see Éponine, serve as a bridge between the Salpêtrière and Les Madelonettes.

It happened, that at precisely that moment, as proofs were wanting in the investigation directed against Thénardier in the matter of his daughters, Éponine and Azelma were released. When Éponine came out, Magnon, who was watching the gate of the Madelonettes, handed her Brujon's note to Babet, charging her to look into the matter.

Éponine went to the Rue Plumet, recognized the gate and the garden, observed the house, spied, lurked, and, a few days later, brought to Magnon, who delivers in the Rue Clocheperce, a biscuit, which

Magnon transmitted to Babet's mistress in the Salpêtrière. A biscuit, in the shady symbolism of prisons, signifies: Nothing to be done.

So that in less than a week from that time, as Brujon and Babet met in the circle of La Force, the one on his way to the examination, the other on his way from it:—

"Well?" asked Brujon, "the Rue P.?"

"Biscuit," replied Babet. Thus did the fœtus of crime engendered by Brujon in La Force miscarry.

This miscarriage had its consequences, however, which were perfectly distinct from Brujon's programme. The reader will see what they were.

Often when we think we are knotting one thread, we are tying quite another.

III

APPARITION TO FATHER MABEUF

Marius no longer went to see any one, but he sometimes encountered Father Mabeuf by chance.

While Marius was slowly descending those melancholy steps which may be called the cellar stairs, and which lead to places without light, where the happy can be heard walking overhead, M. Mabeuf was descending on his side.

The *Flora of Cauteretz* no longer sold at all. The experiments on indigo had not been successful in the little garden of Austerlitz, which had a bad exposure. M. Mabeuf could cultivate there only a few plants which love shade and dampness. Nevertheless, he did not become discouraged. He had obtained a corner in the Jardin des Plantes, with a good exposure, to make his trials with indigo "at his own expense." For this purpose he had pawned his copperplates of the *Flora*. He had reduced his breakfast to two eggs, and he left one of these for his old servant, to whom he had paid no wages for the last fifteen months. And often his breakfast was his only meal. He no longer smiled with his infantile smile, he had grown morose and no longer received visitors. Marius did well not to dream of going thither. Sometimes, at the hour when M. Mabeuf was on his way to the Jardin des Plantes, the old man and the young man passed each other on the Boulevard de l'Hôpital. They did not speak, and only exchanged a melancholy sign of the head. A heart-breaking thing it is that there comes a moment when misery looses bonds! Two men who have been friends become two chance passers-by.

Royol the bookseller was dead. M. Mabeuf no longer knew his books, his garden, or his indigo: these were the three forms which happiness, pleasure, and hope had assumed for him. This sufficed him for his living. He said to himself: "When I shall have made my balls of blueing, I shall be rich, I will withdraw my copperplates from the pawn-shop, I will put my *Flora* in vogue again with trickery, plenty of money and advertisements in the newspapers and I will buy, I know well where, a copy of Pierre de Médine's *Art de Naviguer*, with wood-cuts, edition of 1655." In the meantime, he toiled all day over his plot of indigo, and at night he returned home to water his garden, and to read his books. At that epoch, M. Mabeuf was nearly eighty years of age.

One evening he had a singular apparition.

He had returned home while it was still broad daylight. Mother Plutarque, whose health was declining, was ill and in bed. He had dined on a bone, on which a little meat lingered, and a bit of bread that he had found on the kitchen table, and had seated himself on an overturned stone post, which took the place of a bench in his garden.

Near this bench there rose, after the fashion in orchard-gardens, a sort of large chest, of beams and planks, much dilapidated, a rabbit-hutch on the ground floor, a fruit-closet on the first. There was nothing in the hutch, but there were a few apples in the fruit-closet,—the remains of the winter's provision.

M. Mabeuf had set himself to turning over and reading, with the aid of his glasses, two books of which he was passionately fond and in which, a serious thing at his age, he was interested. His natural timidity rendered him accessible to the acceptance of superstitions in a certain degree. The first of these books was the famous treatise of President Delancre, *De l'Inconstance des Démons*; the other was a quarto by Mutor de la Rubaudière, *Sur les Diables de Vauvert et les Gobelins de la Bièvre*. This last-mentioned old volume interested him all the more, because his garden had been one of the spots haunted by goblins in former times. The twilight had begun to whiten what was on high and to blacken all below. As he read, over the top of the book which he held in his hand, Father Mabeuf was surveying his plants, and among others a magnificent rhododendron which was one of his consolations; four days of heat, wind, and sun without a drop of rain, had passed; the stalks were bending, the buds drooping, the leaves falling; all this needed water, the rhododendron was particularly sad. Father Mabeuf was one of those persons for whom plants have souls. The old man had toiled all day over his indigo plot, he was worn out with fatigue, but he rose, laid his books on the bench, and walked, all bent over and with tottering footsteps, to the well, but when he had grasped the chain, he could not even draw it sufficiently to unhook it. Then he turned round and cast a glance of anguish toward heaven which was becoming studded with stars.

The evening had that serenity which overwhelms the troubles of man beneath an indescribably mournful and eternal joy. The night promised to be as arid as the day had been.

"Stars everywhere!" thought the old man; "not the tiniest cloud! Not a drop of water!"

And his head, which had been upraised for a moment, fell back upon his breast.

He raised it again, and once more looked at the sky, murmuring:—

"A tear of dew! A little pity!"

He tried again to unhook the chain of the well, and could not.

At that moment, he heard a voice saying:—

"Father Mabeuf, would you like to have me water your garden for you?"

At the same time, a noise as of a wild animal passing became audible in the hedge, and he beheld emerging from the shrubbery a sort of tall, slender girl, who drew herself up in front of him and stared boldly at him. She had less the air of a human being than of a form which had just blossomed forth from the twilight.

Before Father Mabeuf, who was easily terrified, and who was, as we have said, quick to take alarm, was able to reply by a single syllable, this being, whose movements had a sort of odd abruptness in the darkness, had unhooked the chain, plunged in and withdrawn the bucket, and filled the watering-pot, and the goodman beheld this apparition, which had bare feet and a tattered petticoat, running about among the flower-beds distributing life around her. The sound of the watering-pot on the leaves filled Father Mabeuf's soul with ecstasy. It seemed to him that the rhododendron was happy now.

The first bucketful emptied, the girl drew a second, then a third. She watered the whole garden.

There was something about her, as she thus ran about among paths, where her outline appeared perfectly black, waving her angular arms, and with her fichu all in rags, that resembled a bat.

When she had finished, Father Mabeuf approached her with tears in his eyes, and laid his hand on her brow.

"God will bless you," said he, "you are an angel since you take care of the flowers."

"No," she replied. "I am the devil, but that's all the same to me."

The old man exclaimed, without either waiting for or hearing her response:—

"What a pity that I am so unhappy and so poor, and that I can do nothing for you!"

"You can do something," said she.

"What?"

"Tell me where M. Marius lives."

The old man did not understand. "What Monsieur Marius?"

He raised his glassy eyes and seemed to be seeking something that had vanished.

"A young man who used to come here."

In the meantime, M. Mabeuf had searched his memory.

"Ah! yes—" he exclaimed. "I know what you mean. Wait! Monsieur Marius—the Baron Marius Pontmercy, parbleu! He lives,—or rather, he no longer lives,—ah well, I don't know."

As he spoke, he had bent over to train a branch of rhododendron, and he continued:—

"Hold, I know now. He very often passes along the boulevard, and goes in the direction of the Glacière, Rue Croulebarbe. The meadow of the Lark. Go there. It is not hard to meet him."

When M. Mabeuf straightened himself up, there was no longer any one there; the girl had disappeared.

He was decidedly terrified.

"Really," he thought, "if my garden had not been watered, I should think that she was a spirit."

An hour later, when he was in bed, it came back to him, and as he fell asleep, at that confused moment when thought, like that fabulous bird which changes itself into a fish in order to cross the sea, little by little assumes the form of a dream in order to traverse slumber, he said to himself in a bewildered way:—

"In sooth, that greatly resembles what Rubaudière narrates of the goblins. Could it have been a goblin?"

IV

An Apparition to Marius

Some days after this visit of a "spirit" to Farmer Mabeuf, one morning,—it was on a Monday, the day when Marius borrowed the hundred-sou piece from Courfeyrac for Thénardier—Marius had put this coin in his pocket, and before carrying it to the clerk's office, he had gone "to take a little stroll," in the hope that this would make him work on his return. It was always thus, however. As soon as he rose, he seated himself before a book and a sheet of paper in order to scribble some translation; his task at that epoch consisted in turning into French a celebrated quarrel between Germans, the Gans and Savigny controversy; he took Savigny, he took Gans, read four lines, tried to write one, could not, saw a star between him and his paper, and rose from his chair, saying: "I shall go out. That will put me in spirits."

And off he went to the Lark's meadow.

There he beheld more than ever the star, and less than ever Savigny and Gans.

He returned home, tried to take up his work again, and did not succeed; there was no means of re-knotting a single one of the threads which were broken in his brain; then he said to himself: "I will not go out to-morrow. It prevents my working." And he went out every day.

He lived in the Lark's meadow more than in Courfeyrac's lodgings. That was his real address: Boulevard de la Santé, at the seventh tree from the Rue Croulebarbe.

That morning he had quitted the seventh tree and had seated himself on the parapet of the River des Gobelins. A cheerful sunlight penetrated the freshly unfolded and luminous leaves.

He was dreaming of "Her." And his meditation turning to a reproach, fell back upon himself; he reflected dolefully on his idleness, his paralysis of soul, which was gaining on him, and of that night which was growing more dense every moment before him, to such a point that he no longer even saw the sun.

Nevertheless, athwart this painful extrication of indistinct ideas which was not even a monologue, so feeble had action become in him, and he had no longer the force to care to despair, athwart this melancholy absorption, sensations from without did reach him. He heard behind him, beneath him, on both banks of the river, the laundresses of the Gobelins beating their linen, and above his head, the birds chattering and singing in the elm-trees. On the one hand, the sound of liberty, the careless happiness of the leisure which has wings; on the other, the sound of toil. What caused him to meditate deeply, and almost reflect, were two cheerful sounds.

All at once, in the midst of his dejected ecstasy, he heard a familiar voice saying:—

"Come! Here he is!"

He raised his eyes, and recognized that wretched child who had come to him one morning, the elder of the Thénardier daughters, Éponine; he knew her name now. Strange to say, she had grown poorer and prettier, two steps which it had not seemed within her power to take. She had accomplished a double progress, towards the light and towards distress. She was barefooted and in rags, as on the day when she had so resolutely entered his chamber, only her rags were two months older now, the holes were larger, the tatters more sordid. It was the same harsh voice, the same brow dimmed and wrinkled with tan, the same free, wild, and vacillating glance. She had besides, more than formerly, in her face that indescribably terrified and lamentable something which sojourn in a prison adds to wretchedness.

She had bits of straw and hay in her hair, not like Ophelia through having gone mad from the contagion of Hamlet's madness, but because she had slept in the loft of some stable.

And in spite of it all, she was beautiful. What a star art thou, O youth!

In the meantime, she had halted in front of Marius with a trace of joy in her livid countenance, and something which resembled a smile.

She stood for several moments as though incapable of speech.

"So I have met you at last!" she said at length. "Father Mabeuf was right, it was on this boulevard! How I have hunted for you! If you only knew! Do you know? I have been in the jug. A fortnight! They let me out! seeing that there was nothing against me, and that, moreover, I had not reached years of discretion. I lack two months of it. Oh! how I have hunted for you! These six weeks! So you don't live down there any more?"

"No," said Marius.

"Ah! I understand. Because of that affair. Those take-downs are disagreeable. You cleared out. Come now! Why do you wear old hats like this! A young man like you ought to have fine clothes. Do you know, Monsieur Marius, Father Mabeuf calls you Baron Marius, I don't know what. It isn't true that you are a baron? Barons are old fellows, they go to the Luxembourg, in front of the château, where there is the most sun, and they read the *Quotidienne* for a sou. I once carried a letter to a baron of that sort. He was over a hundred years old. Say, where do you live now?"

Marius made no reply.

"Ah!" she went on, "you have a hole in your shirt. I must sew it up for you."

She resumed with an expression which gradually clouded over:—

"You don't seem glad to see me."

Marius held his peace; she remained silent for a moment, then exclaimed:—

"But if I choose, nevertheless, I could force you to look glad!"

"What?" demanded Marius. "What do you mean?"

"Ah! you used to call me *thou*," she retorted.

"Well, then, what dost thou mean?"

She bit her lips; she seemed to hesitate, as though a prey to some sort of inward conflict. At last she appeared to come to a decision.

"So much the worse, I don't care. You have a melancholy air, I want you to be pleased. Only promise me that you will smile. I want to see you smile and hear you say: 'Ah, well, that's good.' Poor Mr. Marius! you know? You promised me that you would give me anything I like—"

"Yes! Only speak!"

She looked Marius full in the eye, and said:—

"I have the address."

Marius turned pale. All the blood flowed back to his heart.

"What address?"

"The address that you asked me to get!"

She added, as though with an effort:—

"The address—you know very well!"

"Yes!" stammered Marius.

"Of that young lady."

This word uttered, she sighed deeply.

Marius sprang from the parapet on which he had been sitting and seized her hand distractedly.

"Oh! Well! lead me thither! Tell me! Ask of me anything you wish! Where is it?"

VICTOR HUGO

"Come with me," she responded. "I don't know the street or number very well; it is in quite the other direction from here, but I know the house well, I will take you to it."

She withdrew her hand and went on, in a tone which could have rent the heart of an observer, but which did not even graze Marius in his intoxicated and ecstatic state:—

"Oh! how glad you are!"

A cloud swept across Marius' brow. He seized Éponine by the arm:—

"Swear one thing to me!"

"Swear!" said she, "what does that mean? Come! You want me to swear?"

And she laughed.

"Your father! promise me, Éponine! Swear to me that you will not give this address to your father!"

She turned to him with a stupefied air.

"Éponine! How do you know that my name is Éponine?"

"Promise what I tell you!"

But she did not seem to hear him.

"That's nice! You have called me Éponine!"

Marius grasped both her arms at once.

"But answer me, in the name of Heaven! pay attention to what I am saying to you, swear to me that you will not tell your father this address that you know!"

"My father!" said she. "Ah yes, my father! Be at ease. He's in close confinement. Besides, what do I care for my father!"

"But you do not promise me!" exclaimed Marius.

"Let go of me!" she said, bursting into a laugh, "how you do shake me! Yes! Yes! I promise that! I swear that to you! What is that to me? I will not tell my father the address. There! Is that right? Is that it?"

"Nor to any one?" said Marius.

"Nor to any one."

"Now," resumed Marius, "take me there."

"Immediately?"

"Immediately."

"Come along. Ah! how pleased he is!" said she.

After a few steps she halted.

"You are following me too closely, Monsieur Marius. Let me go on ahead, and follow me so, without seeming to do it. A nice young man like you must not be seen with a woman like me."

No tongue can express all that lay in that word, *woman*, thus pronounced by that child.

She proceeded a dozen paces and then halted once more; Marius joined her. She addressed him sideways, and without turning towards him:—

"By the way, you know that you promised me something?"

Marius fumbled in his pocket. All that he owned in the world was the five francs intended for Thénardier the father. He took them and laid them in Éponine's hand.

She opened her fingers and let the coin fall to the ground, and gazed at him with a gloomy air.

"I don't want your money," said she.

BOOK THIRD
THE HOUSE IN THE RUE PLUMET

I

The House with a Secret

About the middle of the last century, a chief justice in the Parliament of Paris having a mistress and concealing the fact, for at that period the grand seignors displayed their mistresses, and the bourgeois concealed them, had "a little house" built in the Faubourg Saint-Germain, in the deserted Rue Blomet, which is now called Rue Plumet, not far from the spot which was then designated as *Combat des Animaux*.

This house was composed of a single-storied pavilion; two rooms on the ground floor, two chambers on the first floor, a kitchen downstairs, a boudoir upstairs, an attic under the roof, the whole preceded by a garden with a large gate opening on the street. This garden was about an acre and a half in extent. This was all that could be seen by passers-by; but behind the pavilion there was a narrow courtyard, and at the end of the courtyard a low building consisting of two rooms and a cellar, a sort of preparation destined to conceal a child and nurse in case of need. This building communicated in the rear by a masked door which opened by a secret spring, with a long, narrow, paved winding corridor, open to the sky, hemmed in with two lofty walls, which, hidden with wonderful art, and lost as it were between garden enclosures and cultivated land, all of whose angles and detours it followed, ended in another door, also with a secret lock which opened a quarter of a league away, almost in another quarter, at the solitary extremity of the Rue du Babylone.

Through this the chief justice entered, so that even those who were spying on him and following him would merely have observed that the justice betook himself every day in a mysterious way somewhere, and would never have suspected that to go to the Rue de Babylone was to go to the Rue Blomet. Thanks to clever purchasers of land, the magistrate had been able to make a secret, sewer-like passage on his own property, and consequently, without interference. Later on, he had sold in little parcels, for gardens and market gardens, the lots of ground adjoining the corridor, and the proprietors of these lots on both sides thought they had a party wall before their eyes, and did not even suspect the long, paved ribbon winding between two walls amid their flower-beds and their orchards. Only the birds beheld this curiosity. It is probable that the linnets and tomtits of the last century gossiped a great deal about the chief justice.

The pavilion, built of stone in the taste of Mansard, wainscoted and furnished in the Watteau style, rocaille on the inside, old-fashioned on the outside, walled in with a triple hedge of flowers, had something discreet, coquettish, and solemn about it, as befits a caprice of love and magistracy.

This house and corridor, which have now disappeared, were in existence fifteen years ago. In '93 a coppersmith had purchased the house with the idea of demolishing it, but had not been able to pay the price; the nation made him bankrupt. So that it was the house which demolished the coppersmith. After that, the house remained uninhabited, and fell slowly to ruin, as does every dwelling to which the presence of man does not communicate life. It had remained fitted with its old furniture, was always for sale or to let, and the ten or a dozen people who passed through the Rue Plumet were warned of the fact by a yellow and illegible bit of writing which had hung on the garden wall since 1819.

Towards the end of the Restoration, these same passers-by might have noticed that the bill had disappeared, and even that the shutters on the first floor were open. The house was occupied, in fact. The windows had short curtains, a sign that there was a woman about.

In the month of October, 1829, a man of a certain age had presented himself and had hired the house just as it stood, including, of course, the back building and the lane which ended in the Rue de Babylone. He had had the secret openings of the two doors to this passage repaired. The house, as we have just mentioned, was still very nearly furnished with the justice's old fitting; the new tenant had ordered some repairs, had added what was lacking here and there, had replaced the paving-stones in the yard, bricks in the floors, steps in the stairs, missing bits in the inlaid floors and the glass in the lattice windows, and had finally installed himself there with a young girl and an elderly maid-servant, without commotion, rather like a person who is slipping in than like a man who is entering his own house. The neighbors did not gossip about him, for the reason that there were no neighbors.

This unobtrusive tenant was Jean Valjean, the young girl was Cosette. The servant was a woman named Toussaint, whom Jean Valjean had saved from the hospital and from wretchedness, and who was elderly, a stammerer, and from the provinces, three qualities which had decided Jean Valjean to take her with him. He had hired the house under the name of M. Fauchelevent, independent gentleman. In all that has been related heretofore, the reader has, doubtless, been no less prompt than Thénardier to recognize Jean Valjean.

Why had Jean Valjean quitted the convent of the Petit-Picpus? What had happened?

Nothing had happened.

It will be remembered that Jean Valjean was happy in the convent, so happy that his conscience finally took the alarm. He saw Cosette every day, he felt paternity spring up and develop within him more and more, he brooded over the soul of that child, he said to himself that she was his, that nothing could take her from him, that this would last indefinitely, that she would certainly become a nun, being thereto gently incited every day, that thus the convent was henceforth the universe for her as it was for him, that he should grow old there, and that she would grow up there, that she would grow old there, and that he should die there; that, in short, delightful hope, no separation was possible. On reflecting upon this, he fell into perplexity. He interrogated himself. He asked himself if all that happiness were really his, if it were not composed of the happiness of another, of the happiness of that child which he, an old man, was confiscating and stealing; if that were not theft? He said to himself, that this child had a right to know life before renouncing it, that to deprive her in advance, and in some sort without consulting her, of all joys, under the pretext of saving her from all trials, to take advantage of her ignorance of her isolation, in order to make an artificial vocation germinate in her, was to rob a human creature of its nature and to lie to God. And who knows if, when she came to be aware of all this some day, and found herself a nun to her sorrow, Cosette would not come to hate him? A last, almost selfish thought, and less heroic than the rest, but which was intolerable to him. He resolved to quit the convent.

He resolved on this; he recognized with anguish, the fact that it was necessary. As for objections, there were none. Five years' sojourn between these four walls and of disappearance had necessarily destroyed or dispersed the elements of fear. He could return tranquilly among men. He had grown old, and all had undergone a change. Who would recognize him now? And then, to face the worst, there was danger only for himself, and he had no right to condemn Cosette to the cloister for the reason that he had been condemned to the galleys. Besides, what is danger in comparison with the right? Finally, nothing prevented his being prudent and taking his precautions.

As for Cosette's education, it was almost finished and complete.

His determination once taken, he awaited an opportunity. It was not long in presenting itself. Old Fauchelevent died.

Jean Valjean demanded an audience with the revered prioress and told her that, having come into a little inheritance at the death of his brother, which permitted him henceforth to live without working, he should leave the service of the convent and take his daughter with him; but that, as it was not just that Cosette, since she had not taken the vows, should have received her education gratuitously, he humbly begged the Reverend Prioress to see fit that he should offer to the community, as indemnity, for the five years which Cosette had spent there, the sum of five thousand francs.

It was thus that Jean Valjean quitted the convent of the Perpetual Adoration.

On leaving the convent, he took in his own arms the little valise the key to which he still wore on his person, and would permit no porter to touch it. This puzzled Cosette, because of the odor of embalming which proceeded from it.

Let us state at once, that this trunk never quitted him more. He always had it in his chamber. It was the first and only thing sometimes, that he carried off in his moving when he moved about. Cosette laughed at it, and called this valise his *inseparable*, saying: "I am jealous of it."

Nevertheless, Jean Valjean did not reappear in the open air without profound anxiety.

He discovered the house in the Rue Plumet, and hid himself from sight there. Henceforth he was in the possession of the name:—Ultime Fauchelevent.

At the same time he hired two other apartments in Paris, in order that he might attract less attention than if he were to remain always in the same quarter, and so that he could, at need, take himself off at the slightest disquietude which should assail him, and in short, so that he might not again be caught unprovided as on the night when he had so miraculously escaped from Javert. These two apartments were very pitiable, poor in appearance, and in two quarters which were far remote from each other, the one in the Rue de l'Ouest, the other in the Rue de l'Homme Armé.

He went from time to time, now to the Rue de l'Homme Armé, now to the Rue de l'Ouest, to pass a month or six weeks, without taking Toussaint. He had himself served by the porters, and gave himself out as a gentleman from the suburbs, living on his funds, and having a little temporary resting-place in town. This lofty virtue had three domiciles in Paris for the sake of escaping from the police.

II

JEAN VALJEAN AS A NATIONAL GUARD

However, properly speaking, he lived in the Rue Plumet, and he had arranged his existence there in the following fashion:—

Cosette and the servant occupied the pavilion; she had the big sleeping-room with the painted pier-glasses, the boudoir with the gilded fillets, the justice's drawing-room furnished with tapestries and vast armchairs; she had the garden. Jean Valjean had a canopied bed of antique damask in three colors and a beautiful Persian rug purchased in the Rue du Figuier-Saint-Paul at Mother Gaucher's, put into Cosette's chamber, and, in order to redeem the severity of these magnificent old things, he had amalgamated with this bric-à-brac all the gay and graceful little pieces of furniture suitable to young girls, an étagère, a bookcase filled with gilt-edged books, an inkstand, a blotting-book, paper, a work-table incrusted with mother of pearl, a silver-gilt dressing-case, a toilet service in Japanese porcelain. Long damask curtains with a red foundation and three colors, like those on the bed, hung at the windows of the first floor. On the ground floor, the curtains were of tapestry. All winter long, Cosette's little house was heated from top to bottom. Jean Valjean inhabited the sort of porter's lodge which was situated at the end of the back courtyard, with a mattress on a folding-bed, a white wood table, two straw chairs, an earthenware water-jug, a few old volumes on a shelf, his beloved valise in one corner, and never any fire. He dined with Cosette, and he had a loaf of black bread on the table for his own use.

When Toussaint came, he had said to her: "It is the young lady who is the mistress of this house."—"And you, monsieur?" Toussaint replied in amazement.—"I am a much better thing than the master, I am the father."

Cosette had been taught housekeeping in the convent, and she regulated their expenditure, which was very modest. Every day, Jean Valjean put his arm through Cosette's and took her for a walk. He led her to the Luxembourg, to the least frequented walk, and every Sunday he took her to mass at Saint-Jacques-du-Haut-Pas, because that was a long way off. As it was a very poor quarter, he bestowed alms largely there, and the poor people surrounded him in church, which had drawn down upon him Thénardier's epistle: "To the benevolent gentleman of the church of Saint-Jacques-du-Haut-Pas." He was fond of taking Cosette to visit the poor and the sick. No stranger ever entered the house in the Rue Plumet. Toussaint brought their provisions, and Jean Valjean went himself for water to a fountain nearby on the boulevard. Their wood and wine were put into a half-subterranean hollow lined with rock-work which lay near the Rue de Babylone and which had formerly served the chief-justice as a grotto; for at the epoch of follies and "Little Houses" no love was without a grotto.

In the door opening on the Rue de Babylone, there was a box destined for the reception of letters and papers; only, as the three inhabitants of the pavilion in the Rue Plumet received neither papers nor letters, the entire usefulness of that box, formerly the go-between of a love affair, and the confidant of a love-lorn lawyer, was now limited to the tax-collector's notices, and the summons of the guard. For M. Fauchelevent, independent gentleman, belonged to the national guard; he had not been able to escape through the fine meshes of the census of 1831. The municipal information collected at that time had even reached the convent of the Petit-Picpus, a sort of impenetrable and holy cloud, whence Jean Valjean had emerged in venerable guise, and, consequently, worthy of mounting guard in the eyes of the town-hall.

Three or four times a year, Jean Valjean donned his uniform and mounted guard; he did this willingly, however; it was a correct disguise which mixed him with every one, and yet left him solitary. Jean Valjean had just attained his sixtieth birthday, the age of legal exemption; but he did not appear to be over fifty; moreover, he had no desire to escape his sergeant-major nor to quibble with Comte de Lobau; he possessed no civil status, he was concealing his name, he was concealing his identity, so he concealed his age, he concealed everything; and, as we have just said, he willingly did his duty as a national guard; the sum of his ambition lay in resembling any other man who paid his taxes. This man had for his ideal, within, the angel, without, the bourgeois.

Let us note one detail, however; when Jean Valjean went out with Cosette, he dressed as the reader has already seen, and had the air of a retired officer. When he went out alone, which was generally at night, he was always dressed in a workingman's trousers and blouse, and wore a cap which concealed his face. Was this precaution or humility? Both. Cosette was accustomed to the enigmatical side of her destiny, and hardly noticed her father's peculiarities. As for Toussaint, she venerated Jean Valjean, and thought everything he did right.

One day, her butcher, who had caught a glimpse of Jean Valjean, said to her: "That's a queer fish." She replied: "He's a saint."

Neither Jean Valjean nor Cosette nor Toussaint ever entered or emerged except by the door on the Rue de Babylone. Unless seen through the garden gate it would have been difficult to guess that they lived in the Rue Plumet. That gate was always closed. Jean Valjean had left the garden uncultivated, in order not to attract attention.

In this, possibly, he made a mistake.

III

Foliis AC Frondibus

The garden thus left to itself for more than half a century had become extraordinary and charming. The passers-by of forty years ago halted to gaze at it, without a suspicion of the secrets which it hid in its fresh and verdant depths. More than one dreamer of that epoch often allowed his thoughts and his eyes to penetrate indiscreetly between the bars of that ancient, padlocked gate, twisted, tottering, fastened to two green and moss-covered pillars, and oddly crowned with a pediment of undecipherable arabesque.

There was a stone bench in one corner, one or two mouldy statues, several lattices which had lost their nails with time, were rotting on the wall, and there were no walks nor turf; but there was enough grass everywhere. Gardening had taken its departure, and nature had returned. Weeds abounded, which was a great piece of luck for a poor corner of land. The festival of gilliflowers was something splendid. Nothing in this garden obstructed the sacred effort of things towards life; venerable growth reigned there among them. The trees had bent over towards the nettles, the plant had sprung upward, the branch had inclined, that which crawls on the earth had gone in search of that which expands in the air, that which floats on the wind had bent over towards that which trails in the moss; trunks, boughs, leaves, fibres, clusters, tendrils, shoots, spines, thorns, had mingled, crossed, married, confounded themselves in each other; vegetation in a deep and close embrace, had celebrated and accomplished there, under the well-pleased eye of the Creator, in that enclosure three hundred feet square, the holy mystery of fraternity, symbol of the human fraternity. This garden was no longer a garden, it was a colossal thicket, that is to say, something as impenetrable as a forest, as peopled as a city, quivering like a nest, sombre like a cathedral, fragrant like a bouquet, solitary as a tomb, living as a throng.

In Floréal this enormous thicket, free behind its gate and within its four walls, entered upon the secret labor of germination, quivered in the rising sun, almost like an animal which drinks in the breaths of cosmic love, and which feels the sap of April rising and boiling in its veins, and shakes to the wind its enormous wonderful green locks, sprinkled on the damp earth, on the defaced statues, on the crumbling steps of the pavilion, and even on the pavement of the deserted street, flowers like stars, dew like pearls, fecundity, beauty, life, joy, perfumes. At midday, a thousand white butterflies took refuge there, and it was a divine spectacle to see that living summer snow whirling about there in flakes amid the shade. There, in those gay shadows of verdure, a throng of innocent voices spoke sweetly to the soul, and what the twittering forgot to say the humming completed. In the evening, a dreamy vapor exhaled from the garden and enveloped it; a shroud of mist, a calm and celestial sadness covered it; the intoxicating perfume of the honeysuckles and convolvulus poured out from every part of it, like an exquisite and subtle poison; the last appeals of the woodpeckers and the wagtails were audible as they dozed among the branches; one felt the sacred intimacy of the birds and the trees; by day the wings rejoice the leaves, by night the leaves protect the wings.

In winter the thicket was black, dripping, bristling, shivering, and allowed some glimpse of the house. Instead of flowers on the branches and dew in the flowers, the long silvery tracks of the snails were visible on the cold, thick carpet of yellow leaves; but in any fashion, under any aspect, at all seasons, spring, winter, summer, autumn, this tiny enclosure breathed forth melancholy, contemplation, solitude, liberty, the absence of man, the presence of God; and the rusty old gate had the air of saying: "This garden belongs to me."

It was of no avail that the pavements of Paris were there on every side, the classic and splendid hotels of the Rue de Varennes a couple of paces away, the dome of the Invalides close at hand, the Chamber of Deputies not far off; the carriages of the Rue de Bourgogne and of the Rue Saint-Dominique rumbled luxuriously, in vain, in the vicinity, in vain did the yellow, brown, white, and red omnibuses cross each other's course at the neighboring crossroads; the Rue Plumet was the desert; and the death of the former proprietors, the revolution which had passed over it, the crumbling away of ancient fortunes, absence, forgetfulness, forty years of abandonment and widowhood, had sufficed to restore to this privileged spot ferns, mulleins, hemlock, yarrow, tall weeds, great crimped plants, with large leaves of pale green cloth, lizards, beetles, uneasy and rapid insects; to cause to spring forth from the depths of the earth and to reappear between those four walls a certain indescribable and savage grandeur; and for nature, which disconcerts the petty arrangements of man, and which sheds herself

VICTOR HUGO

always thoroughly where she diffuses herself at all, in the ant as well as in the eagle, to blossom out in a petty little Parisian garden with as much rude force and majesty as in a virgin forest of the New World.

Nothing is small, in fact; any one who is subject to the profound and penetrating influence of nature knows this. Although no absolute satisfaction is given to philosophy, either to circumscribe the cause or to limit the effect, the contemplator falls into those unfathomable ecstasies caused by these decompositions of force terminating in unity. Everything toils at everything.

Algebra is applied to the clouds; the radiation of the star profits the rose; no thinker would venture to affirm that the perfume of the hawthorn is useless to the constellations. Who, then, can calculate the course of a molecule? How do we know that the creation of worlds is not determined by the fall of grains of sand? Who knows the reciprocal ebb and flow of the infinitely great and the infinitely little, the reverberations of causes in the precipices of being, and the avalanches of creation? The tiniest worm is of importance; the great is little, the little is great; everything is balanced in necessity; alarming vision for the mind. There are marvellous relations between beings and things; in that inexhaustible whole, from the sun to the grub, nothing despises the other; all have need of each other. The light does not bear away terrestrial perfumes into the azure depths, without knowing what it is doing; the night distributes stellar essences to the sleeping flowers. All birds that fly have round their leg the thread of the infinite. Germination is complicated with the bursting forth of a meteor and with the peck of a swallow cracking its egg, and it places on one level the birth of an earthworm and the advent of Socrates. Where the telescope ends, the microscope begins. Which of the two possesses the larger field of vision? Choose. A bit of mould is a pleiad of flowers; a nebula is an ant-hill of stars. The same promiscuousness, and yet more unprecedented, exists between the things of the intelligence and the facts of substance. Elements and principles mingle, combine, wed, multiply with each other, to such a point that the material and the moral world are brought eventually to the same clearness. The phenomenon is perpetually returning upon itself. In the vast cosmic exchanges the universal life goes and comes in unknown quantities, rolling entirely in the invisible mystery of effluvia, employing everything, not losing a single dream, not a single slumber, sowing an animalcule here, crumbling to bits a planet there, oscillating and winding, making of light a force and of thought an element, disseminated and invisible, dissolving all, except that geometrical point, the *I*; bringing everything back to the soul-atom; expanding everything in God, entangling all activity, from summit to base, in the obscurity of a dizzy mechanism, attaching the flight of an insect to the movement of the earth, subordinating, who knows? Were it only by the identity of the law, the evolution of the comet in the firmament to the whirling of the infusoria in the drop of water. A machine made of mind. Enormous gearing, the prime motor of which is the gnat, and whose final wheel is the zodiac.

IV

CHANGE OF GATE

It seemed that this garden, created in olden days to conceal wanton mysteries, had been transformed and become fitted to shelter chaste mysteries. There were no longer either arbors, or bowling greens, or tunnels, or grottos; there was a magnificent, dishevelled obscurity falling like a veil over all. Paphos had been made over into Eden. It is impossible to say what element of repentance had rendered this retreat wholesome. This flower-girl now offered her blossom to the soul. This coquettish garden, formerly decidedly compromised, had returned to virginity and modesty. A justice assisted by a gardener, a goodman who thought that he was a continuation of Lamoignon, and another goodman who thought that he was a continuation of Lenôtre, had turned it about, cut, ruffled, decked, moulded it to gallantry; nature had taken possession of it once more, had filled it with shade, and had arranged it for love.

There was, also, in this solitude, a heart which was quite ready. Love had only to show himself; he had here a temple composed of verdure, grass, moss, the sight of birds, tender shadows, agitated branches, and a soul made of sweetness, of faith, of candor, of hope, of aspiration, and of illusion.

Cosette had left the convent when she was still almost a child; she was a little more than fourteen, and she was at the "ungrateful age"; we have already said, that with the exception of her eyes, she was homely rather than pretty; she had no ungraceful feature, but she was awkward, thin, timid and bold at once, a grown-up little girl, in short.

Her education was finished, that is to say, she has been taught religion, and even and above all, devotion; then "history," that is to say the thing that bears that name in convents, geography, grammar, the participles, the kings of France, a little music, a little drawing, etc.; but in all other respects she was utterly ignorant, which is a great charm and a great peril. The soul of a young girl should not be left in the dark; later on, mirages that are too abrupt and too lively are formed there, as in a dark chamber. She should be gently and discreetly enlightened, rather with the reflection of realities than with their harsh and direct light. A useful and graciously austere half-light which dissipates puerile fears and obviates falls. There is nothing but the maternal instinct, that admirable intuition composed of the memories of the virgin and the experience of the woman, which knows how this half-light is to be created and of what it should consist.

Nothing supplies the place of this instinct. All the nuns in the world are not worth as much as one mother in the formation of a young girl's soul.

Cosette had had no mother. She had only had many mothers, in the plural.

As for Jean Valjean, he was, indeed, all tenderness, all solicitude; but he was only an old man and he knew nothing at all.

Now, in this work of education, in this grave matter of preparing a woman for life, what science is required to combat that vast ignorance which is called innocence!

Nothing prepares a young girl for passions like the convent. The convent turns the thoughts in the direction of the unknown. The heart, thus thrown back upon itself, works downward within itself, since it cannot overflow, and grows deep, since it cannot expand. Hence visions, suppositions, conjectures, outlines of romances, a desire for adventures, fantastic constructions, edifices built wholly in the inner obscurity of the mind, sombre and secret abodes where the passions immediately find a lodgement as soon as the open gate permits them to enter. The convent is a compression which, in order to triumph over the human heart, should last during the whole life.

On quitting the convent, Cosette could have found nothing more sweet and more dangerous than the house in the Rue Plumet. It was the continuation of solitude with the beginning of liberty; a garden that was closed, but a nature that was acrid, rich, voluptuous, and fragrant; the same dreams as in the convent, but with glimpses of young men; a grating, but one that opened on the street.

Still, when she arrived there, we repeat, she was only a child. Jean Valjean gave this neglected garden over to her. "Do what you like with it," he said to her. This amused Cosette; she turned over all the clumps and all the stones, she hunted for "beasts"; she played in it, while awaiting the time when she would dream in it; she loved this garden for the insects that she found beneath her feet amid the grass, while awaiting the day when she would love it for the stars that she would see through the boughs above her head.

VICTOR HUGO

And then, she loved her father, that is to say, Jean Valjean, with all her soul, with an innocent filial passion which made the goodman a beloved and charming companion to her. It will be remembered that M. Madeleine had been in the habit of reading a great deal. Jean Valjean had continued this practice; he had come to converse well; he possessed the secret riches and the eloquence of a true and humble mind which has spontaneously cultivated itself. He retained just enough sharpness to season his kindness; his mind was rough and his heart was soft. During their conversations in the Luxembourg, he gave her explanations of everything, drawing on what he had read, and also on what he had suffered. As she listened to him, Cosette's eyes wandered vaguely about.

This simple man sufficed for Cosette's thought, the same as the wild garden sufficed for her eyes. When she had had a good chase after the butterflies, she came panting up to him and said: "Ah! How I have run!" He kissed her brow.

Cosette adored the goodman. She was always at his heels. Where Jean Valjean was, there happiness was. Jean Valjean lived neither in the pavilion nor the garden; she took greater pleasure in the paved back courtyard, than in the enclosure filled with flowers, and in his little lodge furnished with straw-seated chairs than in the great drawing-room hung with tapestry, against which stood tufted easy-chairs. Jean Valjean sometimes said to her, smiling at his happiness in being importuned: "Do go to your own quarters! Leave me alone a little!"

She gave him those charming and tender scoldings which are so graceful when they come from a daughter to her father.

"Father, I am very cold in your rooms; why don't you have a carpet here and a stove?"

"Dear child, there are so many people who are better than I and who have not even a roof over their heads."

"Then why is there a fire in my rooms, and everything that is needed?"

"Because you are a woman and a child."

"Bah! must men be cold and feel uncomfortable?"

"Certain men."

"That is good, I shall come here so often that you will be obliged to have a fire."

And again she said to him:—

"Father, why do you eat horrible bread like that?"

"Because, my daughter."

"Well, if you eat it, I will eat it too."

Then, in order to prevent Cosette eating black bread, Jean Valjean ate white bread.

Cosette had but a confused recollection of her childhood. She prayed morning and evening for her mother whom she had never known. The Thénardiers had remained with her as two hideous figures in a dream. She remembered that she had gone "one day, at night," to fetch water in a forest. She thought that it had been very far from Paris. It seemed to her that she had begun to live in an abyss, and that it was Jean Valjean who had rescued her from it. Her childhood produced upon her the effect of a time when there had been nothing around her but millepeds, spiders, and serpents. When she meditated in the evening, before falling asleep, as she had not a very clear idea that she was Jean Valjean's daughter, and that he was her father, she fancied that the soul of her mother had passed into that good man and had come to dwell near her.

When he was seated, she leaned her cheek against his white hair, and dropped a silent tear, saying to herself: "Perhaps this man is my mother."

Cosette, although this is a strange statement to make, in the profound ignorance of a girl brought up in a convent,—maternity being also absolutely unintelligible to virginity,—had ended by fancying that she had had as little mother as possible. She did not even know her mother's name. Whenever she asked Jean Valjean, Jean Valjean remained silent. If she repeated her question, he responded with a smile. Once she insisted; the smile ended in a tear.

This silence on the part of Jean Valjean covered Fantine with darkness.

Was it prudence? Was it respect? Was it a fear that he should deliver this name to the hazards of another memory than his own?

So long as Cosette had been small, Jean Valjean had been willing to talk to her of her mother; when she became a young girl, it was impossible for him to do so. It seemed to him that he no longer dared. Was it because of Cosette? Was it because of Fantine? He felt a certain religious horror at letting that shadow enter Cosette's thought; and of placing a third in their destiny. The more sacred this shade was to him, the more did it seem that it was to be feared. He thought of Fantine, and felt himself overwhelmed with silence.

Through the darkness, he vaguely perceived something which appeared to have its finger on its lips. Had all the modesty which had been in Fantine, and which had violently quitted her during her lifetime, returned to rest upon her after her death, to watch in indignation over the peace of that dead woman, and in its shyness, to keep her in her grave? Was Jean Valjean unconsciously submitting to the pressure? We who believe in death, are not among the number who will reject this mysterious explanation.

Hence the impossibility of uttering, even for Cosette, that name of Fantine.

One day Cosette said to him:—

"Father, I saw my mother in a dream last night. She had two big wings. My mother must have been almost a saint during her life."

"Through martyrdom," replied Jean Valjean.

However, Jean Valjean was happy.

When Cosette went out with him, she leaned on his arm, proud and happy, in the plenitude of her heart. Jean Valjean felt his heart melt within him with delight, at all these sparks of a tenderness so exclusive, so wholly satisfied with himself alone. The poor man trembled, inundated with angelic joy; he declared to himself ecstatically that this would last all their lives; he told himself that he really had not suffered sufficiently to merit so radiant a bliss, and he thanked God, in the depths of his soul, for having permitted him to be loved thus, he, a wretch, by that innocent being.

V

The Rose Perceives that it is an Engine of War

One day, Cosette chanced to look at herself in her mirror, and she said to herself: "Really!" It seemed to her almost that she was pretty. This threw her in a singularly troubled state of mind. Up to that moment she had never thought of her face. She saw herself in her mirror, but she did not look at herself. And then, she had so often been told that she was homely; Jean Valjean alone said gently: "No indeed! no indeed!" At all events, Cosette had always thought herself homely, and had grown up in that belief with the easy resignation of childhood. And here, all at once, was her mirror saying to her, as Jean Valjean had said: "No indeed!" That night, she did not sleep. "What if I were pretty!" she thought. "How odd it would be if I were pretty!" And she recalled those of her companions whose beauty had produced a sensation in the convent, and she said to herself: "What! Am I to be like Mademoiselle So-and-So?"

The next morning she looked at herself again, not by accident this time, and she was assailed with doubts: "Where did I get such an idea?" said she; "no, I am ugly." She had not slept well, that was all, her eyes were sunken and she was pale. She had not felt very joyous on the preceding evening in the belief that she was beautiful, but it made her very sad not to be able to believe in it any longer. She did not look at herself again, and for more than a fortnight she tried to dress her hair with her back turned to the mirror.

In the evening, after dinner, she generally embroidered in wool or did some convent needlework in the drawing-room, and Jean Valjean read beside her. Once she raised her eyes from her work, and was rendered quite uneasy by the manner in which her father was gazing at her.

On another occasion, she was passing along the street, and it seemed to her that some one behind her, whom she did not see, said: "A pretty woman! but badly dressed." "Bah!" she thought, "he does not mean me. I am well dressed and ugly." She was then wearing a plush hat and her merino gown.

At last, one day when she was in the garden, she heard poor old Toussaint saying: "Do you notice how pretty Cosette is growing, sir?" Cosette did not hear her father's reply, but Toussaint's words caused a sort of commotion within her. She fled from the garden, ran up to her room, flew to the looking-glass,—it was three months since she had looked at herself,—and gave vent to a cry. She had just dazzled herself.

She was beautiful and lovely; she could not help agreeing with Toussaint and her mirror. Her figure was formed, her skin had grown white, her hair was lustrous, an unaccustomed splendor had been lighted in her blue eyes. The consciousness of her beauty burst upon her in an instant, like the sudden advent of daylight; other people noticed it also, Toussaint had said so, it was evidently she of whom the passer-by had spoken, there could no longer be any doubt of that; she descended to the garden again, thinking herself a queen, imagining that she heard the birds singing, though it was winter, seeing the sky gilded, the sun among the trees, flowers in the thickets, distracted, wild, in inexpressible delight.

Jean Valjean, on his side, experienced a deep and undefinable oppression at heart.

In fact, he had, for some time past, been contemplating with terror that beauty which seemed to grow more radiant every day on Cosette's sweet face. The dawn that was smiling for all was gloomy for him.

Cosette had been beautiful for a tolerably long time before she became aware of it herself. But, from the very first day, that unexpected light which was rising slowly and enveloping the whole of the young girl's person, wounded Jean Valjean's sombre eye. He felt that it was a change in a happy life, a life so happy that he did not dare to move for fear of disarranging something. This man, who had passed through all manner of distresses, who was still all bleeding from the bruises of fate, who had been almost wicked and who had become almost a saint, who, after having dragged the chain of the galleys, was now dragging the invisible but heavy chain of indefinite misery, this man whom the law had not released from its grasp and who could be seized at any moment and brought back from the obscurity of his virtue to the broad daylight of public opprobrium, this man accepted all, excused all, pardoned all, and merely asked of Providence, of man, of the law, of society, of nature, of the world, one thing, that Cosette might love him!

That Cosette might continue to love him! That God would not prevent the heart of the child from coming to him, and from remaining with him! Beloved by Cosette, he felt that he was healed, rested, appeased, loaded with benefits, recompensed, crowned. Beloved by Cosette, it was well with him! He asked nothing more! Had any one said to him: "Do you want anything better?" he would have answered: "No." God might have said to him: "Do you desire heaven?" and he would have replied: "I should lose by it."

Everything which could affect this situation, if only on the surface, made him shudder like the beginning of something new. He had never known very distinctly himself what the beauty of a woman means; but he understood instinctively, that it was something terrible.

He gazed with terror on this beauty, which was blossoming out ever more triumphant and superb beside him, beneath his very eyes, on the innocent and formidable brow of that child, from the depths of her homeliness, of his old age, of his misery, of his reprobation.

He said to himself: "How beautiful she is! What is to become of me?"

There, moreover, lay the difference between his tenderness and the tenderness of a mother. What he beheld with anguish, a mother would have gazed upon with joy.

The first symptoms were not long in making their appearance.

On the very morrow of the day on which she had said to herself: "Decidedly I am beautiful!" Cosette began to pay attention to her toilet. She recalled the remark of that passer-by: "Pretty, but badly dressed," the breath of an oracle which had passed beside her and had vanished, after depositing in her heart one of the two germs which are destined, later on, to fill the whole life of woman, coquetry. Love is the other.

With faith in her beauty, the whole feminine soul expanded within her. She conceived a horror for her merinos, and shame for her plush hat. Her father had never refused her anything. She at once acquired the whole science of the bonnet, the gown, the mantle, the boot, the cuff, the stuff which is in fashion, the color which is becoming, that science which makes of the Parisian woman something so charming, so deep, and so dangerous. The words *heady woman* were invented for the Parisienne.

In less than a month, little Cosette, in that Thebaid of the Rue de Babylone, was not only one of the prettiest, but one of the "best dressed" women in Paris, which means a great deal more.

She would have liked to encounter her "passer-by," to see what he would say, and to "teach him a lesson!" The truth is, that she was ravishing in every respect, and that she distinguished the difference between a bonnet from Gérard and one from Herbaut in the most marvellous way.

Jean Valjean watched these ravages with anxiety. He who felt that he could never do anything but crawl, walk at the most, beheld wings sprouting on Cosette.

Moreover, from the mere inspection of Cosette's toilet, a woman would have recognized the fact that she had no mother. Certain little proprieties, certain special conventionalities, were not observed by Cosette. A mother, for instance, would have told her that a young girl does not dress in damask.

The first day that Cosette went out in her black damask gown and mantle, and her white crape bonnet, she took Jean Valjean's arm, gay, radiant, rosy, proud, dazzling. "Father," she said, "how do you like me in this guise?" Jean Valjean replied in a voice which resembled the bitter voice of an envious man: "Charming!" He was the same as usual during their walk. On their return home, he asked Cosette:—

"Won't you put on that other gown and bonnet again,—you know the ones I mean?"

This took place in Cosette's chamber. Cosette turned towards the wardrobe where her cast-off schoolgirl's clothes were hanging.

"That disguise!" said she. "Father, what do you want me to do with it? Oh no, the idea! I shall never put on those horrors again. With that machine on my head, I have the air of Madame Mad-dog."

Jean Valjean heaved a deep sigh.

From that moment forth, he noticed that Cosette, who had always heretofore asked to remain at home, saying: "Father, I enjoy myself more here with you," now was always asking to go out. In fact, what is the use of having a handsome face and a delicious costume if one does not display them?

He also noticed that Cosette had no longer the same taste for the back garden. Now she preferred the garden, and did not dislike to promenade back and forth in front of the railed fence. Jean Valjean, who was shy, never set foot in the garden. He kept to his back yard, like a dog.

Cosette, in gaining the knowledge that she was beautiful, lost the grace of ignoring it. An exquisite grace, for beauty enhanced by ingenuousness is ineffable, and nothing is so adorable as a dazzling and innocent creature who walks along, holding in her hand the key to paradise without being conscious of it. But what she had lost in ingenuous grace, she gained in pensive and serious charm. Her whole person, permeated with the joy of youth, of innocence, and of beauty, breathed forth a splendid melancholy.

It was at this epoch that Marius, after the lapse of six months, saw her once more at the Luxembourg.

VI

The Battle Begun

Cosette in her shadow, like Marius in his, was all ready to take fire. Destiny, with its mysterious and fatal patience, slowly drew together these two beings, all charged and all languishing with the stormy electricity of passion, these two souls which were laden with love as two clouds are laden with lightning, and which were bound to overflow and mingle in a look like the clouds in a flash of fire.

The glance has been so much abused in love romances that it has finally fallen into disrepute. One hardly dares to say, nowadays, that two beings fell in love because they looked at each other. That is the way people do fall in love, nevertheless, and the only way. The rest is nothing, but the rest comes afterwards. Nothing is more real than these great shocks which two souls convey to each other by the exchange of that spark.

At that particular hour when Cosette unconsciously darted that glance which troubled Marius, Marius had no suspicion that he had also launched a look which disturbed Cosette.

He caused her the same good and the same evil.

She had been in the habit of seeing him for a long time, and she had scrutinized him as girls scrutinize and see, while looking elsewhere. Marius still considered Cosette ugly, when she had already begun to think Marius handsome. But as he paid no attention to her, the young man was nothing to her.

Still, she could not refrain from saying to herself that he had beautiful hair, beautiful eyes, handsome teeth, a charming tone of voice when she heard him conversing with his comrades, that he held himself badly when he walked, if you like, but with a grace that was all his own, that he did not appear to be at all stupid, that his whole person was noble, gentle, simple, proud, and that, in short, though he seemed to be poor, yet his air was fine.

On the day when their eyes met at last, and said to each other those first, obscure, and ineffable things which the glance lisps, Cosette did not immediately understand. She returned thoughtfully to the house in the Rue de l'Ouest, where Jean Valjean, according to his custom, had come to spend six weeks. The next morning, on waking, she thought of that strange young man, so long indifferent and icy, who now seemed to pay attention to her, and it did not appear to her that this attention was the least in the world agreeable to her. She was, on the contrary, somewhat incensed at this handsome and disdainful individual. A substratum of war stirred within her. It struck her, and the idea caused her a wholly childish joy, that she was going to take her revenge at last.

Knowing that she was beautiful, she was thoroughly conscious, though in an indistinct fashion, that she possessed a weapon. Women play with their beauty as children do with a knife. They wound themselves.

The reader will recall Marius' hesitations, his palpitations, his terrors. He remained on his bench and did not approach. This vexed Cosette. One day, she said to Jean Valjean: "Father, let us stroll about a little in that direction." Seeing that Marius did not come to her, she went to him. In such cases, all women resemble Mahomet. And then, strange to say, the first symptom of true love in a young man is timidity; in a young girl it is boldness. This is surprising, and yet nothing is more simple. It is the two sexes tending to approach each other and assuming, each the other's qualities.

That day, Cosette's glance drove Marius beside himself, and Marius' glance set Cosette to trembling. Marius went away confident, and Cosette uneasy. From that day forth, they adored each other.

The first thing that Cosette felt was a confused and profound melancholy. It seemed to her that her soul had become black since the day before. She no longer recognized it. The whiteness of soul in young girls, which is composed of coldness and gayety, resembles snow. It melts in love, which is its sun.

Cosette did not know what love was. She had never heard the word uttered in its terrestrial sense. On the books of profane music which entered the convent, *amour* (love) was replaced by *tambour* (drum) or *pandour*. This created enigmas which exercised the imaginations of the *big girls*, such as: *Ah, how delightful is the drum!* or, *Pity is not a pandour*. But Cosette had left the convent too early to have occupied herself much with the "drum." Therefore, she did not know what name to give to what she now felt. Is any one the less ill because one does not know the name of one's malady?

She loved with all the more passion because she loved ignorantly. She did not know whether it was a good thing or a bad thing, useful or dangerous, eternal or temporary, allowable or prohibited; she loved. She would have been greatly astonished, had any one said to her: "You do not sleep? But that is forbidden! You do not eat? Why, that is very bad! You have oppressions and palpitations of the heart? That must not be! You blush and turn pale, when a certain being clad in black appears at the end of a certain green walk? But that is abominable!" She would not have understood, and she would have replied: "What fault is there of mine in a matter in which I have no power and of which I know nothing?"

It turned out that the love which presented itself was exactly suited to the state of her soul. It was a sort of admiration at a distance, a mute contemplation, the deification of a stranger. It was the apparition of youth to youth, the dream of nights become a reality yet remaining a dream, the longed-for phantom realized and made flesh at last, but having as yet, neither name, nor fault, nor spot, nor exigence, nor defect; in a word, the distant lover who lingered in the ideal, a chimæra with a form. Any nearer and more palpable meeting would have alarmed Cosette at this first stage, when she was still half immersed in the exaggerated mists of the cloister. She had all the fears of children and all the fears of nuns combined. The spirit of the convent, with which she had been permeated for the space of five years, was still in the process of slow evaporation from her person, and made everything tremble around her. In this situation he was not a lover, he was not even an admirer, he was a vision. She set herself to adoring Marius as something charming, luminous, and impossible.

As extreme innocence borders on extreme coquetry, she smiled at him with all frankness.

Every day, she looked forward to the hour for their walk with impatience, she found Marius there, she felt herself unspeakably happy, and thought in all sincerity that she was expressing her whole thought when she said to Jean Valjean:—

"What a delicious garden that Luxembourg is!"

Marius and Cosette were in the dark as to one another. They did not address each other, they did not salute each other, they did not know each other; they saw each other; and like stars of heaven which are separated by millions of leagues, they lived by gazing at each other.

It was thus that Cosette gradually became a woman and developed, beautiful and loving, with a consciousness of her beauty, and in ignorance of her love. She was a coquette to boot through her ignorance.

VII

To One Sadness Oppose a Sadness and a Half

All situations have their instincts. Old and eternal Mother Nature warned Jean Valjean in a dim way of the presence of Marius. Jean Valjean shuddered to the very bottom of his soul. Jean Valjean saw nothing, knew nothing, and yet he scanned with obstinate attention, the darkness in which he walked, as though he felt on one side of him something in process of construction, and on the other, something which was crumbling away. Marius, also warned, and, in accordance with the deep law of God, by that same Mother Nature, did all he could to keep out of sight of "the father." Nevertheless, it came to pass that Jean Valjean sometimes espied him. Marius' manners were no longer in the least natural. He exhibited ambiguous prudence and awkward daring. He no longer came quite close to them as formerly. He seated himself at a distance and pretended to be reading; why did he pretend that? Formerly he had come in his old coat, now he wore his new one every day; Jean Valjean was not sure that he did not have his hair curled, his eyes were very queer, he wore gloves; in short, Jean Valjean cordially detested this young man.

Cosette allowed nothing to be divined. Without knowing just what was the matter with her she was convinced that there was something in it, and that it must be concealed.

There was a coincidence between the taste for the toilet which had recently come to Cosette, and the habit of new clothes developed by that stranger which was very repugnant to Jean Valjean. It might be accidental, no doubt, certainly, but it was a menacing accident.

He never opened his mouth to Cosette about this stranger. One day, however, he could not refrain from so doing, and, with that vague despair which suddenly casts the lead into the depths of its despair, he said to her: "What a very pedantic air that young man has!"

Cosette, but a year before only an indifferent little girl, would have replied: "Why, no, he is charming." Ten years later, with the love of Marius in her heart, she would have answered: "A pedant, and insufferable to the sight! You are right!"—At the moment in life and the heart which she had then attained, she contented herself with replying, with supreme calmness: "That young man!"

As though she now beheld him for the first time in her life.

"How stupid I am!" thought Jean Valjean. "She had not noticed him. It is I who have pointed him out to her."

Oh, simplicity of the old! oh, the depth of children!

It is one of the laws of those fresh years of suffering and trouble, of those vivacious conflicts between a first love and the first obstacles, that the young girl does not allow herself to be caught in any trap whatever, and that the young man falls into every one. Jean Valjean had instituted an undeclared war against Marius, which Marius, with the sublime stupidity of his passion and his age, did not divine. Jean Valjean laid a host of ambushes for him; he changed his hour, he changed his bench, he forgot his handkerchief, he came alone to the Luxembourg; Marius dashed headlong into all these snares; and to all the interrogation marks planted by Jean Valjean in his pathway, he ingenuously answered "yes." But Cosette remained immured in her apparent unconcern and in her imperturbable tranquillity, so that Jean Valjean arrived at the following conclusion: "That ninny is madly in love with Cosette, but Cosette does not even know that he exists."

Nonetheless did he bear in his heart a mournful tremor. The minute when Cosette would love might strike at any moment. Does not everything begin with indifference?

Only once did Cosette make a mistake and alarm him. He rose from his seat to depart, after a stay of three hours, and she said: "What, already?"

Jean Valjean had not discontinued his trips to the Luxembourg, as he did not wish to do anything out of the way, and as, above all things, he feared to arouse Cosette; but during the hours which were so sweet to the lovers, while Cosette was sending her smile to the intoxicated Marius, who perceived nothing else now, and who now saw nothing in all the world but an adored and radiant face, Jean Valjean was fixing on Marius flashing and terrible eyes. He, who had finally come to believe himself incapable of a malevolent feeling, experienced moments when Marius was present, in which he thought he was becoming savage and ferocious once more, and he felt the old depths of his soul, which had formerly contained so much wrath, opening once more and rising up against that young man. It almost seemed to him that unknown craters were forming in his bosom.

What! he was there, that creature! What was he there for? He came creeping about, smelling out, examining, trying! He came, saying: "Hey! Why not?" He came to prowl about his, Jean Valjean's, life! to prowl about his happiness, with the purpose of seizing it and bearing it away!

Jean Valjean added: "Yes, that's it! What is he in search of? An adventure! What does he want? A love affair! A love affair! And I? What! I have been first, the most wretched of men, and then the most unhappy, and I have traversed sixty years of life on my knees, I have suffered everything that man can suffer, I have grown old without having been young, I have lived without a family, without relatives, without friends, without life, without children, I have left my blood on every stone, on every bramble, on every mile-post, along every wall, I have been gentle, though others have been hard to me, and kind, although others have been malicious, I have become an honest man once more, in spite of everything, I have repented of the evil that I have done and have forgiven the evil that has been done to me, and at the moment when I receive my recompense, at the moment when it is all over, at the moment when I am just touching the goal, at the moment when I have what I desire, it is well, it is good, I have paid, I have earned it, all this is to take flight, all this will vanish, and I shall lose Cosette, and I shall lose my life, my joy, my soul, because it has pleased a great booby to come and lounge at the Luxembourg."

Then his eyes were filled with a sad and extraordinary gleam.

It was no longer a man gazing at a man; it was no longer an enemy surveying an enemy. It was a dog scanning a thief.

The reader knows the rest. Marius pursued his senseless course. One day he followed Cosette to the Rue de l'Ouest. Another day he spoke to the porter. The porter, on his side, spoke, and said to Jean Valjean: "Monsieur, who is that curious young man who is asking for you?" On the morrow Jean Valjean bestowed on Marius that glance which Marius at last perceived. A week later, Jean Valjean had taken his departure. He swore to himself that he would never again set foot either in the Luxembourg or in the Rue de l'Ouest. He returned to the Rue Plumet.

Cosette did not complain, she said nothing, she asked no questions, she did not seek to learn his reasons; she had already reached the point where she was afraid of being divined, and of betraying herself. Jean Valjean had no experience of these miseries, the only miseries which are charming and the only ones with which he was not acquainted; the consequence was that he did not understand the grave significance of Cosette's silence.

He merely noticed that she had grown sad, and he grew gloomy. On his side and on hers, inexperience had joined issue.

Once he made a trial. He asked Cosette:—

"Would you like to come to the Luxembourg?"

A ray illuminated Cosette's pale face.

"Yes," said she.

They went thither. Three months had elapsed. Marius no longer went there. Marius was not there.

On the following day, Jean Valjean asked Cosette again:—

"Would you like to come to the Luxembourg?"

She replied, sadly and gently:—

"No."

Jean Valjean was hurt by this sadness, and heart-broken at this gentleness.

What was going on in that mind which was so young and yet already so impenetrable? What was on its way there within? What was taking place in Cosette's soul? Sometimes, instead of going to bed, Jean Valjean remained seated on his pallet, with his head in his hands, and he passed whole nights asking himself: "What has Cosette in her mind?" and in thinking of the things that she might be thinking about.

Oh! at such moments, what mournful glances did he cast towards that cloister, that chaste peak, that abode of angels, that inaccessible glacier of virtue! How he contemplated, with despairing ecstasy, that convent garden, full of ignored flowers and cloistered virgins, where all perfumes and all souls mount straight to heaven! How he adored that Eden forever closed against him, whence he had voluntarily and madly emerged! How he regretted his abnegation and his folly in having brought Cosette back into the world, poor hero of sacrifice, seized and hurled to the earth by his very self-devotion! How he said to himself, "What have I done?"

However, nothing of all this was perceptible to Cosette. No ill-temper, no harshness. His face was always serene and kind. Jean Valjean's manners were more tender and more paternal than ever. If anything could have betrayed his lack of joy, it was his increased suavity.

On her side, Cosette languished. She suffered from the absence of Marius as she had rejoiced in his presence, peculiarly, without exactly being conscious of it. When Jean Valjean ceased to take her on their customary strolls, a feminine instinct murmured confusedly, at the bottom of her heart, that she must not seem to set store on the Luxembourg garden, and that if this proved to be a matter of indifference to her, her father would take her thither once more. But days, weeks, months, elapsed. Jean Valjean had tacitly accepted Cosette's tacit consent. She regretted it. It was too late. So Marius had disappeared; all was over. The day on which she returned to the Luxembourg, Marius was no longer there. What was to be done? Should she ever find him again? She felt an anguish at her heart, which nothing relieved, and which augmented every day; she no longer knew whether it was winter or summer, whether it was raining or shining, whether the birds were singing, whether it was the season for dahlias or daisies, whether the Luxembourg was more charming than the Tuileries, whether the linen which the laundress brought home was starched too much or not enough, whether Toussaint had done "her marketing" well or ill; and she remained dejected, absorbed, attentive to but a single thought, her eyes vague and staring as when one gazes by night at a black and fathomless spot where an apparition has vanished.

However, she did not allow Jean Valjean to perceive anything of this, except her pallor.

She still wore her sweet face for him.

This pallor sufficed but too thoroughly to trouble Jean Valjean. Sometimes he asked her:—

"What is the matter with you?"

She replied: "There is nothing the matter with me."

And after a silence, when she divined that he was sad also, she would add:—

"And you, father—is there anything wrong with you?"

"With me? Nothing," said he.

These two beings who had loved each other so exclusively, and with so touching an affection, and who had lived so long for each other now suffered side by side, each on the other's account; without acknowledging it to each other, without anger towards each other, and with a smile.

VIII

THE CHAIN-GANG

Jean Valjean was the more unhappy of the two. Youth, even in its sorrows, always possesses its own peculiar radiance.

At times, Jean Valjean suffered so greatly that he became puerile. It is the property of grief to cause the childish side of man to reappear. He had an unconquerable conviction that Cosette was escaping from him. He would have liked to resist, to retain her, to arouse her enthusiasm by some external and brilliant matter. These ideas, puerile, as we have just said, and at the same time senile, conveyed to him, by their very childishness, a tolerably just notion of the influence of gold lace on the imaginations of young girls. He once chanced to see a general on horseback, in full uniform, pass along the street, Comte Coutard, the commandant of Paris. He envied that gilded man; what happiness it would be, he said to himself, if he could put on that suit which was an incontestable thing; and if Cosette could behold him thus, she would be dazzled, and when he had Cosette on his arm and passed the gates of the Tuileries, the guard would present arms to him, and that would suffice for Cosette, and would dispel her idea of looking at young men.

An unforeseen shock was added to these sad reflections.

In the isolated life which they led, and since they had come to dwell in the Rue Plumet, they had contracted one habit. They sometimes took a pleasure trip to see the sun rise, a mild species of enjoyment which befits those who are entering life and those who are quitting it.

For those who love solitude, a walk in the early morning is equivalent to a stroll by night, with the cheerfulness of nature added. The streets are deserted and the birds are singing. Cosette, a bird herself, liked to rise early. These matutinal excursions were planned on the preceding evening. He proposed, and she agreed. It was arranged like a plot, they set out before daybreak, and these trips were so many small delights for Cosette. These innocent eccentricities please young people.

Jean Valjean's inclination led him, as we have seen, to the least frequented spots, to solitary nooks, to forgotten places. There then existed, in the vicinity of the barriers of Paris, a sort of poor meadows, which were almost confounded with the city, where grew in summer sickly grain, and which, in autumn, after the harvest had been gathered, presented the appearance, not of having been reaped, but peeled. Jean Valjean loved to haunt these fields. Cosette was not bored there. It meant solitude to him and liberty to her. There, she became a little girl once more, she could run and almost play; she took off her hat, laid it on Jean Valjean's knees, and gathered bunches of flowers. She gazed at the butterflies on the flowers, but did not catch them; gentleness and tenderness are born with love, and the young girl who cherishes within her breast a trembling and fragile ideal has mercy on the wing of a butterfly. She wove garlands of poppies, which she placed on her head, and which, crossed and penetrated with sunlight, glowing until they flamed, formed for her rosy face a crown of burning embers.

Even after their life had grown sad, they kept up their custom of early strolls.

One morning in October, therefore, tempted by the serene perfection of the autumn of 1831, they set out, and found themselves at break of day near the Barrière du Maine. It was not dawn, it was daybreak; a delightful and stern moment. A few constellations here and there in the deep, pale azure, the earth all black, the heavens all white, a quiver amid the blades of grass, everywhere the mysterious chill of twilight. A lark, which seemed mingled with the stars, was carolling at a prodigious height, and one would have declared that that hymn of pettiness calmed immensity. In the East, the Val-de-Grâce projected its dark mass on the clear horizon with the sharpness of steel; Venus dazzlingly brilliant was rising behind that dome and had the air of a soul making its escape from a gloomy edifice.

All was peace and silence; there was no one on the road; a few stray laborers, of whom they caught barely a glimpse, were on their way to their work along the side-paths.

Jean Valjean was sitting in a cross-walk on some planks deposited at the gate of a timber-yard. His face was turned towards the highway, his back towards the light; he had forgotten the sun which was on the point of rising; he had sunk into one of those profound absorptions in which the mind becomes concentrated, which imprison even the eye, and which are equivalent to four walls. There are meditations which may be called vertical; when one is at the bottom of them, time is required to return to earth. Jean Valjean had plunged into one of these reveries. He was thinking of Cosette, of the happiness that was possible if nothing came between him and her, of the light with which she filled his life, a light which was but the emanation of her soul. He was almost happy in his reverie. Cosette, who was standing beside him, was gazing at the clouds as they turned rosy.

All at once Cosette exclaimed: "Father, I should think some one was coming yonder." Jean Valjean raised his eyes.

Cosette was right. The causeway which leads to the ancient Barrière du Maine is a prolongation, as the reader knows, of the Rue de Sèvres, and is cut at right angles by the inner boulevard. At the elbow of the causeway and the boulevard, at the spot where it branches, they heard a noise which it was difficult to account for at that hour, and a sort of confused pile made its appearance. Some shapeless thing which was coming from the boulevard was turning into the road.

It grew larger, it seemed to move in an orderly manner, though it was bristling and quivering; it seemed to be a vehicle, but its load could not be distinctly made out. There were horses, wheels, shouts; whips were cracking. By degrees the outlines became fixed, although bathed in shadows. It was a vehicle, in fact, which had just turned from the boulevard into the highway, and which was directing its course towards the barrier near which sat Jean Valjean; a second, of the same aspect, followed, then a third, then a fourth; seven chariots made their appearance in succession, the heads of the horses touching the rear of the wagon in front. Figures were moving on these vehicles, flashes were visible through the dusk as though there were naked swords there, a clanking became audible which resembled the rattling of chains, and as this something advanced, the sound of voices waxed louder, and it turned into a terrible thing such as emerges from the cave of dreams.

As it drew nearer, it assumed a form, and was outlined behind the trees with the pallid hue of an apparition; the mass grew white; the day, which was slowly dawning, cast a wan light on this swarming heap which was at once both sepulchral and living, the heads of the figures turned into the faces of corpses, and this is what it proved to be:—

Seven wagons were driving in a file along the road. The first six were singularly constructed. They resembled coopers' drays; they consisted of long ladders placed on two wheels and forming barrows at their rear extremities. Each dray, or rather let us say, each ladder, was attached to four horses harnessed tandem. On these ladders strange clusters of men were being drawn. In the faint light, these men were to be divined rather than seen. Twenty-four on each vehicle, twelve on a side, back to back, facing the passers-by, their legs dangling in the air,—this was the manner in which these men were travelling, and behind their backs they had something which clanked, and which was a chain, and on their necks something which shone, and which was an iron collar. Each man had his collar, but the chain was for all; so that if these four and twenty men had occasion to alight from the dray and walk, they were seized with a sort of inexorable unity, and were obliged to wind over the ground with the chain for a backbone, somewhat after the fashion of millepeds. In the back and front of each vehicle, two men armed with muskets stood erect, each holding one end of the chain under his foot. The iron necklets were square. The seventh vehicle, a huge rack-sided baggage wagon, without a hood, had four wheels and six horses, and carried a sonorous pile of iron boilers, cast-iron pots, braziers, and chains, among which were mingled several men who were pinioned and stretched at full length, and who seemed to be ill. This wagon, all lattice-work, was garnished with dilapidated hurdles which appeared to have served for former punishments. These vehicles kept to the middle of the road. On each side marched a double hedge of guards of infamous aspect, wearing three-cornered hats, like the soldiers under the Directory, shabby, covered with spots and holes, muffled in uniforms of veterans and the trousers of undertakers' men, half gray, half blue, which were almost hanging in rags, with red epaulets, yellow shoulder belts, short sabres, muskets, and cudgels; they were a species of soldier-blackguards. These myrmidons seemed composed of the abjectness of the beggar and the authority of the executioner. The one who appeared to be their chief held a postilion's whip in his hand. All these details, blurred by the dimness of dawn, became more and more clearly outlined as the light increased. At the head and in the rear of the convoy rode mounted gendarmes, serious and with sword in fist.

This procession was so long that when the first vehicle reached the barrier, the last was barely debauching from the boulevard. A throng, sprung, it is impossible to say whence, and formed in a twinkling, as is frequently the case in Paris, pressed forward from both sides of the road and looked on. In the neighboring lanes the shouts of people calling to each other and the wooden shoes of market-gardeners hastening up to gaze were audible.

The men massed upon the drays allowed themselves to be jolted along in silence. They were livid with the chill of morning. They all wore linen trousers, and their bare feet were thrust into wooden shoes. The rest of their costume was a fantasy of wretchedness. Their accoutrements were horribly incongruous; nothing is more funereal than the harlequin in rags. Battered felt hats, tarpaulin caps, hideous woollen nightcaps, and, side by side with a short blouse, a black coat broken at the elbow; many wore women's headgear, others had baskets on their heads; hairy breasts were visible, and through the rent in their garments tattooed designs could be descried; temples of Love, flaming hearts, Cupids; eruptions and unhealthy red blotches could also be seen. Two or three had a straw rope attached to the cross-bar of the dray, and suspended under them like a stirrup, which supported their feet. One of them held in his hand and raised to his mouth something which had the appearance of a black stone and which he seemed to be gnawing; it was bread which he was eating. There were no eyes there which were not either dry, dulled, or flaming with an evil light. The escort troop cursed, the men in chains did not utter a syllable; from time to time the sound of a blow became audible as the cudgels descended on shoulder-blades or skulls; some of these men were yawning; their rags were terrible; their feet hung down, their shoulders oscillated, their heads clashed together, their fetters clanked, their eyes glared ferociously, their fists clenched or fell open inertly like the hands of corpses; in the rear of the convoy ran a band of children screaming with laughter.

This file of vehicles, whatever its nature was, was mournful. It was evident that to-morrow, that an hour hence, a pouring rain might descend, that it might be followed by another and another, and that their dilapidated garments would be drenched, that once soaked, these men would not get dry again, that once chilled, they would not again get warm, that their linen trousers would be glued to their bones by the downpour, that the water would fill their shoes, that no lashes from the whips would be able to prevent their jaws from chattering, that the chain would continue to bind them by the neck, that their legs would continue to dangle, and it was impossible not to shudder at the sight of these human beings thus bound and passive beneath the cold clouds of autumn, and delivered over to the rain, to the blast, to all the furies of the air, like trees and stones.

Blows from the cudgel were not omitted even in the case of the sick men, who lay there knotted with ropes and motionless on the seventh wagon, and who appeared to have been tossed there like sacks filled with misery.

Suddenly, the sun made its appearance; the immense light of the Orient burst forth, and one would have said that it had set fire to all those ferocious heads. Their tongues were unloosed; a conflagration of grins, oaths, and songs exploded. The broad horizontal sheet of light severed the file in two parts, illuminating heads and bodies, leaving feet and wheels in the obscurity. Thoughts made their appearance on these faces; it was a terrible moment; visible demons with their masks removed, fierce souls laid bare. Though lighted up, this wild throng remained in gloom. Some, who were gay, had in their mouths quills through which they blew vermin over the crowd, picking out the women; the dawn accentuated these lamentable profiles with the blackness of its shadows; there was not one of these creatures who was not deformed by reason of wretchedness; and the whole was so monstrous that one would have said that the sun's brilliancy had been changed into the glare of the lightning. The wagon-load which headed the line had struck up a song, and were shouting at the top of their voices with a haggard joviality, a pot-pourri by Desaugiers, then famous, called *The Vestal*; the trees shivered mournfully; in the cross-lanes, countenances of bourgeois listened in an idiotic delight to these coarse strains droned by spectres.

All sorts of distress met in this procession as in chaos; here were to be found the facial angles of every sort of beast, old men, youths, bald heads, gray beards, cynical monstrosities, sour resignation, savage grins, senseless attitudes, snouts surmounted by caps, heads like those of young girls with corkscrew curls on the temples, infantile visages, and by reason of that, horrible thin skeleton faces, to which death alone was lacking. On the first cart was a negro, who had been a slave, in all probability, and who could make a comparison of his chains. The frightful leveller from below, shame, had passed over these brows; at that degree of abasement, the last transformations were suffered by all in their extremest depths, and ignorance, converted into dulness, was the equal of intelligence converted into despair. There was no choice possible between these men who appeared to the eye as the flower of the mud. It was evident that the person who had had the ordering of that unclean procession had not classified them. These beings had been fettered and coupled pell-mell, in alphabetical disorder, probably, and loaded hap-hazard on those carts. Nevertheless, horrors, when grouped together, always end by evolving a result; all additions of wretched men give a sum total, each chain exhaled a common soul, and each dray-load had its own physiognomy. By the side of the one where they were singing, there was one where they were howling; a third where they were begging; one could be seen in which they were gnashing their

VICTOR HUGO

teeth; another load menaced the spectators, another blasphemed God; the last was as silent as the tomb. Dante would have thought that he beheld his seven circles of hell on the march. The march of the damned to their tortures, performed in sinister wise, not on the formidable and flaming chariot of the Apocalypse, but, what was more mournful than that, on the gibbet cart.

One of the guards, who had a hook on the end of his cudgel, made a pretence from time to time, of stirring up this mass of human filth. An old woman in the crowd pointed them out to her little boy five years old, and said to him: "Rascal, let that be a warning to you!"

As the songs and blasphemies increased, the man who appeared to be the captain of the escort cracked his whip, and at that signal a fearful dull and blind flogging, which produced the sound of hail, fell upon the seven dray-loads; many roared and foamed at the mouth; which redoubled the delight of the street urchins who had hastened up, a swarm of flies on these wounds.

Jean Valjean's eyes had assumed a frightful expression. They were no longer eyes; they were those deep and glassy objects which replace the glance in the case of certain wretched men, which seem unconscious of reality, and in which flames the reflection of terrors and of catastrophes. He was not looking at a spectacle, he was seeing a vision. He tried to rise, to flee, to make his escape; he could not move his feet. Sometimes, the things that you see seize upon you and hold you fast. He remained nailed to the spot, petrified, stupid, asking himself, athwart confused and inexpressible anguish, what this sepulchral persecution signified, and whence had come that pandemonium which was pursuing him. All at once, he raised his hand to his brow, a gesture habitual to those whose memory suddenly returns; he remembered that this was, in fact, the usual itinerary, that it was customary to make this detour in order to avoid all possibility of encountering royalty on the road to Fontainebleau, and that, five and thirty years before, he had himself passed through that barrier.

Cosette was no less terrified, but in a different way. She did not understand; what she beheld did not seem to her to be possible; at length she cried:—

"Father! What are those men in those carts?"

Jean Valjean replied: "Convicts."

"Whither are they going?"

"To the galleys."

At that moment, the cudgelling, multiplied by a hundred hands, became zealous, blows with the flat of the sword were mingled with it, it was a perfect storm of whips and clubs; the convicts bent before it, a hideous obedience was evoked by the torture, and all held their peace, darting glances like chained wolves.

Cosette trembled in every limb; she resumed:—

"Father, are they still men?"

"Sometimes," answered the unhappy man.

It was the chain-gang, in fact, which had set out before daybreak from Bicêtre, and had taken the road to Mans in order to avoid Fontainebleau, where the King then was. This caused the horrible journey to last three or four days longer; but torture may surely be prolonged with the object of sparing the royal personage a sight of it.

Jean Valjean returned home utterly overwhelmed. Such encounters are shocks, and the memory that they leave behind them resembles a thorough shaking up.

Nevertheless, Jean Valjean did not observe that, on his way back to the Rue de Babylone with Cosette, the latter was plying him with other questions on the subject of what they had just seen; perhaps he was too much absorbed in his own dejection to notice her words and reply to them. But when Cosette was leaving him in the evening, to betake herself to bed, he heard her say in a low voice, and as though talking to herself: "It seems to me, that if I were to find one of those men in my pathway, oh, my God, I should die merely from the sight of him close at hand."

Fortunately, chance ordained that on the morrow of that tragic day, there was some official solemnity apropos of I know not what,— fêtes in Paris, a review in the Champ de Mars, jousts on the Seine, theatrical performances in the Champs-Élysées, fireworks at the Arc de l'Étoile, illuminations everywhere. Jean Valjean did violence to his habits, and took Cosette to see these rejoicings, for the purpose of diverting her from the memory of the day before, and of effacing, beneath the smiling tumult of all Paris, the abominable thing which had passed before her. The review with which the festival was spiced made the presence of uniforms perfectly natural; Jean Valjean donned his uniform of a national guard with the vague inward feeling of a man who is betaking himself to shelter. However, this trip seemed to attain its object. Cosette, who made it her law to please her father, and to whom, moreover, all spectacles were a novelty, accepted this diversion with the light and easy good grace of youth, and did not pout too disdainfully at that flutter of enjoyment called a public fête; so that Jean Valjean was able to believe that he had succeeded, and that no trace of that hideous vision remained.

Some days later, one morning, when the sun was shining brightly, and they were both on the steps leading to the garden, another infraction of the rules which Jean Valjean seemed to have imposed upon himself, and to the custom of remaining in her chamber which melancholy had caused Cosette to adopt, Cosette, in a wrapper, was standing erect in that negligent attire of early morning which envelops young girls in an adorable way and which produces the effect of a cloud drawn over a star; and, with her head bathed in light, rosy after a good sleep, submitting to the gentle glances of the tender old man, she was picking a daisy to pieces. Cosette did not know the delightful legend, *I love a little, passionately, etc.*—who was there who could have taught her? She was handling the flower instinctively, innocently, without a suspicion that to pluck a daisy apart is to do the same by a heart. If there were a fourth, and smiling Grace called Melancholy, she would have worn the air of that Grace. Jean Valjean was fascinated by the contemplation of those tiny fingers on that flower, and forgetful of everything in the radiance emitted by that child. A red-breast was warbling in the thicket, on one side. White cloudlets floated across the sky, so gayly, that one would have said that they had just been set at liberty. Cosette went on attentively tearing the leaves from her flower; she seemed to be thinking about something; but whatever it was, it must be something charming; all at once she turned her head over her shoulder with the delicate languor of a swan, and said to Jean Valjean: "Father, what are the galleys like?"

BOOK FOURTH
SUCCOR FROM BELOW MAY TURN OUT
TO BE SUCCOR FROM ON HIGH

I

A Wound Without, Healing Within

Thus their life clouded over by degrees.

But one diversion, which had formerly been a happiness, remained to them, which was to carry bread to those who were hungry, and clothing to those who were cold. Cosette often accompanied Jean Valjean on these visits to the poor, on which they recovered some remnants of their former free intercourse; and sometimes, when the day had been a good one, and they had assisted many in distress, and cheered and warmed many little children, Cosette was rather merry in the evening. It was at this epoch that they paid their visit to the Jondrette den.

On the day following that visit, Jean Valjean made his appearance in the pavilion in the morning, calm as was his wont, but with a large wound on his left arm which was much inflamed, and very angry, which resembled a burn, and which he explained in some way or other. This wound resulted in his being detained in the house for a month with fever. He would not call in a doctor. When Cosette urged him, "Call the dog-doctor," said he.

Cosette dressed the wound morning and evening with so divine an air and such angelic happiness at being of use to him, that Jean Valjean felt all his former joy returning, his fears and anxieties dissipating, and he gazed at Cosette, saying: "Oh! what a kindly wound! Oh! what a good misfortune!"

Cosette on perceiving that her father was ill, had deserted the pavilion and again taken a fancy to the little lodging and the back courtyard. She passed nearly all her days beside Jean Valjean and read to him the books which he desired. Generally they were books of travel. Jean Valjean was undergoing a new birth; his happiness was reviving in these ineffable rays; the Luxembourg, the prowling young stranger, Cosette's coldness,—all these clouds upon his soul were growing dim. He had reached the point where he said to himself: "I imagined all that. I am an old fool."

His happiness was so great that the horrible discovery of the Thénardiers made in the Jondrette hovel, unexpected as it was, had, after a fashion, glided over him unnoticed. He had succeeded in making his escape; all trace of him was lost—what more did he care for! he only thought of those wretched beings to pity them. "Here they are in prison, and henceforth they will be incapacitated for doing any harm," he thought, "but what a lamentable family in distress!"

As for the hideous vision of the Barrière du Maine, Cosette had not referred to it again.

Sister Sainte-Mechtilde had taught Cosette music in the convent; Cosette had the voice of a linnet with a soul, and sometimes, in the evening, in the wounded man's humble abode, she warbled melancholy songs which delighted Jean Valjean.

Spring came; the garden was so delightful at that season of the year, that Jean Valjean said to Cosette:—

"You never go there; I want you to stroll in it."

"As you like, father," said Cosette.

And for the sake of obeying her father, she resumed her walks in the garden, generally alone, for, as we have mentioned, Jean Valjean, who was probably afraid of being seen through the fence, hardly ever went there.

Jean Valjean's wound had created a diversion.

When Cosette saw that her father was suffering less, that he was convalescing, and that he appeared to be happy, she experienced a contentment which she did not even perceive, so gently and naturally had it come. Then, it was in the month of March, the days were growing longer, the winter was departing, the winter always bears away with it a portion of our sadness; then came April, that daybreak of summer, fresh as dawn always is, gay like every childhood; a little inclined to weep at times like the new-born being that it is. In that month, nature has charming gleams which pass from the sky, from the trees, from the meadows and the flowers into the heart of man.

Cosette was still too young to escape the penetrating influence of that April joy which bore so strong a resemblance to herself. Insensibly, and without her suspecting the fact, the blackness departed from her spirit. In spring, sad souls grow light, as light falls into cellars at midday. Cosette was no longer sad. However, though this was so, she did not account for it to herself. In the morning, about ten o'clock, after breakfast, when she had succeeded in enticing her father into the garden for a quarter of an hour, and when she was pacing up and down in the sunlight in front of the steps, supporting his left arm for him, she did not perceive that she laughed every moment and that she was happy.

Jean Valjean, intoxicated, beheld her growing fresh and rosy once more.

"Oh! What a good wound!" he repeated in a whisper.

And he felt grateful to the Thénardiers.

His wound once healed, he resumed his solitary twilight strolls.

It is a mistake to suppose that a person can stroll alone in that fashion in the uninhabited regions of Paris without meeting with some adventure.

II

Mother Plutarque Finds No Difficulty in Explaining a Phenomenon

One evening, little Gavroche had had nothing to eat; he remembered that he had not dined on the preceding day either; this was becoming tiresome. He resolved to make an effort to secure some supper. He strolled out beyond the Salpêtrière into deserted regions; that is where windfalls are to be found; where there is no one, one always finds something. He reached a settlement which appeared to him to be the village of Austerlitz.

In one of his preceding lounges he had noticed there an old garden haunted by an old man and an old woman, and in that garden, a passable apple-tree. Beside the apple-tree stood a sort of fruit-house, which was not securely fastened, and where one might contrive to get an apple. One apple is a supper; one apple is life. That which was Adam's ruin might prove Gavroche's salvation. The garden abutted on a solitary, unpaved lane, bordered with brushwood while awaiting the arrival of houses; the garden was separated from it by a hedge.

Gavroche directed his steps towards this garden; he found the lane, he recognized the apple-tree, he verified the fruit-house, he examined the hedge; a hedge means merely one stride. The day was declining, there was not even a cat in the lane, the hour was propitious. Gavroche began the operation of scaling the hedge, then suddenly paused. Some one was talking in the garden. Gavroche peeped through one of the breaks in the hedge.

A couple of paces distant, at the foot of the hedge on the other side, exactly at the point where the gap which he was meditating would have been made, there was a sort of recumbent stone which formed a bench, and on this bench was seated the old man of the garden, while the old woman was standing in front of him. The old woman was grumbling. Gavroche, who was not very discreet, listened.

"Monsieur Mabeuf!" said the old woman.

"Mabeuf!" thought Gavroche, "that name is a perfect farce."

VICTOR HUGO

The old man who was thus addressed, did not stir. The old woman repeated:—

"Monsieur Mabeuf!"

The old man, without raising his eyes from the ground, made up his mind to answer:—

"What is it, Mother Plutarque?"

"Mother Plutarque!" thought Gavroche, "another farcical name."

Mother Plutarque began again, and the old man was forced to accept the conversation:—

"The landlord is not pleased."

"Why?"

"We owe three quarters rent."

"In three months, we shall owe him for four quarters."

"He says that he will turn you out to sleep."

"I will go."

"The green-grocer insists on being paid. She will no longer leave her fagots. What will you warm yourself with this winter? We shall have no wood."

"There is the sun."

"The butcher refuses to give credit; he will not let us have any more meat."

"That is quite right. I do not digest meat well. It is too heavy."

"What shall we have for dinner?"

"Bread."

"The baker demands a settlement, and says, 'no money, no bread.'"

"That is well."

"What will you eat?"

"We have apples in the apple-room."

"But, Monsieur, we can't live like that without money."

"I have none."

The old woman went away, the old man remained alone. He fell into thought. Gavroche became thoughtful also. It was almost dark.

The first result of Gavroche's meditation was, that instead of scaling the hedge, he crouched down under it. The branches stood apart a little at the foot of the thicket.

"Come," exclaimed Gavroche mentally, "here's a nook!" and he curled up in it. His back was almost in contact with Father Mabeuf's bench. He could hear the octogenarian breathe.

Then, by way of dinner, he tried to sleep.

It was a cat-nap, with one eye open. While he dozed, Gavroche kept on the watch.

The twilight pallor of the sky blanched the earth, and the lane formed a livid line between two rows of dark bushes.

All at once, in this whitish band, two figures made their appearance. One was in front, the other some distance in the rear.

"There come two creatures," muttered Gavroche.

The first form seemed to be some elderly bourgeois, who was bent and thoughtful, dressed more than plainly, and who was walking slowly because of his age, and strolling about in the open evening air.

The second was straight, firm, slender. It regulated its pace by that of the first; but in the voluntary slowness of its gait, suppleness and agility were discernible. This figure had also something fierce and disquieting about it, the whole shape was that of what was then called *an elegant*; the hat was of good shape, the coat black, well cut, probably of fine cloth, and well fitted in at the waist. The head was held erect with a sort of robust grace, and beneath the hat the pale profile of a young man could be made out in the dim light. The profile had a rose in its mouth. This second form was well known to Gavroche; it was Montparnasse.

He could have told nothing about the other, except that he was a respectable old man.

Gavroche immediately began to take observations.

One of these two pedestrians evidently had a project connected with the other. Gavroche was well placed to watch the course of events. The bedroom had turned into a hiding-place at a very opportune moment.

Montparnasse on the hunt at such an hour, in such a place, betokened something threatening. Gavroche felt his gamin's heart moved with compassion for the old man.

What was he to do? Interfere? One weakness coming to the aid of another! It would be merely a laughing matter for Montparnasse. Gavroche did not shut his eyes to the fact that the old man, in the first place, and the child in the second, would make but two mouthfuls for that redoubtable ruffian eighteen years of age.

While Gavroche was deliberating, the attack took place, abruptly and hideously. The attack of the tiger on the wild ass, the attack of the spider on the fly. Montparnasse suddenly tossed away his rose, bounded upon the old man, seized him by the collar, grasped and clung to him, and Gavroche with difficulty restrained a scream. A moment later one of these men was underneath the other, groaning, struggling, with a knee of marble upon his breast. Only, it was not just what Gavroche had expected. The one who lay on the earth was Montparnasse; the one who was on top was the old man. All this took place a few paces distant from Gavroche.

The old man had received the shock, had returned it, and that in such a terrible fashion, that in a twinkling, the assailant and the assailed had exchanged rôles.

"Here's a hearty veteran!" thought Gavroche.

He could not refrain from clapping his hands. But it was applause wasted. It did not reach the combatants, absorbed and deafened as they were, each by the other, as their breath mingled in the struggle.

Silence ensued. Montparnasse ceased his struggles. Gavroche indulged in this aside: "Can he be dead!"

The goodman had not uttered a word, nor given vent to a cry. He rose to his feet, and Gavroche heard him say to Montparnasse:—

"Get up."

Montparnasse rose, but the goodman held him fast. Montparnasse's attitude was the humiliated and furious attitude of the wolf who has been caught by a sheep.

Gavroche looked on and listened, making an effort to reinforce his eyes with his ears. He was enjoying himself immensely.

He was repaid for his conscientious anxiety in the character of a spectator. He was able to catch on the wing a dialogue which borrowed from the darkness an indescribably tragic accent. The goodman questioned, Montparnasse replied.

"How old are you?"

"Nineteen."

"You are strong and healthy. Why do you not work?"

"It bores me."

"What is your trade?"

"An idler."

"Speak seriously. Can anything be done for you? What would you like to be?"

"A thief."

A pause ensued. The old man seemed absorbed in profound thought. He stood motionless, and did not relax his hold on Montparnasse.

Every moment the vigorous and agile young ruffian indulged in the twitchings of a wild beast caught in a snare. He gave a jerk, tried a crook of the knee, twisted his limbs desperately, and made efforts to escape.

The old man did not appear to notice it, and held both his arms with one hand, with the sovereign indifference of absolute force.

The old man's reverie lasted for some time, then, looking steadily at Montparnasse, he addressed to him in a gentle voice, in the midst of the darkness where they stood, a solemn harangue, of which Gavroche did not lose a single syllable:—

"My child, you are entering, through indolence, on one of the most laborious of lives. Ah! You declare yourself to be an idler! prepare to toil. There is a certain formidable machine, have you seen it? It is the rolling-mill. You must be on your guard against it, it is crafty and ferocious; if it catches hold of the skirt of your coat, you will be drawn in bodily. That machine is laziness. Stop while there is yet time, and save yourself! Otherwise, it is all over with you; in a short time you will be among the gearing. Once entangled, hope for nothing more. Toil, lazybones! there is no more repose for you! The iron hand of implacable toil has seized you. You do not wish to earn your living, to have a task, to fulfil a duty! It bores you to be like other men? Well! You will be different. Labor is the law; he who rejects it will find ennui his torment. You do not wish to be a workingman, you will be a slave. Toil lets go of you on one side only to grasp you again on the other. You do not desire to be its friend, you shall be its negro slave. Ah! You would have none of the honest weariness of men, you shall have the sweat of the damned. Where others sing, you will rattle in your throat. You will see afar off, from below, other men at work; it will seem to you that they are resting. The laborer, the harvester, the sailor, the blacksmith, will appear to you in glory like the blessed spirits in paradise. What radiance surrounds the forge! To guide the plough, to bind the sheaves, is joy. The bark at liberty in the wind, what delight! Do you, lazy idler, delve, drag on, roll, march! Drag your halter. You are a beast of burden in the team of hell! Ah! To do nothing is your object. Well, not a week, not a day, not an hour shall you have free from oppression. You will be able to lift nothing without anguish. Every minute that passes will make your muscles crack. What is a feather to others will be a rock to you. The simplest things will become steep acclivities. Life will become monstrous all about you. To go, to come, to breathe, will be just so many terrible labors. Your lungs will produce on you the effect of weighing a hundred pounds. Whether you shall walk here rather than there, will become a problem that must be solved. Any one who wants to go out simply gives his door a push, and there he is in the open air. If you wish to go out, you will be obliged to pierce

VICTOR HUGO

your wall. What does every one who wants to step into the street do? He goes downstairs; you will tear up your sheets, little by little you will make of them a rope, then you will climb out of your window, and you will suspend yourself by that thread over an abyss, and it will be night, amid storm, rain, and the hurricane, and if the rope is too short, but one way of descending will remain to you, to fall. To drop hap-hazard into the gulf, from an unknown height, on what? On what is beneath, on the unknown. Or you will crawl up a chimney-flue, at the risk of burning; or you will creep through a sewer-pipe, at the risk of drowning; I do not speak of the holes that you will be obliged to mask, of the stones which you will have to take up and replace twenty times a day, of the plaster that you will have to hide in your straw pallet. A lock presents itself; the bourgeois has in his pocket a key made by a locksmith. If you wish to pass out, you will be condemned to execute a terrible work of art; you will take a large sou, you will cut it in two plates; with what tools? You will have to invent them. That is your business. Then you will hollow out the interior of these plates, taking great care of the outside, and you will make on the edges a thread, so that they can be adjusted one upon the other like a box and its cover. The top and bottom thus screwed together, nothing will be suspected. To the overseers it will be only a sou; to you it will be a box. What will you put in this box? A small bit of steel. A watch-spring, in which you will have cut teeth, and which will form a saw. With this saw, as long as a pin, and concealed in a sou, you will cut the bolt of the lock, you will sever bolts, the padlock of your chain, and the bar at your window, and the fetter on your leg. This masterpiece finished, this prodigy accomplished, all these miracles of art, address, skill, and patience executed, what will be your recompense if it becomes known that you are the author? The dungeon. There is your future. What precipices are idleness and pleasure! Do you know that to do nothing is a melancholy resolution? To live in idleness on the property of society! to be useless, that is to say, pernicious! This leads straight to the depth of wretchedness. Woe to the man who desires to be a parasite! He will become vermin! Ah! So it does not please you to work? Ah! You have but one thought, to drink well, to eat well, to sleep well. You will drink water, you will eat black bread, you will sleep on a plank with a fetter whose cold touch you will feel on your flesh all night long, riveted to your limbs. You will break those fetters, you will flee. That is well. You will crawl on your belly through the brushwood, and you will eat grass like the beasts of the forest. And you will be recaptured. And then you will pass years in a dungeon, riveted to a wall, groping for your jug that you may drink, gnawing at a horrible loaf of darkness which dogs would not touch, eating beans that the worms have eaten before you. You will be a wood-louse in a cellar. Ah! Have pity on yourself, you miserable young child, who were sucking at nurse less than twenty years ago, and who have, no doubt, a mother still alive! I conjure you, listen to me, I entreat you. You desire fine black cloth, varnished shoes, to have your hair curled and sweet-smelling oils on your locks, to please low women, to be handsome. You will be shaven clean, and you will wear a red blouse and wooden shoes. You want rings on your fingers, you will have an iron necklet on your neck. If you glance at a woman, you will receive a blow. And you will enter there at the age of twenty. And you will come out at fifty! You will enter young, rosy, fresh, with brilliant eyes, and all your white teeth, and your handsome, youthful hair; you will come out broken, bent, wrinkled, toothless, horrible, with white locks! Ah! my poor child, you are on the wrong road; idleness is counselling you badly; the hardest of all work is thieving. Believe me, do not undertake that painful profession of an idle man. It is not comfortable to become a rascal. It is less disagreeable to be an honest man. Now go, and ponder on what I have said to you. By the way, what did you want of me? My purse? Here it is."

And the old man, releasing Montparnasse, put his purse in the latter's hand; Montparnasse weighed it for a moment, after which he allowed it to slide gently into the back pocket of his coat, with the same mechanical precaution as though he had stolen it.

All this having been said and done, the goodman turned his back and tranquilly resumed his stroll.

"The blockhead!" muttered Montparnasse.

Who was this goodman? The reader has, no doubt, already divined.

Montparnasse watched him with amazement, as he disappeared in the dusk. This contemplation was fatal to him.

While the old man was walking away, Gavroche drew near.

Gavroche had assured himself, with a sidelong glance, that Father Mabeuf was still sitting on his bench, probably sound asleep. Then the gamin emerged from his thicket, and began to crawl after Montparnasse in the dark, as the latter stood there motionless. In this manner he came up to Montparnasse without being seen or heard, gently insinuated his hand into the back pocket of that frock-coat of fine black cloth, seized the purse, withdrew his hand, and having recourse once more to his crawling, he slipped away like an adder through the shadows. Montparnasse, who had no reason to be on his guard, and who was engaged in thought for the first time in his life, perceived nothing. When Gavroche had once more attained the point where Father Mabeuf was, he flung the purse over the hedge, and fled as fast as his legs would carry him.

The purse fell on Father Mabeuf's foot. This commotion roused him.

He bent over and picked up the purse.

He did not understand in the least, and opened it.

The purse had two compartments; in one of them there was some small change; in the other lay six napoleons.

M. Mabeuf, in great alarm, referred the matter to his housekeeper.

"That has fallen from heaven," said Mother Plutarque.

BOOK FIFTH
THE END OF WHICH DOES NOT
RESEMBLE THE BEGINNING

I

Solitude and the Barracks Combined

Cosette's grief, which had been so poignant and lively four or five months previously, had, without her being conscious of the fact, entered upon its convalescence. Nature, spring, youth, love for her father, the gayety of the birds and flowers, caused something almost resembling forgetfulness to filter gradually, drop by drop, into that soul, which was so virgin and so young. Was the fire wholly extinct there? Or was it merely that layers of ashes had formed? The truth is, that she hardly felt the painful and burning spot any longer.

One day she suddenly thought of Marius: "Why!" said she, "I no longer think of him."

That same week, she noticed a very handsome officer of lancers, with a wasp-like waist, a delicious uniform, the cheeks of a young girl, a sword under his arm, waxed moustaches, and a glazed schapka, passing the gate. Moreover, he had light hair, prominent blue eyes, a round face, was vain, insolent and good-looking; quite the reverse of Marius. He had a cigar in his mouth. Cosette thought that this officer doubtless belonged to the regiment in barracks in the Rue de Babylone.

On the following day, she saw him pass again. She took note of the hour.

From that time forth, was it chance? she saw him pass nearly every day.

The officer's comrades perceived that there was, in that "badly kept" garden, behind that malicious rococo fence, a very pretty creature, who was almost always there when the handsome lieutenant,—who is not unknown to the reader, and whose name was Théodule Gillenormand,—passed by.

"See here!" they said to him, "there's a little creature there who is making eyes at you, look."

"Have I the time," replied the lancer, "to look at all the girls who look at me?"

This was at the precise moment when Marius was descending heavily towards agony, and was saying: "If I could but see her before I die!"— Had his wish been realized, had he beheld Cosette at that moment gazing at the lancer, he would not have been able to utter a word, and he would have expired with grief.

Whose fault was it? No one's.

Marius possessed one of those temperaments which bury themselves in sorrow and there abide; Cosette was one of those persons who plunge into sorrow and emerge from it again.

Cosette was, moreover, passing through that dangerous period, the fatal phase of feminine reverie abandoned to itself, in which the isolated heart of a young girl resembles the tendrils of the vine which cling, as chance directs, to the capital of a marble column or to the post of a wine-shop: A rapid and decisive moment, critical for every orphan, be she rich or poor, for wealth does not prevent a bad choice; misalliances are made in very high circles, real misalliance is that of souls; and as many an unknown young man, without name, without birth, without fortune, is a marble column which bears up a temple of grand sentiments and grand ideas, so such and such a man of the world satisfied and opulent, who has polished boots and varnished words, if looked at not outside, but inside, a thing which is reserved for his wife, is nothing more than a block obscurely haunted by violent, unclean, and vinous passions; the post of a drinking-shop.

What did Cosette's soul contain? Passion calmed or lulled to sleep; something limpid, brilliant, troubled to a certain depth, and gloomy lower down. The image of the handsome officer was reflected in the surface. Did a souvenir linger in the depths?—Quite at the bottom?—Possibly. Cosette did not know.

A singular incident supervened.

II

COSETTE'S APPREHENSIONS

During the first fortnight in April, Jean Valjean took a journey. This, as the reader knows, happened from time to time, at very long intervals. He remained absent a day or two days at the utmost. Where did he go? No one knew, not even Cosette. Once only, on the occasion of one of these departures, she had accompanied him in a hackney-coach as far as a little blind-alley at the corner of which she read: *Impasse de la Planchette*. There he alighted, and the coach took Cosette back to the Rue de Babylone. It was usually when money was lacking in the house that Jean Valjean took these little trips.

So Jean Valjean was absent. He had said: "I shall return in three days."

That evening, Cosette was alone in the drawing-room. In order to get rid of her ennui, she had opened her piano-organ, and had begun to sing, accompanying herself the while, the chorus from *Euryanthe*: "Hunters astray in the wood!" which is probably the most beautiful thing in all the sphere of music. When she had finished, she remained wrapped in thought.

All at once, it seemed to her that she heard the sound of footsteps in the garden.

It could not be her father, he was absent; it could not be Toussaint, she was in bed, and it was ten o'clock at night.

She stepped to the shutter of the drawing-room, which was closed, and laid her ear against it.

It seemed to her that it was the tread of a man, and that he was walking very softly.

She mounted rapidly to the first floor, to her own chamber, opened a small wicket in her shutter, and peeped into the garden. The moon was at the full. Everything could be seen as plainly as by day.

There was no one there.

She opened the window. The garden was absolutely calm, and all that was visible was that the street was deserted as usual.

Cosette thought that she had been mistaken. She thought that she had heard a noise. It was a hallucination produced by the melancholy and magnificent chorus of Weber, which lays open before the mind terrified depths, which trembles before the gaze like a dizzy forest, and in which one hears the crackling of dead branches beneath the uneasy tread of the huntsmen of whom one catches a glimpse through the twilight.

She thought no more about it.

Moreover, Cosette was not very timid by nature. There flowed in her veins some of the blood of the bohemian and the adventuress who runs barefoot. It will be remembered that she was more of a lark than a dove. There was a foundation of wildness and bravery in her.

On the following day, at an earlier hour, towards nightfall, she was strolling in the garden. In the midst of the confused thoughts which occupied her, she fancied that she caught for an instant a sound similar to that of the preceding evening, as though some one were walking beneath the trees in the dusk, and not very far from her; but she told herself that nothing so closely resembles a step on the grass as the friction of two branches which have moved from side to side, and she paid no heed to it. Besides, she could see nothing.

She emerged from "the thicket"; she had still to cross a small lawn to regain the steps.

The moon, which had just risen behind her, cast Cosette's shadow in front of her upon this lawn, as she came out from the shrubbery.

Cosette halted in alarm.

Beside her shadow, the moon outlined distinctly upon the turf another shadow, which was particularly startling and terrible, a shadow which had a round hat.

It was the shadow of a man, who must have been standing on the border of the clump of shrubbery, a few paces in the rear of Cosette.

She stood for a moment without the power to speak, or cry, or call, or stir, or turn her head.

Then she summoned up all her courage, and turned round resolutely.

There was no one there.

She glanced on the ground. The figure had disappeared.

She re-entered the thicket, searched the corners boldly, went as far as the gate, and found nothing.

She felt herself absolutely chilled with terror. Was this another hallucination? What! Two days in succession! One hallucination might pass, but two hallucinations? The disquieting point about it was, that the shadow had assuredly not been a phantom. Phantoms do not wear round hats.

On the following day Jean Valjean returned. Cosette told him what she thought she had heard and seen. She wanted to be reassured and to see her father shrug his shoulders and say to her: "You are a little goose."

Jean Valjean grew anxious.

"It cannot be anything," said he.

He left her under some pretext, and went into the garden, and she saw him examining the gate with great attention.

During the night she woke up; this time she was sure, and she distinctly heard some one walking close to the flight of steps beneath her window. She ran to her little wicket and opened it. In point of fact, there was a man in the garden, with a large club in his hand. Just as she was about to scream, the moon lighted up the man's profile. It was her father. She returned to her bed, saying to herself: "He is very uneasy!"

Jean Valjean passed that night and the two succeeding nights in the garden. Cosette saw him through the hole in her shutter.

On the third night, the moon was on the wane, and had begun to rise later; at one o'clock in the morning, possibly, she heard a loud burst of laughter and her father's voice calling her:—

"Cosette!"

She jumped out of bed, threw on her dressing-gown, and opened her window.

Her father was standing on the grass-plot below.

"I have waked you for the purpose of reassuring you," said he; "look, there is your shadow with the round hat."

And he pointed out to her on the turf a shadow cast by the moon, and which did indeed, bear considerable resemblance to the spectre of a man wearing a round hat. It was the shadow produced by a chimney-pipe of sheet iron, with a hood, which rose above a neighboring roof.

Cosette joined in his laughter, all her lugubrious suppositions were allayed, and the next morning, as she was at breakfast with her father, she made merry over the sinister garden haunted by the shadows of iron chimney-pots.

Jean Valjean became quite tranquil once more; as for Cosette, she did not pay much attention to the question whether the chimney-pot was really in the direction of the shadow which she had seen, or thought she had seen, and whether the moon had been in the same spot in the sky.

She did not question herself as to the peculiarity of a chimney-pot which is afraid of being caught in the act, and which retires when some one looks at its shadow, for the shadow had taken the alarm when

Cosette had turned round, and Cosette had thought herself very sure of this. Cosette's serenity was fully restored. The proof appeared to her to be complete, and it quite vanished from her mind, whether there could possibly be any one walking in the garden during the evening or at night.

A few days later, however, a fresh incident occurred.

III

Enriched with Commentaries by Toussaint

In the garden, near the railing on the street, there was a stone bench, screened from the eyes of the curious by a plantation of yoke-elms, but which could, in case of necessity, be reached by an arm from the outside, past the trees and the gate.

One evening during that same month of April, Jean Valjean had gone out; Cosette had seated herself on this bench after sundown. The breeze was blowing briskly in the trees, Cosette was meditating; an objectless sadness was taking possession of her little by little, that invincible sadness evoked by the evening, and which arises, perhaps, who knows, from the mystery of the tomb which is ajar at that hour.

Perhaps Fantine was within that shadow.

Cosette rose, slowly made the tour of the garden, walking on the grass drenched in dew, and saying to herself, through the species of melancholy somnambulism in which she was plunged: "Really, one needs wooden shoes for the garden at this hour. One takes cold."

She returned to the bench.

As she was about to resume her seat there, she observed on the spot which she had quitted, a tolerably large stone which had, evidently, not been there a moment before.

Cosette gazed at the stone, asking herself what it meant. All at once the idea occurred to her that the stone had not reached the bench all by itself, that some one had placed it there, that an arm had been thrust through the railing, and this idea appeared to alarm her. This time, the fear was genuine; the stone was there. No doubt was possible; she did not touch it, fled without glancing behind her, took refuge in the house, and immediately closed with shutter, bolt, and bar the door-like window opening on the flight of steps. She inquired of Toussaint:—

"Has my father returned yet?"

"Not yet, Mademoiselle."

(We have already noted once for all the fact that Toussaint stuttered. May we be permitted to dispense with it for the future. The musical notation of an infirmity is repugnant to us.)

Jean Valjean, a thoughtful man, and given to nocturnal strolls, often returned quite late at night.

"Toussaint," went on Cosette, "are you careful to thoroughly barricade the shutters opening on the garden, at least with bars, in the evening, and to put the little iron things in the little rings that close them?"

"Oh! be easy on that score, Miss."

Toussaint did not fail in her duty, and Cosette was well aware of the fact, but she could not refrain from adding:—

"It is so solitary here."

"So far as that is concerned," said Toussaint, "it is true. We might be assassinated before we had time to say *ouf!* And Monsieur does not sleep in the house, to boot. But fear nothing, Miss, I fasten the shutters up like prisons. Lone women! That is enough to make one shudder, I believe you! Just imagine, what if you were to see men enter your chamber at night and say: 'Hold your tongue!' and begin to cut your throat. It's not the dying so much; you die, for one must die, and that's all right; it's the abomination of feeling those people touch you. And then, their knives; they can't be able to cut well with them! Ah, good gracious!"

"Be quiet," said Cosette. "Fasten everything thoroughly."

Cosette, terrified by the melodrama improvised by Toussaint, and possibly, also, by the recollection of the apparitions of the past week, which recurred to her memory, dared not even say to her: "Go and look at the stone which has been placed on the bench!" for fear of opening the garden gate and allowing "the men" to enter. She saw that all the doors and windows were carefully fastened, made Toussaint go all over the house from garret to cellar, locked herself up in her own chamber, bolted her door, looked under her couch, went to bed and slept badly. All night long she saw that big stone, as large as a mountain and full of caverns.

At sunrise,—the property of the rising sun is to make us laugh at all our terrors of the past night, and our laughter is in direct proportion to our terror which they have caused,—at sunrise Cosette, when she woke, viewed her fright as a nightmare, and said to herself: "What have I been thinking of? It is like the footsteps that I thought I heard a week or two ago in the garden at night! It is like the shadow of the chimney-pot! Am I becoming a coward?" The sun, which was glowing through the crevices in her shutters, and turning the damask curtains crimson, reassured her to such an extent that everything vanished from her thoughts, even the stone.

"There was no more a stone on the bench than there was a man in a round hat in the garden; I dreamed about the stone, as I did all the rest."

She dressed herself, descended to the garden, ran to the bench, and broke out in a cold perspiration. The stone was there.

But this lasted only for a moment. That which is terror by night is curiosity by day.

"Bah!" said she, "come, let us see what it is."

She lifted the stone, which was tolerably large. Beneath it was something which resembled a letter. It was a white envelope. Cosette seized it. There was no address on one side, no seal on the other. Yet the envelope, though unsealed, was not empty. Papers could be seen inside.

Cosette examined it. It was no longer alarm, it was no longer curiosity; it was a beginning of anxiety.

Cosette drew from the envelope its contents, a little notebook of paper, each page of which was numbered and bore a few lines in a very fine and rather pretty handwriting, as Cosette thought.

Cosette looked for a name; there was none. To whom was this addressed? To her, probably, since a hand had deposited the packet on her bench. From whom did it come? An irresistible fascination took possession of her; she tried to turn away her eyes from the leaflets which were trembling in her hand, she gazed at the sky, the street, the acacias all bathed in light, the pigeons fluttering over a neighboring roof, and then her glance suddenly fell upon the manuscript, and she said to herself that she must know what it contained.

This is what she read.

IV

A Heart Beneath a Stone

The reduction of the universe to a single being, the expansion of a single being even to God, that is love.

Love is the salutation of the angels to the stars.

How sad is the soul, when it is sad through love!

What a void in the absence of the being who, by herself alone fills the world! Oh! how true it is that the beloved being becomes God. One could comprehend that God might be jealous of this had not God the Father of all evidently made creation for the soul, and the soul for love.

The glimpse of a smile beneath a white crape bonnet with a lilac curtain is sufficient to cause the soul to enter into the palace of dreams.

God is behind everything, but everything hides God. Things are black, creatures are opaque. To love a being is to render that being transparent.

Certain thoughts are prayers. There are moments when, whatever the attitude of the body may be, the soul is on its knees.

Parted lovers beguile absence by a thousand chimerical devices, which possess, however, a reality of their own. They are prevented from seeing each other, they cannot write to each other; they discover a multitude of mysterious means to correspond. They send each other the song of the birds, the perfume of the flowers, the smiles of children, the light of the sun, the sighings of the breeze, the rays of stars, all creation. And why not? All the works of God are made to serve love. Love is sufficiently potent to charge all nature with its messages.

Oh Spring! Thou art a letter that I write to her.

The future belongs to hearts even more than it does to minds. Love, that is the only thing that can occupy and fill eternity. In the infinite, the inexhaustible is requisite.

Love participates of the soul itself. It is of the same nature. Like it, it is the divine spark; like it, it is incorruptible, indivisible, imperishable. It is a point of fire that exists within us, which is immortal and infinite, which nothing can confine, and which nothing can extinguish. We feel it burning even to the very marrow of our bones, and we see it beaming in the very depths of heaven.

Oh Love! Adorations! voluptuousness of two minds which understand each other, of two hearts which exchange with each other, of two glances which penetrate each other! You will come to me, will you not, bliss! strolls by twos in the solitudes! Blessed and radiant days! I have sometimes dreamed that from time to time hours detached themselves from the lives of the angels and came here below to traverse the destinies of men.

God can add nothing to the happiness of those who love, except to give them endless duration. After a life of love, an eternity of love is, in fact, an augmentation; but to increase in intensity even the ineffable felicity which love bestows on the soul even in this world, is impossible, even to God. God is the plenitude of heaven; love is the plenitude of man.

You look at a star for two reasons, because it is luminous, and because it is impenetrable. You have beside you a sweeter radiance and a greater mystery, woman.

All of us, whoever we may be, have our respirable beings. We lack air and we stifle. Then we die. To die for lack of love is horrible. Suffocation of the soul.

When love has fused and mingled two beings in a sacred and angelic unity, the secret of life has been discovered so far as they are concerned; they are no longer anything more than the two boundaries of the same destiny; they are no longer anything but the two wings of the same spirit. Love, soar.

On the day when a woman as she passes before you emits light as she walks, you are lost, you love. But one thing remains for you to do: to think of her so intently that she is constrained to think of you.

What love commences can be finished by God alone.

True love is in despair and is enchanted over a glove lost or a handkerchief found, and eternity is required for its devotion and its hopes. It is composed both of the infinitely great and the infinitely little.

If you are a stone, be adamant; if you are a plant, be the sensitive plant; if you are a man, be love.

Nothing suffices for love. We have happiness, we desire paradise; we possess paradise, we desire heaven.

Oh ye who love each other, all this is contained in love. Understand how to find it there. Love has contemplation as well as heaven, and more than heaven, it has voluptuousness.

"Does she still come to the Luxembourg?" "No, sir." "This is the church where she attends mass, is it not?" "She no longer comes here."

"Does she still live in this house?" "She has moved away." "Where has she gone to dwell?"

"She did not say."

What a melancholy thing not to know the address of one's soul!

Love has its childishness, other passions have their pettinesses. Shame on the passions which belittle man! Honor to the one which makes a child of him!

There is one strange thing, do you know it? I dwell in the night. There is a being who carried off my sky when she went away.

Oh! would that we were lying side by side in the same grave, hand in hand, and from time to time, in the darkness, gently caressing a finger,—that would suffice for my eternity!

Ye who suffer because ye love, love yet more. To die of love, is to live in it.

Love. A sombre and starry transfiguration is mingled with this torture. There is ecstasy in agony.

Oh joy of the birds! It is because they have nests that they sing.

Love is a celestial respiration of the air of paradise.

Deep hearts, sage minds, take life as God has made it; it is a long trial, an incomprehensible preparation for an unknown destiny. This destiny, the true one, begins for a man with the first step inside the tomb. Then something appears to him, and he begins to distinguish the definitive. The definitive, meditate upon that word. The living perceive the infinite; the definitive permits itself to be seen only by the dead. In the meanwhile, love and suffer, hope and contemplate. Woe, alas! to him who shall have loved only bodies, forms, appearances! Death will deprive him of all. Try to love souls, you will find them again.

I encountered in the street, a very poor young man who was in love. His hat was old, his coat was worn, his elbows were in holes; water trickled through his shoes, and the stars through his soul.

What a grand thing it is to be loved! What a far grander thing it is to love! The heart becomes heroic, by dint of passion. It is no longer composed of anything but what is pure; it no longer rests on anything that is not elevated and great. An unworthy thought can no more germinate in it, than a nettle on a glacier. The serene and lofty soul, inaccessible to vulgar passions and emotions, dominating the clouds and the shades of this world, its follies, its lies, its hatreds, its vanities, its miseries, inhabits the blue of heaven, and no longer feels anything but profound and subterranean shocks of destiny, as the crests of mountains feel the shocks of earthquake.

If there did not exist some one who loved, the sun would become extinct.

V

COSETTE AFTER THE LETTER

As Cosette read, she gradually fell into thought. At the very moment when she raised her eyes from the last line of the note-book, the handsome officer passed triumphantly in front of the gate,—it was his hour; Cosette thought him hideous.

She resumed her contemplation of the book. It was written in the most charming of chirography, thought Cosette; in the same hand, but with divers inks, sometimes very black, again whitish, as when ink has been added to the inkstand, and consequently on different days. It was, then, a mind which had unfolded itself there, sigh by sigh, irregularly, without order, without choice, without object, hap-hazard. Cosette had never read anything like it. This manuscript, in which she already perceived more light than obscurity, produced upon her the effect of a half-open sanctuary. Each one of these mysterious lines shone before her eyes and inundated her heart with a strange radiance. The education which she had received had always talked to her of the soul, and never of love, very much as one might talk of the firebrand and not of the flame. This manuscript of fifteen pages suddenly and sweetly revealed to her all of love, sorrow, destiny, life, eternity, the beginning, the end. It was as if a hand had opened and suddenly flung upon her a handful of rays of light. In these few lines she felt a passionate, ardent, generous, honest nature, a sacred will, an immense sorrow, and an immense despair, a suffering heart, an ecstasy fully expanded. What was this manuscript? A letter. A letter without name, without address, without date, without signature, pressing and disinterested, an enigma composed of truths, a message of love made to be brought by an angel and read by a virgin, an appointment made beyond the bounds of earth, the love-letter of a phantom to a shade. It was an absent one, tranquil and dejected, who seemed ready to take refuge in death and who sent to the absent love, his lady, the secret of fate, the key of life, love. This had been written with one foot in the grave and one finger in heaven. These lines, which had fallen one by one on the paper, were what might be called drops of soul.

Now, from whom could these pages come? Who could have penned them?

Cosette did not hesitate a moment. One man only.

He!

Day had dawned once more in her spirit; all had reappeared. She felt an unheard-of joy, and a profound anguish. It was he! he who had written! he was there! it was he whose arm had been thrust through that railing! While she was forgetful of him, he had found her again! But had she forgotten him? No, never! She was foolish to have thought so for a single moment. She had always loved him, always adored him. The fire had been smothered, and had smouldered for a time, but she saw all plainly now; it had but made headway, and now it had burst forth afresh, and had inflamed her whole being. This note-book was like a spark which had fallen from that other soul into hers. She felt the conflagration starting up once more.

She imbued herself thoroughly with every word of the manuscript: "Oh yes!" said she, "how perfectly I recognize all that! That is what I had already read in his eyes." As she was finishing it for the third time, Lieutenant Théodule passed the gate once more, and rattled his spurs upon the pavement. Cosette was forced to raise her eyes. She thought him insipid, silly, stupid, useless, foppish, displeasing, impertinent, and extremely ugly. The officer thought it his duty to smile at her.

She turned away as in shame and indignation. She would gladly have thrown something at his head.

She fled, re-entered the house, and shut herself up in her chamber to peruse the manuscript once more, to learn it by heart, and to dream. When she had thoroughly mastered it she kissed it and put it in her bosom.

All was over, Cosette had fallen back into deep, seraphic love. The abyss of Eden had yawned once more.

All day long, Cosette remained in a sort of bewilderment. She scarcely thought, her ideas were in the state of a tangled skein in her brain, she could not manage to conjecture anything, she hoped through a tremor, what? vague things. She dared make herself no promises, and she did not wish to refuse herself anything. Flashes of pallor passed over her countenance, and shivers ran through her frame. It seemed to her, at intervals, that she was entering the land of chimæras; she said to herself: "Is this reality?" Then she felt of the dear paper within her bosom under her gown, she pressed it to her heart, she felt its angles against her flesh; and if Jean Valjean had seen her at the moment, he would have shuddered in the presence of that luminous and unknown joy, which overflowed from beneath her eyelids.—"Oh yes!" she thought, "it is certainly he! This comes from him, and is for me!"

And she told herself that an intervention of the angels, a celestial chance, had given him back to her.

Oh transfiguration of love! Oh dreams! That celestial chance, that intervention of the angels, was a pellet of bread tossed by one thief to another thief, from the Charlemagne Courtyard to the Lion's Ditch, over the roofs of La Force.

VI

OLD PEOPLE ARE MADE TO GO OUT OPPORTUNELY

When evening came, Jean Valjean went out; Cosette dressed herself. She arranged her hair in the most becoming manner, and she put on a dress whose bodice had received one snip of the scissors too much, and which, through this slope, permitted a view of the beginning of her throat, and was, as young girls say, "a trifle indecent." It was not in the least indecent, but it was prettier than usual. She made her toilet thus without knowing why she did so.

Did she mean to go out? No.

Was she expecting a visitor? No.

At dusk, she went down to the garden. Toussaint was busy in her kitchen, which opened on the back yard.

She began to stroll about under the trees, thrusting aside the branches from time to time with her hand, because there were some which hung very low.

In this manner she reached the bench.

The stone was still there.

She sat down, and gently laid her white hand on this stone as though she wished to caress and thank it.

All at once, she experienced that indefinable impression which one undergoes when there is some one standing behind one, even when she does not see the person.

She turned her head and rose to her feet.

It was he.

His head was bare. He appeared to have grown thin and pale. His black clothes were hardly discernible. The twilight threw a wan light on his fine brow, and covered his eyes in shadows. Beneath a veil of incomparable sweetness, he had something about him that suggested death and night. His face was illuminated by the light of the dying day, and by the thought of a soul that is taking flight.

He seemed to be not yet a ghost, and he was no longer a man.

He had flung away his hat in the thicket, a few paces distant.

Cosette, though ready to swoon, uttered no cry. She retreated slowly, for she felt herself attracted. He did not stir. By virtue of something ineffable and melancholy which enveloped him, she felt the look in his eyes which she could not see.

Cosette, in her retreat, encountered a tree and leaned against it. Had it not been for this tree, she would have fallen.

Then she heard his voice, that voice which she had really never heard, barely rising above the rustle of the leaves, and murmuring:—

"Pardon me, here I am. My heart is full. I could not live on as I was living, and I have come. Have you read what I placed there on the bench? Do you recognize me at all? Have no fear of me. It is a long time, you remember the day, since you looked at me at the Luxembourg, near the Gladiator. And the day when you passed before me? It was on the 16th of June and the 2d of July. It is nearly a year ago. I have not seen you for a long time. I inquired of the woman who let the chairs, and she told me that she no longer saw you. You lived in the Rue de l'Ouest, on the third floor, in the front apartments of a new house,—you see that I know! I followed you. What else was there for me to do? And then you disappeared. I thought I saw you pass once, while I was reading the newspapers under the arcade of the Odéon. I ran after you. But no. It was a person who had a bonnet like yours. At night I came hither. Do not be afraid, no one sees me. I come to gaze upon your windows near at hand. I walk very softly, so that you may not hear, for you might be alarmed. The other evening I was behind you, you turned round, I fled. Once, I heard you singing. I was happy. Did it affect you because I heard you singing through the shutters? That could not hurt you. No, it is not so? You see, you are my angel! Let me come sometimes; I think that I am going to die. If you only knew! I adore you. Forgive me, I speak to you, but I do not know what I am saying; I may have displeased you; have I displeased you?"

"Oh! my mother!" said she.

And she sank down as though on the point of death.

He grasped her, she fell, he took her in his arms, he pressed her close, without knowing what he was doing. He supported her, though he was tottering himself. It was as though his brain were full of smoke; lightnings darted between his lips; his ideas vanished; it seemed to him that he was accomplishing some religious act, and that he was committing a profanation. Moreover, he had not the least passion for this lovely woman whose force he felt against his breast. He was beside himself with love.

VICTOR HUGO

She took his hand and laid it on her heart. He felt the paper there, he stammered:—

"You love me, then?"

She replied in a voice so low that it was no longer anything more than a barely audible breath:—

"Hush! Thou knowest it!"

And she hid her blushing face on the breast of the superb and intoxicated young man.

He fell upon the bench, and she beside him. They had no words more. The stars were beginning to gleam. How did it come to pass that their lips met? How comes it to pass that the birds sing, that snow melts, that the rose unfolds, that May expands, that the dawn grows white behind the black trees on the shivering crest of the hills?

A kiss, and that was all.

Both started, and gazed into the darkness with sparkling eyes.

They felt neither the cool night, nor the cold stone, nor the damp earth, nor the wet grass; they looked at each other, and their hearts were full of thoughts. They had clasped hands unconsciously.

She did not ask him, she did not even wonder, how he had entered there, and how he had made his way into the garden. It seemed so simple to her that he should be there!

From time to time, Marius' knee touched Cosette's knee, and both shivered.

At intervals, Cosette stammered a word. Her soul fluttered on her lips like a drop of dew on a flower.

Little by little they began to talk to each other. Effusion followed silence, which is fulness. The night was serene and splendid overhead. These two beings, pure as spirits, told each other everything, their dreams, their intoxications, their ecstasies, their chimæras, their weaknesses, how they had adored each other from afar, how they had longed for each other, their despair when they had ceased to see each other. They confided to each other in an ideal intimacy, which nothing could augment, their most secret and most mysterious thoughts. They related to each other, with candid faith in their illusions, all that love, youth, and the remains of childhood which still lingered about them, suggested to their minds. Their two hearts poured themselves out into each other in such wise, that at the expiration of a quarter of an hour, it was the young man who had the young girl's soul, and the young girl who had the young man's soul. Each became permeated with the other, they were enchanted with each other, they dazzled each other.

When they had finished, when they had told each other everything, she laid her head on his shoulder and asked him:—

"What is your name?"

"My name is Marius," said he. "And yours?"

"My name is Cosette."

BOOK SIXTH
LITTLE GAVROCHE

I

The Malicious Playfulness of the Wind

Since 1823, when the tavern of Montfermeil was on the way to shipwreck and was being gradually engulfed, not in the abyss of a bankruptcy, but in the cesspool of petty debts, the Thénardier pair had had two other children; both males. That made five; two girls and three boys.

Madame Thénardier had got rid of the last two, while they were still young and very small, with remarkable luck.

Got rid of is the word. There was but a mere fragment of nature in that woman. A phenomenon, by the way, of which there is more than one example extant. Like the Maréchale de La Mothe-Houdancourt, the Thénardier was a mother to her daughters only. There her maternity ended. Her hatred of the human race began with her own sons. In the direction of her sons her evil disposition was uncompromising, and her heart had a lugubrious wall in that quarter. As the reader has seen, she detested the eldest; she cursed the other two. Why? Because. The most terrible of motives, the most unanswerable of retorts—Because. "I have no need of a litter of squalling brats," said this mother.

Let us explain how the Thénardiers had succeeded in getting rid of their last two children; and even in drawing profit from the operation.

The woman Magnon, who was mentioned a few pages further back, was the same one who had succeeded in making old Gillenormand support the two children which she had had. She lived on the Quai des Célestins, at the corner of this ancient street of the Petit-Musc which afforded her the opportunity of changing her evil repute into good odor. The reader will remember the great epidemic of croup which ravaged the river districts of the Seine in Paris thirty-five years ago, and of which science took advantage to make experiments on a grand scale as to the efficacy of inhalations of alum, so beneficially replaced at the present day by the external tincture of iodine. During this epidemic, the Magnon lost both her boys, who were still very young, one in the morning, the other in the evening of the same day. This was a blow. These children were precious to their mother; they represented eighty francs a month. These eighty francs were punctually paid in the name of

M. Gillenormand, by collector of his rents, M. Barge, a retired tip-staff, in the Rue du Roi-de-Sicile. The children dead, the income was at an end. The Magnon sought an expedient. In that dark free-masonry of evil of which she formed a part, everything is known, all secrets are kept, and all lend mutual aid. Magnon needed two children; the Thénardiers had two. The same sex, the same age. A good arrangement for the one, a good investment for the other. The little Thénardiers became little Magnons. Magnon quitted the Quai des Célestins and went to live in the Rue Clocheperce. In Paris, the identity which binds an individual to himself is broken between one street and another.

The registry office being in no way warned, raised no objections, and the substitution was effected in the most simple manner in the world. Only, the Thénardier exacted for this loan of her children, ten francs a month, which Magnon promised to pay, and which she actually did pay. It is unnecessary to add that M. Gillenormand continued to perform his compact. He came to see the children every six months. He did not perceive the change. "Monsieur," Magnon said to him, "how much they resemble you!"

Thénardier, to whom avatars were easy, seized this occasion to become Jondrette. His two daughters and Gavroche had hardly had time to discover that they had two little brothers. When a certain degree of misery is reached, one is overpowered with a sort of spectral indifference, and one regards human beings as though they were spectres. Your nearest relations are often no more for you than vague shadowy forms, barely outlined against a nebulous background of life and easily confounded again with the invisible.

On the evening of the day when she had handed over her two little ones to Magnon, with express intention of renouncing them forever, the Thénardier had felt, or had appeared to feel, a scruple. She said to her husband: "But this is abandoning our children!" Thénardier, masterful and phlegmatic, cauterized the scruple with this saying: "Jean Jacques Rousseau did even better!" From scruples, the mother proceeded to uneasiness: "But what if the police were to annoy us? Tell me, Monsieur Thénardier, is what we have done permissible?" Thénardier replied: "Everything is permissible. No one will see anything but true blue in it. Besides, no one has any interest in looking closely after children who have not a sou."

Magnon was a sort of fashionable woman in the sphere of crime. She was careful about her toilet. She shared her lodgings, which were furnished in an affected and wretched style, with a clever gallicized English thief. This English woman, who had become a naturalized Parisienne, recommended by very wealthy relations, intimately connected with the medals in the Library and Mademoiselle Mar's diamonds, became celebrated later on in judicial accounts. She was called *Mamselle Miss*.

The two little creatures who had fallen to Magnon had no reason to complain of their lot. Recommended by the eighty francs, they were well cared for, as is everything from which profit is derived; they were neither badly clothed, nor badly fed; they were treated almost like "little gentlemen,"—better by their false mother than by their real one. Magnon played the lady, and talked no thieves' slang in their presence.

Thus passed several years. Thénardier augured well from the fact. One day, he chanced to say to Magnon as she handed him his monthly stipend of ten francs: "The father must give them some education."

All at once, these two poor children, who had up to that time been protected tolerably well, even by their evil fate, were abruptly hurled into life and forced to begin it for themselves.

A wholesale arrest of malefactors, like that in the Jondrette garret, necessarily complicated by investigations and subsequent incarcerations, is a veritable disaster for that hideous and occult counter-society which pursues its existence beneath public society; an adventure of this description entails all sorts of catastrophes in that sombre world. The Thénardier catastrophe involved the catastrophe of Magnon.

One day, a short time after Magnon had handed to Éponine the note relating to the Rue Plumet, a sudden raid was made by the police in the Rue Clocheperce; Magnon was seized, as was also Mamselle Miss; and all the inhabitants of the house, which was of a suspicious character, were gathered into the net. While this was going on, the two little boys were playing in the back yard, and saw nothing of the raid. When they tried to enter the house again, they found the door fastened and the house empty. A cobbler opposite called them to him, and delivered to them a paper which "their mother" had left for them. On this paper there was an address: *M. Barge, collector of rents, Rue du Roi-de-Sicile, No.* 8. The proprietor of the stall said to them: "You cannot live here any longer. Go there. It is nearby. The first street on the left. Ask your way from this paper."

The children set out, the elder leading the younger, and holding in his hand the paper which was to guide them. It was cold, and his benumbed little fingers could not close very firmly, and they did not keep a very good hold on the paper. At the corner of the Rue Clocheperce, a gust of wind tore it from him, and as night was falling, the child was not able to find it again.

They began to wander aimlessly through the streets.

II

In Which Little Gavroche Extracts Profit from Napoleon the Great

Spring in Paris is often traversed by harsh and piercing breezes which do not precisely chill but freeze one; these north winds which sadden the most beautiful days produce exactly the effect of those puffs of cold air which enter a warm room through the cracks of a badly fitting door or window. It seems as though the gloomy door of winter had remained ajar, and as though the wind were pouring through it. In the spring of 1832, the epoch when the first great epidemic of this century broke out in Europe, these north gales were more harsh and piercing than ever. It was a door even more glacial than that of winter which was ajar. It was the door of the sepulchre. In these winds one felt the breath of the cholera.

From a meteorological point of view, these cold winds possessed this peculiarity, that they did not preclude a strong electric tension. Frequent storms, accompanied by thunder and lightning, burst forth at this epoch.

One evening, when these gales were blowing rudely, to such a degree that January seemed to have returned and that the bourgeois had resumed their cloaks, Little Gavroche, who was always shivering gayly under his rags, was standing as though in ecstasy before a wig-maker's shop in the vicinity of the Orme-Saint-Gervais. He was adorned with a woman's woollen shawl, picked up no one knows where, and which he had converted into a neck comforter. Little Gavroche appeared to be engaged in intent admiration of a wax bride, in a low-necked dress, and crowned with orange-flowers, who was revolving in the window, and displaying her smile to passers-by, between two argand lamps; but in reality, he was taking an observation of the shop, in order to discover whether he could not "prig" from the shop-front a cake of soap, which he would then proceed to sell for a sou to a "hair-dresser" in the suburbs. He had often managed to breakfast off of such a roll. He called his species of work, for which he possessed special aptitude, "shaving barbers."

While contemplating the bride, and eyeing the cake of soap, he muttered between his teeth: "Tuesday. It was not Tuesday. Was it Tuesday? Perhaps it was Tuesday. Yes, it was Tuesday."

No one has ever discovered to what this monologue referred.

Yes, perchance, this monologue had some connection with the last occasion on which he had dined, three days before, for it was now Friday.

The barber in his shop, which was warmed by a good stove, was shaving a customer and casting a glance from time to time at the enemy, that freezing and impudent street urchin both of whose hands were in his pockets, but whose mind was evidently unsheathed.

While Gavroche was scrutinizing the shop-window and the cakes of windsor soap, two children of unequal stature, very neatly dressed, and still smaller than himself, one apparently about seven years of age, the other five, timidly turned the handle and entered the shop, with a request for something or other, alms possibly, in a plaintive murmur which resembled a groan rather than a prayer. They both spoke at once, and their words were unintelligible because sobs broke the voice of the younger, and the teeth of the elder were chattering with cold. The barber wheeled round with a furious look, and without abandoning his razor, thrust back the elder with his left hand and the younger with his knee, and slammed his door, saying: "The idea of coming in and freezing everybody for nothing!"

The two children resumed their march in tears. In the meantime, a cloud had risen; it had begun to rain.

Little Gavroche ran after them and accosted them:—

"What's the matter with you, brats?"

"We don't know where we are to sleep," replied the elder.

"Is that all?" said Gavroche. "A great matter, truly. The idea of bawling about that. They must be greenies!"

And adopting, in addition to his superiority, which was rather bantering, an accent of tender authority and gentle patronage:—

"Come along with me, young 'uns!"

"Yes, sir," said the elder.

And the two children followed him as they would have followed an archbishop. They had stopped crying.

Gavroche led them up the Rue Saint-Antoine in the direction of the Bastille.

As Gavroche walked along, he cast an indignant backward glance at the barber's shop.

"That fellow has no heart, the whiting," he muttered. "He's an Englishman."

A woman who caught sight of these three marching in a file, with Gavroche at their head, burst into noisy laughter. This laugh was wanting in respect towards the group.

"Good day, Mamselle Omnibus," said Gavroche to her.

An instant later, the wig-maker occurred to his mind once more, and he added:—

"I am making a mistake in the beast; he's not a whiting, he's a serpent. Barber, I'll go and fetch a locksmith, and I'll have a bell hung to your tail."

This wig-maker had rendered him aggressive. As he strode over a gutter, he apostrophized a bearded portress who was worthy to meet Faust on the Brocken, and who had a broom in her hand.

"Madam," said he, "so you are going out with your horse?"

And thereupon, he spattered the polished boots of a pedestrian.

"You scamp!" shouted the furious pedestrian.

Gavroche elevated his nose above his shawl.

"Is Monsieur complaining?"

"Of you!" ejaculated the man.

"The office is closed," said Gavroche, "I do not receive any more complaints."

In the meanwhile, as he went on up the street, he perceived a beggar-girl, thirteen or fourteen years old, and clad in so short a gown that her knees were visible, lying thoroughly chilled under a porte-cochère. The little girl was getting to be too old for such a thing. Growth does play these tricks. The petticoat becomes short at the moment when nudity becomes indecent.

"Poor girl!" said Gavroche. "She hasn't even trousers. Hold on, take this."

And unwinding all the comfortable woollen which he had around his neck, he flung it on the thin and purple shoulders of the beggar-girl, where the scarf became a shawl once more.

The child stared at him in astonishment, and received the shawl in silence. When a certain stage of distress has been reached in his misery, the poor man no longer groans over evil, no longer returns thanks for good.

That done: "Brrr!" said Gavroche, who was shivering more than Saint Martin, for the latter retained one-half of his cloak.

At this *brrr!* the downpour of rain, redoubled in its spite, became furious. The wicked skies punish good deeds.

"Ah, come now!" exclaimed Gavroche, "what's the meaning of this? It's re-raining! Good Heavens, if it goes on like this, I shall stop my subscription."

And he set out on the march once more.

"It's all right," he resumed, casting a glance at the beggar-girl, as she coiled up under the shawl, "she's got a famous peel."

And looking up at the clouds he exclaimed:—

"Caught!"

The two children followed close on his heels.

As they were passing one of these heavy grated lattices, which indicate a baker's shop, for bread is put behind bars like gold, Gavroche turned round:—

"Ah, by the way, brats, have we dined?"

"Monsieur," replied the elder, "we have had nothing to eat since this morning."

"So you have neither father nor mother?" resumed Gavroche majestically.

"Excuse us, sir, we have a papa and a mamma, but we don't know where they are."

"Sometimes that's better than knowing where they are," said Gavroche, who was a thinker.

"We have been wandering about these two hours," continued the elder, "we have hunted for things at the corners of the streets, but we have found nothing."

"I know," ejaculated Gavroche, "it's the dogs who eat everything."

He went on, after a pause:—

"Ah! we have lost our authors. We don't know what we have done with them. This should not be, gamins. It's stupid to let old people stray off like that. Come now! we must have a snooze all the same."

However, he asked them no questions. What was more simple than that they should have no dwelling place!

The elder of the two children, who had almost entirely recovered the prompt heedlessness of childhood, uttered this exclamation:—

"It's queer, all the same. Mamma told us that she would take us to get a blessed spray on Palm Sunday."

"Bosh," said Gavroche.

"Mamma," resumed the elder, "is a lady who lives with Mamselle Miss."

"Tanflûte!" retorted Gavroche.

Meanwhile he had halted, and for the last two minutes he had been feeling and fumbling in all sorts of nooks which his rags contained.

At last he tossed his head with an air intended to be merely satisfied, but which was triumphant, in reality.

"Let us be calm, young 'uns. Here's supper for three."

And from one of his pockets he drew forth a sou.

Without allowing the two urchins time for amazement, he pushed both of them before him into the baker's shop, and flung his sou on the counter, crying:—

"Boy! five centimes' worth of bread."

The baker, who was the proprietor in person, took up a loaf and a knife.

"In three pieces, my boy!" went on Gavroche.

And he added with dignity:—

"There are three of us."

And seeing that the baker, after scrutinizing the three customers, had taken down a black loaf, he thrust his finger far up his nose with an inhalation as imperious as though he had had a pinch of the great Frederick's snuff on the tip of his thumb, and hurled this indignant apostrophe full in the baker's face:—

"Keksekça?"

Those of our readers who might be tempted to espy in this interpellation of Gavroche's to the baker a Russian or a Polish word, or one of those savage cries which the Yoways and the Botocudos hurl at each other from bank to bank of a river, athwart the solitudes, are warned that it is a word which they (our readers) utter every day, and which takes the place of the phrase: "Qu'est-ce que c'est que cela?" The baker understood perfectly, and replied:—

"Well! It's bread, and very good bread of the second quality."

"You mean *larton brutal* (black bread)!" retorted Gavroche, calmly and coldly disdainful. "White bread, boy! white bread (*larton savonné*)! I'm standing treat."

The baker could not repress a smile, and as he cut the white bread he surveyed them in a compassionate way which shocked Gavroche.

"Come, now, baker's boy!" said he, "what are you taking our measure like that for?"

All three of them placed end to end would have hardly made a measure.

When the bread was cut, the baker threw the sou into his drawer, and Gavroche said to the two children:—

"Grub away."

The little boys stared at him in surprise.

Gavroche began to laugh.

"Ah! hullo, that's so! they don't understand yet, they're too small."

And he repeated:—

"Eat away."

At the same time, he held out a piece of bread to each of them.

And thinking that the elder, who seemed to him the more worthy of his conversation, deserved some special encouragement and ought to be relieved from all hesitation to satisfy his appetite, he added, as he handed him the largest share:—

"Ram that into your muzzle."

One piece was smaller than the others; he kept this for himself.

The poor children, including Gavroche, were famished. As they tore their bread apart in big mouthfuls, they blocked up the shop of the baker, who, now that they had paid their money, looked angrily at them.

"Let's go into the street again," said Gavroche.

They set off once more in the direction of the Bastille.

From time to time, as they passed the lighted shop-windows, the smallest halted to look at the time on a leaden watch which was suspended from his neck by a cord.

"Well, he is a very green 'un," said Gavroche.

Then, becoming thoughtful, he muttered between his teeth:—

"All the same, if I had charge of the babes I'd lock 'em up better than that."

Just as they were finishing their morsel of bread, and had reached the angle of that gloomy Rue des Ballets, at the other end of which the low and threatening wicket of La Force was visible:—

"Hullo, is that you, Gavroche?" said some one.

"Hullo, is that you, Montparnasse?" said Gavroche.

A man had just accosted the street urchin, and the man was no other than Montparnasse in disguise, with blue spectacles, but recognizable to Gavroche.

"The bow-wows!" went on Gavroche, "you've got a hide the color of a linseed plaster, and blue specs like a doctor. You're putting on style, 'pon my word!"

"Hush!" ejaculated Montparnasse, "not so loud."

And he drew Gavroche hastily out of range of the lighted shops.

The two little ones followed mechanically, holding each other by the hand.

When they were ensconced under the arch of a porte-cochère, sheltered from the rain and from all eyes:—

"Do you know where I'm going?" demanded Montparnasse.

"To the Abbey of Ascend-with-Regret," replied Gavroche.

"Joker!"

And Montparnasse went on:—

"I'm going to find Babet."

"Ah!" exclaimed Gavroche, "so her name is Babet."

Montparnasse lowered his voice:—

"Not she, he."

"Ah! Babet."

"Yes, Babet."

"I thought he was buckled."

"He has undone the buckle," replied Montparnasse.

And he rapidly related to the gamin how, on the morning of that very day, Babet, having been transferred to La Conciergerie, had made his escape, by turning to the left instead of to the right in "the police office."

Gavroche expressed his admiration for this skill.

"What a dentist!" he cried.

Montparnasse added a few details as to Babet's flight, and ended with:—

"Oh! That's not all."

Gavroche, as he listened, had seized a cane that Montparnasse held in his hand, and mechanically pulled at the upper part, and the blade of a dagger made its appearance.

"Ah!" he exclaimed, pushing the dagger back in haste, "you have brought along your gendarme disguised as a bourgeois."

Montparnasse winked.

"The deuce!" resumed Gavroche, "so you're going to have a bout with the bobbies?"

"You can't tell," replied Montparnasse with an indifferent air. "It's always a good thing to have a pin about one."

Gavroche persisted:—

"What are you up to to-night?"

Again Montparnasse took a grave tone, and said, mouthing every syllable: "Things."

And abruptly changing the conversation:—

"By the way!"

"What?"

"Something happened t'other day. Fancy. I meet a bourgeois. He makes me a present of a sermon and his purse. I put it in my pocket. A minute later, I feel in my pocket. There's nothing there."

"Except the sermon," said Gavroche.

"But you," went on Montparnasse, "where are you bound for now?"

Gavroche pointed to his two protégés, and said:—

"I'm going to put these infants to bed."

"Whereabouts is the bed?"

"At my house."

"Where's your house?"

"At my house."

"So you have a lodging?"

"Yes, I have."

"And where is your lodging?"

"In the elephant," said Gavroche.

Montparnasse, though not naturally inclined to astonishment, could not restrain an exclamation.

"In the elephant!"

"Well, yes, in the elephant!" retorted Gavroche. "Kekçaa?"

This is another word of the language which no one writes, and which every one speaks.

Kekçaa signifies: *Qu'est que c'est que cela a?* (What's the matter with that?)

The urchin's profound remark recalled Montparnasse to calmness and good sense. He appeared to return to better sentiments with regard to Gavroche's lodging.

"Of course," said he, "yes, the elephant. Is it comfortable there?"

"Very," said Gavroche. "It's really bully there. There ain't any draughts, as there are under the bridges."

"How do you get in?"

"Oh, I get in."

"So there is a hole?" demanded Montparnasse.

"Parbleu! I should say so. But you mustn't tell. It's between the fore legs. The bobbies haven't seen it."

"And you climb up? Yes, I understand."

"A turn of the hand, cric, crac, and it's all over, no one there."

VICTOR HUGO

After a pause, Gavroche added:—

"I shall have a ladder for these children."

Montparnasse burst out laughing:—

"Where the devil did you pick up those young 'uns?"

Gavroche replied with great simplicity:—

"They are some brats that a wig-maker made me a present of."

Meanwhile, Montparnasse had fallen to thinking:—

"You recognized me very readily," he muttered.

He took from his pocket two small objects which were nothing more than two quills wrapped in cotton, and thrust one up each of his nostrils. This gave him a different nose.

"That changes you," remarked Gavroche, "you are less homely so, you ought to keep them on all the time."

Montparnasse was a handsome fellow, but Gavroche was a tease.

"Seriously," demanded Montparnasse, "how do you like me so?"

The sound of his voice was different also. In a twinkling, Montparnasse had become unrecognizable.

"Oh! Do play Porrichinelle for us!" exclaimed Gavroche.

The two children, who had not been listening up to this point, being occupied themselves in thrusting their fingers up their noses, drew near at this name, and stared at Montparnasse with dawning joy and admiration.

Unfortunately, Montparnasse was troubled.

He laid his hand on Gavroche's shoulder, and said to him, emphasizing his words: "Listen to what I tell you, boy! if I were on the square with my dog, my knife, and my wife, and if you were to squander ten sous on me, I wouldn't refuse to work, but this isn't Shrove Tuesday."

This odd phrase produced a singular effect on the gamin. He wheeled round hastily, darted his little sparkling eyes about him with profound attention, and perceived a police sergeant standing with his back to them a few paces off. Gavroche allowed an: "Ah! good!" to escape him, but immediately suppressed it, and shaking Montparnasse's hand:—

"Well, good evening," said he, "I'm going off to my elephant with my brats. Supposing that you should need me some night, you can come and hunt me up there. I lodge on the entresol. There is no porter. You will inquire for Monsieur Gavroche."

"Very good," said Montparnasse.

And they parted, Montparnasse betaking himself in the direction of the Grève, and Gavroche towards the Bastille. The little one of five, dragged along by his brother who was dragged by Gavroche, turned his head back several times to watch "Porrichinelle" as he went.

The ambiguous phrase by means of which Montparnasse had warned Gavroche of the presence of the policeman, contained no other talisman than the assonance *dig* repeated five or six times in different forms. This syllable, *dig*, uttered alone or artistically mingled with the words of a phrase, means: "Take care, we can no longer talk freely." There was besides, in Montparnasse's sentence, a literary beauty which was lost upon Gavroche, that is *mon dogue, ma dague et ma digue*, a slang expression of the Temple, which signifies my dog, my knife, and my wife, greatly in vogue among clowns and the red-tails in the great century when Molière wrote and Callot drew.

Twenty years ago, there was still to be seen in the southwest corner of the Place de la Bastille, near the basin of the canal, excavated in the ancient ditch of the fortress-prison, a singular monument, which has already been effaced from the memories of Parisians, and which deserved to leave some trace, for it was the idea of a "member of the Institute, the General-in-chief of the army of Egypt."

We say monument, although it was only a rough model. But this model itself, a marvellous sketch, the grandiose skeleton of an idea of Napoleon's, which successive gusts of wind have carried away and thrown, on each occasion, still further from us, had become historical and had acquired a certain definiteness which contrasted with its provisional aspect. It was an elephant forty feet high, constructed of timber and masonry, bearing on its back a tower which resembled a house, formerly painted green by some dauber, and now painted black by heaven, the wind, and time. In this deserted and unprotected corner of the place, the broad brow of the colossus, his trunk, his tusks, his tower, his enormous crupper, his four feet, like columns produced, at night, under the starry heavens, a surprising and terrible form. It was a sort of symbol of popular force. It was sombre, mysterious, and immense. It was some mighty, visible phantom, one knew not what, standing erect beside the invisible spectre of the Bastille.

Few strangers visited this edifice, no passer-by looked at it. It was falling into ruins; every season the plaster which detached itself from its sides formed hideous wounds upon it. "The ædiles," as the expression ran in elegant dialect, had forgotten it ever since 1814. There it stood in its corner, melancholy, sick, crumbling, surrounded by a rotten palisade, soiled continually by drunken coachmen; cracks meandered athwart its belly, a lath projected from its tail, tall grass flourished between its legs; and, as the level of the place had been rising all around it for a space of thirty years, by that slow and continuous movement which insensibly elevates the soil of large towns, it stood in a hollow, and it looked as though the ground were giving way beneath it. It was unclean, despised, repulsive, and superb, ugly in the eyes of the bourgeois, melancholy in the eyes of the thinker. There was something about it of the dirt which is on the point of being swept out, and something of the majesty which is on the point of being decapitated. As we have said, at night, its aspect changed. Night is the real element of everything that is dark. As soon as twilight descended, the old elephant became transfigured; he assumed a tranquil and redoubtable appearance in the formidable serenity of the shadows. Being of the past, he belonged to night; and obscurity was in keeping with his grandeur.

This rough, squat, heavy, hard, austere, almost misshapen, but assuredly majestic monument, stamped with a sort of magnificent and savage gravity, has disappeared, and left to reign in peace, a sort of gigantic stove, ornamented with its pipe, which has replaced the sombre fortress with its nine towers, very much as the bourgeoisie replaces the feudal classes. It is quite natural that a stove should be the symbol of an epoch in which a pot contains power. This epoch will pass away, people have already begun to understand that, if there can be force in a boiler, there can be no force except in the brain; in other words, that which leads and drags on the world, is not locomotives, but ideas. Harness locomotives to ideas,—that is well done; but do not mistake the horse for the rider.

At all events, to return to the Place de la Bastille, the architect of this elephant succeeded in making a grand thing out of plaster; the architect of the stove has succeeded in making a pretty thing out of bronze.

This stove-pipe, which has been baptized by a sonorous name, and called the column of July, this monument of a revolution that miscarried, was still enveloped in 1832, in an immense shirt of woodwork, which we regret, for our part, and by a vast plank enclosure, which completed the task of isolating the elephant.

It was towards this corner of the place, dimly lighted by the reflection of a distant street lamp, that the gamin guided his two "brats."

The reader must permit us to interrupt ourselves here and to remind him that we are dealing with simple reality, and that twenty years ago, the tribunals were called upon to judge, under the charge of vagabondage, and mutilation of a public monument, a child who had been caught asleep in this very elephant of the Bastille. This fact noted, we proceed.

On arriving in the vicinity of the colossus, Gavroche comprehended the effect which the infinitely great might produce on the infinitely small, and said:—

"Don't be scared, infants."

Then he entered through a gap in the fence into the elephant's enclosure and helped the young ones to clamber through the breach. The two children, somewhat frightened, followed Gavroche without uttering a word, and confided themselves to this little Providence in rags which had given them bread and had promised them a shelter.

There, extended along the fence, lay a ladder which by day served the laborers in the neighboring timber-yard. Gavroche raised it with remarkable vigor, and placed it against one of the elephant's forelegs. Near the point where the ladder ended, a sort of black hole in the belly of the colossus could be distinguished.

Gavroche pointed out the ladder and the hole to his guests, and said to them:—

"Climb up and go in."

The two little boys exchanged terrified glances.

"You're afraid, brats!" exclaimed Gavroche.

And he added:—

"You shall see!"

He clasped the rough leg of the elephant, and in a twinkling, without deigning to make use of the ladder, he had reached the aperture. He entered it as an adder slips through a crevice, and disappeared within, and an instant later, the two children saw his head, which looked pale, appear vaguely, on the edge of the shadowy hole, like a wan and whitish spectre.

"Well!" he exclaimed, "climb up, young 'uns! You'll see how snug it is here! Come up, you!" he said to the elder, "I'll lend you a hand."

The little fellows nudged each other, the gamin frightened and inspired them with confidence at one and the same time, and then, it was raining very hard. The elder one undertook the risk. The younger, on seeing his brother climbing up, and himself left alone between the paws of this huge beast, felt greatly inclined to cry, but he did not dare.

The elder lad climbed, with uncertain steps, up the rungs of the ladder; Gavroche, in the meanwhile, encouraging him with exclamations like a fencing-master to his pupils, or a muleteer to his mules.

"Don't be afraid!—That's it!—Come on!—Put your feet there!—Give us your hand here!—Boldly!"

And when the child was within reach, he seized him suddenly and vigorously by the arm, and pulled him towards him.

"Nabbed!" said he.

The brat had passed through the crack.

"Now," said Gavroche, "wait for me. Be so good as to take a seat, Monsieur."

And making his way out of the hole as he had entered it, he slipped down the elephant's leg with the agility of a monkey, landed on his feet in the grass, grasped the child of five round the body, and planted him fairly in the middle of the ladder, then he began to climb up behind him, shouting to the elder:—

"I'm going to boost him, do you tug."

And in another instant, the small lad was pushed, dragged, pulled, thrust, stuffed into the hole, before he had time to recover himself, and Gavroche, entering behind him, and repulsing the ladder with a kick which sent it flat on the grass, began to clap his hands and to cry:—

"Here we are! Long live General Lafayette!"

This explosion over, he added:—

"Now, young 'uns, you are in my house."

Gavroche was at home, in fact.

Oh, unforeseen utility of the useless! Charity of great things! Goodness of giants! This huge monument, which had embodied an idea of the Emperor's, had become the box of a street urchin. The brat had been accepted and sheltered by the colossus. The bourgeois decked out in their Sunday finery who passed the elephant of the Bastille, were fond of saying as they scanned it disdainfully with their prominent eyes: "What's the good of that?" It served to save from the cold, the frost, the hail, and rain, to shelter from the winds of winter, to preserve from slumber in the mud which produces fever, and from slumber in the snow which produces death, a little being who had no father, no mother, no bread, no clothes, no refuge. It served to receive the innocent whom society repulsed. It served to diminish public crime. It was a lair open to one against whom all doors were shut. It seemed as though the miserable old mastodon, invaded by vermin and oblivion, covered with warts, with mould, and ulcers, tottering, worm-eaten, abandoned, condemned, a sort of mendicant colossus, asking alms in vain with a benevolent look in the midst of the crossroads, had taken pity on that other mendicant, the poor pygmy, who roamed without shoes to his feet, without a roof over his head, blowing on his fingers, clad in rags, fed on rejected scraps. That was what the elephant of the Bastille was good for. This idea of Napoleon, disdained by men, had been taken back by God. That which had been merely illustrious, had become august. In order to realize his thought, the Emperor should have had porphyry, brass, iron, gold, marble; the old collection of planks, beams and plaster sufficed for God. The Emperor had had the dream of a genius; in that Titanic elephant, armed, prodigious, with trunk uplifted, bearing its tower and scattering on all sides its merry and vivifying waters, he wished to incarnate the people. God had done a grander thing with it, he had lodged a child there.

The hole through which Gavroche had entered was a breach which was hardly visible from the outside, being concealed, as we have stated, beneath the elephant's belly, and so narrow that it was only cats and homeless children who could pass through it.

"Let's begin," said Gavroche, "by telling the porter that we are not at home."

And plunging into the darkness with the assurance of a person who is well acquainted with his apartments, he took a plank and stopped up the aperture.

Again Gavroche plunged into the obscurity. The children heard the crackling of the match thrust into the phosphoric bottle. The chemical match was not yet in existence; at that epoch the Fumade steel represented progress.

A sudden light made them blink; Gavroche had just managed to ignite one of those bits of cord dipped in resin which are called *cellar rats*. The *cellar rat*, which emitted more smoke than light, rendered the interior of the elephant confusedly visible.

Gavroche's two guests glanced about them, and the sensation which they experienced was something like that which one would feel if shut up in the great tun of Heidelberg, or, better still, like what Jonah must have felt in the biblical belly of the whale. An entire and gigantic skeleton appeared enveloping them. Above, a long brown beam, whence started at regular distances, massive, arching ribs, represented the vertebral column with its sides, stalactites of plaster depended from them like entrails, and vast spiders' webs stretching from side to side, formed dirty diaphragms. Here and there, in the corners, were visible large blackish spots which had the appearance of being alive, and which changed places rapidly with an abrupt and frightened movement.

VICTOR HUGO

Fragments which had fallen from the elephant's back into his belly had filled up the cavity, so that it was possible to walk upon it as on a floor.

The smaller child nestled up against his brother, and whispered to him:—

"It's black."

This remark drew an exclamation from Gavroche. The petrified air of the two brats rendered some shock necessary.

"What's that you are gabbling about there?" he exclaimed. "Are you scoffing at me? Are you turning up your noses? Do you want the Tuileries? Are you brutes? Come, say! I warn you that I don't belong to the regiment of simpletons. Ah, come now, are you brats from the Pope's establishment?"

A little roughness is good in cases of fear. It is reassuring. The two children drew close to Gavroche.

Gavroche, paternally touched by this confidence, passed from grave to gentle, and addressing the smaller:—

"Stupid," said he, accenting the insulting word, with a caressing intonation, "it's outside that it is black. Outside it's raining, here it does not rain; outside it's cold, here there's not an atom of wind; outside there are heaps of people, here there's no one; outside there ain't even the moon, here there's my candle, confound it!"

The two children began to look upon the apartment with less terror; but Gavroche allowed them no more time for contemplation.

"Quick," said he.

And he pushed them towards what we are very glad to be able to call the end of the room.

There stood his bed.

Gavroche's bed was complete; that is to say, it had a mattress, a blanket, and an alcove with curtains.

The mattress was a straw mat, the blanket a rather large strip of gray woollen stuff, very warm and almost new. This is what the alcove consisted of:—

Three rather long poles, thrust into and consolidated, with the rubbish which formed the floor, that is to say, the belly of the elephant, two in front and one behind, and united by a rope at their summits, so as to form a pyramidal bundle. This cluster supported a trellis-work of brass wire which was simply placed upon it, but artistically applied, and held by fastenings of iron wire, so that it enveloped all three holes. A row of very heavy stones kept this network down to the floor so that nothing could pass under it. This grating was nothing else than a piece of the brass screens with which aviaries are covered in menageries. Gavroche's bed stood as in a cage, behind this net. The whole resembled an Esquimaux tent.

This trellis-work took the place of curtains.

Gavroche moved aside the stones which fastened the net down in front, and the two folds of the net which lapped over each other fell apart.

"Down on all fours, brats!" said Gavroche.

He made his guests enter the cage with great precaution, then he crawled in after them, pulled the stones together, and closed the opening hermetically again.

All three had stretched out on the mat. Gavroche still had the *cellar rat* in his hand.

"Now," said he, "go to sleep! I'm going to suppress the candelabra."

"Monsieur," the elder of the brothers asked Gavroche, pointing to the netting, "what's that for?"

"That," answered Gavroche gravely, "is for the rats. Go to sleep!"

Nevertheless, he felt obliged to add a few words of instruction for the benefit of these young creatures, and he continued:—

"It's a thing from the Jardin des Plantes. It's used for fierce animals. There's a whole shopful of them there. All you've got to do is to climb over a wall, crawl through a window, and pass through a door. You can get as much as you want."

As he spoke, he wrapped the younger one up bodily in a fold of the blanket, and the little one murmured:—

"Oh! how good that is! It's warm!"

Gavroche cast a pleased eye on the blanket.

"That's from the Jardin des Plantes, too," said he. "I took that from the monkeys."

And, pointing out to the eldest the mat on which he was lying, a very thick and admirably made mat, he added:—

"That belonged to the giraffe."

After a pause he went on:—

"The beasts had all these things. I took them away from them. It didn't trouble them. I told them: 'It's for the elephant.'"

He paused, and then resumed:—

"You crawl over the walls and you don't care a straw for the government. So there now!"

The two children gazed with timid and stupefied respect on this intrepid and ingenious being, a vagabond like themselves, isolated like themselves, frail like themselves, who had something admirable and all-powerful about him, who seemed supernatural to them, and whose physiognomy was composed of all the grimaces of an old mountebank, mingled with the most ingenuous and charming smiles.

"Monsieur," ventured the elder timidly, "you are not afraid of the police, then?"

Gavroche contented himself with replying:—

"Brat! Nobody says 'police,' they say 'bobbies.'"

The smaller had his eyes wide open, but he said nothing. As he was on the edge of the mat, the elder being in the middle, Gavroche tucked the blanket round him as a mother might have done, and heightened the mat under his head with old rags, in such a way as to form a pillow for the child. Then he turned to the elder:—

"Hey! We're jolly comfortable here, ain't we?"

"Ah, yes!" replied the elder, gazing at Gavroche with the expression of a saved angel.

The two poor little children who had been soaked through, began to grow warm once more.

"Ah, by the way," continued Gavroche, "what were you bawling about?"

And pointing out the little one to his brother:—

"A mite like that, I've nothing to say about, but the idea of a big fellow like you crying! It's idiotic; you looked like a calf."

"Gracious," replied the child, "we have no lodging."

"Bother!" retorted Gavroche, "you don't say 'lodgings,' you say 'crib.'"

"And then, we were afraid of being alone like that at night."

"You don't say 'night,' you say 'darkmans.'"

"Thank you, sir," said the child.

"Listen," went on Gavroche, "you must never bawl again over anything. I'll take care of you. You shall see what fun we'll have. In summer, we'll go to the Glacière with Navet, one of my pals, we'll bathe in the Gare, we'll run stark naked in front of the rafts on the bridge at Austerlitz,—that makes the laundresses raging. They scream, they get mad, and if you only knew how ridiculous they are! We'll go and see the man-skeleton. And then I'll take you to the play. I'll take you to see Frédérick Lemaître. I have tickets, I know some of the actors, I even played in a piece once. There were a lot of us fellers, and we ran under a cloth, and that made the sea. I'll get you an engagement at my theatre. We'll go to see the savages. They ain't real, those savages ain't. They wear pink tights that go all in wrinkles, and you can see where their elbows have been darned with white. Then, we'll go to the Opera. We'll get in with the hired applauders. The Opera claque is well managed. I wouldn't associate with the claque on the boulevard. At the Opera, just fancy! some of them pay twenty sous, but they're ninnies. They're called dishclouts. And then we'll go to see the guillotine work. I'll show you the executioner. He lives in the Rue des Marais. Monsieur Sanson. He has a letter-box at his door. Ah! we'll have famous fun!"

At that moment a drop of wax fell on Gavroche's finger, and recalled him to the realities of life.

"The deuce!" said he, "there's the wick giving out. Attention! I can't spend more than a sou a month on my lighting. When a body goes to bed, he must sleep. We haven't the time to read M. Paul de Kock's romances. And besides, the light might pass through the cracks of the porte-cochère, and all the bobbies need to do is to see it."

"And then," remarked the elder timidly,—he alone dared talk to Gavroche, and reply to him, "a spark might fall in the straw, and we must look out and not burn the house down."

"People don't say 'burn the house down,'" remarked Gavroche, "they say 'blaze the crib.'"

The storm increased in violence, and the heavy downpour beat upon the back of the colossus amid claps of thunder. "You're taken in, rain!" said Gavroche. "It amuses me to hear the decanter run down the legs of the house. Winter is a stupid; it wastes its merchandise, it loses its labor, it can't wet us, and that makes it kick up a row, old water-carrier that it is."

This allusion to the thunder, all the consequences of which Gavroche, in his character of a philosopher of the nineteenth century, accepted, was followed by a broad flash of lightning, so dazzling that a hint of it entered the belly of the elephant through the crack. Almost at the same instant, the thunder rumbled with great fury. The two little creatures uttered a shriek, and started up so eagerly that the network came near being displaced, but Gavroche turned his bold face to them, and took advantage of the clap of thunder to burst into a laugh.

"Calm down, children. Don't topple over the edifice. That's fine, first-class thunder; all right. That's no slouch of a streak of lightning. Bravo for the good God! Deuce take it! It's almost as good as it is at the Ambigu."

VICTOR HUGO

That said, he restored order in the netting, pushed the two children gently down on the bed, pressed their knees, in order to stretch them out at full length, and exclaimed:—

"Since the good God is lighting his candle, I can blow out mine. Now, babes, now, my young humans, you must shut your peepers. It's very bad not to sleep. It'll make you swallow the strainer, or, as they say, in fashionable society, stink in the gullet. Wrap yourself up well in the hide! I'm going to put out the light. Are you ready?"

"Yes," murmured the elder, "I'm all right. I seem to have feathers under my head."

"People don't say 'head,'" cried Gavroche, "they say 'nut'."

The two children nestled close to each other, Gavroche finished arranging them on the mat, drew the blanket up to their very ears, then repeated, for the third time, his injunction in the hieratical tongue:—

"Shut your peepers!"

And he snuffed out his tiny light.

Hardly had the light been extinguished, when a peculiar trembling began to affect the netting under which the three children lay.

It consisted of a multitude of dull scratches which produced a metallic sound, as if claws and teeth were gnawing at the copper wire. This was accompanied by all sorts of little piercing cries.

The little five-year-old boy, on hearing this hubbub overhead, and chilled with terror, jogged his brother's elbow; but the elder brother had already shut his peepers, as Gavroche had ordered. Then the little one, who could no longer control his terror, questioned Gavroche, but in a very low tone, and with bated breath:—

"Sir?"

"Hey?" said Gavroche, who had just closed his eyes.

"What is that?"

"It's the rats," replied Gavroche.

And he laid his head down on the mat again.

The rats, in fact, who swarmed by thousands in the carcass of the elephant, and who were the living black spots which we have already mentioned, had been held in awe by the flame of the candle, so long as it had been lighted; but as soon as the cavern, which was the same as their city, had returned to darkness, scenting what the good story-teller Perrault calls "fresh meat," they had hurled themselves in throngs on Gavroche's tent, had climbed to the top of it, and had begun to bite the meshes as though seeking to pierce this new-fangled trap.

Still the little one could not sleep.

"Sir?" he began again.

"Hey?" said Gavroche.

"What are rats?"

"They are mice."

This explanation reassured the child a little. He had seen white mice in the course of his life, and he was not afraid of them. Nevertheless, he lifted up his voice once more.

"Sir?"

"Hey?" said Gavroche again.

"Why don't you have a cat?"

"I did have one," replied Gavroche, "I brought one here, but they ate her."

This second explanation undid the work of the first, and the little fellow began to tremble again.

The dialogue between him and Gavroche began again for the fourth time:—

"Monsieur?"

"Hey?"

"Who was it that was eaten?"

"The cat."

"And who ate the cat?"

"The rats."

"The mice?"

"Yes, the rats."

The child, in consternation, dismayed at the thought of mice which ate cats, pursued:—

"Sir, would those mice eat us?"

"Wouldn't they just!" ejaculated Gavroche.

The child's terror had reached its climax. But Gavroche added:—

"Don't be afraid. They can't get in. And besides, I'm here! Here, catch hold of my hand. Hold your tongue and shut your peepers!"

At the same time Gavroche grasped the little fellow's hand across his brother. The child pressed the hand close to him, and felt reassured. Courage and strength have these mysterious ways of communicating themselves. Silence reigned round them once more, the sound of their voices had frightened off the rats; at the expiration of a few minutes, they came raging back, but in vain, the three little fellows were fast asleep and heard nothing more.

The hours of the night fled away. Darkness covered the vast Place de la Bastille. A wintry gale, which mingled with the rain, blew in gusts, the patrol searched all the doorways, alleys, enclosures, and obscure nooks, and in their search for nocturnal vagabonds they passed in silence before the elephant; the monster, erect, motionless, staring open-eyed into the shadows, had the appearance of dreaming happily over his good deed; and sheltered from heaven and from men the three poor sleeping children.

In order to understand what is about to follow, the reader must remember, that, at that epoch, the Bastille guard-house was situated at the other end of the square, and that what took place in the vicinity of the elephant could neither be seen nor heard by the sentinel.

Towards the end of that hour which immediately precedes the dawn, a man turned from the Rue Saint-Antoine at a run, made the circuit of the enclosure of the column of July, and glided between the palings until he was underneath the belly of the elephant. If any light had illuminated that man, it might have been divined from the thorough manner in which he was soaked that he had passed the night in the rain. Arrived beneath the elephant, he uttered a peculiar cry, which did not belong to any human tongue, and which a paroquet alone could have imitated. Twice he repeated this cry, of whose orthography the following barely conveys an idea:—

"Kirikikiou!"

At the second cry, a clear, young, merry voice responded from the belly of the elephant:—

"Yes!"

Almost immediately, the plank which closed the hole was drawn aside, and gave passage to a child who descended the elephant's leg, and fell briskly near the man. It was Gavroche. The man was Montparnasse.

As for his cry of *Kirikikiou*,—that was, doubtless, what the child had meant, when he said:—

"You will ask for Monsieur Gavroche."

On hearing it, he had waked with a start, had crawled out of his "alcove," pushing apart the netting a little, and carefully drawing it together again, then he had opened the trap, and descended.

The man and the child recognized each other silently amid the gloom: Montparnasse confined himself to the remark:—

"We need you. Come, lend us a hand."

The lad asked for no further enlightenment.

"I'm with you," said he.

And both took their way towards the Rue Saint-Antoine, whence Montparnasse had emerged, winding rapidly through the long file of market-gardeners' carts which descend towards the markets at that hour.

The market-gardeners, crouching, half-asleep, in their wagons, amid the salads and vegetables, enveloped to their very eyes in their mufflers on account of the beating rain, did not even glance at these strange pedestrians.

III

The Vicissitudes of Flight

This is what had taken place that same night at the La Force:—

An escape had been planned between Babet, Brujon, Guelemer, and Thénardier, although Thénardier was in close confinement. Babet had arranged the matter for his own benefit, on the same day, as the reader has seen from Montparnasse's account to Gavroche. Montparnasse was to help them from outside.

Brujon, after having passed a month in the punishment cell, had had time, in the first place, to weave a rope, in the second, to mature a plan. In former times, those severe places where the discipline of the prison delivers the convict into his own hands, were composed of four stone walls, a stone ceiling, a flagged pavement, a camp bed, a grated window, and a door lined with iron, and were called *dungeons*; but the dungeon was judged to be too terrible; nowadays they are composed of an iron door, a grated window, a camp bed, a flagged pavement, four stone walls, and a stone ceiling, and are called *chambers of punishment*. A little light penetrates towards midday. The inconvenient point about these chambers which, as the reader sees, are not dungeons, is that they allow the persons who should be at work to think.

So Brujon meditated, and he emerged from the chamber of punishment with a rope. As he had the name of being very dangerous in the Charlemagne courtyard, he was placed in the New Building. The first thing he found in the New Building was Guelemer, the second was a nail; Guelemer, that is to say, crime; a nail, that is to say, liberty. Brujon, of whom it is high time that the reader should have a complete idea, was, with an appearance of delicate health and a profoundly premeditated languor, a polished, intelligent sprig, and a thief, who had a caressing glance, and an atrocious smile. His glance resulted from his will, and his smile from his nature. His first studies in his art had been directed to roofs. He had made great progress in the industry of the men who tear off lead, who plunder the roofs and despoil the gutters by the process called *double pickings*.

The circumstance which put the finishing touch on the moment peculiarly favorable for an attempt at escape, was that the roofers were re-laying and re-jointing, at that very moment, a portion of the slates on the prison. The Saint-Bernard courtyard was no longer absolutely isolated from the Charlemagne and the Saint-Louis courts. Up above there were scaffoldings and ladders; in other words, bridges and stairs in the direction of liberty.

The New Building, which was the most cracked and decrepit thing to be seen anywhere in the world, was the weak point in the prison. The walls were eaten by saltpetre to such an extent that the authorities had been obliged to line the vaults of the dormitories with a sheathing of wood, because stones were in the habit of becoming detached and falling on the prisoners in their beds. In spite of this antiquity, the authorities committed the error of confining in the New Building the most troublesome prisoners, of placing there "the hard cases," as they say in prison parlance.

The New Building contained four dormitories, one above the other, and a top story which was called the Bel-Air (Fine-Air). A large chimney-flue, probably from some ancient kitchen of the Dukes de la Force, started from the ground floor, traversed all four stories, cut the dormitories, where it figured as a flattened pillar, into two portions, and finally pierced the roof.

Guelemer and Brujon were in the same dormitory. They had been placed, by way of precaution, on the lower story. Chance ordained that the heads of their beds should rest against the chimney.

Thénardier was directly over their heads in the top story known as Fine-Air. The pedestrian who halts on the Rue Culture-Sainte-Catherine, after passing the barracks of the firemen, in front of the porte-cochère of the bathing establishment, beholds a yard full of flowers and shrubs in wooden boxes, at the extremity of which spreads out a little white rotunda with two wings, brightened up with green shutters, the bucolic dream of Jean Jacques.

Not more than ten years ago, there rose above that rotunda an enormous black, hideous, bare wall by which it was backed up.

This was the outer wall of La Force.

This wall, beside that rotunda, was Milton viewed through Berquin.

Lofty as it was, this wall was overtopped by a still blacker roof, which could be seen beyond. This was the roof of the New Building. There one could descry four dormer-windows, guarded with bars; they were the windows of the Fine-Air.

A chimney pierced the roof; this was the chimney which traversed the dormitories.

The Bel-Air, that top story of the New Building, was a sort of large hall, with a Mansard roof, guarded with triple gratings and double doors of sheet iron, which were studded with enormous bolts. When one entered from the north end, one had on one's left the four dormer-windows, on one's right, facing the windows, at regular intervals, four square, tolerably vast cages, separated by narrow passages, built of masonry to about the height of the elbow, and the rest, up to the roof, of iron bars.

Thénardier had been in solitary confinement in one of these cages since the night of the 3d of February. No one was ever able to discover how, and by what connivance, he succeeded in procuring, and secreting a bottle of wine, invented, so it is said, by Desrues, with which a narcotic is mixed, and which the band of the *Endormeurs*, or *Sleep-compellers*, rendered famous.

There are, in many prisons, treacherous employees, half-jailers, half-thieves, who assist in escapes, who sell to the police an unfaithful service, and who turn a penny whenever they can.

On that same night, then, when Little Gavroche picked up the two lost children, Brujon and Guelemer, who knew that Babet, who had escaped that morning, was waiting for them in the street as well as Montparnasse, rose softly, and with the nail which Brujon had found, began to pierce the chimney against which their beds stood. The rubbish fell on Brujon's bed, so that they were not heard. Showers mingled with thunder shook the doors on their hinges, and created in the prison a terrible and opportune uproar. Those of the prisoners who woke, pretended to fall asleep again, and left Guelemer and Brujon to their own devices. Brujon was adroit; Guelemer was vigorous. Before any sound had reached the watcher, who was sleeping in the grated cell which opened into the dormitory, the wall had been pierced, the chimney scaled, the iron grating which barred the upper orifice of the flue forced, and the two redoubtable ruffians were on the roof. The wind and rain redoubled, the roof was slippery.

"What a good night to leg it!" said Brujon.

An abyss six feet broad and eighty feet deep separated them from the surrounding wall. At the bottom of this abyss, they could see the musket of a sentinel gleaming through the gloom. They fastened one end of the rope which Brujon had spun in his dungeon to the stumps of the iron bars which they had just wrenched off, flung the other over the outer wall, crossed the abyss at one bound, clung to the coping of the wall, got astride of it, let themselves slip, one after the other, along the rope, upon a little roof which touches the bath-house, pulled their rope after them, jumped down into the courtyard of the bath-house, traversed it, pushed open the porter's wicket, beside which hung his rope, pulled this, opened the porte-cochère, and found themselves in the street.

Three-quarters of an hour had not elapsed since they had risen in bed in the dark, nail in hand, and their project in their heads.

A few moments later they had joined Babet and Montparnasse, who were prowling about the neighborhood.

They had broken their rope in pulling it after them, and a bit of it remained attached to the chimney on the roof. They had sustained no other damage, however, than that of scratching nearly all the skin off their hands.

That night, Thénardier was warned, without any one being able to explain how, and was not asleep.

Towards one o'clock in the morning, the night being very dark, he saw two shadows pass along the roof, in the rain and squalls, in front of the dormer-window which was opposite his cage. One halted at the window, long enough to dart in a glance. This was Brujon.

Thénardier recognized him, and understood. This was enough.

Thénardier, rated as a burglar, and detained as a measure of precaution under the charge of organizing a nocturnal ambush, with armed force, was kept in sight. The sentry, who was relieved every two hours, marched up and down in front of his cage with loaded musket. The Fine-Air was lighted by a skylight. The prisoner had on his feet fetters weighing fifty pounds. Every day, at four o'clock in the afternoon, a jailer, escorted by two dogs,—this was still in vogue at that time,—entered his cage, deposited beside his bed a loaf of black bread weighing two pounds, a jug of water, a bowl filled with rather thin bouillon, in which swam a few Mayagan beans, inspected his irons and tapped the bars. This man and his dogs made two visits during the night.

Thénardier had obtained permission to keep a sort of iron bolt which he used to spike his bread into a crack in the wall, "in order to preserve it from the rats," as he said. As Thénardier was kept in sight, no objection had been made to this spike. Still, it was remembered afterwards, that one of the jailers had said: "It would be better to let him have only a wooden spike."

At two o'clock in the morning, the sentinel, who was an old soldier, was relieved, and replaced by a conscript. A few moments later, the man with the dogs paid his visit, and went off without noticing anything, except, possibly, the excessive youth and "the rustic air" of the "raw recruit." Two hours afterwards, at four o'clock, when they came to relieve the conscript, he was found asleep on the floor, lying like a log near Thénardier's cage. As for Thénardier, he was no longer there. There was a hole in the ceiling of his cage, and, above it, another hole in the roof. One of the planks of his bed had been wrenched off, and probably carried away with him, as it was not found. They also seized in his cell a half-empty bottle which contained the remains of the stupefying wine with which the soldier had been drugged. The soldier's bayonet had disappeared.

At the moment when this discovery was made, it was assumed that Thénardier was out of reach. The truth is, that he was no longer in the New Building, but that he was still in great danger.

Thénardier, on reaching the roof of the New Building, had found the remains of Brujon's rope hanging to the bars of the upper trap of the chimney, but, as this broken fragment was much too short, he had not been able to escape by the outer wall, as Brujon and Guelemer had done.

When one turns from the Rue des Ballets into the Rue du Roi-de-Sicile, one almost immediately encounters a repulsive ruin. There stood on that spot, in the last century, a house of which only the back wall now remains, a regular wall of masonry, which rises to the height of the third story between the adjoining buildings. This ruin can be recognized by two large square windows which are still to be seen there; the middle one, that nearest the right gable, is barred with a worm-eaten beam adjusted like a prop. Through these windows there was formerly visible a lofty and lugubrious wall, which was a fragment of the outer wall of La Force.

The empty space on the street left by the demolished house is half-filled by a fence of rotten boards, shored up by five stone posts. In this recess lies concealed a little shanty which leans against the portion of the ruin which has remained standing. The fence has a gate, which, a few years ago, was fastened only by a latch.

It was the crest of this ruin that Thénardier had succeeded in reaching, a little after one o'clock in the morning.

How had he got there? That is what no one has ever been able to explain or understand. The lightning must, at the same time, have hindered and helped him. Had he made use of the ladders and scaffoldings of the slaters to get from roof to roof, from enclosure to enclosure, from compartment to compartment, to the buildings of the Charlemagne court, then to the buildings of the Saint-Louis court, to the outer wall, and thence to the hut on the Rue du Roi-de-Sicile? But in that itinerary there existed breaks which seemed to render it an impossibility. Had he placed the plank from his bed like a bridge from the roof of the Fine-Air to the outer wall, and crawled flat, on his belly on the coping of the outer wall the whole distance round the prison as far as the hut? But the outer wall of La Force formed a crenellated and unequal line; it mounted and descended, it dropped at the firemen's barracks, it rose towards the bath-house, it was cut in twain by buildings, it was not even of the same height on the Hotel Lamoignon as on the Rue Pavée; everywhere occurred falls and right angles; and then, the sentinels must have espied the dark form of the fugitive; hence, the route taken by Thénardier still remains rather inexplicable. In two manners, flight was impossible. Had Thénardier, spurred on by that thirst for liberty which changes precipices into ditches, iron bars into wattles of osier, a legless man into an athlete, a gouty man into a bird, stupidity into instinct, instinct into intelligence, and intelligence into genius, had Thénardier invented a third mode? No one has ever found out.

The marvels of escape cannot always be accounted for. The man who makes his escape, we repeat, is inspired; there is something of the star and of the lightning in the mysterious gleam of flight; the effort towards deliverance is no less surprising than the flight towards the sublime, and one says of the escaped thief: "How did he contrive to scale that wall?" in the same way that one says of Corneille: "Where did he find *the means of dying?*"

At all events, dripping with perspiration, drenched with rain, with his clothes hanging in ribbons, his hands flayed, his elbows bleeding, his knees torn, Thénardier had reached what children, in their figurative language, call *the edge* of the wall of the ruin, there he had stretched himself out at full length, and there his strength had failed him. A steep escarpment three stories high separated him from the pavement of the street.

The rope which he had was too short.

There he waited, pale, exhausted, desperate with all the despair which he had undergone, still hidden by the night, but telling himself

VICTOR HUGO

that the day was on the point of dawning, alarmed at the idea of hearing the neighboring clock of Saint-Paul strike four within a few minutes, an hour when the sentinel was relieved and when the latter would be found asleep under the pierced roof, staring in horror at a terrible depth, at the light of the street lanterns, the wet, black pavement, that pavement longed for yet frightful, which meant death, and which meant liberty.

He asked himself whether his three accomplices in flight had succeeded, if they had heard him, and if they would come to his assistance. He listened. With the exception of the patrol, no one had passed through the street since he had been there. Nearly the whole of the descent of the market-gardeners from Montreuil, from Charonne, from Vincennes, and from Bercy to the markets was accomplished through the Rue Saint-Antoine.

Four o'clock struck. Thénardier shuddered. A few moments later, that terrified and confused uproar which follows the discovery of an escape broke forth in the prison. The sound of doors opening and shutting, the creaking of gratings on their hinges, a tumult in the guard-house, the hoarse shouts of the turnkeys, the shock of musket-butts on the pavement of the courts, reached his ears. Lights ascended and descended past the grated windows of the dormitories, a torch ran along the ridge-pole of the top story of the New Building, the firemen belonging in the barracks on the right had been summoned. Their helmets, which the torch lighted up in the rain, went and came along the roofs. At the same time, Thénardier perceived in the direction of the Bastille a wan whiteness lighting up the edge of the sky in doleful wise.

He was on top of a wall ten inches wide, stretched out under the heavy rains, with two gulfs to right and left, unable to stir, subject to the giddiness of a possible fall, and to the horror of a certain arrest, and his thoughts, like the pendulum of a clock, swung from one of these ideas to the other: "Dead if I fall, caught if I stay." In the midst of this anguish, he suddenly saw, the street being still dark, a man who was gliding along the walls and coming from the Rue Pavée, halt in the recess above which Thénardier was, as it were, suspended. Here this man was joined by a second, who walked with the same caution, then by a third, then by a fourth. When these men were re-united, one of them lifted the latch of the gate in the fence, and all four entered the enclosure in which the shanty stood. They halted directly under Thénardier. These men had evidently chosen this vacant space in order that they might consult without being seen by the passers-by or by the sentinel who guards the wicket of La Force a few paces distant. It must be added, that the rain kept this sentinel blocked in his box. Thénardier, not being able to distinguish their visages, lent an ear to their words with the desperate attention of a wretch who feels himself lost.

Thénardier saw something resembling a gleam of hope flash before his eyes,—these men conversed in slang.

The first said in a low but distinct voice:—

"Let's cut. What are we up to here?"

The second replied: "It's raining hard enough to put out the very devil's fire. And the bobbies will be along instanter. There's a soldier on guard yonder. We shall get nabbed here."

These two words, *icigo* and *icicaille*, both of which mean *ici*, and which belong, the first to the slang of the barriers, the second to the slang of the Temple, were flashes of light for Thénardier. By the *icigo* he recognized Brujon, who was a prowler of the barriers, by the *icicaille* he knew Babet, who, among his other trades, had been an old-clothes broker at the Temple.

The antique slang of the great century is no longer spoken except in the Temple, and Babet was really the only person who spoke it in all its purity. Had it not been for the *icicaille*, Thénardier would not have recognized him, for he had entirely changed his voice.

In the meanwhile, the third man had intervened.

"There's no hurry yet, let's wait a bit. How do we know that he doesn't stand in need of us?"

By this, which was nothing but French, Thénardier recognized Montparnasse, who made it a point in his elegance to understand all slangs and to speak none of them.

As for the fourth, he held his peace, but his huge shoulders betrayed him. Thénardier did not hesitate. It was Guelemer.

Brujon replied almost impetuously but still in a low tone:—

"What are you jabbering about? The tavern-keeper hasn't managed to cut his stick. He don't tumble to the racket, that he don't! You have to be a pretty knowing cove to tear up your shirt, cut up your sheet to make a rope, punch holes in doors, get up false papers, make false keys, file your irons, hang out your cord, hide yourself, and disguise yourself! The old fellow hasn't managed to play it, he doesn't understand how to work the business."

Babet added, still in that classical slang which was spoken by Poulailler and Cartouche, and which is to the bold, new, highly colored and risky argot used by Brujon what the language of Racine is to the language of André Chenier:—

"Your tavern-keeper must have been nabbed in the act. You have to be knowing. He's only a greenhorn. He must have let himself be taken in by a bobby, perhaps even by a sheep who played it on him as his pal. Listen, Montparnasse, do you hear those shouts in the prison? You have seen all those lights. He's recaptured, there! He'll get off with twenty years. I ain't afraid, I ain't a coward, but there ain't anything more to do, or otherwise they'd lead us a dance. Don't get mad, come with us, let's go drink a bottle of old wine together."

"One doesn't desert one's friends in a scrape," grumbled Montparnasse.

"I tell you he's nabbed!" retorted Brujon. "At the present moment, the inn-keeper ain't worth a ha'penny. We can't do nothing for him. Let's be off. Every minute I think a bobby has got me in his fist."

Montparnasse no longer offered more than a feeble resistance; the fact is, that these four men, with the fidelity of ruffians who never abandon each other, had prowled all night long about La Force, great as was their peril, in the hope of seeing Thénardier make his appearance on the top of some wall. But the night, which was really growing too fine,—for the downpour was such as to render all the streets deserted,— the cold which was overpowering them, their soaked garments, their hole-ridden shoes, the alarming noise which had just burst forth in the prison, the hours which had elapsed, the patrol which they had encountered, the hope which was vanishing, all urged them to beat a retreat. Montparnasse himself, who was, perhaps, almost Thénardier's son-in-law, yielded. A moment more, and they would be gone. Thénardier was panting on his wall like the shipwrecked sufferers of the *Méduse* on their raft when they beheld the vessel which had appeared in sight vanish on the horizon.

He dared not call to them; a cry might be heard and ruin everything. An idea occurred to him, a last idea, a flash of inspiration; he drew from his pocket the end of Brujon's rope, which he had detached from the chimney of the New Building, and flung it into the space enclosed by the fence.

This rope fell at their feet.

"A widow," said Babet.

"My tortouse!" said Brujon.

"The tavern-keeper is there," said Montparnasse.

They raised their eyes. Thénardier thrust out his head a very little.

"Quick!" said Montparnasse, "have you the other end of the rope, Brujon?"

"Yes."

"Knot the two pieces together, we'll fling him the rope, he can fasten it to the wall, and he'll have enough of it to get down with."

Thénardier ran the risk, and spoke:—

"I am paralyzed with cold."

"We'll warm you up."

"I can't budge."

"Let yourself slide, we'll catch you."

"My hands are benumbed."

"Only fasten the rope to the wall."

"I can't."

"Then one of us must climb up," said Montparnasse.

"Three stories!" ejaculated Brujon.

An ancient plaster flue, which had served for a stove that had been used in the shanty in former times, ran along the wall and mounted almost to the very spot where they could see Thénardier. This flue, then much damaged and full of cracks, has since fallen, but the marks of it are still visible.

It was very narrow.

"One might get up by the help of that," said Montparnasse.

"By that flue?" exclaimed Babet, "a grown-up cove, never! it would take a brat."

"A brat must be got," resumed Brujon.

"Where are we to find a young 'un?" said Guelemer.

"Wait," said Montparnasse. "I've got the very article."

He opened the gate of the fence very softly, made sure that no one was passing along the street, stepped out cautiously, shut the gate behind him, and set off at a run in the direction of the Bastille.

Seven or eight minutes elapsed, eight thousand centuries to Thénardier; Babet, Brujon, and Guelemer did not open their lips; at last the gate opened once more, and Montparnasse appeared, breathless, and followed by Gavroche. The rain still rendered the street completely deserted.

Little Gavroche entered the enclosure and gazed at the forms of these ruffians with a tranquil air. The water was dripping from his hair. Guelemer addressed him:—

"Are you a man, young 'un?"

Gavroche shrugged his shoulders, and replied:—

"A young 'un like me's a man, and men like you are babes."

"The brat's tongue's well hung!" exclaimed Babet.

"The Paris brat ain't made of straw," added Brujon.

"What do you want?" asked Gavroche.

Montparnasse answered:—

"Climb up that flue."

"With this rope," said Babet.

"And fasten it," continued Brujon.

"To the top of the wall," went on Babet.

"To the cross-bar of the window," added Brujon.

"And then?" said Gavroche.

"There!" said Guelemer.

The gamin examined the rope, the flue, the wall, the windows, and made that indescribable and disdainful noise with his lips which signifies:—

"Is that all!"

"There's a man up there whom you are to save," resumed Montparnasse.

"Will you?" began Brujon again.

"Greenhorn!" replied the lad, as though the question appeared a most unprecedented one to him.

And he took off his shoes.

Guelemer seized Gavroche by one arm, set him on the roof of the shanty, whose worm-eaten planks bent beneath the urchin's weight, and handed him the rope which Brujon had knotted together during Montparnasse's absence. The gamin directed his steps towards the flue, which it was easy to enter, thanks to a large crack which touched the roof. At the moment when he was on the point of ascending, Thénardier, who saw life and safety approaching, bent over the edge of the wall; the first light of dawn struck white upon his brow dripping with sweat, upon his livid cheek-bones, his sharp and savage nose, his bristling gray beard, and Gavroche recognized him.

"Hullo! it's my father! Oh, that won't hinder."

And taking the rope in his teeth, he resolutely began the ascent.

He reached the summit of the hut, bestrode the old wall as though it had been a horse, and knotted the rope firmly to the upper cross-bar of the window.

A moment later, Thénardier was in the street.

As soon as he touched the pavement, as soon as he found himself out of danger, he was no longer either weary, or chilled or trembling; the terrible things from which he had escaped vanished like smoke, all that strange and ferocious mind awoke once more, and stood erect and free, ready to march onward.

These were this man's first words:—

"Now, whom are we to eat?"

It is useless to explain the sense of this frightfully transparent remark, which signifies both to kill, to assassinate, and to plunder. *To eat*, true sense: *to devour*.

"Let's get well into a corner," said Brujon. "Let's settle it in three words, and part at once. There was an affair that promised well in the Rue Plumet, a deserted street, an isolated house, an old rotten gate on a garden, and lone women."

"Well! why not?" demanded Thénardier.

"Your girl, Éponine, went to see about the matter," replied Babet.

"And she brought a biscuit to Magnon," added Guelemer. "Nothing to be made there."

"The girl's no fool," said Thénardier. "Still, it must be seen to."

"Yes, yes," said Brujon, "it must be looked up."

In the meanwhile, none of the men seemed to see Gavroche, who, during this colloquy, had seated himself on one of the fence-posts; he waited a few moments, thinking that perhaps his father would turn towards him, then he put on his shoes again, and said:—

"Is that all? You don't want any more, my men? Now you're out of your scrape. I'm off. I must go and get my brats out of bed."

And off he went.

The five men emerged, one after another, from the enclosure.

When Gavroche had disappeared at the corner of the Rue des Ballets, Babet took Thénardier aside.

"Did you take a good look at that young 'un?" he asked.

"What young 'un?"

"The one who climbed the wall and carried you the rope."

"Not particularly."

"Well, I don't know, but it strikes me that it was your son."

"Bah!" said Thénardier, "do you think so?"

BOOK SEVENTH
SLANG

I

Origin

Pigritia is a terrible word.

It engenders a whole world, *la pègre*, for which read *theft*, and a hell, *la pègrenne*, for which read *hunger*.

Thus, idleness is the mother.

She has a son, theft, and a daughter, hunger.

Where are we at this moment? In the land of slang.

What is slang? It is at one and the same time, a nation and a dialect; it is theft in its two kinds; people and language.

When, four and thirty years ago, the narrator of this grave and sombre history introduced into a work written with the same aim as this a thief who talked argot, there arose amazement and clamor.— "What! How! Argot! Why, argot is horrible! It is the language of prisons, galleys, convicts, of everything that is most abominable in society!" etc., etc.

We have never understood this sort of objections.

Since that time, two powerful romancers, one of whom is a profound observer of the human heart, the other an intrepid friend of the people, Balzac and Eugène Sue, having represented their ruffians as talking their natural language, as the author of *The Last Day of a Condemned Man* did in 1828, the same objections have been raised. People repeated: "What do authors mean by that revolting dialect? Slang is odious! Slang makes one shudder!"

Who denies that? Of course it does.

When it is a question of probing a wound, a gulf, a society, since when has it been considered wrong to go too far? to go to the bottom? We have always thought that it was sometimes a courageous act, and, at least, a simple and useful deed, worthy of the sympathetic attention which duty accepted and fulfilled merits. Why should one not explore everything, and study everything? Why should one halt on the way? The halt is a matter depending on the sounding-line, and not on the leadsman.

Certainly, too, it is neither an attractive nor an easy task to undertake an investigation into the lowest depths of the social order, where terra firma comes to an end and where mud begins, to rummage in those vague, murky waves, to follow up, to seize and to fling, still quivering, upon the pavement that abject dialect which is dripping with filth when thus brought to the light, that pustulous vocabulary each word of which seems an unclean ring from a monster of the mire and the shadows. Nothing is more lugubrious than the contemplation thus in its nudity, in the broad light of thought, of the horrible swarming of slang. It seems, in fact, to be a sort of horrible beast made for the night which has just been torn from its cesspool. One thinks one beholds a frightful, living, and bristling thicket which quivers, rustles, wavers, returns to shadow, threatens and glares. One word resembles a claw, another an extinguished and bleeding eye, such and such a phrase seems to move like the claw of a crab. All this is alive with the hideous vitality of things which have been organized out of disorganization.

Now, when has horror ever excluded study? Since when has malady banished medicine? Can one imagine a naturalist refusing to study the viper, the bat, the scorpion, the centipede, the tarantula, and one who would cast them back into their darkness, saying: "Oh! how ugly that is!" The thinker who should turn aside from slang would resemble a surgeon who should avert his face from an ulcer or a wart. He would be like a philologist refusing to examine a fact in language, a philosopher hesitating to scrutinize a fact in humanity. For, it must be stated to those who are ignorant of the case, that argot is both a literary phenomenon and a social result. What is slang, properly speaking? It is the language of wretchedness.

We may be stopped; the fact may be put to us in general terms, which is one way of attenuating it; we may be told, that all trades, professions, it may be added, all the accidents of the social hierarchy and all forms of intelligence, have their own slang. The merchant who says: "Montpellier not active, Marseilles fine quality," the broker on 'change who says: "Assets at end of current month," the gambler who says: *"Tiers et tout, refait de pique,"* the sheriff of the Norman Isles who says: "The holder in fee reverting to his landed estate cannot claim the fruits of that estate during the hereditary seizure of the real estate by the mortgagor," the playwright who says: "The piece was hissed," the comedian who says: "I've made a hit," the philosopher who says: "Phenomenal triplicity," the huntsman who says: *"Voileci allais, Voileci fuyant,"* the phrenologist who says: "Amativeness, combativeness, secretiveness," the infantry soldier who says: "My shooting-iron," the cavalry-man who says: "My turkey-cock," the fencing-master who says: "Tierce, quarte, break," the printer who says: "My shooting-stick and galley,"—all, printer, fencing-master, cavalry dragoon, infantry-man, phrenologist, huntsman, philosopher, comedian, playwright, sheriff, gambler, stock-broker, and merchant, speak slang. The painter who says: "My grinder," the notary who says: "My Skip-the-Gutter," the hairdresser who says: "My mealyback," the cobbler who says: "My cub," talks slang. Strictly speaking, if one absolutely insists on the point, all the different fashions of saying the right and the left, the sailor's *port* and *starboard*, the scene-shifter's *court-side*, and *garden-side*, the beadle's *Gospel-side* and *Epistle-side*, are slang. There is the slang of the affected lady as well as of the *précieuses*. The Hotel Rambouillet nearly adjoins the Cour des Miracles. There is a slang of duchesses, witness this phrase contained in a love-letter from a very great lady and a very pretty woman of the Restoration: "You will find in this gossip a fultitude of reasons why I should libertize." Diplomatic ciphers are slang; the pontifical chancellery by using 26 for Rome, *grkztntgzyal* for despatch, and *abfxustgrnogrkzu tu XI.* for the Duc de Modena, speaks slang. The physicians of the Middle Ages who, for carrot, radish, and turnip, said *Opoponach, perfroschinum, reptitalmus, dracatholicum, angelorum, postmegorum*, talked slang. The sugar-manufacturer who says: "Loaf, clarified, lumps, bastard, common, burnt,"—this honest manufacturer talks slang. A certain school of criticism twenty years ago, which used to say: "Half of the works of Shakespeare consists of plays upon words and puns,"—talked slang. The poet, and the artist who, with profound understanding, would designate M. de Montmorency as "a bourgeois," if he were not a judge of verses and statues, speak slang. The classic Academician who calls flowers "Flora," fruits, "Pomona," the sea, "Neptune," love, "fires," beauty, "charms," a horse, "a courser," the white or tricolored cockade, "the rose of Bellona," the three-cornered hat, "Mars' triangle,"—that classical Academician talks slang. Algebra, medicine, botany, have each their slang. The tongue which is employed on board ship, that wonderful language of the sea, which is so complete and so picturesque, which was spoken by Jean Bart, Duquesne, Suffren, and Duperré, which mingles with the whistling of the rigging, the sound of the speaking-trumpets, the shock of the boarding-irons, the roll of the sea, the wind, the gale, the cannon, is wholly a heroic and dazzling slang, which is to the fierce slang of the thieves what the lion is to the jackal.

No doubt. But say what we will, this manner of understanding the word *slang* is an extension which every one will not admit. For our part, we reserve to the word its ancient and precise, circumscribed and determined significance, and we restrict slang to slang. The veritable slang and the slang that is pre-eminently slang, if the two words can be coupled thus, the slang immemorial which was a kingdom, is nothing else, we repeat, than the homely, uneasy, crafty, treacherous, venomous, cruel, equivocal, vile, profound, fatal tongue of wretchedness. There exists, at the extremity of all abasement and all misfortunes, a last misery which revolts and makes up its mind to enter into conflict with the whole mass of fortunate facts and reigning rights; a fearful conflict, where, now cunning, now violent, unhealthy and ferocious at one and the same time, it attacks the social order with pin-pricks through vice, and with club-blows through crime. To meet the needs of this conflict, wretchedness has invented a language of combat, which is slang.

To keep afloat and to rescue from oblivion, to hold above the gulf, were it but a fragment of some language which man has spoken and which would, otherwise, be lost, that is to say, one of the elements, good or bad, of which civilization is composed, or by which it is complicated, to extend the records of social observation; is to serve civilization itself. This service Plautus rendered, consciously or unconsciously, by making two Carthaginian soldiers talk Phœnician; that service Molière rendered, by making so many of his characters talk Levantine and all sorts of dialects. Here objections spring up afresh. Phœnician, very good! Levantine, quite right! Even dialect, let that pass! They are tongues which have belonged to nations or provinces; but slang! What is the use of preserving slang? What is the good of assisting slang "to survive"?

To this we reply in one word, only. Assuredly, if the tongue which a nation or a province has spoken is worthy of interest, the language which has been spoken by a misery is still more worthy of attention and study.

It is the language which has been spoken, in France, for example, for more than four centuries, not only by a misery, but by every possible human misery.

And then, we insist upon it, the study of social deformities and infirmities, and the task of pointing them out with a view to remedy, is not a business in which choice is permitted. The historian of manners and ideas has no less austere a mission than the historian of events. The latter has the surface of civilization, the conflicts of crowns, the births of princes, the marriages of kings, battles, assemblages, great public men, revolutions in the daylight, everything on the exterior; the other historian has the interior, the depths, the people who toil, suffer, wait, the oppressed woman, the agonizing child, the secret war between man and man, obscure ferocities, prejudices, plotted iniquities, the subterranean, the indistinct tremors of multitudes, the die-of-hunger, the counter-blows of the law, the secret evolution of souls, the go-bare-foot, the bare-armed, the disinherited, the orphans, the unhappy, and the infamous, all the forms which roam through the darkness. He must descend with his heart full of charity, and severity at the same time, as a brother and as a judge, to those impenetrable casemates where crawl, pell-mell, those who bleed and those who deal the blow, those who weep and those who curse, those who fast and those who devour, those who endure evil and those who inflict it. Have these historians of hearts and souls duties at all inferior to the historians of external facts? Does any one think that Alighieri has any fewer things to say than Machiavelli? Is the under side of civilization any less important than the upper side merely because it is deeper and more sombre? Do we really know the mountain well when we are not acquainted with the cavern?

Let us say, moreover, parenthetically, that from a few words of what precedes a marked separation might be inferred between the two classes of historians which does not exist in our mind. No one is a good historian of the patent, visible, striking, and public life of peoples, if he is not, at the same time, in a certain measure, the historian of their deep and hidden life; and no one is a good historian of the interior unless he understands how, at need, to be the historian of the exterior also. The history of manners and ideas permeates the history of events, and this is true reciprocally. They constitute two different orders of facts which correspond to each other, which are always interlaced, and which often bring forth results. All the lineaments which providence traces on the surface of a nation have their parallels, sombre but distinct, in their depths, and all convulsions of the depths produce ebullitions on the surface. True history being a mixture of all things, the true historian mingles in everything.

Man is not a circle with a single centre; he is an ellipse with a double focus. Facts form one of these, and ideas the other.

Slang is nothing but a dressing-room where the tongue having some bad action to perform, disguises itself. There it clothes itself in word-masks, in metaphor-rags. In this guise it becomes horrible.

One finds it difficult to recognize. Is it really the French tongue, the great human tongue? Behold it ready to step upon the stage and to retort upon crime, and prepared for all the employments of the repertory of evil. It no longer walks, it hobbles; it limps on the crutch of the Court of Miracles, a crutch metamorphosable into a club; it is called vagrancy; every sort of spectre, its dressers, have painted its face, it crawls and rears, the double gait of the reptile. Henceforth, it is apt at all rôles, it is made suspicious by the counterfeiter, covered with verdigris by the forger, blacked by the soot of the incendiary; and the murderer applies its rouge.

When one listens, by the side of honest men, at the portals of society, one overhears the dialogues of those who are on the outside. One distinguishes questions and replies. One perceives, without understanding it, a hideous murmur, sounding almost like human accents, but more nearly resembling a howl than an articulate word. It is slang. The words are misshapen and stamped with an indescribable and fantastic bestiality. One thinks one hears hydras talking.

It is unintelligible in the dark. It gnashes and whispers, completing the gloom with mystery. It is black in misfortune, it is blacker still in crime; these two blacknesses amalgamated, compose slang. Obscurity in the atmosphere, obscurity in acts, obscurity in voices. Terrible, toad-like tongue which goes and comes, leaps, crawls, slobbers, and stirs about in monstrous wise in that immense gray fog composed of rain and night, of hunger, of vice, of falsehood, of injustice, of nudity, of suffocation, and of winter, the high noonday of the miserable.

Let us have compassion on the chastised. Alas! Who are we ourselves? Who am I who now address you? Who are you who are listening to me? And are you very sure that we have done nothing before we were born? The earth is not devoid of resemblance to a jail. Who knows whether man is not a recaptured offender against divine justice? Look closely at life. It is so made, that everywhere we feel the sense of punishment.

Are you what is called a happy man? Well! you are sad every day. Each day has its own great grief or its little care. Yesterday you were trembling for a health that is dear to you, to-day you fear for your own; to-morrow it will be anxiety about money, the day after to-morrow the diatribe of a slanderer, the day after that, the misfortune of some friend; then the prevailing weather, then something that has been broken or lost, then a pleasure with which your conscience and your vertebral column reproach you; again, the course of public affairs. This without reckoning in the pains of the heart. And so it goes on. One cloud is dispelled, another forms. There is hardly one day out of a hundred which is wholly joyous and sunny. And you belong to that small class who are happy! As for the rest of mankind, stagnating night rests upon them.

Thoughtful minds make but little use of the phrase: the fortunate and the unfortunate. In this world, evidently the vestibule of another, there are no fortunate.

The real human division is this: the luminous and the shady. To diminish the number of the shady, to augment the number of the luminous,—that is the object. That is why we cry: Education! science! To teach reading, means to light the fire; every syllable spelled out sparkles.

However, he who says light does not, necessarily, say joy. People suffer in the light; excess burns. The flame is the enemy of the wing. To burn without ceasing to fly,—therein lies the marvel of genius.

When you shall have learned to know, and to love, you will still suffer. The day is born in tears. The luminous weep, if only over those in darkness.

II

Roots

S lang is the tongue of those who sit in darkness.

Thought is moved in its most sombre depths, social philosophy is bidden to its most poignant meditations, in the presence of that enigmatic dialect at once so blighted and rebellious. Therein lies chastisement made visible. Every syllable has an air of being marked. The words of the vulgar tongue appear therein wrinkled and shrivelled, as it were, beneath the hot iron of the executioner. Some seem to be still smoking. Such and such a phrase produces upon you the effect of the shoulder of a thief branded with the fleur-de-lys, which has suddenly been laid bare. Ideas almost refuse to be expressed in these substantives which are fugitives from justice. Metaphor is sometimes so shameless, that one feels that it has worn the iron neck-fetter.

Moreover, in spite of all this, and because of all this, this strange dialect has by rights, its own compartment in that great impartial case of pigeon-holes where there is room for the rusty farthing as well as for the gold medal, and which is called literature. Slang, whether the public admit the fact or not has its syntax and its poetry. It is a language. Yes, by the deformity of certain terms, we recognize the fact that it was chewed by Mandrin, and by the splendor of certain metonymies, we feel that Villon spoke it.

That exquisite and celebrated verse—

> *Mais où sont les neiges d'antan?*
> *But where are the snows of years gone by?*

is a verse of slang. *Antan—ante annum—*is a word of Thunes slang, which signified the past year, and by extension, *formerly.* Thirty-five years ago, at the epoch of the departure of the great chain-gang, there could be read in one of the cells at Bicêtre, this maxim engraved with a nail on the wall by a king of Thunes condemned to the galleys: *Les dabs d'antan trimaient siempre pour la pierre du Coësre.* This means *Kings in days gone by always went and had themselves anointed.* In the opinion of that king, anointment meant the galleys.

The word *décarade*, which expresses the departure of heavy vehicles at a gallop, is attributed to Villon, and it is worthy of him. This word, which strikes fire with all four of its feet, sums up in a masterly onomatopœia the whole of La Fontaine's admirable verse:—

> *Six forts chevaux tiraient un coche.*
> *Six stout horses drew a coach.*

From a purely literary point of view, few studies would prove more curious and fruitful than the study of slang. It is a whole language within a language, a sort of sickly excrescence, an unhealthy graft which has produced a vegetation, a parasite which has its roots in the old Gallic trunk, and whose sinister foliage crawls all over one side of the language. This is what may be called the first, the vulgar aspect of slang. But, for those who study the tongue as it should be studied, that is to say, as geologists study the earth, slang appears like a veritable alluvial deposit. According as one digs a longer or shorter distance into it, one finds in slang, below the old popular French, Provençal, Spanish, Italian, Levantine, that language of the Mediterranean ports, English and German, the Romance language in its three varieties, French, Italian, and Romance Romance, Latin, and finally Basque and Celtic. A profound and unique formation. A subterranean edifice erected in common by all the miserable. Each accursed race has deposited its layer, each suffering has dropped its stone there, each heart has contributed its pebble. A throng of evil, base, or irritated souls, who have traversed life and have vanished into eternity, linger there almost entirely visible still beneath the form of some monstrous word.

Do you want Spanish? The old Gothic slang abounded in it. Here is *boffete*, a box on the ear, which is derived from *bofeton; vantane*, window (later on *vanterne*), which comes from *vantana; gat*, cat, which comes from *gato; acite*, oil, which comes from *aceyte*. Do you want Italian? Here is *spade*, sword, which comes from *spada; carvel*, boat, which comes from *caravella*. Do you want English? Here is *bichot*, which comes from *bishop; raille*, spy, which comes from *rascal, rascalion; pilche*, a case, which comes from *pilcher*, a sheath. Do you want German? Here is the *caleur*, the waiter, *kellner*; the *hers*, the master, *herzog* (duke). Do you want Latin? Here is *frangir*, to break, *frangere; affurer*, to steal, *fur; cadene*, chain, *catena*. There is one word which crops up in every language of the continent, with a sort of mysterious power and authority. It is the word *magnus*; the Scotchman makes of it his *mac*, which designates the chief of the clan; Mac-Farlane, Mac-Callumore, the great Farlane, the great Callumore; slang turns it into *meck* and later *le meg*, that is to say, God. Would you like Basque? Here is *gahisto*, the devil, which comes from *gaïztoa*, evil; *sorgabon*, good night, which comes from *gabon*, good evening. Do you want Celtic? Here is *blavin*, a handkerchief, which comes from *blavet*, gushing water; *ménesse*, a woman (in a bad sense), which comes from *meinec*, full of stones; *barant*, brook, from *baranton*, fountain; *goffeur*, locksmith, from *goff*, blacksmith; *guedouze*, death, which comes from *guenn-du*, black-white. Finally, would you like history? Slang calls crowns *les maltèses*, a souvenir of the coin in circulation on the galleys of Malta.

In addition to the philological origins just indicated, slang possesses other and still more natural roots, which spring, so to speak, from the mind of man itself.

In the first place, the direct creation of words. Therein lies the mystery of tongues. To paint with words, which contains figures one knows not how or why, is the primitive foundation of all human languages, what may be called their granite.

Slang abounds in words of this description, immediate words, words created instantaneously no one knows either where or by whom, without etymology, without analogies, without derivatives, solitary, barbarous, sometimes hideous words, which at times possess a singular power of expression and which live. The executioner, *le taule*; the forest, *le sabri*; fear, flight, *taf*; the lackey, *le larbin*; the mineral, the prefect, the minister, *pharos*; the devil, *le rabouin*. Nothing is stranger than these words which both mask and reveal. Some, *le rabouin*, for example, are at the same time grotesque and terrible, and produce on you the effect of a cyclopean grimace.

In the second place, metaphor. The peculiarity of a language which is desirous of saying all yet concealing all is that it is rich in figures. Metaphor is an enigma, wherein the thief who is plotting a stroke, the prisoner who is arranging an escape, take refuge. No idiom is more metaphorical than slang: *dévisser le coco* (to unscrew the nut), to twist the neck; *tortiller* (to wriggle), to eat; *être gerbé*, to be tried; *a rat*, a bread thief; *il lansquine*, it rains, a striking, ancient figure which partly bears its date about it, which assimilates long oblique lines of rain, with the dense and slanting pikes of the lancers, and which compresses into a single word the popular expression: it rains halberds. Sometimes, in proportion as slang progresses from the first epoch to the second, words pass from the primitive and savage sense to the metaphorical sense. The devil ceases to be *le rabouin*, and becomes *le boulanger* (the baker), who puts the bread into the oven. This is more witty, but less grand, something like Racine after Corneille, like Euripides after Æschylus. Certain slang phrases which participate in the two epochs and have at once the barbaric character and the metaphorical character resemble phantasmagories. *Les sorgueuers vont solliciter des gails à la lune*—the prowlers are going to steal horses by night,—this passes before the mind like a group of spectres. One knows not what one sees.

In the third place, the expedient. Slang lives on the language. It uses it in accordance with its fancy, it dips into it hap-hazard, and it often confines itself, when occasion arises, to alter it in a gross and summary fashion. Occasionally, with the ordinary words thus deformed and complicated with words of pure slang, picturesque phrases are formed, in which there can be felt the mixture of the two preceding elements, the direct creation and the metaphor: *le cab jaspine, je marronne que la roulotte de Pantin trime dans le sabri*, the dog is barking, I suspect that the diligence for Paris is passing through the woods. *Le dab est sinve, la dabuge est merloussière, la fée est bative*, the bourgeois is stupid, the bourgeoise is cunning, the daughter is pretty. Generally, to throw listeners off the track, slang confines itself to adding to all the words of the language without distinction, an ignoble tail, a termination in *aille*, in *orgue*, in *iergue*, or in *uche*. Thus: *Vousiergue trouvaille bonorgue ce gigotmuche?* Do you think that leg of mutton good? A phrase addressed by Cartouche to a turnkey in order to find out whether the sum offered for his escape suited him.

The termination in *mar* has been added recently.

Slang, being the dialect of corruption, quickly becomes corrupted itself. Besides this, as it is always seeking concealment, as soon as it feels that it is understood, it changes its form. Contrary to what happens with every other vegetation, every ray of light which falls upon it kills whatever it touches. Thus slang is in constant process of decomposition and recomposition; an obscure and rapid work which never pauses. It passes over more ground in ten years than a language in ten centuries. Thus *le larton* (bread) becomes *le lartif; le gail* (horse) becomes *le gaye; la fertanche* (straw) becomes *la fertille; le momignard* (brat), *le momacque; les fiques* (duds), *frusques; la chique* (the church), *l'égrugeoir; le colabre* (neck), *le colas*. The devil is at first, *gahisto*, then *le rabouin*, then *the baker*; the priest is a *ratichon*, then the boar (*le sanglier*); the dagger is *le vingt-deux* (twenty-two), then *le surin*, then *le lingre*; the police are *railles*, then *roussins*, then *rousses*, then *marchands de lacets* (dealers in stay-laces), then *coquers*, then *cognes*; the executioner is *le taule*, then *Charlot, l'atigeur*, then *le becquillard*. In the seventeenth century, to fight was "to give each other snuff"; in the nineteenth it is "to chew each other's throats." There have been twenty different phrases between these two extremes. Cartouche's talk would have been Hebrew to Lacenaire. All the words of this language are perpetually engaged in flight like the men who utter them.

Still, from time to time, and in consequence of this very movement, the ancient slang crops up again and becomes new once more. It has its headquarters where it maintains its sway. The Temple preserved the slang of the seventeenth century; Bicêtre, when it was a prison, preserved the slang of Thunes. There one could hear the termination in *anche* of the old Thuneurs. *Boyanches-tu* (bois-tu), do you drink? But perpetual movement remains its law, nevertheless.

If the philosopher succeeds in fixing, for a moment, for purposes of observation, this language which is incessantly evaporating, he falls into doleful and useful meditation. No study is more efficacious and more fecund in instruction. There is not a metaphor, not an analogy, in slang, which does not contain a lesson. Among these men, to beat means to feign; one beats a malady; ruse is their strength.

For them, the idea of the man is not separated from the idea of darkness. The night is called *la sorgue*; man, *l'orgue*. Man is a derivative of the night.

They have taken up the practice of considering society in the light of an atmosphere which kills them, of a fatal force, and they speak of their liberty as one would speak of his health. A man under arrest is a *sick man*; one who is condemned is a *dead man*.

The most terrible thing for the prisoner within the four walls in which he is buried, is a sort of glacial chastity, and he calls the dungeon the *castus*. In that funereal place, life outside always presents itself under its most smiling aspect. The prisoner has irons on his feet; you think, perhaps, that his thought is that it is with the feet that one walks? No; he is thinking that it is with the feet that one dances; so, when he has succeeded in severing his fetters, his first idea is that now he can dance, and he calls the saw the *bastringue* (public-house ball).—A name is a centre; profound assimilation.—The ruffian has two heads, one of which reasons out his actions and leads him all his life long, and the other which he has upon his shoulders on the day of his death; he calls the head which counsels him in crime *la sorbonne*, and the head which expiates it *la tronche*.—When a man has no longer anything but rags upon his body and vices in his heart, when he has arrived at that double moral and material degradation which the word blackguard characterizes in its two acceptations, he is ripe for crime; he is like a well-whetted knife; he has two cutting edges, his distress and his malice; so slang does not say a blackguard, it says *un réguisé*.—What are the galleys? A brazier of damnation, a hell. The convict calls himself a *fagot*.—And finally, what name do malefactors give to their prison? The *college*. A whole penitentiary system can be evolved from that word.

Does the reader wish to know where the majority of the songs of the galleys, those refrains called in the special vocabulary *lirlonfa*, have had their birth?

Let him listen to what follows:—

There existed at the Châtelet in Paris a large and long cellar. This cellar was eight feet below the level of the Seine. It had neither windows nor air-holes, its only aperture was the door; men could enter there, air could not. This vault had for ceiling a vault of stone, and for floor ten inches of mud. It was flagged; but the pavement had rotted and cracked under the oozing of the water. Eight feet above the floor, a long and massive beam traversed this subterranean excavation from side to side; from this beam hung, at short distances apart, chains three feet long, and at the end of these chains there were rings for the neck. In this vault, men who had been condemned to the galleys were incarcerated until the day of their departure for Toulon. They were thrust under this beam, where each one found his fetters swinging in the darkness and waiting for him.

The chains, those pendant arms, and the necklets, those open hands, caught the unhappy wretches by the throat. They were rivetted and left there. As the chain was too short, they could not lie down. They remained motionless in that cavern, in that night, beneath that beam, almost hanging, forced to unheard-of efforts to reach their bread, jug, or their vault overhead, mud even to mid-leg, filth flowing to their very calves, broken asunder with fatigue, with thighs and knees giving way, clinging fast to the chain with their hands in order to obtain some rest, unable to sleep except when standing erect, and awakened every moment by the strangling of the collar; some woke no more. In order to eat, they pushed the bread, which was flung to them in the mud, along their leg with their heel until it reached their hand.

How long did they remain thus? One month, two months, six months sometimes; one stayed a year. It was the antechamber of the galleys. Men were put there for stealing a hare from the king. In this sepulchre-hell, what did they do? What man can do in a sepulchre, they went through the agonies of death, and what can man do in hell, they sang; for song lingers where there is no longer any hope. In the waters of Malta, when a galley was approaching, the song could be heard before the sound of the oars. Poor Survincent, the poacher, who had gone through the prison-cellar of the Châtelet, said: "It was the rhymes that kept me up." Uselessness of poetry. What is the good of rhyme?

It is in this cellar that nearly all the slang songs had their birth. It is from the dungeon of the Grand-Châtelet of Paris that comes the melancholy refrain of the Montgomery galley: *"Timaloumisaine, timaloumison."* The majority of these songs are melancholy; some are gay; one is tender:—

> Icicaille est la theatre   Here is the theatre
> Du petit dardant.   Of the little archer (Cupid).

Do what you will, you cannot annihilate that eternal relic in the heart of man, love.

In this world of dismal deeds, people keep their secrets. The secret is the thing above all others. The secret, in the eyes of these wretches, is unity which serves as a base of union. To betray a secret is to tear from each member of this fierce community something of his own personality. To inform against, in the energetic slang dialect, is called: "to eat the bit." As though the informer drew to himself a little of the substance of all and nourished himself on a bit of each one's flesh.

What does it signify to receive a box on the ear? Commonplace metaphor replies: "It is to see thirty-six candles." Here slang intervenes and takes it up: Candle, *camoufle.* Thereupon, the ordinary tongue gives *camouflet* as the synonym for *soufflet.* Thus, by a sort of infiltration from below upwards, with the aid of metaphor, that incalculable, trajectory slang mounts from the cavern to the Academy; and Poulailler saying: "I light my *camoufle,*" causes Voltaire to write: "Langleviel La Beaumelle deserves a hundred *camouflets.*"

Researches in slang mean discoveries at every step. Study and investigation of this strange idiom lead to the mysterious point of intersection of regular society with society which is accursed.

The thief also has his food for cannon, stealable matter, you, I, whoever passes by; *le pantre*. (*Pan,* everybody.)

Slang is language turned convict.

That the thinking principle of man be thrust down ever so low, that it can be dragged and pinioned there by obscure tyrannies of fatality, that it can be bound by no one knows what fetters in that abyss, is sufficient to create consternation.

Oh, poor thought of miserable wretches!

Alas! will no one come to the succor of the human soul in that darkness? Is it her destiny there to await forever the mind, the liberator, the immense rider of Pegasi and hippogriffs, the combatant of heroes of the dawn who shall descend from the azure between two wings, the radiant knight of the future? Will she forever summon in vain to her assistance the lance of light of the ideal? Is she condemned to hear the fearful approach of Evil through the density of the gulf, and to catch glimpses, nearer and nearer at hand, beneath the hideous water of that dragon's head, that maw streaked with foam, and that writhing undulation of claws, swellings, and rings? Must it remain there, without a gleam of light, without hope, given over to that terrible approach, vaguely scented out by the monster, shuddering, dishevelled, wringing its arms, forever chained to the rock of night, a sombre Andromeda white and naked amid the shadows!

III

SLANG WHICH WEEPS AND SLANG WHICH LAUGHS

A s the reader perceives, slang in its entirety, slang of four hundred years ago, like the slang of to-day, is permeated with that sombre, symbolical spirit which gives to all words a mien which is now mournful, now menacing. One feels in it the wild and ancient sadness of those vagrants of the Court of Miracles who played at cards with packs of their own, some of which have come down to us. The eight of clubs, for instance, represented a huge tree bearing eight enormous trefoil leaves, a sort of fantastic personification of the forest. At the foot of this tree a fire was burning, over which three hares were roasting a huntsman on a spit, and behind him, on another fire, hung a steaming pot, whence emerged the head of a dog. Nothing can be more melancholy than these reprisals in painting, by a pack of cards, in the presence of stakes for the roasting of smugglers and of the cauldron for the boiling of counterfeiters. The diverse forms assumed by thought in the realm of slang, even song, even raillery, even menace, all partook of this powerless and dejected character. All the songs, the melodies of some of which have been collected, were humble and lamentable to the point of evoking tears. The *pègre* is always the poor *pègre*, and he is always the hare in hiding, the fugitive mouse, the flying bird. He hardly complains, he contents himself with sighing; one of his moans has come down to us: "I do not understand how God, the father of men, can torture his children and his grandchildren and hear them cry, without himself suffering torture." The wretch, whenever he has time to think, makes himself small before the low, and frail in the presence of society; he lies down flat on his face, he entreats, he appeals to the side of compassion; we feel that he is conscious of his guilt.

Towards the middle of the last century a change took place, prison songs and thieves' ritournelles assumed, so to speak, an insolent and jovial mien. The plaintive *maluré* was replaced by the *larifla*. We find in the eighteenth century, in nearly all the songs of the galleys and prisons, a diabolical and enigmatical gayety. We hear this strident and lilting refrain which we should say had been lighted up by a phosphorescent gleam, and which seems to have been flung into the forest by a will-o'-the-wisp playing the fife:—

Miralabi suslababo
Mirliton ribonribette
Surlababi mirlababo
Mirliton ribonribo.

This was sung in a cellar or in a nook of the forest while cutting a man's throat.

A serious symptom. In the eighteenth century, the ancient melancholy of the dejected classes vanishes. They began to laugh. They rally the *grand meg* and the *grand dab*. Given Louis XV they call the King of France "le Marquis de Pantin." And behold, they are almost gay. A sort of gleam proceeds from these miserable wretches, as though their consciences were not heavy within them any more. These lamentable tribes of darkness have no longer merely the desperate audacity of actions, they possess the heedless audacity of mind. A sign that they are losing the sense of their criminality, and that they feel, even among thinkers and dreamers, some indefinable support which the latter themselves know not of. A sign that theft and pillage are beginning to filter into doctrines and sophisms, in such a way as to lose somewhat of their ugliness, while communicating much of it to sophisms and doctrines. A sign, in short, of some outbreak which is prodigious and near unless some diversion shall arise.

Let us pause a moment. Whom are we accusing here? Is it the eighteenth century? Is it philosophy? Certainly not. The work of the eighteenth century is healthy and good and wholesome. The encyclopedists, Diderot at their head; the physiocrates, Turgot at their head; the philosophers, Voltaire at their head; the Utopians, Rousseau at their head,—these are four sacred legions. Humanity's immense advance towards the light is due to them. They are the four vanguards of the human race, marching towards the four cardinal points of progress. Diderot towards the beautiful, Turgot towards the useful, Voltaire towards the true, Rousseau towards the just. But by the side of and above the philosophers, there were the sophists, a venomous vegetation mingled with a healthy growth, hemlock in the virgin forest. While the executioner was burning the great books of the liberators of the century on the grand staircase of the court-house, writers now forgotten were publishing, with the King's sanction, no one knows what strangely disorganizing writings, which were eagerly read by the unfortunate. Some of these publications, odd to say, which were patronized by a prince, are to be found in the Secret Library. These facts, significant but unknown, were imperceptible on the surface. Sometimes, in the very obscurity of a fact lurks its danger. It is obscure because it is underhand. Of all these writers, the one who probably then excavated in the masses the most unhealthy gallery was Restif de La Bretonne.

This work, peculiar to the whole of Europe, effected more ravages in Germany than anywhere else. In Germany, during a given period, summed up by Schiller in his famous drama *The Robbers*, theft and pillage rose up in protest against property and labor, assimilated certain specious and false elementary ideas, which, though just in appearance, were absurd in reality, enveloped themselves in these ideas, disappeared within them, after a fashion, assumed an abstract name, passed into the state of theory, and in that shape circulated among the laborious, suffering, and honest masses, unknown even to the imprudent chemists who had prepared the mixture, unknown even to the masses who accepted it. Whenever a fact of this sort presents itself, the case is grave. Suffering engenders wrath; and while the prosperous classes blind themselves or fall asleep, which is the same thing as shutting one's eyes, the hatred of the unfortunate classes lights its torch at some aggrieved or ill-made spirit which dreams in a corner, and sets itself to the scrutiny of society. The scrutiny of hatred is a terrible thing.

Hence, if the ill-fortune of the times so wills it, those fearful commotions which were formerly called *jacqueries*, beside which purely political agitations are the merest child's play, which are no longer the conflict of the oppressed and the oppressor, but the revolt of discomfort against comfort. Then everything crumbles.

Jacqueries are earthquakes of the people.

It is this peril, possibly imminent towards the close of the eighteenth century, which the French Revolution, that immense act of probity, cut short.

The French Revolution, which is nothing else than the idea armed with the sword, rose erect, and, with the same abrupt movement, closed the door of ill and opened the door of good.

It put a stop to torture, promulgated the truth, expelled miasma, rendered the century healthy, crowned the populace.

It may be said of it that it created man a second time, by giving him a second soul, the right.

The nineteenth century has inherited and profited by its work, and to-day, the social catastrophe to which we lately alluded is simply impossible. Blind is he who announces it! Foolish is he who fears it! Revolution is the vaccine of Jacquerie.

Thanks to the Revolution, social conditions have changed. Feudal and monarchical maladies no longer run in our blood. There is no more of the Middle Ages in our constitution. We no longer live in the days when terrible swarms within made irruptions, when one heard beneath his feet the obscure course of a dull rumble, when indescribable elevations from mole-like tunnels appeared on the surface of civilization, where the soil cracked open, where the roofs of caverns yawned, and where one suddenly beheld monstrous heads emerging from the earth.

The revolutionary sense is a moral sense. The sentiment of right, once developed, develops the sentiment of duty. The law of all is liberty, which ends where the liberty of others begins, according to Robespierre's admirable definition. Since '89, the whole people has been dilating into a sublime individual; there is not a poor man, who, possessing his right, has not his ray of sun; the die-of-hunger feels within him the honesty of France; the dignity of the citizen is an internal armor; he who is free is scrupulous; he who votes reigns. Hence incorruptibility; hence the miscarriage of unhealthy lusts; hence eyes heroically lowered before temptations. The revolutionary wholesomeness is such, that on a day of deliverance, a 14th of July, a 10th of August, there is no longer any populace. The first cry of the enlightened and increasing throngs is: death to thieves! Progress is an honest man; the ideal and the absolute do not filch pocket-handkerchiefs. By whom were the wagons containing the wealth of the Tuileries escorted in 1848? By the rag-pickers of the Faubourg Saint-Antoine. Rags mounted guard over the treasure. Virtue rendered these tatterdemalions resplendent. In those wagons in chests, hardly closed, and some, even, half-open, amid a hundred dazzling caskets, was that ancient crown of France, studded with diamonds, surmounted by the carbuncle of royalty, by the Regent diamond, which was worth thirty millions. Barefooted, they guarded that crown.

Hence, no more Jacquerie. I regret it for the sake of the skilful. The old fear has produced its last effects in that quarter; and henceforth it can no longer be employed in politics. The principal spring of the red spectre is broken. Every one knows it now. The scare-crow scares no longer. The birds take liberties with the mannikin, foul creatures alight upon it, the bourgeois laugh at it.

IV

The Two Duties: To Watch and To Hope

This being the case, is all social danger dispelled? Certainly not. There is no Jacquerie; society may rest assured on that point; blood will no longer rush to its head. But let society take heed to the manner in which it breathes. Apoplexy is no longer to be feared, but phthisis is there. Social phthisis is called misery.

One can perish from being undermined as well as from being struck by lightning.

Let us not weary of repeating, and sympathetic souls must not forget that this is the first of fraternal obligations, and selfish hearts must understand that the first of political necessities consists in thinking first of all of the disinherited and sorrowing throngs, in solacing, airing, enlightening, loving them, in enlarging their horizon to a magnificent extent, in lavishing upon them education in every form, in offering them the example of labor, never the example of idleness, in diminishing the individual burden by enlarging the notion of the universal aim, in setting a limit to poverty without setting a limit to wealth, in creating vast fields of public and popular activity, in having, like Briareus, a hundred hands to extend in all directions to the oppressed and the feeble, in employing the collective power for that grand duty of opening workshops for all arms, schools for all aptitudes, and laboratories for all degrees of intelligence, in augmenting salaries, diminishing trouble, balancing what should be and what is, that is to say, in proportioning enjoyment to effort and a glut to need; in a word, in evolving from the social apparatus more light and more comfort for the benefit of those who suffer and those who are ignorant.

And, let us say it, all this is but the beginning. The true question is this: labor cannot be a law without being a right.

We will not insist upon this point; this is not the proper place for that.

If nature calls itself Providence, society should call itself foresight.

Intellectual and moral growth is no less indispensable than material improvement. To know is a sacrament, to think is the prime necessity, truth is nourishment as well as grain. A reason which fasts from science and wisdom grows thin. Let us enter equal complaint against stomachs and minds which do not eat. If there is anything more heart-breaking than a body perishing for lack of bread, it is a soul which is dying from hunger for the light.

The whole of progress tends in the direction of solution. Some day we shall be amazed. As the human race mounts upward, the deep layers emerge naturally from the zone of distress. The obliteration of misery will be accomplished by a simple elevation of level.

We should do wrong were we to doubt this blessed consummation.

The past is very strong, it is true, at the present moment. It censures. This rejuvenation of a corpse is surprising. Behold, it is walking and advancing. It seems a victor; this dead body is a conqueror. He arrives with his legions, superstitions, with his sword, despotism, with his banner, ignorance; a while ago, he won ten battles. He advances, he threatens, he laughs, he is at our doors. Let us not despair, on our side. Let us sell the field on which Hannibal is encamped.

What have we to fear, we who believe?

No such thing as a back-flow of ideas exists any more than there exists a return of a river on its course.

But let those who do not desire a future reflect on this matter. When they say "no" to progress, it is not the future but themselves that they are condemning. They are giving themselves a sad malady; they are inoculating themselves with the past. There is but one way of rejecting To-morrow, and that is to die.

Now, no death, that of the body as late as possible, that of the soul never,—this is what we desire.

Yes, the enigma will utter its word, the sphinx will speak, the problem will be solved.

Yes, the people, sketched out by the eighteenth century, will be finished by the nineteenth. He who doubts this is an idiot! The future blossoming, the near blossoming forth of universal well-being, is a divinely fatal phenomenon.

Immense combined propulsions direct human affairs and conduct them within a given time to a logical state, that is to say, to a state of equilibrium; that is to say, to equity. A force composed of earth and heaven results from humanity and governs it; this force is a worker of miracles; marvellous issues are no more difficult to it than extraordinary vicissitudes. Aided by science, which comes from one man, and by the event, which comes from another, it is not greatly alarmed by these contradictions in the attitude of problems, which seem impossibilities to the vulgar herd. It is no less skilful at causing a solution to spring forth from the reconciliation of ideas, than a lesson from the reconciliation of facts, and we may expect anything from that mysterious power of progress, which brought the Orient and the Occident face to face one fine day, in the depths of a sepulchre, and made the imaums converse with Bonaparte in the interior of the Great Pyramid.

In the meantime, let there be no halt, no hesitation, no pause in the grandiose onward march of minds. Social philosophy consists essentially in science and peace. Its object is, and its result must be, to dissolve wrath by the study of antagonisms. It examines, it scrutinizes, it analyzes; then it puts together once more, it proceeds by means of reduction, discarding all hatred.

More than once, a society has been seen to give way before the wind which is let loose upon mankind; history is full of the shipwrecks of nations and empires; manners, customs, laws, religions,—and some fine day that unknown force, the hurricane, passes by and bears them all away. The civilizations of India, of Chaldea, of Persia, of Syria, of Egypt, have disappeared one after the other. Why? We know not. What are the causes of these disasters? We do not know. Could these societies have been saved? Was it their fault? Did they persist in the fatal vice which destroyed them? What is the amount of suicide in these terrible deaths of a nation and a race? Questions to which there exists no reply. Darkness enwraps condemned civilizations. They sprung a leak, then they sank. We have nothing more to say; and it is with a sort of terror that we look on, at the bottom of that sea which is called the past, behind those colossal waves, at the shipwreck of those immense vessels, Babylon, Nineveh, Tarsus, Thebes, Rome, beneath the fearful gusts which emerge from all the mouths of the shadows. But shadows are there, and light is here. We are not acquainted with the maladies of these ancient civilizations, we do not know the infirmities of our own. Everywhere upon it we have the right of light, we contemplate its beauties, we lay bare its defects. Where it is ill, we probe; and the sickness once diagnosed, the study of the cause leads to the discovery of the remedy. Our civilization, the work of twenty centuries, is its law and its prodigy; it is worth the trouble of saving. It will be saved. It is already much to have solaced it; its enlightenment is yet another point. All the labors of modern social philosophies must converge towards this point. The thinker of to-day has a great duty—to auscultate civilization.

We repeat, that this auscultation brings encouragement; it is by this persistence in encouragement that we wish to conclude these pages, an austere interlude in a mournful drama. Beneath the social mortality, we feel human imperishableness. The globe does not perish, because it has these wounds, craters, eruptions, sulphur pits, here and there, nor because of a volcano which ejects its pus. The maladies of the people do not kill man.

And yet, any one who follows the course of social clinics shakes his head at times. The strongest, the tenderest, the most logical have their hours of weakness.

Will the future arrive? It seems as though we might almost put this question, when we behold so much terrible darkness. Melancholy face-to-face encounter of selfish and wretched. On the part of the selfish, the prejudices, shadows of costly education, appetite increasing through intoxication, a giddiness of prosperity which dulls, a fear of suffering which, in some, goes as far as an aversion for the suffering, an implacable satisfaction, the *I* so swollen that it bars the soul; on the side of the wretched covetousness, envy, hatred of seeing others enjoy, the profound impulses of the human beast towards assuaging its desires, hearts full of mist, sadness, need, fatality, impure and simple ignorance.

Shall we continue to raise our eyes to heaven? is the luminous point which we distinguish there one of those which vanish? The ideal is frightful to behold, thus lost in the depths, small, isolated, imperceptible, brilliant, but surrounded by those great, black menaces, monstrously heaped around it; yet no more in danger than a star in the maw of the clouds.

BOOK EIGHTH
ENCHANTMENTS AND DESOLATIONS

I

FULL LIGHT

The reader has probably understood that Éponine, having recognized through the gate, the inhabitant of that Rue Plumet whither Magnon had sent her, had begun by keeping the ruffians away from the Rue Plumet, and had then conducted Marius thither, and that, after many days spent in ecstasy before that gate, Marius, drawn on by that force which draws the iron to the magnet and a lover towards the stones of which is built the house of her whom he loves, had finally entered Cosette's garden as Romeo entered the garden of Juliet. This had even proved easier for him than for Romeo; Romeo was obliged to scale a wall, Marius had only to use a little force on one of the bars of the decrepit gate which vacillated in its rusty recess, after the fashion of old people's teeth. Marius was slender and readily passed through.

As there was never any one in the street, and as Marius never entered the garden except at night, he ran no risk of being seen.

Beginning with that blessed and holy hour when a kiss betrothed these two souls, Marius was there every evening. If, at that period of her existence, Cosette had fallen in love with a man in the least unscrupulous or debauched, she would have been lost; for there are generous natures which yield themselves, and Cosette was one of them. One of woman's magnanimities is to yield. Love, at the height where it is absolute, is complicated with some indescribably celestial blindness of modesty. But what dangers you run, O noble souls! Often you give the heart, and we take the body. Your heart remains with you, you gaze upon it in the gloom with a shudder. Love has no middle course; it either ruins or it saves. All human destiny lies in this dilemma. This dilemma, ruin, or safety, is set forth no more inexorably by any fatality than by love. Love is life, if it is not death. Cradle; also coffin. The same sentiment says "yes" and "no" in the human heart. Of all the things that God has made, the human heart is the one which sheds the most light, alas! and the most darkness.

God willed that Cosette's love should encounter one of the loves which save.

Throughout the whole of the month of May of that year 1832, there were there, in every night, in that poor, neglected garden, beneath that thicket which grew thicker and more fragrant day by day, two beings composed of all chastity, all innocence, overflowing with all the felicity of heaven, nearer to the archangels than to mankind, pure, honest, intoxicated, radiant, who shone for each other amid the shadows. It seemed to Cosette that Marius had a crown, and to Marius that Cosette had a nimbus. They touched each other, they gazed at each other, they clasped each other's hands, they pressed close to each other; but there was a distance which they did not pass. Not that they respected it; they did not know of its existence. Marius was conscious of a barrier, Cosette's innocence; and Cosette of a support, Marius' loyalty. The first kiss had also been the last. Marius, since that time, had not gone further than to touch Cosette's hand, or her kerchief, or a lock of her hair, with his lips. For him, Cosette was a perfume and not a woman. He inhaled her. She refused nothing, and he asked nothing. Cosette was happy, and Marius was satisfied. They lived in this ecstatic state which can be described as the dazzling of one soul by another soul. It was the ineffable first embrace of two maiden souls in the ideal. Two swans meeting on the Jungfrau.

At that hour of love, an hour when voluptuousness is absolutely mute, beneath the omnipotence of ecstasy, Marius, the pure and seraphic Marius, would rather have gone to a woman of the town than have raised Cosette's robe to the height of her ankle. Once, in the moonlight, Cosette stooped to pick up something on the ground, her bodice fell apart and permitted a glimpse of the beginning of her throat. Marius turned away his eyes.

What took place between these two beings? Nothing. They adored each other.

At night, when they were there, that garden seemed a living and a sacred spot. All flowers unfolded around them and sent them incense; and they opened their souls and scattered them over the flowers. The wanton and vigorous vegetation quivered, full of strength and intoxication, around these two innocents, and they uttered words of love which set the trees to trembling.

What words were these? Breaths. Nothing more. These breaths sufficed to trouble and to touch all nature round about. Magic power which we should find it difficult to understand were we to read in a book these conversations which are made to be borne away and dispersed like smoke wreaths by the breeze beneath the leaves. Take from those murmurs of two lovers that melody which proceeds from the soul and which accompanies them like a lyre, and what remains is nothing more than a shade; you say: "What! is that all!" eh! yes, childish prattle, repetitions, laughter at nothing, nonsense, everything that is deepest and most sublime in the world! The only things which are worth the trouble of saying and hearing!

The man who has never heard, the man who has never uttered these absurdities, these paltry remarks, is an imbecile and a malicious fellow. Cosette said to Marius:—

"Dost thou know?—"

(In all this and athwart this celestial maidenliness, and without either of them being able to say how it had come about, they had begun to call each other *thou*.)

"Dost thou know? My name is Euphrasie."

"Euphrasie? Why, no, thy name is Cosette."

"Oh! Cosette is a very ugly name that was given to me when I was a little thing. But my real name is Euphrasie. Dost thou like that name— Euphrasie?"

"Yes. But Cosette is not ugly."

"Do you like it better than Euphrasie?"

"Why, yes."

"Then I like it better too. Truly, it is pretty, Cosette. Call me Cosette."

And the smile that she added made of this dialogue an idyl worthy of a grove situated in heaven. On another occasion she gazed intently at him and exclaimed:—

"Monsieur, you are handsome, you are good-looking, you are witty, you are not at all stupid, you are much more learned than I am, but I bid you defiance with this word: I love you!"

And Marius, in the very heavens, thought he heard a strain sung by a star.

Or she bestowed on him a gentle tap because he coughed, and she said to him:—

"Don't cough, sir; I will not have people cough on my domain without my permission. It's very naughty to cough and to disturb me. I want you to be well, because, in the first place, if you were not well, I should be very unhappy. What should I do then?"

And this was simply divine.

Once Marius said to Cosette:—

"Just imagine, I thought at one time that your name was Ursule."

This made both of them laugh the whole evening.

In the middle of another conversation, he chanced to exclaim:—

"Oh! One day, at the Luxembourg, I had a good mind to finish breaking up a veteran!" But he stopped short, and went no further. He would have been obliged to speak to Cosette of her garter, and that was impossible. This bordered on a strange theme, the flesh, before which that immense and innocent love recoiled with a sort of sacred fright.

Marius pictured life with Cosette to himself like this, without anything else; to come every evening to the Rue Plumet, to displace the old and accommodating bar of the chief-justice's gate, to sit elbow to elbow on that bench, to gaze through the trees at the scintillation of the on-coming night, to fit a fold of the knee of his trousers into the ample fall of Cosette's gown, to caress her thumb-nail, to call her *thou*, to smell of the same flower, one after the other, forever, indefinitely. During this time, clouds passed above their heads. Every time that the wind blows it bears with it more of the dreams of men than of the clouds of heaven.

This chaste, almost shy love was not devoid of gallantry, by any means. To pay compliments to the woman whom a man loves is the first method of bestowing caresses, and he is half audacious who tries it. A compliment is something like a kiss through a veil. Voluptuousness mingles there with its sweet tiny point, while it hides itself. The heart draws back before voluptuousness only to love the more. Marius' blandishments, all saturated with fancy, were, so to speak, of azure hue. The birds when they fly up yonder, in the direction of the angels, must hear such words. There were mingled with them, nevertheless, life, humanity, all the positiveness of which Marius was capable. It was what is said in the bower, a prelude to what will be said in the chamber; a lyrical effusion, strophe and sonnet intermingled, pleasing hyperboles of cooing, all the refinements of adoration arranged in a bouquet and exhaling a celestial perfume, an ineffable twitter of heart to heart.

"Oh!" murmured Marius, "how beautiful you are! I dare not look at you. It is all over with me when I contemplate you. You are a grace. I know not what is the matter with me. The hem of your gown, when the tip of your shoe peeps from beneath, upsets me. And then, what an enchanted gleam when you open your thought even but a little! You talk astonishingly good sense. It seems to me at times that you are a dream. Speak, I listen, I admire. Oh Cosette! how strange it is and how charming! I am really beside myself. You are adorable, Mademoiselle. I study your feet with the microscope and your soul with the telescope."

And Cosette answered:—

"I have been loving a little more all the time that has passed since this morning."

Questions and replies took care of themselves in this dialogue, which always turned with mutual consent upon love, as the little pith figures always turn on their peg.

Cosette's whole person was ingenuousness, ingenuity, transparency, whiteness, candor, radiance. It might have been said of Cosette that she was clear. She produced on those who saw her the sensation of April and dawn. There was dew in her eyes. Cosette was a condensation of the auroral light in the form of a woman.

It was quite simple that Marius should admire her, since he adored her. But the truth is, that this little school-girl, fresh from the convent, talked with exquisite penetration and uttered, at times, all sorts of true and delicate sayings. Her prattle was conversation. She never made a mistake about anything, and she saw things justly. The woman feels and speaks with the tender instinct of the heart, which is infallible.

No one understands so well as a woman, how to say things that are, at once, both sweet and deep. Sweetness and depth, they are the whole of woman; in them lies the whole of heaven.

In this full felicity, tears welled up to their eyes every instant. A crushed lady-bug, a feather fallen from a nest, a branch of hawthorn broken, aroused their pity, and their ecstasy, sweetly mingled with melancholy, seemed to ask nothing better than to weep. The most sovereign symptom of love is a tenderness that is, at times, almost unbearable.

And, in addition to this,—all these contradictions are the lightning play of love,—they were fond of laughing, they laughed readily and with a delicious freedom, and so familiarly that they sometimes presented the air of two boys.

Still, though unknown to hearts intoxicated with purity, nature is always present and will not be forgotten. She is there with her brutal and sublime object; and however great may be the innocence of souls, one feels in the most modest private interview, the adorable and mysterious shade which separates a couple of lovers from a pair of friends.

They idolized each other.

The permanent and the immutable are persistent. People live, they smile, they laugh, they make little grimaces with the tips of their lips, they interlace their fingers, they call each other *thou*, and that does not prevent eternity.

Two lovers hide themselves in the evening, in the twilight, in the invisible, with the birds, with the roses; they fascinate each other in the darkness with their hearts which they throw into their eyes, they murmur, they whisper, and in the meantime, immense librations of the planets fill the infinite universe.

II

THE BEWILDERMENT OF
PERFECT HAPPINESS

They existed vaguely, frightened at their happiness. They did not notice the cholera which decimated Paris precisely during that very month. They had confided in each other as far as possible, but this had not extended much further than their names. Marius had told Cosette that he was an orphan, that his name was Marius Pontmercy, that he was a lawyer, that he lived by writing things for publishers, that his father had been a colonel, that the latter had been a hero, and that he, Marius, was on bad terms with his grandfather who was rich. He had also hinted at being a baron, but this had produced no effect on Cosette. She did not know the meaning of the word. Marius was Marius. On her side, she had confided to him that she had been brought up at the Petit-Picpus convent, that her mother, like his own, was dead, that her father's name was M. Fauchelevent, that he was very good, that he gave a great deal to the poor, but that he was poor himself, and that he denied himself everything though he denied her nothing.

Strange to say, in the sort of symphony which Marius had lived since he had been in the habit of seeing Cosette, the past, even the most recent past, had become so confused and distant to him, that what Cosette told him satisfied him completely. It did not even occur to him to tell her about the nocturnal adventure in the hovel, about Thénardier, about the burn, and about the strange attitude and singular flight of her father. Marius had momentarily forgotten all this; in the evening he did not even know that there had been a morning, what he had done, where he had breakfasted, nor who had spoken to him; he had songs in his ears which rendered him deaf to every other thought; he only existed at the hours when he saw Cosette. Then, as he was in heaven, it was quite natural that he should forget earth. Both bore languidly the indefinable burden of immaterial pleasures. Thus lived these somnambulists who are called lovers.

Alas! Who is there who has not felt all these things? Why does there come an hour when one emerges from this azure, and why does life go on afterwards?

Loving almost takes the place of thinking. Love is an ardent forgetfulness of all the rest. Then ask logic of passion if you will. There is no more absolute logical sequence in the human heart than there is a perfect geometrical figure in the celestial mechanism. For Cosette and Marius nothing existed except Marius and Cosette. The universe around them had fallen into a hole. They lived in a golden minute. There was nothing before them, nothing behind. It hardly occurred to Marius that Cosette had a father. His brain was dazzled and obliterated. Of what did these lovers talk then? We have seen, of the flowers, and the swallows, the setting sun and the rising moon, and all sorts of important things. They had told each other everything except everything. The everything of lovers is nothing. But the father, the realities, that lair, the ruffians, that adventure, to what purpose? And was he very sure that this nightmare had actually existed? They were two, and they adored each other, and beyond that there was nothing. Nothing else existed. It is probable that this vanishing of hell in our rear is inherent to the arrival of paradise. Have we beheld demons? Are there any? Have we trembled? Have we suffered? We no longer know. A rosy cloud hangs over it.

So these two beings lived in this manner, high aloft, with all that improbability which is in nature; neither at the nadir nor at the zenith, between man and seraphim, above the mire, below the ether, in the clouds; hardly flesh and blood, soul and ecstasy from head to foot; already too sublime to walk the earth, still too heavily charged with humanity to disappear in the blue, suspended like atoms which are waiting to be precipitated; apparently beyond the bounds of destiny; ignorant of that rut; yesterday, to-day, to-morrow; amazed, rapturous, floating, soaring; at times so light that they could take their flight out into the infinite; almost prepared to soar away to all eternity. They slept wide-awake, thus sweetly lulled. Oh! splendid lethargy of the real overwhelmed by the ideal.

Sometimes, beautiful as Cosette was, Marius shut his eyes in her presence. The best way to look at the soul is through closed eyes.

Marius and Cosette never asked themselves whither this was to lead them. They considered that they had already arrived. It is a strange claim on man's part to wish that love should lead to something.

III

The Beginning of Shadow

Jean Valjean suspected nothing.

Cosette, who was rather less dreamy than Marius, was gay, and that sufficed for Jean Valjean's happiness. The thoughts which Cosette cherished, her tender preoccupations, Marius' image which filled her heart, took away nothing from the incomparable purity of her beautiful, chaste, and smiling brow. She was at the age when the virgin bears her love as the angel his lily. So Jean Valjean was at ease. And then, when two lovers have come to an understanding, things always go well; the third party who might disturb their love is kept in a state of perfect blindness by a restricted number of precautions which are always the same in the case of all lovers. Thus, Cosette never objected to any of Jean Valjean's proposals. Did she want to take a walk? "Yes, dear little father." Did she want to stay at home? Very good. Did he wish to pass the evening with Cosette? She was delighted. As he always went to bed at ten o'clock, Marius did not come to the garden on such occasions until after that hour, when, from the street, he heard Cosette open the long glass door on the veranda. Of course, no one ever met Marius in the daytime. Jean Valjean never even dreamed any longer that Marius was in existence. Only once, one morning, he chanced to say to Cosette: "Why, you have whitewash on your back!" On the previous evening, Marius, in a transport, had pushed Cosette against the wall.

Old Toussaint, who retired early, thought of nothing but her sleep, and was as ignorant of the whole matter as Jean Valjean.

Marius never set foot in the house. When he was with Cosette, they hid themselves in a recess near the steps, in order that they might neither be seen nor heard from the street, and there they sat, frequently contenting themselves, by way of conversation, with pressing each other's hands twenty times a minute as they gazed at the branches of the trees. At such times, a thunderbolt might have fallen thirty paces from them, and they would not have noticed it, so deeply was the reverie of the one absorbed and sunk in the reverie of the other.

Limpid purity. Hours wholly white; almost all alike. This sort of love is a recollection of lily petals and the plumage of the dove.

The whole extent of the garden lay between them and the street. Every time that Marius entered and left, he carefully adjusted the bar of the gate in such a manner that no displacement was visible.

He usually went away about midnight, and returned to Courfeyrac's lodgings. Courfeyrac said to Bahorel:—

"Would you believe it? Marius comes home nowadays at one o'clock in the morning."

Bahorel replied:—

"What do you expect? There's always a petard in a seminary fellow."

At times, Courfeyrac folded his arms, assumed a serious air, and said to Marius:—

"You are getting irregular in your habits, young man."

Courfeyrac, being a practical man, did not take in good part this reflection of an invisible paradise upon Marius; he was not much in the habit of concealed passions; it made him impatient, and now and then he called upon Marius to come back to reality.

One morning, he threw him this admonition:—

"My dear fellow, you produce upon me the effect of being located in the moon, the realm of dreams, the province of illusions, capital, soap-bubble. Come, be a good boy, what's her name?"

But nothing could induce Marius "to talk." They might have torn out his nails before one of the two sacred syllables of which that ineffable name, Cosette, was composed. True love is as luminous as the dawn and as silent as the tomb. Only, Courfeyrac saw this change in Marius, that his taciturnity was of the beaming order.

During this sweet month of May, Marius and Cosette learned to know these immense delights. To dispute and to say *you* for *thou*, simply that they might say *thou* the better afterwards. To talk at great length with very minute details, of persons in whom they took not the slightest interest in the world; another proof that in that ravishing opera called love, the libretto counts for almost nothing;

For Marius, to listen to Cosette discussing finery;

For Cosette, to listen to Marius talk in politics;

To listen, knee pressed to knee, to the carriages rolling along the Rue de Babylone;

To gaze upon the same planet in space, or at the same glowworm gleaming in the grass;

To hold their peace together; a still greater delight than conversation; Etc., etc.

In the meantime, divers complications were approaching.

One evening, Marius was on his way to the rendezvous, by way of the Boulevard des Invalides. He habitually walked with drooping head. As he was on the point of turning the corner of the Rue Plumet, he heard some one quite close to him say:—

"Good evening, Monsieur Marius."

He raised his head and recognized Éponine.

This produced a singular effect upon him. He had not thought of that girl a single time since the day when she had conducted him to the Rue Plumet, he had not seen her again, and she had gone completely out of his mind. He had no reasons for anything but gratitude towards her, he owed her his happiness, and yet, it was embarrassing to him to meet her.

It is an error to think that passion, when it is pure and happy, leads man to a state of perfection; it simply leads him, as we have noted, to a state of oblivion. In this situation, man forgets to be bad, but he also forgets to be good. Gratitude, duty, matters essential and important to be remembered, vanish. At any other time, Marius would have behaved quite differently to Éponine. Absorbed in Cosette, he had not even clearly put it to himself that this Éponine was named Éponine Thénardier, and that she bore the name inscribed in his father's will, that name, for which, but a few months before, he would have so ardently sacrificed himself. We show Marius as he was. His father himself was fading out of his soul to some extent, under the splendor of his love.

He replied with some embarrassment:—

"Ah! so it's you, Éponine?"

"Why do you call me *you?* Have I done anything to you?"

"No," he answered.

Certainly, he had nothing against her. Far from it. Only, he felt that he could not do otherwise, now that he used *thou* to Cosette, than say *you* to Éponine.

As he remained silent, she exclaimed:—

"Say—"

Then she paused. It seemed as though words failed that creature formerly so heedless and so bold. She tried to smile and could not. Then she resumed:—

"Well?"

Then she paused again, and remained with downcast eyes.

"Good evening, Mr. Marius," said she suddenly and abruptly; and away she went.

IV

A Cab Runs in English and Barks in Slang

The following day was the 3d of June, 1832, a date which it is necessary to indicate on account of the grave events which at that epoch hung on the horizon of Paris in the state of lightning-charged clouds. Marius, at nightfall, was pursuing the same road as on the preceding evening, with the same thoughts of delight in his heart, when he caught sight of Éponine approaching, through the trees of the boulevard. Two days in succession—this was too much. He turned hastily aside, quitted the boulevard, changed his course and went to the Rue Plumet through the Rue Monsieur.

This caused Éponine to follow him to the Rue Plumet, a thing which she had not yet done. Up to that time, she had contented herself with watching him on his passage along the boulevard without ever seeking to encounter him. It was only on the evening before that she had attempted to address him.

So Éponine followed him, without his suspecting the fact. She saw him displace the bar and slip into the garden.

She approached the railing, felt of the bars one after the other, and readily recognized the one which Marius had moved.

She murmured in a low voice and in gloomy accents:—

"None of that, Lisette!"

She seated herself on the underpinning of the railing, close beside the bar, as though she were guarding it. It was precisely at the point where the railing touched the neighboring wall. There was a dim nook there, in which Éponine was entirely concealed.

She remained thus for more than an hour, without stirring and without breathing, a prey to her thoughts.

Towards ten o'clock in the evening, one of the two or three persons who passed through the Rue Plumet, an old, belated bourgeois who was making haste to escape from this deserted spot of evil repute, as he skirted the garden railings and reached the angle which it made with the wall, heard a dull and threatening voice saying:—

"I'm no longer surprised that he comes here every evening."

The passer-by cast a glance around him, saw no one, dared not peer into the black niche, and was greatly alarmed. He redoubled his pace.

This passer-by had reason to make haste, for a very few instants later, six men, who were marching separately and at some distance from each other, along the wall, and who might have been taken for a gray patrol, entered the Rue Plumet.

The first to arrive at the garden railing halted, and waited for the others; a second later, all six were reunited.

These men began to talk in a low voice.

"This is the place," said one of them.

"Is there a *cab* (dog) in the garden?" asked another.

"I don't know. In any case, I have fetched a ball that we'll make him eat."

"Have you some putty to break the pane with?"

"Yes."

"The railing is old," interpolated a fifth, who had the voice of a ventriloquist.

"So much the better," said the second who had spoken. "It won't screech under the saw, and it won't be hard to cut."

The sixth, who had not yet opened his lips, now began to inspect the gate, as Éponine had done an hour earlier, grasping each bar in succession, and shaking them cautiously.

Thus he came to the bar which Marius had loosened. As he was on the point of grasping this bar, a hand emerged abruptly from the darkness, fell upon his arm; he felt himself vigorously thrust aside by a push in the middle of his breast, and a hoarse voice said to him, but not loudly:—

"There's a dog."

At the same moment, he perceived a pale girl standing before him.

The man underwent that shock which the unexpected always brings. He bristled up in hideous wise; nothing is so formidable to behold as ferocious beasts who are uneasy; their terrified air evokes terror.

He recoiled and stammered:—

"What jade is this?"

"Your daughter."

It was, in fact, Éponine, who had addressed Thénardier.

At the apparition of Éponine, the other five, that is to say, Claquesous, Guelemer, Babet, Brujon, and Montparnasse had noiselessly drawn near, without precipitation, without uttering a word, with the sinister slowness peculiar to these men of the night.

Some indescribable but hideous tools were visible in their hands. Guelemer held one of those pairs of curved pincers which prowlers call *fanchons*.

"Ah, see here, what are you about there? What do you want with us? Are you crazy?" exclaimed Thénardier, as loudly as one can exclaim and still speak low; "what have you come here to hinder our work for?"

Éponine burst out laughing, and threw herself on his neck.

"I am here, little father, because I am here. Isn't a person allowed to sit on the stones nowadays? It's you who ought not to be here. What have you come here for, since it's a biscuit? I told Magnon so. There's nothing to be done here. But embrace me, my good little father! It's a long time since I've seen you! So you're out?"

Thénardier tried to disentangle himself from Éponine's arms, and grumbled:—

"That's good. You've embraced me. Yes, I'm out. I'm not in. Now, get away with you."

But Éponine did not release her hold, and redoubled her caresses.

"But how did you manage it, little pa? You must have been very clever to get out of that. Tell me about it! And my mother? Where is mother? Tell me about mamma."

Thénardier replied:—

"She's well. I don't know, let me alone, and be off, I tell you."

"I won't go, so there now," pouted Éponine like a spoiled child; "you send me off, and it's four months since I saw you, and I've hardly had time to kiss you."

And she caught her father round the neck again.

"Come, now, this is stupid!" said Babet.

"Make haste!" said Guelemer, "the cops may pass."

The ventriloquist's voice repeated his distich:—

"Nous n' sommes pas le jour de l'an,

"This isn't New Year's day

A bécoter papa, maman."

To peck at pa and ma."

Éponine turned to the five ruffians.

"Why, it's Monsieur Brujon. Good day, Monsieur Babet. Good day, Monsieur Claquesous. Don't you know me, Monsieur Guelemer? How goes it, Montparnasse?"

"Yes, they know you!" ejaculated Thénardier. "But good day, good evening, sheer off! leave us alone!"

"It's the hour for foxes, not for chickens," said Montparnasse.

"You see the job we have on hand here," added Babet.

Éponine caught Montparnasse's hand.

"Take care," said he, "you'll cut yourself, I've a knife open."

"My little Montparnasse," responded Éponine very gently, "you must have confidence in people. I am the daughter of my father, perhaps. Monsieur Babet, Monsieur Guelemer, I'm the person who was charged to investigate this matter."

It is remarkable that Éponine did not talk slang. That frightful tongue had become impossible to her since she had known Marius.

She pressed in her hand, small, bony, and feeble as that of a skeleton, Guelemer's huge, coarse fingers, and continued:—

"You know well that I'm no fool. Ordinarily, I am believed. I have rendered you service on various occasions. Well, I have made inquiries; you will expose yourselves to no purpose, you see. I swear to you that there is nothing in this house."

"There are lone women," said Guelemer.

"No, the persons have moved away."

"The candles haven't, anyway!" ejaculated Babet.

And he pointed out to Éponine, across the tops of the trees, a light which was wandering about in the mansard roof of the pavilion. It was Toussaint, who had stayed up to spread out some linen to dry.

Éponine made a final effort.

"Well," said she, "they're very poor folks, and it's a hovel where there isn't a sou."

"Go to the devil!" cried Thénardier. "When we've turned the house upside down and put the cellar at the top and the attic below, we'll tell you what there is inside, and whether it's francs or sous or half-farthings."

And he pushed her aside with the intention of entering.

"My good friend, Mr. Montparnasse," said Éponine, "I entreat you, you are a good fellow, don't enter."

"Take care, you'll cut yourself," replied Montparnasse.

Thénardier resumed in his decided tone:—

"Decamp, my girl, and leave men to their own affairs!"

Éponine released Montparnasse's hand, which she had grasped again, and said:—

"So you mean to enter this house?"

"Rather!" grinned the ventriloquist.

Then she set her back against the gate, faced the six ruffians who were armed to the teeth, and to whom the night lent the visages of demons, and said in a firm, low voice:—

"Well, I don't mean that you shall."

They halted in amazement. The ventriloquist, however, finished his grin. She went on:—

"Friends! Listen well. This is not what you want. Now I'm talking. In the first place, if you enter this garden, if you lay a hand on this gate, I'll scream, I'll beat on the door, I'll rouse everybody, I'll have the whole six of you seized, I'll call the police."

"She'd do it, too," said Thénardier in a low tone to Brujon and the ventriloquist.

She shook her head and added:—

"Beginning with my father!"

Thénardier stepped nearer.

"Not so close, my good man!" said she.

He retreated, growling between his teeth:—

"Why, what's the matter with her?"

And he added:—

"Bitch!"

She began to laugh in a terrible way:—

"As you like, but you shall not enter here. I'm not the daughter of a dog, since I'm the daughter of a wolf. There are six of you, what matters that to me? You are men. Well, I'm a woman. You don't frighten me. I tell you that you shan't enter this house, because it doesn't suit me. If you approach, I'll bark. I told you, I'm the dog, and I don't care a straw for you. Go your way, you bore me! Go where you please, but don't come here, I forbid it! You can use your knives. I'll use kicks; it's all the same to me, come on!"

She advanced a pace nearer the ruffians, she was terrible, she burst out laughing:—

"Pardine! I'm not afraid. I shall be hungry this summer, and I shall be cold this winter. Aren't they ridiculous, these ninnies of men, to think they can scare a girl! What! Scare? Oh, yes, much! Because you have finical poppets of mistresses who hide under the bed when you put on a big voice, forsooth! I ain't afraid of anything, that I ain't!"

She fastened her intent gaze upon Thénardier and said:—

"Not even of you, father!"

Then she continued, as she cast her blood-shot, spectre-like eyes upon the ruffians in turn:—

"What do I care if I'm picked up to-morrow morning on the pavement of the Rue Plumet, killed by the blows of my father's club, or whether I'm found a year from now in the nets at Saint-Cloud or the Isle of Swans in the midst of rotten old corks and drowned dogs?"

She was forced to pause; she was seized by a dry cough, her breath came from her weak and narrow chest like the death-rattle.

She resumed:—

"I have only to cry out, and people will come, and then slap, bang! There are six of you; I represent the whole world."

Thénardier made a movement towards her.

"Don't approach!" she cried.

He halted, and said gently:—

"Well, no; I won't approach, but don't speak so loud. So you intend to hinder us in our work, my daughter? But we must earn our living all the same. Have you no longer any kind feeling for your father?"

"You bother me," said Éponine.

"But we must live, we must eat—"

"Burst!"

So saying, she seated herself on the underpinning of the fence and hummed:—

> "Mon bras si dodu,   "My arm so plump,
> Ma jambe bien faite   My leg well formed,
> Et le temps perdu."   And time wasted."

She had set her elbow on her knee and her chin in her hand, and she swung her foot with an air of indifference. Her tattered gown permitted a view of her thin shoulder-blades. The neighboring street lantern illuminated her profile and her attitude. Nothing more resolute and more surprising could be seen.

The six rascals, speechless and gloomy at being held in check by a girl, retreated beneath the shadow cast by the lantern, and held counsel with furious and humiliated shrugs.

In the meantime she stared at them with a stern but peaceful air.

"There's something the matter with her," said Babet. "A reason. Is she in love with the dog? It's a shame to miss this, anyway. Two women, an old fellow who lodges in the back-yard, and curtains that ain't so bad at the windows. The old cove must be a Jew. I think the job's a good one."

"Well, go in, then, the rest of you," exclaimed Montparnasse. "Do the job. I'll stay here with the girl, and if she fails us—"

He flashed the knife, which he held open in his hand, in the light of the lantern.

Thénardier said not a word, and seemed ready for whatever the rest pleased.

Brujon, who was somewhat of an oracle, and who had, as the reader knows, "put up the job," had not as yet spoken. He seemed thoughtful. He had the reputation of not sticking at anything, and it was known that he had plundered a police post simply out of bravado. Besides this he made verses and songs, which gave him great authority.

Babet interrogated him:—

"You say nothing, Brujon?"

Brujon remained silent an instant longer, then he shook his head in various ways, and finally concluded to speak:—

"See here; this morning I came across two sparrows fighting, this evening I jostled a woman who was quarrelling. All that's bad. Let's quit."

They went away.

As they went, Montparnasse muttered:—

"Never mind! if they had wanted, I'd have cut her throat."

Babet responded

"I wouldn't. I don't hit a lady."

At the corner of the street they halted and exchanged the following enigmatical dialogue in a low tone:—

"Where shall we go to sleep to-night?"

"Under Pantin (Paris)."

"Have you the key to the gate, Thénardier?"

"Pardi."

Éponine, who never took her eyes off of them, saw them retreat by the road by which they had come. She rose and began to creep after them along the walls and the houses. She followed them thus as far as the boulevard.

There they parted, and she saw these six men plunge into the gloom, where they appeared to melt away.

VICTOR HUGO

V

Things of the Night

After the departure of the ruffians, the Rue Plumet resumed its tranquil, nocturnal aspect. That which had just taken place in this street would not have astonished a forest. The lofty trees, the copses, the heaths, the branches rudely interlaced, the tall grass, exist in a sombre manner; the savage swarming there catches glimpses of sudden apparitions of the invisible; that which is below man distinguishes, through the mists, that which is beyond man; and the things of which we living beings are ignorant there meet face to face in the night. Nature, bristling and wild, takes alarm at certain approaches in which she fancies that she feels the supernatural. The forces of the gloom know each other, and are strangely balanced by each other. Teeth and claws fear what they cannot grasp. Blood-drinking bestiality, voracious appetites, hunger in search of prey, the armed instincts of nails and jaws which have for source and aim the belly, glare and smell out uneasily the impassive spectral forms straying beneath a shroud, erect in its vague and shuddering robe, and which seem to them to live with a dead and terrible life. These brutalities, which are only matter, entertain a confused fear of having to deal with the immense obscurity condensed into an unknown being. A black figure barring the way stops the wild beast short. That which emerges from the cemetery intimidates and disconcerts that which emerges from the cave; the ferocious fear the sinister; wolves recoil when they encounter a ghoul.

VI

Marius Becomes Practical Once More to the Extent of Giving Cosette His Address

While this sort of a dog with a human face was mounting guard over the gate, and while the six ruffians were yielding to a girl, Marius was by Cosette's side.

Never had the sky been more studded with stars and more charming, the trees more trembling, the odor of the grass more penetrating; never had the birds fallen asleep among the leaves with a sweeter noise; never had all the harmonies of universal serenity responded more thoroughly to the inward music of love; never had Marius been more captivated, more happy, more ecstatic.

But he had found Cosette sad; Cosette had been weeping. Her eyes were red.

This was the first cloud in that wonderful dream.

Marius' first word had been: "What is the matter?"

And she had replied: "This."

Then she had seated herself on the bench near the steps, and while he tremblingly took his place beside her, she had continued:—

"My father told me this morning to hold myself in readiness, because he has business, and we may go away from here."

Marius shivered from head to foot.

When one is at the end of one's life, to die means to go away; when one is at the beginning of it, to go away means to die.

For the last six weeks, Marius had little by little, slowly, by degrees, taken possession of Cosette each day. As we have already explained, in the case of first love, the soul is taken long before the body; later on, one takes the body long before the soul; sometimes one does not take the soul at all; the Faublas and the Prudhommes add: "Because there is none"; but the sarcasm is, fortunately, a blasphemy. So Marius possessed Cosette, as spirits possess, but he enveloped her with all his soul, and seized her jealously with incredible conviction. He possessed her smile, her breath, her perfume, the profound radiance of her blue eyes, the sweetness of her skin when he touched her hand, the charming mark which she had on her neck, all her thoughts. Therefore, he possessed all Cosette's dreams.

He incessantly gazed at, and he sometimes touched lightly with his breath, the short locks on the nape of her neck, and he declared to himself that there was not one of those short hairs which did not belong to him, Marius. He gazed upon and adored the things that she wore, her knot of ribbon, her gloves, her sleeves, her shoes, her cuffs, as sacred objects of which he was the master. He dreamed that he was the lord of those pretty shell combs which she wore in her hair, and he even said to himself, in confused and suppressed stammerings of voluptuousness which did not make their way to the light, that there was not a ribbon of her gown, not a mesh in her stockings, not a fold in her bodice, which was not his. Beside Cosette he felt himself beside his own property, his own thing, his own despot and his slave. It seemed as though they had so intermingled their souls, that it would have been impossible to tell them apart had they wished to take them back again.—"This is mine." "No, it is mine." "I assure you that you are mistaken. This is my property." "What you are taking as your own is myself."—Marius was something that made a part of Cosette, and Cosette was something which made a part of Marius. Marius felt Cosette within him. To have Cosette, to possess Cosette, this, to him, was not to be distinguished from breathing. It was in the midst of this faith, of this intoxication, of this virgin possession, unprecedented and absolute, of this sovereignty, that these words: "We are going away," fell suddenly, at a blow, and that the harsh voice of reality cried to him: "Cosette is not yours!"

Marius awoke. For six weeks Marius had been living, as we have said, outside of life; those words, *going away!* caused him to re-enter it harshly.

He found not a word to say. Cosette merely felt that his hand was very cold. She said to him in her turn: "What is the matter?"

He replied in so low a tone that Cosette hardly heard him:—

"I did not understand what you said."

She began again:—

"This morning my father told me to settle all my little affairs and to hold myself in readiness, that he would give me his linen to put in a trunk, that he was obliged to go on a journey, that we were to go away, that it is necessary to have a large trunk for me and a small one for him, and that all is to be ready in a week from now, and that we might go to England."

"But this is outrageous!" exclaimed Marius.

It is certain, that, at that moment, no abuse of power, no violence, not one of the abominations of the worst tyrants, no action of Busiris, of Tiberius, or of Henry VIII., could have equalled this in atrocity, in the opinion of Marius; M. Fauchelevent taking his daughter off to England because he had business there.

He demanded in a weak voice:—

"And when do you start?"

"He did not say when."

"And when shall you return?"

"He did not say when."

Marius rose and said coldly:—

"Cosette, shall you go?"

Cosette turned toward him her beautiful eyes, all filled with anguish, and replied in a sort of bewilderment:—

"Where?"

"To England. Shall you go?"

"Why do you say *you* to me?"

"I ask you whether you will go?"

"What do you expect me to do?" she said, clasping her hands.

"So, you will go?"

"If my father goes."

"So, you will go?"

Cosette took Marius' hand, and pressed it without replying.

"Very well," said Marius, "then I will go elsewhere."

Cosette felt rather than understood the meaning of these words. She turned so pale that her face shone white through the gloom. She stammered:—

"What do you mean?"

Marius looked at her, then raised his eyes to heaven, and answered: "Nothing."

When his eyes fell again, he saw Cosette smiling at him. The smile of a woman whom one loves possesses a visible radiance, even at night.

"How silly we are! Marius, I have an idea."

"What is it?"

"If we go away, do you go too! I will tell you where! Come and join me wherever I am."

Marius was now a thoroughly roused man. He had fallen back into reality. He cried to Cosette:—

"Go away with you! Are you mad? Why, I should have to have money, and I have none! Go to England? But I am in debt now, I owe, I don't know how much, more than ten louis to Courfeyrac, one of my friends with whom you are not acquainted! I have an old hat which is not worth three francs, I have a coat which lacks buttons in front, my shirt is all ragged, my elbows are torn, my boots let in the water; for the last six weeks I have not thought about it, and I have not told you about it. You only see me at night, and you give me your love; if you were to see me in the daytime, you would give me a sou! Go to England! Eh! I haven't enough to pay for a passport!"

He threw himself against a tree which was close at hand, erect, his brow pressed close to the bark, feeling neither the wood which flayed his skin, nor the fever which was throbbing in his temples, and there he stood motionless, on the point of falling, like the statue of despair.

He remained a long time thus. One could remain for eternity in such abysses. At last he turned round. He heard behind him a faint stifled noise, which was sweet yet sad.

It was Cosette sobbing.

She had been weeping for more than two hours beside Marius as he meditated.

He came to her, fell at her knees, and slowly prostrating himself, he took the tip of her foot which peeped out from beneath her robe, and kissed it.

She let him have his way in silence. There are moments when a woman accepts, like a sombre and resigned goddess, the religion of love.

"Do not weep," he said.

She murmured:—

"Not when I may be going away, and you cannot come!"

He went on:—

"Do you love me?"

She replied, sobbing, by that word from paradise which is never more charming than amid tears:—

"I adore you!"

He continued in a tone which was an indescribable caress:—

"Do not weep. Tell me, will you do this for me, and cease to weep?"

"Do you love me?" said she.

He took her hand.

"Cosette, I have never given my word of honor to any one, because my word of honor terrifies me. I feel that my father is by my side.

Well, I give you my most sacred word of honor, that if you go away I shall die."

In the tone with which he uttered these words there lay a melancholy so solemn and so tranquil, that Cosette trembled. She felt that chill which is produced by a true and gloomy thing as it passes by. The shock made her cease weeping.

"Now, listen," said he, "do not expect me to-morrow."

"Why?"

"Do not expect me until the day after to-morrow."

"Oh! Why?"

"You will see."

"A day without seeing you! But that is impossible!"

"Let us sacrifice one day in order to gain our whole lives, perhaps."

And Marius added in a low tone and in an aside:—

"He is a man who never changes his habits, and he has never received any one except in the evening."

"Of what man are you speaking?" asked Cosette.

"I? I said nothing."

"What do you hope, then?"

"Wait until the day after to-morrow."

"You wish it?"

"Yes, Cosette."

She took his head in both her hands, raising herself on tiptoe in order to be on a level with him, and tried to read his hope in his eyes.

Marius resumed:—

"Now that I think of it, you ought to know my address: something might happen, one never knows; I live with that friend named Courfeyrac, Rue de la Verrerie, No. 16."

He searched in his pocket, pulled out his penknife, and with the blade he wrote on the plaster of the wall:—

16 Rue de la Verrerie.

In the meantime, Cosette had begun to gaze into his eyes once more.

"Tell me your thought, Marius; you have some idea. Tell it to me. Oh! tell me, so that I may pass a pleasant night."

"This is my idea: that it is impossible that God should mean to part us. Wait; expect me the day after to-morrow."

"What shall I do until then?" said Cosette. "You are outside, you go, and come! How happy men are! I shall remain entirely alone! Oh! How sad I shall be! What is it that you are going to do to-morrow evening? tell me."

"I am going to try something."

"Then I will pray to God and I will think of you here, so that you may be successful. I will question you no further, since you do not wish it. You are my master. I shall pass the evening to-morrow in singing that music from *Euryanthe* that you love, and that you came one evening to listen to, outside my shutters. But day after to-morrow you will come early. I shall expect you at dusk, at nine o'clock precisely, I warn you. Mon Dieu! how sad it is that the days are so long! On the stroke of nine, do you understand, I shall be in the garden."

"And I also."

And without having uttered it, moved by the same thought, impelled by those electric currents which place lovers in continual communication, both being intoxicated with delight even in their sorrow, they fell into each other's arms, without perceiving that their lips met while their uplifted eyes, overflowing with rapture and full of tears, gazed upon the stars.

When Marius went forth, the street was deserted. This was the moment when Éponine was following the ruffians to the boulevard.

While Marius had been dreaming with his head pressed to the tree, an idea had crossed his mind; an idea, alas! that he himself judged to be senseless and impossible. He had come to a desperate decision.

VII

THE OLD HEART AND THE YOUNG HEART IN THE PRESENCE OF EACH OTHER

At that epoch, Father Gillenormand was well past his ninety-first birthday. He still lived with Mademoiselle Gillenormand in the Rue des Filles-du-Calvaire, No. 6, in the old house which he owned. He was, as the reader will remember, one of those antique old men who await death perfectly erect, whom age bears down without bending, and whom even sorrow cannot curve.

Still, his daughter had been saying for some time: "My father is sinking." He no longer boxed the maids' ears; he no longer thumped the landing-place so vigorously with his cane when Basque was slow in opening the door. The Revolution of July had exasperated him for the space of barely six months. He had viewed, almost tranquilly, that coupling of words, in the *Moniteur:* M. Humblot-Conté, peer of France. The fact is, that the old man was deeply dejected. He did not bend, he did not yield; this was no more a characteristic of his physical than of his moral nature, but he felt himself giving way internally. For four years he had been waiting for Marius, with his foot firmly planted, that is the exact word, in the conviction that that good-for-nothing young scamp would ring at his door some day or other; now he had reached the point, where, at certain gloomy hours, he said to himself, that if Marius made him wait much longer—It was not death that was insupportable to him; it was the idea that perhaps he should never see Marius again. The idea of never seeing Marius again had never entered his brain until that day; now the thought began to recur to him, and it chilled him. Absence, as is always the case in genuine and natural sentiments, had only served to augment the grandfather's love for the ungrateful child, who had gone off like a flash. It is during December nights, when the cold stands at ten degrees, that one thinks oftenest of the son.

M. Gillenormand was, or thought himself, above all things, incapable of taking a single step, he—the grandfather, towards his grandson; "I would die rather," he said to himself. He did not consider himself as the least to blame; but he thought of Marius only with profound tenderness, and the mute despair of an elderly, kindly old man who is about to vanish in the dark.

He began to lose his teeth, which added to his sadness.

M. Gillenormand, without however acknowledging it to himself, for it would have rendered him furious and ashamed, had never loved a mistress as he loved Marius.

He had had placed in his chamber, opposite the head of his bed, so that it should be the first thing on which his eyes fell on waking, an old portrait of his other daughter, who was dead, Madame Pontmercy, a portrait which had been taken when she was eighteen. He gazed incessantly at that portrait. One day, he happened to say, as he gazed upon it:—

"I think the likeness is strong."

"To my sister?" inquired Mademoiselle Gillenormand. "Yes, certainly."

The old man added:—

"And to him also."

Once as he sat with his knees pressed together, and his eyes almost closed, in a despondent attitude, his daughter ventured to say to him:—

"Father, are you as angry with him as ever?"

She paused, not daring to proceed further.

"With whom?" he demanded.

"With that poor Marius."

He raised his aged head, laid his withered and emaciated fist on the table, and exclaimed in his most irritated and vibrating tone:—

"Poor Marius, do you say! That gentleman is a knave, a wretched scoundrel, a vain little ingrate, a heartless, soulless, haughty, and wicked man!"

And he turned away so that his daughter might not see the tear that stood in his eye.

Three days later he broke a silence which had lasted four hours, to say to his daughter point-blank:—

"I had the honor to ask Mademoiselle Gillenormand never to mention him to me."

Aunt Gillenormand renounced every effort, and pronounced this acute diagnosis: "My father never cared very much for my sister after her folly. It is clear that he detests Marius."

"After her folly" meant: "after she had married the colonel."

However, as the reader has been able to conjecture, Mademoiselle Gillenormand had failed in her attempt to substitute her favorite, the officer of lancers, for Marius. The substitute, Théodule, had not been a success. M. Gillenormand had not accepted the *quid pro quo*. A vacancy in the heart does not accommodate itself to a stop-gap. Théodule, on his side, though he scented the inheritance, was disgusted at the task of pleasing. The goodman bored the lancer; and the lancer shocked the goodman. Lieutenant Théodule was gay, no doubt, but a chatter-box, frivolous, but vulgar; a high liver, but a frequenter of bad company; he had mistresses, it is true, and he had a great deal to say about them, it is true also; but he talked badly. All his good qualities had a defect. M. Gillenormand was worn out with hearing him tell about the love affairs that he had in the vicinity of the barracks in the Rue de Babylone. And then, Lieutenant Gillenormand sometimes came in his uniform, with the tricolored cockade. This rendered him downright intolerable. Finally, Father Gillenormand had said to his daughter: "I've had enough of that Théodule. I haven't much taste for warriors in time of peace. Receive him if you choose. I don't know but I prefer slashers to fellows that drag their swords. The clash of blades in battle is less dismal, after all, than the clank of the scabbard on the pavement. And then, throwing out your chest like a bully and lacing yourself like a girl, with stays under your cuirass, is doubly ridiculous. When one is a veritable man, one holds equally aloof from swagger and from affected airs. He is neither a blusterer nor a finnicky-hearted man. Keep your Théodule for yourself."

It was in vain that his daughter said to him: "But he is your grandnephew, nevertheless,"—it turned out that M. Gillenormand, who was a grandfather to the very finger-tips, was not in the least a grand-uncle.

In fact, as he had good sense, and as he had compared the two, Théodule had only served to make him regret Marius all the more.

One evening,—it was the 24th of June, which did not prevent Father Gillenormand having a rousing fire on the hearth,—he had dismissed his daughter, who was sewing in a neighboring apartment. He was alone in his chamber, amid its pastoral scenes, with his feet propped on the andirons, half enveloped in his huge screen of coromandel lacquer, with its nine leaves, with his elbow resting on a table where burned two candles under a green shade, engulfed in his tapestry armchair, and in his hand a book which he was not reading. He was dressed, according to his wont, like an *incroyable*, and resembled an antique portrait by Garat. This would have made people run after him in the street, had not his daughter covered him up, whenever he went out, in a vast bishop's wadded cloak, which concealed his attire. At home, he never wore a dressing gown, except when he rose and retired. "It gives one a look of age," said he.

Father Gillenormand was thinking of Marius lovingly and bitterly; and, as usual, bitterness predominated. His tenderness once soured always ended by boiling and turning to indignation. He had reached the point where a man tries to make up his mind and to accept that which rends his heart. He was explaining to himself that there was no longer any reason why Marius should return, that if he intended to return, he should have done it long ago, that he must renounce the idea. He was trying to accustom himself to the thought that all was over, and that he should die without having beheld "that gentleman" again. But his whole nature revolted; his aged paternity would not consent to this. "Well!" said he,—this was his doleful refrain,—"he will not return!" His bald head had fallen upon his breast, and he fixed a melancholy and irritated gaze upon the ashes on his hearth.

In the very midst of his reverie, his old servant Basque entered, and inquired:—

"Can Monsieur receive M. Marius?"

The old man sat up erect, pallid, and like a corpse which rises under the influence of a galvanic shock. All his blood had retreated to his heart. He stammered:—

"M. Marius what?"

"I don't know," replied Basque, intimidated and put out of countenance by his master's air; "I have not seen him. Nicolette came in and said to me: 'There's a young man here; say that it is M. Marius.'"

Father Gillenormand stammered in a low voice:—

"Show him in."

And he remained in the same attitude, with shaking head, and his eyes fixed on the door. It opened once more. A young man entered. It was Marius.

Marius halted at the door, as though waiting to be bidden to enter.

His almost squalid attire was not perceptible in the obscurity caused by the shade. Nothing could be seen but his calm, grave, but strangely sad face.

It was several minutes before Father Gillenormand, dulled with amazement and joy, could see anything except a brightness as when one is in the presence of an apparition. He was on the point of swooning;

he saw Marius through a dazzling light. It certainly was he, it certainly was Marius.

At last! After the lapse of four years! He grasped him entire, so to speak, in a single glance. He found him noble, handsome, distinguished, well-grown, a complete man, with a suitable mien and a charming air. He felt a desire to open his arms, to call him, to fling himself forward; his heart melted with rapture, affectionate words swelled and overflowed his breast; at length all his tenderness came to the light and reached his lips, and, by a contrast which constituted the very foundation of his nature, what came forth was harshness. He said abruptly:—

"What have you come here for?"

Marius replied with embarrassment:—

"Monsieur—"

M. Gillenormand would have liked to have Marius throw himself into his arms. He was displeased with Marius and with himself. He was conscious that he was brusque, and that Marius was cold. It caused the goodman unendurable and irritating anxiety to feel so tender and forlorn within, and only to be able to be hard outside. Bitterness returned. He interrupted Marius in a peevish tone:—

"Then why did you come?"

That "then" signified: *If you do not come to embrace me*. Marius looked at his grandfather, whose pallor gave him a face of marble.

"Monsieur—"

"Have you come to beg my pardon? Do you acknowledge your faults?"

He thought he was putting Marius on the right road, and that "the child" would yield. Marius shivered; it was the denial of his father that was required of him; he dropped his eyes and replied:—

"No, sir."

"Then," exclaimed the old man impetuously, with a grief that was poignant and full of wrath, "what do you want of me?"

Marius clasped his hands, advanced a step, and said in a feeble and trembling voice:—

"Sir, have pity on me."

These words touched M. Gillenormand; uttered a little sooner, they would have rendered him tender, but they came too late. The grandfather rose; he supported himself with both hands on his cane; his lips were white, his brow wavered, but his lofty form towered above Marius as he bowed.

"Pity on you, sir! It is youth demanding pity of the old man of ninety-one! You are entering into life, I am leaving it; you go to the play, to balls, to the café, to the billiard-hall; you have wit, you please the women, you are a handsome fellow; as for me, I spit on my brands in the heart of summer; you are rich with the only riches that are really such, I possess all the poverty of age; infirmity, isolation! You have your thirty-two teeth, a good digestion, bright eyes, strength, appetite, health, gayety, a forest of black hair; I have no longer even white hair, I have lost my teeth, I am losing my legs, I am losing my memory; there are three names of streets that I confound incessantly, the Rue Charlot, the Rue du Chaume, and the Rue Saint-Claude, that is what I have come to; you have before you the whole future, full of sunshine, and I am beginning to lose my sight, so far am I advancing into the night; you are in love, that is a matter of course, I am beloved by no one in all the world; and you ask pity of me! Parbleu! Molière forgot that. If that is the way you jest at the courthouse, Messieurs the lawyers, I sincerely compliment you. You are droll."

And the octogenarian went on in a grave and angry voice:—

"Come, now, what do you want of me?"

"Sir," said Marius, "I know that my presence is displeasing to you, but I have come merely to ask one thing of you, and then I shall go away immediately."

"You are a fool!" said the old man. "Who said that you were to go away?"

This was the translation of the tender words which lay at the bottom of his heart:—

"Ask my pardon! Throw yourself on my neck!"

M. Gillenormand felt that Marius would leave him in a few moments, that his harsh reception had repelled the lad, that his hardness was driving him away; he said all this to himself, and it augmented his grief; and as his grief was straightway converted into wrath, it increased his harshness. He would have liked to have Marius understand, and Marius did not understand, which made the goodman furious.

He began again:—

"What! you deserted me, your grandfather, you left my house to go no one knows whither, you drove your aunt to despair, you went off, it is easily guessed, to lead a bachelor life; it's more convenient, to play the dandy, to come in at all hours, to amuse yourself; you have given me no signs of life, you have contracted debts without even telling me to pay them, you have become a smasher of windows and a blusterer, and, at the end of four years, you come to me, and that is all you have to say to me!"

This violent fashion of driving a grandson to tenderness was productive only of silence on the part of Marius. M. Gillenormand folded his arms; a gesture which with him was peculiarly imperious, and apostrophized Marius bitterly:—

"Let us make an end of this. You have come to ask something of me, you say? Well, what? What is it? Speak!"

"Sir," said Marius, with the look of a man who feels that he is falling over a precipice, "I have come to ask your permission to marry."

M. Gillenormand rang the bell. Basque opened the door half-way.

"Call my daughter."

A second later, the door was opened once more, Mademoiselle Gillenormand did not enter, but showed herself; Marius was standing, mute, with pendant arms and the face of a criminal; M. Gillenormand was pacing back and forth in the room. He turned to his daughter and said to her:—

"Nothing. It is Monsieur Marius. Say good day to him. Monsieur wishes to marry. That's all. Go away."

The curt, hoarse sound of the old man's voice announced a strange degree of excitement. The aunt gazed at Marius with a frightened air, hardly appeared to recognize him, did not allow a gesture or a syllable to escape her, and disappeared at her father's breath more swiftly than a straw before the hurricane.

In the meantime, Father Gillenormand had returned and placed his back against the chimney-piece once more.

"You marry! At one and twenty! You have arranged that! You have only a permission to ask! a formality. Sit down, sir. Well, you have had a revolution since I had the honor to see you last. The Jacobins got the upper hand. You must have been delighted. Are you not a Republican since you are a Baron? You can make that agree. The Republic makes a good sauce for the barony. Are you one of those decorated by July? Have you taken the Louvre at all, sir? Quite near here, in the Rue Saint-Antoine, opposite the Rue des Nonamdières, there is a cannon-ball incrusted in the wall of the third story of a house with this inscription: 'July 28th, 1830.' Go take a look at that. It produces a good effect. Ah! those friends of yours do pretty things. By the way, aren't they erecting a fountain in the place of the monument of M. le Duc de Berry? So you want to marry? Whom? Can one inquire without indiscretion?"

He paused, and, before Marius had time to answer, he added violently:—

"Come now, you have a profession? A fortune made? How much do you earn at your trade of lawyer?"

"Nothing," said Marius, with a sort of firmness and resolution that was almost fierce.

"Nothing? Then all that you have to live upon is the twelve hundred livres that I allow you?"

Marius did not reply. M. Gillenormand continued:—

"Then I understand the girl is rich?"

"As rich as I am."

"What! No dowry?"

"No."

"Expectations?"

"I think not."

"Utterly naked! What's the father?"

"I don't know."

"And what's her name?"

"Mademoiselle Fauchelevent."

"Fauchewhat?"

"Fauchelevent."

"Pttt!" ejaculated the old gentleman.

"Sir!" exclaimed Marius.

M. Gillenormand interrupted him with the tone of a man who is speaking to himself:—

"That's right, one and twenty years of age, no profession, twelve hundred livres a year, Madame la Baronne de Pontmercy will go and purchase a couple of sous' worth of parsley from the fruiterer."

"Sir," repeated Marius, in the despair at the last hope, which was vanishing, "I entreat you! I conjure you in the name of Heaven, with clasped hands, sir, I throw myself at your feet, permit me to marry her!"

The old man burst into a shout of strident and mournful laughter, coughing and laughing at the same time.

"Ah! ah! ah! You said to yourself: 'Pardine! I'll go hunt up that old blockhead, that absurd numskull! What a shame that I'm not twenty-five! How I'd treat him to a nice respectful summons! How nicely I'd get along without him! It's nothing to me, I'd say to him: "You're only too happy to see me, you old idiot, I want to marry, I desire to wed Mamselle No-matter-whom, daughter of Monsieur No-matter-what, I have no shoes, she has no chemise, that just suits; I want to throw my career, my future, my youth, my life to the dogs; I wish to take a plunge into wretchedness with a woman around my neck, that's an idea, and you must consent to it!" and the old fossil will consent.' Go, my lad, do as you like, attach your paving-stone, marry your Pousselevent, your Coupelevent—Never, sir, never!"

"Father—"

"Never!"

At the tone in which that "never" was uttered, Marius lost all hope. He traversed the chamber with slow steps, with bowed head, tottering and more like a dying man than like one merely taking his departure. M. Gillenormand followed him with his eyes, and at the moment when the door opened, and Marius was on the point of going out, he advanced four paces, with the senile vivacity of impetuous and spoiled old gentlemen, seized Marius by the collar, brought him back energetically into the room, flung him into an armchair and said to him:—

"Tell me all about it!"

"It was that single word "father" which had effected this revolution.

Marius stared at him in bewilderment. M. Gillenormand's mobile face was no longer expressive of anything but rough and ineffable good-nature. The grandsire had given way before the grandfather.

"Come, see here, speak, tell me about your love affairs, jabber, tell me everything! Sapristi! how stupid young folks are!"

"Father—" repeated Marius.

The old man's entire countenance lighted up with indescribable radiance.

"Yes, that's right, call me father, and you'll see!"

There was now something so kind, so gentle, so openhearted, and so paternal in this brusqueness, that Marius, in the sudden transition from discouragement to hope, was stunned and intoxicated by it, as it were. He was seated near the table, the light from the candles brought out the dilapidation of his costume, which Father Gillenormand regarded with amazement.

"Well, father—" said Marius.

"Ah, by the way," interrupted M. Gillenormand, "you really have not a penny then? You are dressed like a pickpocket."

He rummaged in a drawer, drew forth a purse, which he laid on the table: "Here are a hundred louis, buy yourself a hat."

"Father," pursued Marius, "my good father, if you only knew! I love her. You cannot imagine it; the first time I saw her was at the Luxembourg, she came there; in the beginning, I did not pay much heed to her, and then, I don't know how it came about, I fell in love with her. Oh! how unhappy that made me! Now, at last, I see her every day, at her own home, her father does not know it, just fancy, they are going away, it is in the garden that we meet, in the evening, her father means to take her to England, then I said to myself: 'I'll go and see my grandfather and tell him all about the affair. I should go mad first, I should die, I should fall ill, I should throw myself into the water. I absolutely must marry her, since I should go mad otherwise.' This is the whole truth, and I do not think that I have omitted anything. She lives in a garden with an iron fence, in the Rue Plumet. It is in the neighborhood of the Invalides."

Father Gillenormand had seated himself, with a beaming countenance, beside Marius. As he listened to him and drank in the sound of his voice, he enjoyed at the same time a protracted pinch of snuff. At the words "Rue Plumet" he interrupted his inhalation and allowed the remainder of his snuff to fall upon his knees.

"The Rue Plumet, the Rue Plumet, did you say?—Let us see!—Are there not barracks in that vicinity?—Why, yes, that's it. Your cousin Théodule has spoken to me about it. The lancer, the officer. A gay girl, my good friend, a gay girl!—Pardieu, yes, the Rue Plumet. It is what used to be called the Rue Blomet.—It all comes back to me now. I have heard of that little girl of the iron railing in the Rue Plumet. In a garden, a Pamela. Your taste is not bad. She is said to be a very tidy creature. Between ourselves, I think that simpleton of a lancer has been courting her a bit. I don't know where he did it. However, that's not to the purpose. Besides, he is not to be believed. He brags, Marius! I think it quite proper that a young man like you should be in love. It's the right thing at your age. I like you better as a lover than as a Jacobin. I like you better in love with a petticoat, sapristi! with twenty petticoats, than with M. de Robespierre. For my part, I will do myself the justice to say, that in the line of *sans-culottes*, I have never loved any one but women. Pretty girls are pretty girls, the deuce! There's no objection to that. As for the little one, she receives you without her father's knowledge. That's in the established order of things. I have had adventures of that same sort myself. More than one. Do you know what is done then? One does not take the matter ferociously; one does not precipitate himself into the tragic; one does not make one's mind to marriage and M. le

Maire with his scarf. One simply behaves like a fellow of spirit. One shows good sense. Slip along, mortals; don't marry. You come and look up your grandfather, who is a good-natured fellow at bottom, and who always has a few rolls of louis in an old drawer; you say to him: 'See here, grandfather.' And the grandfather says: 'That's a simple matter. Youth must amuse itself, and old age must wear out. I have been young, you will be old. Come, my boy, you shall pass it on to your grandson. Here are two hundred pistoles. Amuse yourself, deuce take it!' Nothing better! That's the way the affair should be treated. You don't marry, but that does no harm. You understand me?"

Marius, petrified and incapable of uttering a syllable, made a sign with his head that he did not.

The old man burst out laughing, winked his aged eye, gave him a slap on the knee, stared him full in the face with a mysterious and beaming air, and said to him, with the tenderest of shrugs of the shoulder:—

"Booby! make her your mistress."

Marius turned pale. He had understood nothing of what his grandfather had just said. This twaddle about the Rue Blomet, Pamela, the barracks, the lancer, had passed before Marius like a dissolving view. Nothing of all that could bear any reference to Cosette, who was a lily. The good man was wandering in his mind. But this wandering terminated in words which Marius did understand, and which were a mortal insult to Cosette. Those words, "make her your mistress," entered the heart of the strict young man like a sword.

He rose, picked up his hat which lay on the floor, and walked to the door with a firm, assured step. There he turned round, bowed deeply to his grandfather, raised his head erect again, and said:—

"Five years ago you insulted my father; to-day you have insulted my wife. I ask nothing more of you, sir. Farewell."

Father Gillenormand, utterly confounded, opened his mouth, extended his arms, tried to rise, and before he could utter a word, the door closed once more, and Marius had disappeared.

The old man remained for several minutes motionless and as though struck by lightning, without the power to speak or breathe, as though a clenched fist grasped his throat. At last he tore himself from his armchair, ran, so far as a man can run at ninety-one, to the door, opened it, and cried:—

"Help! Help!"

His daughter made her appearance, then the domestics. He began again, with a pitiful rattle: "Run after him! Bring him back! What have I done to him? He is mad! He is going away! Ah! my God! Ah! my God! This time he will not come back!"

He went to the window which looked out on the street, threw it open with his aged and palsied hands, leaned out more than half-way, while Basque and Nicolette held him behind, and shouted:—

"Marius! Marius! Marius! Marius!"

But Marius could no longer hear him, for at that moment he was turning the corner of the Rue Saint-Louis.

The octogenarian raised his hands to his temples two or three times with an expression of anguish, recoiled tottering, and fell back into an armchair, pulseless, voiceless, tearless, with quivering head and lips which moved with a stupid air, with nothing in his eyes and nothing any longer in his heart except a gloomy and profound something which resembled night.

BOOK NINTH

WHITHER ARE THEY GOING?

I

JEAN VALJEAN

That same day, towards four o'clock in the afternoon, Jean Valjean was sitting alone on the back side of one of the most solitary slopes in the Champ-de-Mars. Either from prudence, or from a desire to meditate, or simply in consequence of one of those insensible changes of habit which gradually introduce themselves into the existence of every one, he now rarely went out with Cosette. He had on his workman's waistcoat, and trousers of gray linen; and his long-visored cap concealed his countenance.

He was calm and happy now beside Cosette; that which had, for a time, alarmed and troubled him had been dissipated; but for the last week or two, anxieties of another nature had come up. One day, while walking on the boulevard, he had caught sight of Thénardier; thanks to his disguise, Thénardier had not recognized him; but since that day, Jean Valjean had seen him repeatedly, and he was now certain that Thénardier was prowling about in their neighborhood.

This had been sufficient to make him come to a decision.

Moreover, Paris was not tranquil: political troubles presented this inconvenient feature, for any one who had anything to conceal in his life, that the police had grown very uneasy and very suspicious, and that while seeking to ferret out a man like Pépin or Morey, they might very readily discover a man like Jean Valjean.

Jean Valjean had made up his mind to quit Paris, and even France, and go over to England.

He had warned Cosette. He wished to set out before the end of the week.

He had seated himself on the slope in the Champ-de-Mars, turning over all sorts of thoughts in his mind,—Thénardier, the police, the journey, and the difficulty of procuring a passport.

He was troubled from all these points of view.

Last of all, an inexplicable circumstance which had just attracted his attention, and from which he had not yet recovered, had added to his state of alarm.

On the morning of that very day, when he alone of the household was stirring, while strolling in the garden before Cosette's shutters were open, he had suddenly perceived on the wall, the following line, engraved, probably with a nail:—

16 Rue de la Verrerie.

This was perfectly fresh, the grooves in the ancient black mortar were white, a tuft of nettles at the foot of the wall was powdered with the fine, fresh plaster.

This had probably been written on the preceding night.

What was this? A signal for others? A warning for himself?

In any case, it was evident that the garden had been violated, and that strangers had made their way into it.

He recalled the odd incidents which had already alarmed the household.

His mind was now filling in this canvas.

He took good care not to speak to Cosette of the line written on the wall, for fear of alarming her.

In the midst of his preoccupations, he perceived, from a shadow cast by the sun, that some one had halted on the crest of the slope immediately behind him.

He was on the point of turning round, when a paper folded in four fell upon his knees as though a hand had dropped it over his head.

He took the paper, unfolded it, and read these words written in large characters, with a pencil:—

"MOVE AWAY FROM YOUR HOUSE."

Jean Valjean sprang hastily to his feet; there was no one on the slope; he gazed all around him and perceived a creature larger than a child, not so large as a man, clad in a gray blouse and trousers of dust-colored cotton velvet, who was jumping over the parapet and who slipped into the moat of the Champ-de-Mars.

Jean Valjean returned home at once, in a very thoughtful mood.

II

Marius

Marius had left M. Gillenormand in despair. He had entered the house with very little hope, and quitted it with immense despair.

However, and those who have observed the depths of the human heart will understand this, the officer, the lancer, the ninny, Cousin Théodule, had left no trace in his mind. Not the slightest. The dramatic poet might, apparently, expect some complications from this revelation made point-blank by the grandfather to the grandson. But what the drama would gain thereby, truth would lose. Marius was at an age when one believes nothing in the line of evil; later on comes the age when one believes everything. Suspicions are nothing else than wrinkles. Early youth has none of them. That which overwhelmed Othello glides innocuous over Candide. Suspect Cosette! There are hosts of crimes which Marius could sooner have committed.

He began to wander about the streets, the resource of those who suffer. He thought of nothing, so far as he could afterwards remember. At two o'clock in the morning he returned to Courfeyrac's quarters and flung himself, without undressing, on his mattress. The sun was shining brightly when he sank into that frightful leaden slumber which permits ideas to go and come in the brain. When he awoke, he saw Courfeyrac, Enjolras, Feuilly, and Combeferre standing in the room with their hats on and all ready to go out.

Courfeyrac said to him:—

"Are you coming to General Lamarque's funeral?"

It seemed to him that Courfeyrac was speaking Chinese.

He went out some time after them. He put in his pocket the pistols which Javert had given him at the time of the adventure on the 3d of February, and which had remained in his hands. These pistols were still loaded. It would be difficult to say what vague thought he had in his mind when he took them with him.

All day long he prowled about, without knowing where he was going; it rained at times, he did not perceive it; for his dinner, he purchased a penny roll at a baker's, put it in his pocket and forgot it. It appears that he took a bath in the Seine without being aware of it. There are moments when a man has a furnace within his skull. Marius was passing through one of those moments. He no longer hoped for anything; this step he had taken since the preceding evening. He waited for night with feverish impatience, he had but one idea clearly before his mind;—this was, that at nine o'clock he should see Cosette. This last happiness now constituted his whole future; after that, gloom. At intervals, as he roamed through the most deserted boulevards, it seemed to him that he heard strange noises in Paris. He thrust his head out of his reverie and said: "Is there fighting on hand?"

At nightfall, at nine o'clock precisely, as he had promised Cosette, he was in the Rue Plumet. When he approached the grating he forgot everything. It was forty-eight hours since he had seen Cosette; he was about to behold her once more; every other thought was effaced, and he felt only a profound and unheard-of joy. Those minutes in which one lives centuries always have this sovereign and wonderful property, that at the moment when they are passing they fill the heart completely.

Marius displaced the bar, and rushed headlong into the garden. Cosette was not at the spot where she ordinarily waited for him. He traversed the thicket, and approached the recess near the flight of steps: "She is waiting for me there," said he. Cosette was not there. He raised his eyes, and saw that the shutters of the house were closed. He made the tour of the garden, the garden was deserted. Then he returned to the house, and, rendered senseless by love, intoxicated, terrified, exasperated with grief and uneasiness, like a master who returns home at an evil hour, he tapped on the shutters. He knocked and knocked again, at the risk of seeing the window open, and her father's gloomy face make its appearance, and demand: "What do you want?" This was nothing in comparison with what he dimly caught a glimpse of. When he had rapped, he lifted up his voice and called Cosette.—"Cosette!" he cried; "Cosette!" he repeated imperiously. There was no reply. All was over. No one in the garden; no one in the house.

Marius fixed his despairing eyes on that dismal house, which was as black and as silent as a tomb and far more empty. He gazed at the stone seat on which he had passed so many adorable hours with Cosette. Then he seated himself on the flight of steps, his heart filled with sweetness and resolution, he blessed his love in the depths of his thought, and he said to himself that, since Cosette was gone, all that there was left for him was to die.

All at once he heard a voice which seemed to proceed from the street, and which was calling to him through the trees:—

"Mr. Marius!"

He started to his feet.

"Hey?" said he.

"Mr. Marius, are you there?"

"Yes."

"Mr. Marius," went on the voice, "your friends are waiting for you at the barricade of the Rue de la Chanvrerie."

This voice was not wholly unfamiliar to him. It resembled the hoarse, rough voice of Éponine. Marius hastened to the gate, thrust aside the movable bar, passed his head through the aperture, and saw some one who appeared to him to be a young man, disappearing at a run into the gloom.

III

M. Mabeuf

Jean Valjean's purse was of no use to M. Mabeuf. M. Mabeuf, in his venerable, infantile austerity, had not accepted the gift of the stars; he had not admitted that a star could coin itself into louis d'or. He had not divined that what had fallen from heaven had come from Gavroche. He had taken the purse to the police commissioner of the quarter, as a lost article placed by the finder at the disposal of claimants. The purse was actually lost. It is unnecessary to say that no one claimed it, and that it did not succor M. Mabeuf.

Moreover, M. Mabeuf had continued his downward course.

His experiments on indigo had been no more successful in the Jardin des Plantes than in his garden at Austerlitz. The year before he had owed his housekeeper's wages; now, as we have seen, he owed three quarters of his rent. The pawnshop had sold the plates of his *Flora* after the expiration of thirteen months. Some coppersmith had made stewpans of them. His copper plates gone, and being unable to complete even the incomplete copies of his *Flora* which were in his possession, he had disposed of the text, at a miserable price, as waste paper, to a second-hand bookseller. Nothing now remained to him of his life's work. He set to work to eat up the money for these copies. When he saw that this wretched resource was becoming exhausted, he gave up his garden and allowed it to run to waste. Before this, a long time before, he had given up his two eggs and the morsel of beef which he ate from time to time. He dined on bread and potatoes. He had sold the last of his furniture, then all duplicates of his bedding, his clothing and his blankets, then his herbariums and prints; but he still retained his most precious books, many of which were of the greatest rarity, among others, *Les Quadrins Historiques de la Bible*, edition of 1560; *La Concordance des Bibles*, by Pierre de Besse; *Les Marguerites de la Marguerite*, of Jean de La Haye, with a dedication to the Queen of Navarre; the book *de la Charge et Dignité de l'Ambassadeur*, by the Sieur de Villiers Hotman; a *Florilegium Rabbinicum* of 1644; a *Tibullus* of 1567, with this magnificent inscription: *Venetiis, in ædibus Manutianis*; and lastly, a Diogenes Laertius, printed at Lyons in 1644, which contained the famous variant of the manuscript 411, thirteenth century, of the Vatican, and those of the two manuscripts of Venice, 393 and 394, consulted with such fruitful results by Henri Estienne, and all the passages in Doric dialect which are only found in the celebrated manuscript of the twelfth century belonging to the Naples Library. M. Mabeuf never had any fire in his chamber, and went to bed at sundown, in order not to consume any candles. It seemed as though he had no longer any neighbors: people avoided him when he went out; he perceived the fact. The wretchedness of a child interests a mother, the wretchedness of a young man interests a young girl, the wretchedness of an old man interests no one. It is, of all distresses, the coldest. Still, Father Mabeuf had not entirely lost his childlike serenity. His eyes acquired some vivacity when they rested on his books, and he smiled when he gazed at the Diogenes Laertius, which was a unique copy. His bookcase with glass doors was the only piece of furniture which he had kept beyond what was strictly indispensable.

One day, Mother Plutarque said to him:—

"I have no money to buy any dinner."

What she called dinner was a loaf of bread and four or five potatoes.

"On credit?" suggested M. Mabeuf.

"You know well that people refuse me."

M. Mabeuf opened his bookcase, took a long look at all his books, one after another, as a father obliged to decimate his children would gaze upon them before making a choice, then seized one hastily, put it in under his arm and went out. He returned two hours later, without anything under his arm, laid thirty sous on the table, and said:—

"You will get something for dinner."

From that moment forth, Mother Plutarque saw a sombre veil, which was never more lifted, descend over the old man's candid face.

On the following day, on the day after, and on the day after that, it had to be done again.

M. Mabeuf went out with a book and returned with a coin. As the second-hand dealers perceived that he was forced to sell, they purchased of him for twenty sous that for which he had paid twenty francs, sometimes at those very shops. Volume by volume, the whole library went the same road. He said at times: "But I am eighty;" as though he cherished some secret hope that he should arrive at the end of his days before reaching the end of his books. His melancholy increased. Once, however, he had a pleasure. He had gone out with a

Robert Estienne, which he had sold for thirty-five sous under the Quai Malaquais, and he returned with an Aldus which he had bought for forty sous in the Rue des Grès.—"I owe five sous," he said, beaming on Mother Plutarque. That day he had no dinner.

He belonged to the Horticultural Society. His destitution became known there. The president of the society came to see him, promised to speak to the Minister of Agriculture and Commerce about him, and did so.—"Why, what!" exclaimed the Minister, "I should think so! An old savant! a botanist! an inoffensive man! Something must be done for him!" On the following day, M. Mabeuf received an invitation to dine with the Minister. Trembling with joy, he showed the letter to Mother Plutarque. "We are saved!" said he. On the day appointed, he went to the Minister's house. He perceived that his ragged cravat, his long, square coat, and his waxed shoes astonished the ushers. No one spoke to him, not even the Minister. About ten o'clock in the evening, while he was still waiting for a word, he heard the Minister's wife, a beautiful woman in a low-necked gown whom he had not ventured to approach, inquire: "Who is that old gentleman?" He returned home on foot at midnight, in a driving rain-storm. He had sold an Elzevir to pay for a carriage in which to go thither.

He had acquired the habit of reading a few pages in his Diogenes Laertius every night, before he went to bed. He knew enough Greek to enjoy the peculiarities of the text which he owned. He had now no other enjoyment. Several weeks passed. All at once, Mother Plutarque fell ill. There is one thing sadder than having no money with which to buy bread at the baker's and that is having no money to purchase drugs at the apothecary's. One evening, the doctor had ordered a very expensive potion. And the malady was growing worse; a nurse was required. M. Mabeuf opened his bookcase; there was nothing there. The last volume had taken its departure. All that was left to him was Diogenes Laertius. He put this unique copy under his arm, and went out. It was the 4th of June, 1832; he went to the Porte Saint-Jacques, to Royal's successor, and returned with one hundred francs. He laid the pile of five-franc pieces on the old serving-woman's nightstand, and returned to his chamber without saying a word.

On the following morning, at dawn, he seated himself on the overturned post in his garden, and he could be seen over the top of the hedge, sitting the whole morning motionless, with drooping head, his eyes vaguely fixed on the withered flower-beds. It rained at intervals; the old man did not seem to perceive the fact.

In the afternoon, extraordinary noises broke out in Paris. They resembled shots and the clamors of a multitude.

Father Mabeuf raised his head. He saw a gardener passing, and inquired:—

"What is it?"

The gardener, spade on back, replied in the most unconcerned tone:—

"It is the riots."

"What riots?"

"Yes, they are fighting."

"Why are they fighting?"

"Ah, good Heavens!" ejaculated the gardener.

"In what direction?" went on M. Mabeuf.

"In the neighborhood of the Arsenal."

Father Mabeuf went to his room, took his hat, mechanically sought for a book to place under his arm, found none, said: "Ah! truly!" and went off with a bewildered air.

BOOK TENTH
THE 5TH OF JUNE, 1832

I

The Surface of the Question

Of what is revolt composed? Of nothing and of everything. Of an electricity disengaged, little by little, of a flame suddenly darting forth, of a wandering force, of a passing breath. This breath encounters heads which speak, brains which dream, souls which suffer, passions which burn, wretchedness which howls, and bears them away.

Whither?

At random. Athwart the state, the laws, athwart prosperity and the insolence of others.

Irritated convictions, embittered enthusiasms, agitated indignations, instincts of war which have been repressed, youthful courage which has been exalted, generous blindness; curiosity, the taste for change, the thirst for the unexpected, the sentiment which causes one to take pleasure in reading the posters for the new play, and love, the prompter's whistle, at the theatre; the vague hatreds, rancors, disappointments, every vanity which thinks that destiny has bankrupted it; discomfort, empty dreams, ambitions that are hedged about, whoever hopes for a downfall, some outcome, in short, at the very bottom, the rabble, that mud which catches fire,—such are the elements of revolt. That which is grandest and that which is basest; the beings who prowl outside of all bounds, awaiting an occasion, bohemians, vagrants, vagabonds of the crossroads, those who sleep at night in a desert of houses with no other roof than the cold clouds of heaven, those who, each day, demand their bread from chance and not from toil, the unknown of poverty and nothingness, the bare-armed, the bare-footed, belong to revolt. Whoever cherishes in his soul a secret revolt against any deed whatever on the part of the state, of life or of fate, is ripe for riot, and, as soon as it makes its appearance, he begins to quiver, and to feel himself borne away with the whirlwind.

Revolt is a sort of waterspout in the social atmosphere which forms suddenly in certain conditions of temperature, and which, as it eddies about, mounts, descends, thunders, tears, razes, crushes, demolishes, uproots, bearing with it great natures and small, the strong man and the feeble mind, the tree trunk and the stalk of straw. Woe to him whom it bears away as well as to him whom it strikes! It breaks the one against the other.

It communicates to those whom it seizes an indescribable and extraordinary power. It fills the firstcomer with the force of events; it converts everything into projectiles. It makes a cannon-ball of a rough stone, and a general of a porter.

If we are to believe certain oracles of crafty political views, a little revolt is desirable from the point of view of power. System: revolt strengthens those governments which it does not overthrow. It puts the army to the test; it consecrates the bourgeoisie, it draws out the muscles of the police; it demonstrates the force of the social framework. It is an exercise in gymnastics; it is almost hygiene. Power is in better health after a revolt, as a man is after a good rubbing down.

Revolt, thirty years ago, was regarded from still other points of view.

There is for everything a theory, which proclaims itself "good sense"; Philintus against Alcestis; mediation offered between the false and the true; explanation, admonition, rather haughty extenuation which, because it is mingled with blame and excuse, thinks itself wisdom, and is often only pedantry. A whole political school called "the golden mean" has been the outcome of this. As between cold water and hot water, it is the lukewarm water party. This school with its false depth, all on the surface, which dissects effects without going back to first causes, chides from its height of a demi-science, the agitation of the public square.

If we listen to this school, "The riots which complicated the affair of 1830 deprived that great event of a portion of its purity. The Revolution of July had been a fine popular gale, abruptly followed by blue sky. They made the cloudy sky reappear. They caused that revolution, at first so remarkable for its unanimity, to degenerate into a quarrel. In the Revolution of July, as in all progress accomplished by fits and starts, there had been secret fractures; these riots rendered them perceptible. It might have been said: 'Ah! this is broken.' After the Revolution of July, one was sensible only of deliverance; after the riots, one was conscious of a catastrophe.

"All revolt closes the shops, depresses the funds, throws the Exchange into consternation, suspends commerce, clogs business, precipitates failures; no more money, private fortunes rendered uneasy, public credit shaken, industry disconcerted, capital withdrawing, work at a discount, fear everywhere; counter-shocks in every town. Hence gulfs. It has been calculated that the first day of a riot costs France twenty millions, the second day forty, the third sixty, a three days' uprising costs one hundred and twenty millions, that is to say, if only the financial result be taken into consideration, it is equivalent to a disaster, a shipwreck or a lost battle, which should annihilate a fleet of sixty ships of the line.

"No doubt, historically, uprisings have their beauty; the war of the pavements is no less grandiose, and no less pathetic, than the war of thickets: in the one there is the soul of forests, in the other the heart of cities; the one has Jean Chouan, the other has a Jeanne. Revolts have illuminated with a red glare all the most original points of the Parisian character, generosity, devotion, stormy gayety, students proving that bravery forms part of intelligence, the National Guard invincible, bivouacs of shopkeepers, fortresses of street urchins, contempt of death on the part of passers-by. Schools and legions clashed together. After all, between the combatants, there was only a difference of age; the race is the same; it is the same stoical men who died at the age of twenty for their ideas, at forty for their families. The army, always a sad thing in civil wars, opposed prudence to audacity. Uprisings, while proving popular intrepidity, also educated the courage of the bourgeois.

"This is well. But is all this worth the bloodshed? And to the bloodshed add the future darkness, progress compromised, uneasiness among the best men, honest liberals in despair, foreign absolutism happy in these wounds dealt to revolution by its own hand, the vanquished of 1830 triumphing and saying: 'We told you so!' Add Paris enlarged, possibly, but France most assuredly diminished. Add, for all must needs be told, the massacres which have too often dishonored the victory of order grown ferocious over liberty gone mad. To sum up all, uprisings have been disastrous."

Thus speaks that approximation to wisdom with which the bourgeoisie, that approximation to the people, so willingly contents itself.

For our parts, we reject this word *uprisings* as too large, and consequently as too convenient. We make a distinction between one popular movement and another popular movement. We do not inquire whether an uprising costs as much as a battle. Why a battle, in the first place? Here the question of war comes up. Is war less of a scourge than an uprising is of a calamity? And then, are all uprisings calamities? And what if the revolt of July did cost a hundred and twenty millions? The establishment of Philip V. in Spain cost France two milliards. Even at the same price, we should prefer the 14th of July. However, we reject these figures, which appear to be reasons and which are only words. An uprising being given, we examine it by itself. In all that is said by the doctrinarian objection above presented, there is no question of anything but effect, we seek the cause.

We will be explicit.

II

THE ROOT OF THE MATTER

There is such a thing as an uprising, and there is such a thing as insurrection; these are two separate phases of wrath; one is in the wrong, the other is in the right. In democratic states, the only ones which are founded on justice, it sometimes happens that the fraction usurps; then the whole rises and the necessary claim of its rights may proceed as far as resort to arms. In all questions which result from collective sovereignty, the war of the whole against the fraction is insurrection; the attack of the fraction against the whole is revolt; according as the Tuileries contain a king or the Convention, they are justly or unjustly attacked. The same cannon, pointed against the populace, is wrong on the 10th of August, and right on the 14th of Vendémiaire. Alike in appearance, fundamentally different in reality; the Swiss defend the false, Bonaparte defends the true. That which universal suffrage has effected in its liberty and in its sovereignty cannot be undone by the street. It is the same in things pertaining purely to civilization; the instinct of the masses, clear-sighted to-day, may be troubled to-morrow. The same fury legitimate when directed against Terray and absurd when directed against Turgot. The destruction of machines, the pillage of warehouses, the breaking of rails, the demolition of docks, the false routes of multitudes, the refusal by the people of justice to progress, Ramus assassinated by students, Rousseau driven out of Switzerland and stoned,—that is revolt. Israel against Moses, Athens against Phocian, Rome against Cicero,—that is an uprising; Paris against the Bastille,—that is insurrection. The soldiers against Alexander, the sailors against Christopher Columbus,—this is the same revolt; impious revolt; why? Because Alexander is doing for Asia with the sword that which Christopher Columbus is doing for America with the compass; Alexander like Columbus, is finding a world. These gifts of a world to civilization are such augmentations of light, that all resistance in that case is culpable. Sometimes the populace counterfeits fidelity to itself. The masses are traitors to the people. Is there, for example, anything stranger than that long and bloody protest of dealers in contraband salt, a legitimate chronic revolt, which, at the decisive moment, on the day of salvation, at the very hour of popular victory, espouses the throne, turns into *chouannerie*, and, from having been an insurrection against, becomes an uprising for, sombre masterpieces of ignorance! The contraband salt dealer escapes the royal gibbets, and with a rope's end round his neck, mounts the white cockade. "Death to the salt duties," brings forth, "Long live the King!" The assassins of Saint-Barthélemy, the cut-throats of September, the manslaughterers of Avignon, the assassins of Coligny, the assassins of Madam Lamballe, the assassins of Brune, Miquelets, Verdets, Cadenettes, the companions of Jéhu, the chevaliers of Brassard,—behold an uprising. La Vendée is a grand, catholic uprising. The sound of right in movement is recognizable, it does not always proceed from the trembling of excited masses; there are mad rages, there are cracked bells, all tocsins do not give out the sound of bronze. The brawl of passions and ignorances is quite another thing from the shock of progress. Show me in what direction you are going. Rise, if you will, but let it be that you may grow great. There is no insurrection except in a forward direction. Any other sort of rising is bad; every violent step towards the rear is a revolt; to retreat is to commit a deed of violence against the human race. Insurrection is a fit of rage on the part of truth; the pavements which the uprising disturbs give forth the spark of right. These pavements bequeath to the uprising only their mud. Danton against Louis XIV is insurrection; Hébert against Danton is revolt.

Hence it results that if insurrection in given cases may be, as Lafayette says, the most holy of duties, an uprising may be the most fatal of crimes.

There is also a difference in the intensity of heat; insurrection is often a volcano, revolt is often only a fire of straw.

Revolt, as we have said, is sometimes found among those in power. Polignac is a rioter; Camille Desmoulins is one of the governing powers.

Insurrection is sometimes resurrection.

The solution of everything by universal suffrage being an absolutely modern fact, and all history anterior to this fact being, for the space of four thousand years, filled with violated right, and the suffering of peoples, each epoch of history brings with it that protest of which it is capable. Under the Cæsars, there was no insurrection, but there was Juvenal.

The *facit indignatio* replaces the Gracchi.

Under the Cæsars, there is the exile to Syene; there is also the man of the *Annales*. We do not speak of the immense exile of Patmos who, on his part also, overwhelms the real world with a protest in the name of the ideal world, who makes of his vision an enormous satire and casts on Rome-Nineveh, on Rome-Babylon, on Rome-Sodom, the flaming reflection of the Apocalypse. John on his rock is the sphinx on its pedestal; we may understand him, he is a Jew, and it is Hebrew; but the man who writes the *Annales* is of the Latin race, let us rather say he is a Roman.

As the Neros reign in a black way, they should be painted to match. The work of the graving-tool alone would be too pale; there must be poured into the channel a concentrated prose which bites.

Despots count for something in the question of philosophers. A word that is chained is a terrible word. The writer doubles and trebles his style when silence is imposed on a nation by its master. From this silence there arises a certain mysterious plenitude which filters into thought and there congeals into bronze. The compression of history produces conciseness in the historian. The granite solidity of such and such a celebrated prose is nothing but the accumulation effected by the tyrant.

Tyranny constrains the writer to conditions of diameter which are augmentations of force. The Ciceronian period, which hardly sufficed for Verres, would be blunted on Caligula. The less spread of sail in the phrase, the more intensity in the blow. Tacitus thinks with all his might.

The honesty of a great heart, condensed in justice and truth, overwhelms as with lightning.

Be it remarked, in passing, that Tacitus is not historically superposed upon Cæsar. The Tiberii were reserved for him. Cæsar and Tacitus are two successive phenomena, a meeting between whom seems to be mysteriously avoided, by the One who, when He sets the centuries on the stage, regulates the entrances and the exits. Cæsar is great, Tacitus is great; God spares these two greatnesses by not allowing them to clash with one another. The guardian of justice, in striking Cæsar, might strike too hard and be unjust. God does not will it. The great wars of Africa and Spain, the pirates of Sicily destroyed, civilization introduced into Gaul, into Britanny, into Germany,—all this glory covers the Rubicon. There is here a sort of delicacy of the divine justice, hesitating to let loose upon the illustrious usurper the formidable historian, sparing Cæsar Tacitus, and according extenuating circumstances to genius.

Certainly, despotism remains despotism, even under the despot of genius. There is corruption under all illustrious tyrants, but the moral pest is still more hideous under infamous tyrants. In such reigns, nothing veils the shame; and those who make examples, Tacitus as well as Juvenal, slap this ignominy which cannot reply, in the face, more usefully in the presence of all humanity.

Rome smells worse under Vitellius than under Sylla. Under Claudius and under Domitian, there is a deformity of baseness corresponding to the repulsiveness of the tyrant. The villainy of slaves is a direct product of the despot; a miasma exhales from these cowering consciences wherein the master is reflected; public powers are unclean; hearts are small; consciences are dull, souls are like vermin; thus it is under Caracalla, thus it is under Commodus, thus it is under Heliogabalus, while, from the Roman Senate, under Cæsar, there comes nothing but the odor of the dung which is peculiar to the eyries of the eagles.

Hence the advent, apparently tardy, of the Tacituses and the Juvenals; it is in the hour for evidence, that the demonstrator makes his appearance.

But Juvenal and Tacitus, like Isaiah in Biblical times, like Dante in the Middle Ages, is man; riot and insurrection are the multitude, which is sometimes right and sometimes wrong.

In the majority of cases, riot proceeds from a material fact; insurrection is always a moral phenomenon. Riot is Masaniello; insurrection, Spartacus. Insurrection borders on mind, riot on the stomach; Gaster grows irritated; but Gaster, assuredly, is not always in the wrong. In questions of famine, riot, Buzançais, for example, holds a true, pathetic, and just point of departure. Nevertheless, it remains a riot. Why? It is because, right at bottom, it was wrong in form. Shy although in the right, violent although strong, it struck at random; it walked like a blind elephant; it left behind it the corpses of old men, of women, and of children; it wished the blood of inoffensive and innocent persons without knowing why. The nourishment of the people is a good object; to massacre them is a bad means.

All armed protests, even the most legitimate, even that of the 10th of August, even that of July 14th, begin with the same troubles. Before the right gets set free, there is foam and tumult. In the beginning, the insurrection is a riot, just as a river is a torrent. Ordinarily it ends in that ocean: revolution. Sometimes, however, coming from those lofty mountains which dominate the moral horizon, justice, wisdom, reason, right, formed of the pure snow of the ideal, after a long fall from rock to rock, after having reflected the sky in its transparency and increased by a hundred affluents in the majestic mien of triumph, insurrection is suddenly lost in some quagmire, as the Rhine is in a swamp.

All this is of the past, the future is another thing. Universal suffrage has this admirable property, that it dissolves riot in its inception, and, by giving the vote to insurrection, it deprives it of its arms. The disappearance of wars, of street wars as well as of wars on the frontiers, such is the inevitable progression. Whatever To-day may be, To-morrow will be peace.

However, insurrection, riot, and points of difference between the former and the latter,—the bourgeois, properly speaking, knows nothing of such shades. In his mind, all is sedition, rebellion pure and simple, the revolt of the dog against his master, an attempt to bite whom must be punished by the chain and the kennel, barking, snapping, until such day as the head of the dog, suddenly enlarged, is outlined vaguely in the gloom face to face with the lion.

Then the bourgeois shouts: "Long live the people!"

This explanation given, what does the movement of June, 1832, signify, so far as history is concerned? Is it a revolt? Is it an insurrection?

It may happen to us, in placing this formidable event on the stage, to say revolt now and then, but merely to distinguish superficial facts, and always preserving the distinction between revolt, the form, and insurrection, the foundation.

This movement of 1832 had, in its rapid outbreak and in its melancholy extinction, so much grandeur, that even those who see in it only an uprising, never refer to it otherwise than with respect. For them, it is like a relic of 1830. Excited imaginations, say they, are not to be calmed in a day. A revolution cannot be cut off short. It must needs undergo some undulations before it returns to a state of rest, like a mountain sinking into the plain. There are no Alps without their Jura, nor Pyrenees without the Asturias.

This pathetic crisis of contemporary history which the memory of Parisians calls "the epoch of the riots," is certainly a characteristic hour amid the stormy hours of this century. A last word, before we enter on the recital.

The facts which we are about to relate belong to that dramatic and living reality, which the historian sometimes neglects for lack of time and space. There, nevertheless, we insist upon it, is life, palpitation, human tremor. Petty details, as we think we have already said, are, so to speak, the foliage of great events, and are lost in the distance of history.

The epoch, surnamed "of the riots," abounds in details of this nature. Judicial inquiries have not revealed, and perhaps have not sounded the depths, for another reason than history. We shall therefore bring to light, among the known and published peculiarities, things which have not heretofore been known, about facts over which have passed the forgetfulness of some, and the death of others. The majority of the actors in these gigantic scenes have disappeared; beginning with the very next day they held their peace; but of what we shall relate, we shall be able to say: "We have seen this." We alter a few names, for history relates and does not inform against, but the deed which we shall paint will be genuine. In accordance with the conditions of the book which we are now writing, we shall show only one side and one episode, and certainly, the least known at that, of the two days, the 5th and the 6th of June, 1832, but we shall do it in such wise that the reader may catch a glimpse, beneath the gloomy veil which we are about to lift, of the real form of this frightful public adventure.

III

A Burial; An Occasion to Be Born Again

In the spring of 1832, although the cholera had been chilling all minds for the last three months and had cast over their agitation an indescribable and gloomy pacification, Paris had already long been ripe for commotion. As we have said, the great city resembles a piece of artillery; when it is loaded, it suffices for a spark to fall, and the shot is discharged. In June, 1832, the spark was the death of General Lamarque.

Lamarque was a man of renown and of action. He had had in succession, under the Empire and under the Restoration, the sorts of bravery requisite for the two epochs, the bravery of the battle-field and the bravery of the tribune. He was as eloquent as he had been valiant; a sword was discernible in his speech. Like Foy, his predecessor, after upholding the command, he upheld liberty; he sat between the left and the extreme left, beloved of the people because he accepted the chances of the future, beloved of the populace because he had served the Emperor well; he was, in company with Comtes Gérard and Drouet, one of Napoleon's marshals *in petto*. The treaties of 1815 removed him as a personal offence. He hated Wellington with a downright hatred which pleased the multitude; and, for seventeen years, he majestically preserved the sadness of Waterloo, paying hardly any attention to intervening events. In his death agony, at his last hour, he clasped to his breast a sword which had been presented to him by the officers of the Hundred Days. Napoleon had died uttering the word *army*, Lamarque uttering the word *country*.

His death, which was expected, was dreaded by the people as a loss, and by the government as an occasion. This death was an affliction. Like everything that is bitter, affliction may turn to revolt. This is what took place.

On the preceding evening, and on the morning of the 5th of June, the day appointed for Lamarque's burial, the Faubourg Saint-Antoine, which the procession was to touch at, assumed a formidable aspect. This tumultuous network of streets was filled with rumors. They armed themselves as best they might. Joiners carried off door-weights of their establishment "to break down doors." One of them had made himself a dagger of a stocking-weaver's hook by breaking off the hook and sharpening the stump. Another, who was in a fever "to attack," slept wholly dressed for three days. A carpenter named Lombier met a comrade, who asked him: "Whither are you going?" "Eh! well, I have no weapons." "What then?" "I'm going to my timber-yard to get my compasses." "What for?" "I don't know," said Lombier. A certain Jacqueline, an expeditious man, accosted some passing artisans: "Come here, you!" He treated them to ten sous' worth of wine and said: "Have you work?" "No." "Go to Filspierre, between the Barrière Charonne and the Barrière Montreuil, and you will find work." At Filspierre's they found cartridges and arms. Certain well-known leaders were going the rounds, that is to say, running from one house to another, to collect their men. At Barthélemy's, near the Barrière du Trône, at Capel's, near the Petit-Chapeau, the drinkers accosted each other with a grave air. They were heard to say: "Have you your pistol?" "Under my blouse." "And you?" "Under my shirt." In the Rue Traversière, in front of the Bland workshop, and in the yard of the Maison-Brulée, in front of tool-maker Bernier's, groups whispered together. Among them was observed a certain Mavot, who never remained more than a week in one shop, as the masters always discharged him "because they were obliged to dispute with him every day." Mavot was killed on the following day at the barricade of the Rue Ménilmontant. Pretot, who was destined to perish also in the struggle, seconded Mavot, and to the question: "What is your object?" he replied: *"Insurrection."* Workmen assembled at the corner of the Rue de Bercy, waited for a certain Lemarin, the revolutionary agent for the Faubourg Saint-Marceau. Watchwords were exchanged almost publicly.

On the 5th of June, accordingly, a day of mingled rain and sun, General Lamarque's funeral procession traversed Paris with official military pomp, somewhat augmented through precaution. Two battalions, with draped drums and reversed arms, ten thousand National Guards, with their swords at their sides, escorted the coffin. The hearse was drawn by young men. The officers of the Invalides came immediately behind it, bearing laurel branches. Then came an innumerable, strange, agitated multitude, the sectionaries of the Friends of the People, the Law School, the Medical School, refugees of all nationalities, and Spanish, Italian, German, and Polish flags, tricolored horizontal banners, every possible sort of banner, children waving green boughs, stone-cutters and carpenters who were on strike at the moment, printers who were recognizable by their paper caps, marching two by two, three by three, uttering cries, nearly all of them brandishing sticks, some brandishing sabres, without order and yet with a single soul, now a tumultuous rout, again a column. Squads chose themselves leaders; a man armed with a pair of pistols in full view, seemed to pass the host in review, and the files separated before him. On the side alleys of the boulevards, in the branches of the trees, on balconies, in windows, on the roofs, swarmed the heads of men, women, and children; all eyes were filled with anxiety. An armed throng was passing, and a terrified throng looked on.

The Government, on its side, was taking observations. It observed with its hand on its sword. Four squadrons of carabineers could be seen in the Place Louis XV in their saddles, with their trumpets at their head, cartridge-boxes filled and muskets loaded, all in readiness to march; in the Latin country and at the Jardin des Plantes, the Municipal Guard echelonned from street to street; at the Halle-aux-Vins, a squadron of dragoons; at the Grève half of the 12th Light Infantry, the other half being at the Bastille; the 6th Dragoons at the Célestins; and the courtyard of the Louvre full of artillery. The remainder of the troops were confined to their barracks, without reckoning the regiments of the environs of Paris. Power being uneasy, held suspended over the menacing multitude twenty-four thousand soldiers in the city and thirty thousand in the banlieue.

Divers reports were in circulation in the cortège. Legitimist tricks were hinted at; they spoke of the Duc de Reichstadt, whom God had marked out for death at that very moment when the populace were designating him for the Empire. One personage, whose name has remained unknown, announced that at a given hour two overseers who had been won over, would throw open the doors of a factory of arms to the people. That which predominated on the uncovered brows of the majority of those present was enthusiasm mingled with dejection. Here and there, also, in that multitude given over to such violent but noble emotions, there were visible genuine visages of criminals and ignoble mouths which said: "Let us plunder!" There are certain agitations which stir up the bottoms of marshes and make clouds of mud rise through the water. A phenomenon to which "well drilled" policemen are no strangers.

The procession proceeded, with feverish slowness, from the house of the deceased, by way of the boulevards as far as the Bastille. It rained from time to time; the rain mattered nothing to that throng. Many incidents, the coffin borne round the Vendome column, stones thrown at the Duc de Fitz-James, who was seen on a balcony with his hat on his head, the Gallic cock torn from a popular flag and dragged in the mire, a policeman wounded with a blow from a sword at the Porte Saint-Martin, an officer of the 12th Light Infantry saying aloud: "I am a Republican," the Polytechnic School coming up unexpectedly against orders to remain at home, the shouts of: "Long live the Polytechnique! Long live the Republic!" marked the passage of the funeral train. At the Bastille, long files of curious and formidable people who descended from the Faubourg Saint-Antoine, effected a junction with the procession, and a certain terrible seething began to agitate the throng.

One man was heard to say to another: "Do you see that fellow with a red beard, he's the one who will give the word when we are to fire." It appears that this red beard was present, at another riot, the Quénisset affair, entrusted with this same function.

The hearse passed the Bastille, traversed the small bridge, and reached the esplanade of the bridge of Austerlitz. There it halted. The crowd, surveyed at that moment with a bird's-eye view, would have presented the aspect of a comet whose head was on the esplanade and whose tail spread out over the Quai Bourdon, covered the Bastille, and was prolonged on the boulevard as far as the Porte Saint-Martin. A circle was traced around the hearse. The vast rout held their peace. Lafayette spoke and bade Lamarque farewell. This was a touching and august instant, all heads uncovered, all hearts beat high.

All at once, a man on horseback, clad in black, made his appearance in the middle of the group with a red flag, others say, with a pike surmounted with a red liberty-cap. Lafayette turned aside his head. Exelmans quitted the procession.

This red flag raised a storm, and disappeared in the midst of it. From the Boulevard Bourdon to the bridge of Austerlitz one of those clamors which resemble billows stirred the multitude. Two prodigious shouts went up: "Lamarque to the Pantheon!—Lafayette to the Town-hall!" Some young men, amid the declamations of the throng, harnessed themselves and began to drag Lamarque in the hearse across the bridge of Austerlitz and Lafayette in a hackney-coach along the Quai Morland.

In the crowd which surrounded and cheered Lafayette, it was noticed that a German showed himself named Ludwig Snyder, who died a centenarian afterwards, who had also been in the war of 1776, and who had fought at Trenton under Washington, and at Brandywine under Lafayette.

In the meantime, the municipal cavalry on the left bank had been set in motion, and came to bar the bridge, on the right bank the dragoons emerged from the Célestins and deployed along the Quai Morland. The men who were dragging Lafayette suddenly caught sight of them at the corner of the quay and shouted: "The dragoons!" The dragoons advanced at a walk, in silence, with their pistols in their holsters, their swords in their scabbards, their guns slung in their leather sockets, with an air of gloomy expectation.

They halted two hundred paces from the little bridge. The carriage in which sat Lafayette advanced to them, their ranks opened and allowed it to pass, and then closed behind it. At that moment the dragoons and the crowd touched. The women fled in terror. What took place during that fatal minute? No one can say. It is the dark moment when two clouds come together. Some declare that a blast of trumpets sounding the charge was heard in the direction of the Arsenal, others that a blow from a dagger was given by a child to a dragoon. The fact is, that three shots were suddenly discharged: the first killed Cholet, chief of the squadron, the second killed an old deaf woman who was in the act of closing her window, the third singed the shoulder of an officer; a woman screamed: "They are beginning too soon!" and all at once, a squadron of dragoons which had remained in the barracks up to this time, was seen to debouch at a gallop with bared swords, through the Rue Bassompierre and the Boulevard Bourdon, sweeping all before them.

Then all is said, the tempest is loosed, stones rain down, a fusillade breaks forth, many precipitate themselves to the bottom of the bank, and pass the small arm of the Seine, now filled in, the timber-yards of the Isle Louviers, that vast citadel ready to hand, bristle with combatants, stakes are torn up, pistol-shots fired, a barricade begun, the young men who are thrust back pass the Austerlitz bridge with the hearse at a run, and the municipal guard, the carabineers rush up, the dragoons ply their swords, the crowd disperses in all directions, a rumor of war flies to all four quarters of Paris, men shout: "To arms!" they run, tumble down, flee, resist. Wrath spreads abroad the riot as wind spreads a fire.

IV

The Ebullitions of Former Days

Nothing is more extraordinary than the first breaking out of a riot. Everything bursts forth everywhere at once. Was it foreseen? Yes. Was it prepared? No. Whence comes it? From the pavements. Whence falls it? From the clouds. Here insurrection assumes the character of a plot; there of an improvisation. The first comer seizes a current of the throng and leads it whither he wills. A beginning full of terror, in which is mingled a sort of formidable gayety. First come clamors, the shops are closed, the displays of the merchants disappear; then come isolated shots; people flee; blows from gun-stocks beat against portes-cochères, servants can be heard laughing in the courtyards of houses and saying: "There's going to be a row!"

A quarter of an hour had not elapsed when this is what was taking place at twenty different spots in Paris at once.

In the Rue Sainte-Croix-de-la-Bretonnerie, twenty young men, bearded and with long hair, entered a dram-shop and emerged a moment later, carrying a horizontal tricolored flag covered with crape, and having at their head three men armed, one with a sword, one with a gun, and the third with a pike.

In the Rue des Nonaindières, a very well-dressed bourgeois, who had a prominent belly, a sonorous voice, a bald head, a lofty brow, a black beard, and one of these stiff moustaches which will not lie flat, offered cartridges publicly to passers-by.

In the Rue Saint-Pierre-Montmartre, men with bare arms carried about a black flag, on which could be read in white letters this inscription: "Republic or Death!" In the Rue des Jeûneurs, Rue du Cadran, Rue Montorgueil, Rue Mandar, groups appeared waving flags on which could be distinguished in gold letters, the word *section* with a number. One of these flags was red and blue with an almost imperceptible stripe of white between.

They pillaged a factory of small-arms on the Boulevard Saint-Martin, and three armorers' shops, the first in the Rue Beaubourg, the second in the Rue Michel-le-Comte, the other in the Rue du Temple. In a few minutes, the thousand hands of the crowd had seized and carried off two hundred and thirty guns, nearly all double-barrelled, sixty-four swords, and eighty-three pistols. In order to provide more arms, one man took the gun, the other the bayonet.

Opposite the Quai de la Grève, young men armed with muskets installed themselves in the houses of some women for the purpose of firing. One of them had a flint-lock. They rang, entered, and set about making cartridges. One of these women relates: "I did not know what cartridges were; it was my husband who told me."

One cluster broke into a curiosity shop in the Rue des Vieilles-Haudriettes, and seized yataghans and Turkish arms.

The body of a mason who had been killed by a gun-shot lay in the Rue de la Perle.

And then on the right bank, the left bank, on the quays, on the boulevards, in the Latin country, in the quarter of the Halles, panting men, artisans, students, members of sections read proclamations and shouted: "To arms!" broke street lanterns, unharnessed carriages, unpaved the streets, broke in the doors of houses, uprooted trees, rummaged cellars, rolled out hogsheads, heaped up paving-stones, rough slabs, furniture and planks, and made barricades.

They forced the bourgeois to assist them in this. They entered the dwellings of women, they forced them to hand over the swords and guns of their absent husbands, and they wrote on the door, with whiting: "The arms have been delivered"; some signed "their names" to receipts for the guns and swords and said: "Send for them to-morrow at the Mayor's office." They disarmed isolated sentinels and National Guardsmen in the streets on their way to the Townhall. They tore the epaulets from officers. In the Rue du Cimitière-Saint-Nicholas, an officer of the National Guard, on being pursued by a crowd armed with clubs and foils, took refuge with difficulty in a house, whence he was only able to emerge at nightfall and in disguise.

In the Quartier Saint-Jacques, the students swarmed out of their hotels and ascended the Rue Saint-Hyacinthe to the Café du Progrèss, or descended to the Café des Sept-Billards, in the Rue des Mathurins. There, in front of the door, young men mounted on the stone corner-posts, distributed arms. They plundered the timber-yard in the Rue Transnonain in order to obtain material for barricades. On a single point the inhabitants resisted, at the corner of the Rue Sainte-Avoye and the Rue Simon-Le-Franc, where they destroyed the barricade with their own hands. At a single point the insurgents yielded; they abandoned a barricade begun in the Rue de Temple after having fired on a detachment of the National Guard, and fled through the Rue de la Corderie. The detachment picked up in the barricade a red flag, a package of cartridges, and three hundred pistol-balls. The National Guardsmen tore up the flag, and carried off its tattered remains on the points of their bayonets.

All that we are here relating slowly and successively took place simultaneously at all points of the city in the midst of a vast tumult, like a mass of tongues of lightning in one clap of thunder. In less than an hour, twenty-seven barricades sprang out of the earth in the quarter of the Halles alone. In the centre was that famous house No. 50, which was the fortress of Jeanne and her six hundred companions, and which, flanked on the one hand by a barricade at Saint-Merry, and on the other by a barricade of the Rue Maubuée, commanded three streets, the Rue des Arcis, the Rue Saint-Martin, and the Rue Aubry-le-Boucher, which it faced. The barricades at right angles fell back, the one of the Rue Montorgueil on the Grande-Truanderie, the other of the Rue Geoffroy-Langevin on the Rue Sainte-Avoye. Without reckoning innumerable barricades in twenty other quarters of Paris, in the Marais, at Mont-Sainte-Geneviève; one in the Rue Ménilmontant, where was visible a porte-cochère torn from its hinges; another near the little bridge of the Hôtel-Dieu made with an "écossais," which had been unharnessed and overthrown, three hundred paces from the Prefecture of Police.

At the barricade of the Rue des Ménétriers, a well-dressed man distributed money to the workmen. At the barricade of the Rue Grenetat, a horseman made his appearance and handed to the one who seemed to be the commander of the barricade what had the appearance of a roll of silver. "Here," said he, "this is to pay expenses, wine, et cætera." A light-haired young man, without a cravat, went from barricade to barricade, carrying pass-words. Another, with a naked sword, a blue police cap on his head, placed sentinels. In the interior, beyond the barricades, the wine-shops and porters' lodges were converted into guard-houses. Otherwise the riot was conducted after the most scientific military tactics. The narrow, uneven, sinuous streets, full of angles and turns, were admirably chosen; the neighborhood of the Halles, in particular, a network of streets more intricate than a forest. The Society of the Friends of the People had, it was said, undertaken to direct the insurrection in the Quartier Sainte-Avoye. A man killed in the Rue du Ponceau who was searched had on his person a plan of Paris.

That which had really undertaken the direction of the uprising was a sort of strange impetuosity which was in the air. The insurrection had abruptly built barricades with one hand, and with the other seized nearly all the posts of the garrison. In less than three hours, like a train of powder catching fire, the insurgents had invaded and occupied, on the right bank, the Arsenal, the Mayoralty of the Place Royale, the whole of the Marais, the Popincourt arms manufactory, la Galiote, the Château-d'Eau, and all the streets near the Halles; on the left bank, the barracks of the Veterans, Sainte-Pélagie, the Place Maubert, the powder magazine of the Deux-Moulins, and all the barriers. At five o'clock in the evening, they were masters of the Bastille, of the Lingerie, of the Blancs-Manteaux; their scouts had reached the Place des Victoires, and menaced the Bank, the Petits-Pères barracks, and the Post-Office. A third of Paris was in the hands of the rioters.

The conflict had been begun on a gigantic scale at all points; and, as a result of the disarming domiciliary visits, and armorers' shops hastily invaded, was, that the combat which had begun with the throwing of stones was continued with gun-shots.

About six o'clock in the evening, the Passage du Saumon became the field of battle. The uprising was at one end, the troops were at the other. They fired from one gate to the other. An observer, a dreamer, the author of this book, who had gone to get a near view of this volcano, found himself in the passage between the two fires. All that he had to protect him from the bullets was the swell of the two half-columns which separate the shops; he remained in this delicate situation for nearly half an hour.

Meanwhile the call to arms was beaten, the National Guard armed in haste, the legions emerged from the Mayoralities, the regiments from their barracks. Opposite the passage de l'Ancre a drummer received a blow from a dagger. Another, in the Rue du Cygne, was assailed by thirty young men who broke his instrument, and took away his sword. Another was killed in the Rue Grenier-Saint-Lazare. In the Rue Michel-le-Comte, three officers fell dead one after the other. Many of the Municipal Guards, on being wounded, in the Rue des Lombards, retreated.

In front of the Cour-Batave, a detachment of National Guards found a red flag bearing the following inscription: *Republican revolution, No. 127.* Was this a revolution, in fact?

The insurrection had made of the centre of Paris a sort of inextricable, tortuous, colossal citadel.

There was the hearth; there, evidently, was the question. All the rest was nothing but skirmishes. The proof that all would be decided there lay in the fact that there was no fighting going on there as yet.

In some regiments, the soldiers were uncertain, which added to the fearful uncertainty of the crisis. They recalled the popular ovation which had greeted the neutrality of the 53d of the Line in July, 1830. Two intrepid men, tried in great wars, the Marshal Lobau and General Bugeaud, were in command, Bugeaud under Lobau. Enormous patrols, composed of battalions of the Line, enclosed in entire companies of the National Guard, and preceded by a commissary of police wearing his scarf of office, went to reconnoitre the streets in rebellion. The insurgents, on their side, placed videttes at the corners of all open spaces, and audaciously sent their patrols outside the barricades. Each side was watching the other. The Government, with an army in its hand, hesitated; the night was almost upon them, and the Saint-Merry tocsin began to make itself heard. The Minister of War at that time, Marshal Soult, who had seen Austerlitz, regarded this with a gloomy air.

These old sailors, accustomed to correct manœuvres and having as resource and guide only tactics, that compass of battles, are utterly disconcerted in the presence of that immense foam which is called public wrath.

The National Guards of the suburbs rushed up in haste and disorder. A battalion of the 12th Light came at a run from Saint-Denis, the 14th of the Line arrived from Courbevoie, the batteries of the Military School had taken up their position on the Carrousel; cannons were descending from Vincennes.

Solitude was formed around the Tuileries. Louis Philippe was perfectly serene.

V

Originality of Paris

During the last two years, as we have said, Paris had witnessed more than one insurrection. Nothing is, generally, more singularly calm than the physiognomy of Paris during an uprising beyond the bounds of the rebellious quarters. Paris very speedily accustoms herself to anything,— it is only a riot,—and Paris has so many affairs on hand, that she does not put herself out for so small a matter. These colossal cities alone can offer such spectacles. These immense enclosures alone can contain at the same time civil war and an odd and indescribable tranquillity. Ordinarily, when an insurrection commences, when the shop-keeper hears the drum, the call to arms, the general alarm, he contents himself with the remark:—

"There appears to be a squabble in the Rue Saint-Martin."

Or:—

"In the Faubourg Saint-Antoine."

Often he adds carelessly:—

"Or somewhere in that direction."

Later on, when the heart-rending and mournful hubbub of musketry and firing by platoons becomes audible, the shopkeeper says:—

"It's getting hot! Hullo, it's getting hot!"

A moment later, the riot approaches and gains in force, he shuts up his shop precipitately, hastily dons his uniform, that is to say, he places his merchandise in safety and risks his own person.

Men fire in a square, in a passage, in a blind alley; they take and re-take the barricade; blood flows, the grape-shot riddles the fronts of the houses, the balls kill people in their beds, corpses encumber the streets. A few streets away, the shock of billiard-balls can be heard in the cafés.

The theatres open their doors and present vaudevilles; the curious laugh and chat a couple of paces distant from these streets filled with war. Hackney-carriages go their way; passers-by are going to a dinner somewhere in town. Sometimes in the very quarter where the fighting is going on.

In 1831, a fusillade was stopped to allow a wedding party to pass.

At the time of the insurrection of 1839, in the Rue Saint-Martin a little, infirm old man, pushing a hand-cart surmounted by a tricolored rag, in which he had carafes filled with some sort of liquid, went and came from barricade to troops and from troops to the barricade, offering his glasses of cocoa impartially,—now to the Government, now to anarchy.

Nothing can be stranger; and this is the peculiar character of uprisings in Paris, which cannot be found in any other capital. To this end, two things are requisite, the size of Paris and its gayety. The city of Voltaire and Napoleon is necessary.

On this occasion, however, in the resort to arms of June 5th, 1832, the great city felt something which was, perhaps, stronger than itself. It was afraid.

Closed doors, windows, and shutters were to be seen everywhere, in the most distant and most "disinterested" quarters. The courageous took to arms, the poltroons hid. The busy and heedless passer-by disappeared. Many streets were empty at four o'clock in the morning.

Alarming details were hawked about, fatal news was disseminated,—that *they* were masters of the Bank;—that there were six hundred of them in the Cloister of Saint-Merry alone, entrenched and embattled in the church; that the line was not to be depended on; that Armand Carrel had been to see Marshal Clausel and that the Marshal had said: "Get a regiment first"; that Lafayette was ill, but that he had said to them, nevertheless: "I am with you. I will follow you wherever there is room for a chair"; that one must be on one's guard; that at night there would be people pillaging isolated dwellings in the deserted corners of Paris (there the imagination of the police, that Anne Radcliffe mixed up with the Government was recognizable); that a battery had been established in the Rue Aubry le Boucher; that Lobau and Bugeaud were putting their heads together, and that, at midnight, or at daybreak at latest, four columns would march simultaneously on the centre of the uprising, the first coming from the Bastille, the second from the Porte Saint-Martin, the third from the Grève, the fourth from the Halles; that perhaps, also, the troops would evacuate Paris and withdraw to the Champ-de-Mars; that no one knew what would happen, but that this time, it certainly was serious.

People busied themselves over Marshal Soult's hesitations. Why did not he attack at once? It is certain that he was profoundly absorbed. The old lion seemed to scent an unknown monster in that gloom.

Evening came, the theatres did not open; the patrols circulated with an air of irritation; passers-by were searched; suspicious persons were arrested. By nine o'clock, more than eight hundred persons had been arrested, the Prefecture of Police was encumbered with them, so was the Conciergerie, so was La Force.

At the Conciergerie in particular, the long vault which is called the Rue de Paris was littered with trusses of straw upon which lay a heap of prisoners, whom the man of Lyons, Lagrange, harangued valiantly. All that straw rustled by all these men, produced the sound of a heavy shower. Elsewhere prisoners slept in the open air in the meadows, piled on top of each other.

Anxiety reigned everywhere, and a certain tremor which was not habitual with Paris.

People barricaded themselves in their houses; wives and mothers were uneasy; nothing was to be heard but this: "Ah! my God! He has not come home!" There was hardly even the distant rumble of a vehicle to be heard.

People listened on their thresholds, to the rumors, the shouts, the tumult, the dull and indistinct sounds, to the things that were said: "It is cavalry," or: "Those are the caissons galloping," to the trumpets, the drums, the firing, and, above all, to that lamentable alarm peal from Saint-Merry.

They waited for the first cannon-shot. Men sprang up at the corners of the streets and disappeared, shouting: "Go home!" And people made haste to bolt their doors. They said: "How will all this end?" From moment to moment, in proportion as the darkness descended, Paris seemed to take on a more mournful hue from the formidable flaming of the revolt.

BOOK ELEVENTH
THE ATOM FRATERNIZES
WITH THE HURRICANE

I

Some Explanations with Regard to the Origin of Gavroche's Poetry. The Influence of an Academician on This Poetry

At the instant when the insurrection, arising from the shock of the populace and the military in front of the Arsenal, started a movement in advance and towards the rear in the multitude which was following the hearse and which, through the whole length of the boulevards, weighed, so to speak, on the head of the procession, there arose a frightful ebb. The rout was shaken, their ranks were broken, all ran, fled, made their escape, some with shouts of attack, others with the pallor of flight. The great river which covered the boulevards divided in a twinkling, overflowed to right and left, and spread in torrents over two hundred streets at once with the roar of a sewer that has broken loose.

At that moment, a ragged child who was coming down through the Rue Ménilmontant, holding in his hand a branch of blossoming laburnum which he had just plucked on the heights of Belleville, caught sight of an old holster-pistol in the show-window of a bric-à-brac merchant's shop.

"Mother What's-your-name, I'm going to borrow your machine."

And off he ran with the pistol.

Two minutes later, a flood of frightened bourgeois who were fleeing through the Rue Amelot and the Rue Basse, encountered the lad brandishing his pistol and singing:—

> *La nuit on ne voit rien,*
> *Le jour on voit très bien,*
> *D'un écrit apocryphe*
> *Le bourgeois s'ébouriffe,*
> *Pratiquez la vertu,*
> *Tutu, chapeau pointu!*

It was little Gavroche on his way to the wars.

On the boulevard he noticed that the pistol had no trigger.

Who was the author of that couplet which served to punctuate his march, and of all the other songs which he was fond of singing on occasion? We know not. Who does know? Himself, perhaps. However, Gavroche was well up in all the popular tunes in circulation, and he mingled with them his own chirpings. An observing urchin and a rogue, he made a potpourri of the voices of nature and the voices of Paris. He combined the repertory of the birds with the repertory of the workshops. He was acquainted with thieves, a tribe contiguous to his own. He had, it appears, been for three months apprenticed to a printer. He had one day executed a commission for M. Baour-Lormian, one of the Forty. Gavroche was a gamin of letters.

Moreover, Gavroche had no suspicion of the fact that when he had offered the hospitality of his elephant to two brats on that villainously rainy night, it was to his own brothers that he had played the part of Providence. His brothers in the evening, his father in the morning; that is what his night had been like. On quitting the Rue des Ballets at daybreak, he had returned in haste to the elephant, had artistically extracted from it the two brats, had shared with them some sort of breakfast which he had invented, and had then gone away, confiding them to that good mother, the street, who had brought him up, almost entirely. On leaving them, he had appointed to meet them at the same spot in the evening, and had left them this discourse by way of a farewell: "I break a cane, otherwise expressed, I cut my stick, or, as they say at the court, I file off. If you don't find papa and mamma, young 'uns, come back here this evening. I'll scramble you up some supper, and I'll give you a shakedown." The two children, picked up by some policeman and placed in the refuge, or stolen by some mountebank, or having simply strayed off in that immense Chinese puzzle of a Paris, did not return. The lowest depths of the actual social world are full of these lost traces. Gavroche did not see them again. Ten or twelve weeks had elapsed since that night. More than once he had scratched the back of his head and said: "Where the devil are my two children?"

In the meantime, he had arrived, pistol in hand, in the Rue du Pont-aux-Choux. He noticed that there was but one shop open in that street, and, a matter worthy of reflection, that was a pastry-cook's shop. This presented a providential occasion to eat another apple-turnover before entering the unknown. Gavroche halted, fumbled in his fob, turned his pocket inside out, found nothing, not even a sou, and began to shout: "Help!"

It is hard to miss the last cake.

Nevertheless, Gavroche pursued his way.

Two minutes later he was in the Rue Saint-Louis. While traversing the Rue du Parc-Royal, he felt called upon to make good the loss of the apple-turnover which had been impossible, and he indulged himself in the immense delight of tearing down the theatre posters in broad daylight.

A little further on, on catching sight of a group of comfortable-looking persons, who seemed to be landed proprietors, he shrugged his shoulders and spit out at random before him this mouthful of philosophical bile as they passed:

"How fat those moneyed men are! They're drunk! They just wallow in good dinners. Ask 'em what they do with their money. They don't know. They eat it, that's what they do! As much as their bellies will hold."

II

GAVROCHE ON THE MARCH

The brandishing of a triggerless pistol, grasped in one's hand in the open street, is so much of a public function that Gavroche felt his fervor increasing with every moment. Amid the scraps of the Marseillaise which he was singing, he shouted:—

"All goes well. I suffer a great deal in my left paw, I'm all broken up with rheumatism, but I'm satisfied, citizens. All that the bourgeois have to do is to bear themselves well, I'll sneeze them out subversive couplets. What are the police spies? Dogs. And I'd just like to have one of them at the end of my pistol. I'm just from the boulevard, my friends. It's getting hot there, it's getting into a little boil, it's simmering. It's time to skim the pot. Forward march, men! Let an impure blood inundate the furrows! I give my days to my country, I shall never see my concubine more, Nini, finished, yes, Nini? But never mind! Long live joy! Let's fight, crebleu! I've had enough of despotism."

At that moment, the horse of a lancer of the National Guard having fallen, Gavroche laid his pistol on the pavement, and picked up the man, then he assisted in raising the horse. After which he picked up his pistol and resumed his way. In the Rue de Thorigny, all was peace and silence. This apathy, peculiar to the Marais, presented a contrast with the vast surrounding uproar. Four gossips were chatting in a doorway.

Scotland has trios of witches, Paris has quartettes of old gossiping hags; and the "Thou shalt be King" could be quite as mournfully hurled at Bonaparte in the Carrefour Baudoyer as at Macbeth on the heath of Armuyr. The croak would be almost identical.

The gossips of the Rue de Thorigny busied themselves only with their own concerns. Three of them were portresses, and the fourth was a rag-picker with her basket on her back.

All four of them seemed to be standing at the four corners of old age, which are decrepitude, decay, ruin, and sadness.

The rag-picker was humble. In this open-air society, it is the rag-picker who salutes and the portress who patronizes. This is caused by the corner for refuse, which is fat or lean, according to the will of the portresses, and after the fancy of the one who makes the heap. There may be kindness in the broom.

This rag-picker was a grateful creature, and she smiled, with what a smile! on the three portresses. Things of this nature were said:—

"Ah, by the way, is your cat still cross?"

"Good gracious, cats are naturally the enemies of dogs, you know. It's the dogs who complain."

"And people also."

"But the fleas from a cat don't go after people."

"That's not the trouble, dogs are dangerous. I remember one year when there were so many dogs that it was necessary to put it in the newspapers. That was at the time when there were at the Tuileries great sheep that drew the little carriage of the King of Rome. Do you remember the King of Rome?"

"I liked the Duc de Bordeau better."

"I knew Louis XVIII. I prefer Louis XVIII."

"Meat is awfully dear, isn't it, Mother Patagon?"

"Ah! don't mention it, the butcher's shop is a horror. A horrible horror—one can't afford anything but the poor cuts nowadays."

Here the rag-picker interposed:—

"Ladies, business is dull. The refuse heaps are miserable. No one throws anything away any more. They eat everything."

"There are poorer people than you, la Vargoulême."

"Ah, that's true," replied the rag-picker, with deference, "I have a profession."

A pause succeeded, and the rag-picker, yielding to that necessity for boasting which lies at the bottom of man, added:—

"In the morning, on my return home, I pick over my basket, I sort my things. This makes heaps in my room. I put the rags in a basket, the cores and stalks in a bucket, the linen in my cupboard, the woollen stuff in my commode, the old papers in the corner of the window, the things that are good to eat in my bowl, the bits of glass in my fireplace, the old shoes behind my door, and the bones under my bed."

Gavroche had stopped behind her and was listening.

"Old ladies," said he, "what do you mean by talking politics?"

He was assailed by a broadside, composed of a quadruple howl.

"Here's another rascal."

"What's that he's got in his paddle? A pistol?"

"Well, I'd like to know what sort of a beggar's brat this is?"

"That sort of animal is never easy unless he's overturning the authorities."

Gavroche disdainfully contented himself, by way of reprisal, with elevating the tip of his nose with his thumb and opening his hand wide.

The rag-picker cried:—

"You malicious, bare-pawed little wretch!"

The one who answered to the name of Patagon clapped her hands together in horror.

"There's going to be evil doings, that's certain. The errand-boy next door has a little pointed beard, I have seen him pass every day with a young person in a pink bonnet on his arm; to-day I saw him pass, and he had a gun on his arm. Mame Bacheux says, that last week there was a revolution at—at—at—where's the calf!—at Pontoise. And then, there you see him, that horrid scamp, with his pistol! It seems that the Célestins are full of pistols. What do you suppose the Government can do with good-for-nothings who don't know how to do anything but contrive ways of upsetting the world, when we had just begun to get a little quiet after all the misfortunes that have happened, good Lord! to that poor queen whom I saw pass in the tumbril! And all this is going to make tobacco dearer. It's infamous! And I shall certainly go to see him beheaded on the guillotine, the wretch!"

"You've got the sniffles, old lady," said Gavroche. "Blow your promontory."

And he passed on. When he was in the Rue Pavée, the rag-picker occurred to his mind, and he indulged in this soliloquy:—

"You're in the wrong to insult the revolutionists, Mother Dust-Heap-Corner. This pistol is in your interests. It's so that you may have more good things to eat in your basket."

All at once, he heard a shout behind him; it was the portress Patagon who had followed him, and who was shaking her fist at him in the distance and crying:—

"You're nothing but a bastard."

"Oh! Come now," said Gavroche, "I don't care a brass farthing for that!"

Shortly afterwards, he passed the Hotel Lamoignon. There he uttered this appeal:—

"Forward march to the battle!"

And he was seized with a fit of melancholy. He gazed at his pistol with an air of reproach which seemed an attempt to appease it:—

"I'm going off," said he, "but you won't go off!"

One dog may distract the attention from another dog. A very gaunt poodle came along at the moment. Gavroche felt compassion for him.

"My poor doggy," said he, "you must have gone and swallowed a cask, for all the hoops are visible."

Then he directed his course towards l'Orme-Saint-Gervais.

III

JUST INDIGNATION OF A HAIR-DRESSER

The worthy hair-dresser who had chased from his shop the two little fellows to whom Gavroche had opened the paternal interior of the elephant was at that moment in his shop engaged in shaving an old soldier of the legion who had served under the Empire. They were talking. The hair-dresser had, naturally, spoken to the veteran of the riot, then of General Lamarque, and from Lamarque they had passed to the Emperor. Thence sprang up a conversation between barber and soldier which Prudhomme, had he been present, would have enriched with arabesques, and which he would have entitled: "Dialogue between the razor and the sword."

"How did the Emperor ride, sir?" said the barber.

"Badly. He did not know how to fall—so he never fell."

"Did he have fine horses? He must have had fine horses!"

"On the day when he gave me my cross, I noticed his beast. It was a racing mare, perfectly white. Her ears were very wide apart, her saddle deep, a fine head marked with a black star, a very long neck, strongly articulated knees, prominent ribs, oblique shoulders and a powerful crupper. A little more than fifteen hands in height."

"A pretty horse," remarked the hair-dresser.

"It was His Majesty's beast."

The hair-dresser felt, that after this observation, a short silence would be fitting, so he conformed himself to it, and then went on:—

"The Emperor was never wounded but once, was he, sir?"

The old soldier replied with the calm and sovereign tone of a man who had been there:—

"In the heel. At Ratisbon. I never saw him so well dressed as on that day. He was as neat as a new sou."

"And you, Mr. Veteran, you must have been often wounded?"

"I?" said the soldier, "ah! not to amount to anything. At Marengo, I received two sabre-blows on the back of my neck, a bullet in the right arm at Austerlitz, another in the left hip at Jena. At Friedland, a thrust from a bayonet, there,—at the Moskowa seven or eight lance-thrusts, no matter where, at Lutzen a splinter of a shell crushed one of my fingers. Ah! and then at Waterloo, a ball from a biscaïen in the thigh, that's all."

"How fine that is!" exclaimed the hair-dresser, in Pindaric accents, "to die on the field of battle! On my word of honor, rather than die in bed, of an illness, slowly, a bit by bit each day, with drugs, cataplasms, syringes, medicines, I should prefer to receive a cannon-ball in my belly!"

"You're not over fastidious," said the soldier.

He had hardly spoken when a fearful crash shook the shop. The show-window had suddenly been fractured.

The wig-maker turned pale.

"Ah, good God!" he exclaimed, "it's one of them!"

"What?"

"A cannon-ball."

"Here it is," said the soldier.

And he picked up something that was rolling about the floor. It was a pebble.

The hair-dresser ran to the broken window and beheld Gavroche fleeing at the full speed, towards the Marché Saint-Jean. As he passed the hair-dresser's shop Gavroche, who had the two brats still in his mind, had not been able to resist the impulse to say good day to him, and had flung a stone through his panes.

"You see!" shrieked the hair-dresser, who from white had turned blue, "that fellow returns and does mischief for the pure pleasure of it. What has any one done to that gamin?"

IV

The Child is Amazed at the Old Man

In the meantime, in the Marché Saint-Jean, where the post had already been disarmed, Gavroche had just "effected a junction" with a band led by Enjolras, Courfeyrac, Combeferre, and Feuilly. They were armed after a fashion. Bahorel and Jean Prouvaire had found them and swelled the group. Enjolras had a double-barrelled hunting-gun, Combeferre the gun of a National Guard bearing the number of his legion, and in his belt, two pistols which his unbuttoned coat allowed to be seen, Jean Prouvaire an old cavalry musket, Bahorel a rifle; Courfeyrac was brandishing an unsheathed sword-cane. Feuilly, with a naked sword in his hand, marched at their head shouting: "Long live Poland!"

They reached the Quai Morland. Cravatless, hatless, breathless, soaked by the rain, with lightning in their eyes. Gavroche accosted them calmly:—

"Where are we going?"

"Come along," said Courfeyrac.

Behind Feuilly marched, or rather bounded, Bahorel, who was like a fish in water in a riot. He wore a scarlet waistcoat, and indulged in the sort of words which break everything. His waistcoat astounded a passer-by, who cried in bewilderment:—

"Here are the reds!"

"The reds, the reds!" retorted Bahorel. "A queer kind of fear, bourgeois. For my part I don't tremble before a poppy, the little red hat inspires me with no alarm. Take my advice, bourgeois, let's leave fear of the red to horned cattle."

He caught sight of a corner of the wall on which was placarded the most peaceable sheet of paper in the world, a permission to eat eggs, a Lenten admonition addressed by the Archbishop of Paris to his "flock."

Bahorel exclaimed:—

"'Flock'; a polite way of saying geese."

And he tore the charge from the nail. This conquered Gavroche. From that instant Gavroche set himself to study Bahorel.

"Bahorel," observed Enjolras, "you are wrong. You should have let that charge alone, he is not the person with whom we have to deal, you are wasting your wrath to no purpose. Take care of your supply. One does not fire out of the ranks with the soul any more than with a gun."

"Each one in his own fashion, Enjolras," retorted Bahorel. "This bishop's prose shocks me; I want to eat eggs without being permitted. Your style is the hot and cold; I am amusing myself. Besides, I'm not wasting myself, I'm getting a start; and if I tore down that charge, Hercle! 'twas only to whet my appetite."

This word, *Hercle*, struck Gavroche. He sought all occasions for learning, and that tearer-down of posters possessed his esteem. He inquired of him:—

"What does *Hercle* mean?"

Bahorel answered:—

"It means cursed name of a dog, in Latin."

Here Bahorel recognized at a window a pale young man with a black beard who was watching them as they passed, probably a Friend of the A B C. He shouted to him:—

"Quick, cartridges, *para bellum*."

"A fine man! that's true," said Gavroche, who now understood Latin.

A tumultuous retinue accompanied them,—students, artists, young men affiliated to the Cougourde of Aix, artisans, longshoremen, armed with clubs and bayonets; some, like Combeferre, with pistols thrust into their trousers.

An old man, who appeared to be extremely aged, was walking in the band.

He had no arms, and he made great haste, so that he might not be left behind, although he had a thoughtful air.

Gavroche caught sight of him:—

"Keksekça?" said he to Courfeyrac.

"He's an old duffer."

It was M. Mabeuf.

V

THE OLD MAN

L et us recount what had taken place.

Enjolras and his friends had been on the Boulevard Bourdon, near the public storehouses, at the moment when the dragoons had made their charge. Enjolras, Courfeyrac, and Combeferre were among those who had taken to the Rue Bassompierre, shouting: "To the barricades!" In the Rue Lesdiguières they had met an old man walking along. What had attracted their attention was that the goodman was walking in a zig-zag, as though he were intoxicated. Moreover, he had his hat in his hand, although it had been raining all the morning, and was raining pretty briskly at the very time. Courfeyrac had recognized Father Mabeuf. He knew him through having many times accompanied Marius as far as his door. As he was acquainted with the peaceful and more than timid habits of the old beadle-book-collector, and was amazed at the sight of him in the midst of that uproar, a couple of paces from the cavalry charges, almost in the midst of a fusillade, hatless in the rain, and strolling about among the bullets, he had accosted him, and the following dialogue had been exchanged between the rioter of fire and the octogenarian:—

"M. Mabeuf, go to your home."

"Why?"

"There's going to be a row."

"That's well."

"Thrusts with the sword and firing, M. Mabeuf."

"That is well."

"Firing from cannon."

"That is good. Where are the rest of you going?"

"We are going to fling the government to the earth."

"That is good."

And he had set out to follow them. From that moment forth he had not uttered a word. His step had suddenly become firm; artisans had offered him their arms; he had refused with a sign of the head. He advanced nearly to the front rank of the column, with the movement of a man who is marching and the countenance of a man who is sleeping.

"What a fierce old fellow!" muttered the students. The rumor spread

VICTOR HUGO

through the troop that he was a former member of the Convention,—
an old regicide. The mob had turned in through the Rue de la Verrerie.

Little Gavroche marched in front with that deafening song which
made of him a sort of trumpet.

He sang:

> *"Voici la lune qui paraît,*
> *Quand irons-nous dans la forêt?*
> *Demandait Charlot à Charlotte.*

> *Tou tou tou*
> *Pour Chatou.*
> *Je n'ai qu'un Dieu, qu'un roi, qu'un liard, et qu'une botte.*

> *"Pour avoir bu de grand matin*
> *La rosée à même le thym,*
> *Deux moineaux étaient en ribotte.*

> *Zi zi zi*
> *Pour Passy.*
> *Je n'ai qu'un Dieu, qu'un roi, qu'un liard, et qu'une botte.*

> *"Et ces deux pauvres petits loups,*
> *Comme deux grives étaient soûls;*
> *Un tigre en riait dans sa grotte.*

> *Don don don*
> *Pour Meudon.*
> *Je n'ai qu'un Dieu, qu'un roi, qu'un liard, et qu'une botte.*

> *"L'un jurait et l'autre sacrait.*
> *Quand irons nous dans la forêt?*
> *Demandait Charlot à Charlotte.*

> *Tin tin tin*
> *Pour Pantin.*
> *Je n'ai qu'un Dieu, qu'un roi, qu'un liard, et qu'une botte."*

They directed their course towards Saint-Merry.

VI

RECRUITS

The band augmented every moment. Near the Rue des Billettes, a man of lofty stature, whose hair was turning gray, and whose bold and daring mien was remarked by Courfeyrac, Enjolras, and Combeferre, but whom none of them knew, joined them. Gavroche, who was occupied in singing, whistling, humming, running on ahead and pounding on the shutters of the shops with the butt of his triggerless pistol; paid no attention to this man.

It chanced that in the Rue de la Verrerie, they passed in front of Courfeyrac's door.

"This happens just right," said Courfeyrac, "I have forgotten my purse, and I have lost my hat."

He quitted the mob and ran up to his quarters at full speed. He seized an old hat and his purse.

He also seized a large square coffer, of the dimensions of a large valise, which was concealed under his soiled linen.

As he descended again at a run, the portress hailed him:—

"Monsieur de Courfeyrac!"

"What's your name, portress?"

The portress stood bewildered.

"Why, you know perfectly well, I'm the concierge; my name is Mother Veuvain."

"Well, if you call me Monsieur de Courfeyrac again, I shall call you Mother de Veuvain. Now speak, what's the matter? What do you want?"

"There is some one who wants to speak with you."

"Who is it?"

"I don't know."

"Where is he?"

"In my lodge."

"The devil!" ejaculated Courfeyrac.

"But the person has been waiting your return for over an hour," said the portress.

At the same time, a sort of pale, thin, small, freckled, and youthful artisan, clad in a tattered blouse and patched trousers of ribbed velvet, and who had rather the air of a girl accoutred as a man than of a man, emerged from the lodge and said to Courfeyrac in a voice which was not the least in the world like a woman's voice:—

"Monsieur Marius, if you please."

"He is not here."

"Will he return this evening?"

"I know nothing about it."

And Courfeyrac added:—

"For my part, I shall not return."

The young man gazed steadily at him and said:—

"Why not?"

"Because."

"Where are you going, then?"

"What business is that of yours?"

"Would you like to have me carry your coffer for you?"

"I am going to the barricades."

"Would you like to have me go with you?"

"If you like!" replied Courfeyrac. "The street is free, the pavements belong to every one."

And he made his escape at a run to join his friends. When he had rejoined them, he gave the coffer to one of them to carry. It was only a quarter of an hour after this that he saw the young man, who had actually followed them.

A mob does not go precisely where it intends. We have explained that a gust of wind carries it away. They overshot Saint-Merry and found themselves, without precisely knowing how, in the Rue Saint-Denis.

BOOK TWELFTH
CORINTHE

I

History of Corinthe from its Foundation

The Parisians who nowadays on entering on the Rue Rambuteau at the end near the Halles, notice on their right, opposite the Rue Mondétour, a basket-maker's shop having for its sign a basket in the form of Napoleon the Great with this inscription:—

Napoleon Is Made
Wholly Of Willow,

have no suspicion of the terrible scenes which this very spot witnessed hardly thirty years ago.

It was there that lay the Rue de la Chanvrerie, which ancient deeds spell Chanverrerie, and the celebrated public-house called *Corinthe*.

The reader will remember all that has been said about the barricade effected at this point, and eclipsed, by the way, by the barricade Saint-Merry. It was on this famous barricade of the Rue de la Chanvrerie, now fallen into profound obscurity, that we are about to shed a little light.

May we be permitted to recur, for the sake of clearness in the recital, to the simple means which we have already employed in the case of Waterloo. Persons who wish to picture to themselves in a tolerably exact manner the constitution of the houses which stood at that epoch near the Pointe Saint-Eustache, at the northeast angle of the Halles of Paris, where to-day lies the embouchure of the Rue Rambuteau, have only to imagine an N touching the Rue Saint-Denis with its summit and the Halles with its base, and whose two vertical bars should form the Rue de la Grande-Truanderie, and the Rue de la Chanvrerie, and whose transverse bar should be formed by the Rue de la Petite-Truanderie. The old Rue Mondétour cut the three strokes of the N at the most crooked angles. So that the labyrinthine confusion of these four streets sufficed to form, on a space three fathoms square, between the Halles and the Rue Saint-Denis on the one hand, and between the Rue du Cygne and the Rue des Prêcheurs on the other, seven islands of houses, oddly cut up, of varying sizes, placed crosswise and hap-hazard, and barely separated, like the blocks of stone in a dock, by narrow crannies.

We say narrow crannies, and we can give no more just idea of those dark, contracted, many-angled alleys, lined with eight-story buildings. These buildings were so decrepit that, in the Rue de la Chanvrerie and the Rue de la Petite-Truanderie, the fronts were shored up with beams running from one house to another. The street was narrow and the gutter broad, the pedestrian there walked on a pavement that was always wet, skirting little stalls resembling cellars, big posts encircled with iron hoops, excessive heaps of refuse, and gates armed with enormous, century-old gratings. The Rue Rambuteau has devastated all that.

The name of Mondétour paints marvellously well the sinuosities of that whole set of streets. A little further on, they are found still better expressed by the *Rue Pirouette*, which ran into the Rue Mondétour.

The passer-by who got entangled from the Rue Saint-Denis in the Rue de la Chanvrerie beheld it gradually close in before him as though he had entered an elongated funnel. At the end of this street, which was very short, he found further passage barred in the direction of the Halles by a tall row of houses, and he would have thought himself in a blind alley, had he not perceived on the right and left two dark cuts through which he could make his escape. This was the Rue Mondétour, which on one side ran into the Rue de Prêcheurs, and on the other into the Rue du Cygne and the Petite-Truanderie. At the bottom of this sort of cul-de-sac, at the angle of the cutting on the right, there was to be seen a house which was not so tall as the rest, and which formed a sort of cape in the street. It is in this house, of two stories only, that an illustrious wine-shop had been merrily installed three hundred years before. This tavern created a joyous noise in the very spot which old Theophilus described in the following couplet:—

> *Là branle le squelette horrible*
> *D'un pauvre amant qui se pendit.*

The situation was good, and tavern-keepers succeeded each other there, from father to son.

In the time of Mathurin Regnier, this cabaret was called the *Pot-aux-Roses*, and as the rebus was then in fashion, it had for its sign-board, a post (*poteau*) painted rose-color. In the last century, the worthy

Natoire, one of the fantastic masters nowadays despised by the stiff school, having got drunk many times in this wine-shop at the very table where Regnier had drunk his fill, had painted, by way of gratitude, a bunch of Corinth grapes on the pink post. The keeper of the cabaret, in his joy, had changed his device and had caused to be placed in gilt letters beneath the bunch these words: "At the Bunch of Corinth Grapes" (*"Au Raisin de Corinthe"*). Hence the name of Corinthe. Nothing is more natural to drunken men than ellipses. The ellipsis is the zig-zag of the phrase. Corinthe gradually dethroned the Pot-aux-Roses. The last proprietor of the dynasty, Father Hucheloup, no longer acquainted even with the tradition, had the post painted blue.

A room on the ground floor, where the bar was situated, one on the first floor containing a billiard-table, a wooden spiral staircase piercing the ceiling, wine on the tables, smoke on the walls, candles in broad daylight,—this was the style of this cabaret. A staircase with a trap-door in the lower room led to the cellar. On the second floor were the lodgings of the Hucheloup family. They were reached by a staircase which was a ladder rather than a staircase, and had for their entrance only a private door in the large room on the first floor. Under the roof, in two mansard attics, were the nests for the servants. The kitchen shared the ground floor with the tap-room.

Father Hucheloup had, possibly, been born a chemist, but the fact is that he was a cook; people did not confine themselves to drinking alone in his wine-shop, they also ate there. Hucheloup had invented a capital thing which could be eaten nowhere but in his house, stuffed carps, which he called *carpes au gras*. These were eaten by the light of a tallow candle or of a lamp of the time of Louis XVI, on tables to which were nailed waxed cloths in lieu of table-cloths. People came thither from a distance. Hucheloup, one fine morning, had seen fit to notify passers-by of this "specialty"; he had dipped a brush in a pot of black paint, and as he was an orthographer on his own account, as well as a cook after his own fashion, he had improvised on his wall this remarkable inscription:—

CARPES HO GRAS.

One winter, the rain-storms and the showers had taken a fancy to obliterate the S which terminated the first word, and the G which began the third; this is what remained:—

Time and rain assisting, a humble gastronomical announcement had become a profound piece of advice.

In this way it came about, that though he knew no French, Father Hucheloup understood Latin, that he had evoked philosophy from his kitchen, and that, desirous simply of effacing Lent, he had equalled Horace. And the striking thing about it was, that that also meant: "Enter my wine-shop."

Nothing of all this is in existence now. The Mondétour labyrinth was disembowelled and widely opened in 1847, and probably no longer exists at the present moment. The Rue de la Chanvrerie and Corinthe have disappeared beneath the pavement of the Rue Rambuteau.

As we have already said, Corinthe was the meeting-place if not the rallying-point, of Courfeyrac and his friends. It was Grantaire who had discovered Corinthe. He had entered it on account of the *Carpe horas*, and had returned thither on account of the *Carpes au gras*. There they drank, there they ate, there they shouted; they did not pay much, they paid badly, they did not pay at all, but they were always welcome. Father Hucheloup was a jovial host.

Hucheloup, that amiable man, as was just said, was a wine-shop-keeper with a moustache; an amusing variety. He always had an ill-tempered air, seemed to wish to intimidate his customers, grumbled at the people who entered his establishment, and had rather the mien of seeking a quarrel with them than of serving them with soup. And yet, we insist upon the word, people were always welcome there. This oddity had attracted customers to his shop, and brought him young men, who said to each other: "Come hear Father Hucheloup growl." He had been a fencing-master. All of a sudden, he would burst out laughing. A big voice, a good fellow. He had a comic foundation under a tragic exterior, he asked nothing better than to frighten you, very much like those snuff-boxes which are in the shape of a pistol. The detonation makes one sneeze.

Mother Hucheloup, his wife, was a bearded and a very homely creature.

About 1830, Father Hucheloup died. With him disappeared the secret of stuffed carps. His inconsolable widow continued to keep the wine-shop. But the cooking deteriorated, and became execrable; the wine, which had always been bad, became fearfully bad. Nevertheless, Courfeyrac and his friends continued to go to Corinthe,—out of pity, as Bossuet said.

The Widow Hucheloup was breathless and misshapen and given to rustic recollections. She deprived them of their flatness by her pronunciation. She had a way of her own of saying things, which spiced her reminiscences of the village and of her springtime. It had formerly been her delight, so she affirmed, to hear the *loups-de-gorge* (*rouges-gorges*) *chanter dans les ogrepines* (*aubépines*)—to hear the redbreasts sing in the hawthorn-trees.

The hall on the first floor, where "the restaurant" was situated, was a large and long apartment encumbered with stools, chairs, benches, and tables, and with a crippled, lame, old billiard-table. It was reached by a spiral staircase which terminated in the corner of the room at a square hole like the hatchway of a ship.

This room, lighted by a single narrow window, and by a lamp that was always burning, had the air of a garret. All the four-footed furniture comported itself as though it had but three legs—the whitewashed walls had for their only ornament the following quatrain in honor of Mame Hucheloup:—

> *Elle étonne à dix pas, elle épouvente à deux,*
> *Une verrue habite en son nez hasardeux;*
> *On tremble à chaque instant qu'elle ne vous la mouche*
> *Et qu'un beau jour son nez ne tombe dans sa bouche.*

This was scrawled in charcoal on the wall.

Mame Hucheloup, a good likeness, went and came from morning till night before this quatrain with the most perfect tranquillity. Two serving-maids, named Matelote and Gibelotte, and who had never been known by any other names, helped Mame Hucheloup to set on the tables the jugs of poor wine, and the various broths which were served to the hungry patrons in earthenware bowls. Matelote, large, plump, redhaired, and noisy, the favorite ex-sultana of the defunct Hucheloup, was homelier than any mythological monster, be it what it may; still, as it becomes the servant to always keep in the rear of the mistress, she was less homely than Mame Hucheloup. Gibelotte, tall, delicate, white with a lymphatic pallor, with circles round her eyes, and drooping lids, always languid and weary, afflicted with what may be called chronic lassitude, the first up in the house and the last in bed, waited on every one, even the other maid, silently and gently, smiling through her fatigue with a vague and sleepy smile.

Before entering the restaurant room, the visitor read on the door the following line written there in chalk by Courfeyrac:—

Régale si tu peux et mange si tu l'oses.

II

Preliminary Gayeties

Laigle de Meaux, as the reader knows, lived more with Joly than elsewhere. He had a lodging, as a bird has one on a branch. The two friends lived together, ate together, slept together. They had everything in common, even Musichetta, to some extent. They were, what the subordinate monks who accompany monks are called, *bini*. On the morning of the 5th of June, they went to Corinthe to breakfast. Joly, who was all stuffed up, had a catarrh which Laigle was beginning to share. Laigle's coat was threadbare, but Joly was well dressed.

It was about nine o'clock in the morning, when they opened the door of Corinthe.

They ascended to the first floor.

Matelote and Gibelotte received them.

"Oysters, cheese, and ham," said Laigle.

And they seated themselves at a table.

The wine-shop was empty; there was no one there but themselves.

Gibelotte, knowing Joly and Laigle, set a bottle of wine on the table.

While they were busy with their first oysters, a head appeared at the hatchway of the staircase, and a voice said:—

"I am passing by. I smell from the street a delicious odor of Brie cheese. I enter." It was Grantaire.

Grantaire took a stool and drew up to the table.

At the sight of Grantaire, Gibelotte placed two bottles of wine on the table.

That made three.

"Are you going to drink those two bottles?" Laigle inquired of Grantaire.

Grantaire replied:—

"All are ingenious, thou alone art ingenuous. Two bottles never yet astonished a man."

The others had begun by eating, Grantaire began by drinking. Half a bottle was rapidly gulped down.

"So you have a hole in your stomach?" began Laigle again.

"You have one in your elbow," said Grantaire.

And after having emptied his glass, he added:—

"Ah, by the way, Laigle of the funeral oration, your coat is old."

"I should hope so," retorted Laigle. "That's why we get on well together, my coat and I. It has acquired all my folds, it does not bind me anywhere, it is moulded on my deformities, it falls in with all my movements, I am only conscious of it because it keeps me warm. Old coats are just like old friends."

"That's true," ejaculated Joly, striking into the dialogue, "an old goat is an old abi" (*ami*, friend).

"Especially in the mouth of a man whose head is stuffed up," said Grantaire.

"Grantaire," demanded Laigle, "have you just come from the boulevard?"

"No."

"We have just seen the head of the procession pass, Joly and I."

"It's a marvellous sight," said Joly.

"How quiet this street is!" exclaimed Laigle. "Who would suspect that Paris was turned upside down? How plainly it is to be seen that in former days there were nothing but convents here! In this neighborhood! Du Breul and Sauval give a list of them, and so does the Abbé Lebeuf. They were all round here, they fairly swarmed, booted and barefooted, shaven, bearded, gray, black, white, Franciscans, Minims, Capuchins, Carmelites, Little Augustines, Great Augustines, old Augustines—there was no end of them."

"Don't let's talk of monks," interrupted Grantaire, "it makes one want to scratch one's self."

Then he exclaimed:—

"Bouh! I've just swallowed a bad oyster. Now hypochondria is taking possession of me again. The oysters are spoiled, the servants are ugly. I hate the human race. I just passed through the Rue Richelieu, in front of the big public library. That pile of oyster-shells which is called a library is disgusting even to think of. What paper! What ink! What scrawling! And all that has been written! What rascal was it who said that man was a featherless biped? And then, I met a pretty girl of my acquaintance, who is as beautiful as the spring, worthy to be called Floréal, and who is delighted, enraptured, as happy as the angels, because a wretch yesterday, a frightful banker all spotted with small-pox, deigned to take a fancy to her! Alas! woman keeps on the watch for a protector as much as for a lover; cats chase mice as well as birds. Two months ago that young woman was virtuous in an attic, she adjusted little brass rings in the eyelet-holes of corsets, what do you call it? She sewed, she had a camp bed, she dwelt beside a pot of flowers, she was contented. Now here she is a bankeress. This transformation took place last night. I met the victim this morning in high spirits. The hideous point about it is, that the jade is as pretty to-day as she was yesterday. Her financier did not show in her face. Roses have this advantage or disadvantage over women, that the traces left upon them by caterpillars are visible. Ah! there is no morality on earth. I call to witness the myrtle, the symbol of love, the laurel, the symbol of air, the olive, that ninny, the symbol of peace, the apple-tree which came nearest rangling Adam with its pips, and the fig-tree, the grandfather of petticoats. As for right, do you know what right is? The Gauls covet Clusium, Rome protects Clusium, and demands what wrong Clusium has done to them. Brennus answers: 'The wrong that Alba did to you, the wrong that Fidenæ did to you, the wrong that the Eques, the Volsci, and the Sabines have done to you. They were your neighbors. The Clusians are ours. We understand neighborliness just as you do. You have stolen Alba, we shall take Clusium.' Rome said: 'You shall not take Clusium.' Brennus took Rome. Then he cried: 'Væ victis!' That is what right is. Ah! what beasts of prey there are in this world! What eagles! It makes my flesh creep."

He held out his glass to Joly, who filled it, then he drank and went on, having hardly been interrupted by this glass of wine, of which no one, not even himself, had taken any notice:—

"Brennus, who takes Rome, is an eagle; the banker who takes the grisette is an eagle. There is no more modesty in the one case than in the other. So we believe in nothing. There is but one reality: drink. Whatever your opinion may be in favor of the lean cock, like the Canton of Uri, or in favor of the fat cock, like the Canton of Glaris, it matters little, drink. You talk to me of the boulevard, of that procession, *et cætera, et cætera*. Come now, is there going to be another revolution? This poverty of means on the part of the good God astounds me. He has to keep greasing the groove of events every moment. There is a hitch, it won't work. Quick, a revolution! The good God has his hands perpetually black with that cart-grease. If I were in his place, I'd be perfectly simple about it, I would not wind up my mechanism every minute, I'd lead the human race in a straightforward way, I'd weave matters mesh by mesh, without breaking the thread, I would have no provisional arrangements, I would have no extraordinary repertory.

What the rest of you call progress advances by means of two motors, men and events. But, sad to say, from time to time, the exceptional becomes necessary. The ordinary troupe suffices neither for event nor for men: among men geniuses are required, among events revolutions. Great accidents are the law; the order of things cannot do without them; and, judging from the apparition of comets, one would be tempted to think that Heaven itself finds actors needed for its performance. At the moment when one expects it the least, God placards a meteor on the wall of the firmament. Some queer star turns up, underlined by an enormous tail. And that causes the death of Cæsar. Brutus deals him a blow with a knife, and God a blow with a comet. *Crac*, and behold an aurora borealis, behold a revolution, behold a great man; '93 in big letters, Napoleon on guard, the comet of 1811 at the head of the poster. Ah! what a beautiful blue theatre all studded with unexpected flashes! Boum! Boum! extraordinary show! Raise your eyes, boobies. Everything is in disorder, the star as well as the drama. Good God, it is too much and not enough. These resources, gathered from exception, seem magnificence and poverty. My friends, Providence has come down to expedients. What does a revolution prove? That God is in a quandry. He effects a *coup d'état* because he, God, has not been able to make both ends meet. In fact, this confirms me in my conjectures as to Jehovah's fortune; and when I see so much distress in heaven and on earth, from the bird who has not a grain of millet to myself without a hundred thousand livres of income, when I see human destiny, which is very badly worn, and even royal destiny, which is threadbare, witness the Prince de Condé hung, when I see winter, which is nothing but a rent in the zenith through which the wind blows, when I see so many rags even in the perfectly new purple of the morning on the crests of hills, when I see the drops of dew, those mock pearls, when I see the frost, that paste, when I see humanity ripped apart and events patched up, and so many spots on the sun and so many holes in the moon, when I see so much misery everywhere, I suspect that God is not rich. The appearance exists, it is true, but I feel that he is hard up. He gives a revolution as a tradesman whose money-box is empty gives a ball. God must not be judged from appearances. Beneath the gilding of heaven I perceive a poverty-stricken universe. Creation is bankrupt. That is why I am discontented. Here it is the 4th of June, it is almost night; ever since this morning I have been waiting for daylight to come; it has not come, and I bet that it won't come all day. This is the inexactness of an ill-paid clerk. Yes, everything is badly arranged, nothing fits anything else, this old world is all warped, I take my stand on the opposition, everything goes awry; the universe is a tease. It's like children, those who want them have none, and those who don't want them have them. Total: I'm vexed. Besides, Laigle de Meaux, that bald-head, offends my sight. It humiliates me to think that I am of the same age as that baldy. However, I criticise, but I do not insult. The universe is what it is. I speak here without evil intent and to ease my conscience. Receive, Eternal Father, the assurance of my distinguished consideration. Ah! by all the saints of Olympus and by all the gods of paradise, I was not intended to be a Parisian, that is to say, to rebound forever, like a shuttlecock between two battledores, from the group of the loungers to the group of the roysterers. I was made to be a Turk, watching oriental houris all day long, executing those exquisite Egyptian dances, as sensuous as the dream of a chaste man, or a Beauceron peasant, or a Venetian gentleman surrounded by gentlewoman, or a petty German prince, furnishing the half of a foot-soldier to the Germanic confederation, and occupying his leisure with drying his breeches on his hedge, that is to say, his frontier. Those are the positions for which I was born! Yes, I have said a Turk, and I will not retract. I do not understand how people can habitually take Turks in bad part; Mohammed had his good points; respect for the inventor of seraglios with houris and paradises with odalisques! Let us not insult Mohammedanism, the only religion which is ornamented with a hen-roost! Now, I insist on a drink. The earth is a great piece of stupidity. And it appears that they are going to fight, all those imbeciles, and to break each other's profiles and to massacre each other in the heart of summer, in the month of June, when they might go off with a creature on their arm, to breathe the immense heaps of new-mown hay in the meadows! Really, people do commit altogether too many follies. An old broken lantern which I have just seen at a bric-à-brac merchant's suggests a reflection to my mind; it is time to enlighten the human race. Yes, behold me sad again. That's what comes of swallowing an oyster and a revolution the wrong way! I am growing melancholy once more. Oh! frightful old world. People strive, turn each other out, prostitute themselves, kill each other, and get used to it!"

And Grantaire, after this fit of eloquence, had a fit of coughing, which was well earned.

"À propos of revolution," said Joly, "it is decidedly abberent that Barius is in lub."

"Does any one know with whom?" demanded Laigle.

"Do."

"No?"

"Do! I tell you."

"Marius' love affairs!" exclaimed Grantaire. "I can imagine it. Marius is a fog, and he must have found a vapor. Marius is of the race of poets. He who says poet, says fool, madman, *Tymbræus Apollo*. Marius and his Marie, or his Marion, or his Maria, or his Mariette. They must make a queer pair of lovers. I know just what it is like. Ecstasies in which they forget to kiss. Pure on earth, but joined in heaven. They are souls possessed of senses. They lie among the stars."

Grantaire was attacking his second bottle and, possibly, his second harangue, when a new personage emerged from the square aperture of the stairs. It was a boy less than ten years of age, ragged, very small, yellow, with an odd phiz, a vivacious eye, an enormous amount of hair drenched with rain, and wearing a contented air.

The child unhesitatingly making his choice among the three, addressed himself to Laigle de Meaux.

"Are you Monsieur Bossuet?"

"That is my nickname," replied Laigle. "What do you want with me?"

"This. A tall blonde fellow on the boulevard said to me: 'Do you know Mother Hucheloup?' I said: 'Yes, Rue Chanvrerie, the old man's widow;' he said to me: 'Go there. There you will find M. Bossuet. Tell him from me: "A B C".' It's a joke that they're playing on you, isn't it. He gave me ten sous."

"Joly, lend me ten sous," said Laigle; and, turning to Grantaire: "Grantaire, lend me ten sous."

This made twenty sous, which Laigle handed to the lad.

"Thank you, sir," said the urchin.

"What is your name?" inquired Laigle.

"Navet, Gavroche's friend."

"Stay with us," said Laigle.

"Breakfast with us," said Grantaire.

The child replied:—

"I can't, I belong in the procession, I'm the one to shout 'Down with Polignac!'"

And executing a prolonged scrape of his foot behind him, which is the most respectful of all possible salutes, he took his departure.

The child gone, Grantaire took the word:—

"That is the pure-bred gamin. There are a great many varieties of the gamin species. The notary's gamin is called Skip-the-Gutter, the cook's gamin is called a scullion, the baker's gamin is called a *mitron*, the lackey's gamin is called a groom, the marine gamin is called the cabin-boy, the soldier's gamin is called the drummer-boy, the painter's gamin is called paint-grinder, the tradesman's gamin is called an errand-boy, the courtesan gamin is called the minion, the kingly gamin is called the dauphin, the god gamin is called the bambino."

In the meantime, Laigle was engaged in reflection; he said half aloud:—

"A B C, that is to say: the burial of Lamarque."

"The tall blonde," remarked Grantaire, "is Enjolras, who is sending you a warning."

"Shall we go?" ejaculated Bossuet.

"It's raiding," said Joly. "I have sworn to go through fire, but not through water. I don't wand to ged a gold."

"I shall stay here," said Grantaire. "I prefer a breakfast to a hearse."

"Conclusion: we remain," said Laigle. "Well, then, let us drink. Besides, we might miss the funeral without missing the riot."

"Ah! the riot, I am with you!" cried Joly.

Laigle rubbed his hands.

"Now we're going to touch up the revolution of 1830. As a matter of fact, it does hurt the people along the seams."

"I don't think much of your revolution," said Grantaire. "I don't execrate this Government. It is the crown tempered by the cotton night-cap. It is a sceptre ending in an umbrella. In fact, I think that to-day, with the present weather, Louis Philippe might utilize his royalty in two directions, he might extend the tip of the sceptre end against the people, and open the umbrella end against heaven."

The room was dark, large clouds had just finished the extinction of daylight. There was no one in the wine-shop, or in the street, every one having gone off "to watch events."

"Is it midday or midnight?" cried Bossuet. "You can't see your hand before your face. Gibelotte, fetch a light."

Grantaire was drinking in a melancholy way.

"Enjolras disdains me," he muttered. "Enjolras said: 'Joly is ill, Grantaire is drunk.' It was to Bossuet that he sent Navet. If he had come for me, I would have followed him. So much the worse for Enjolras! I won't go to his funeral."

This resolution once arrived at, Bossuet, Joly, and Grantaire did not stir from the wine-shop. By two o'clock in the afternoon, the table at which they sat was covered with empty bottles. Two candles were burning on it, one in a flat copper candlestick which was perfectly green, the other in the neck of a cracked carafe. Grantaire had seduced Joly and Bossuet to wine; Bossuet and Joly had conducted Grantaire back towards cheerfulness.

As for Grantaire, he had got beyond wine, that merely moderate inspirer of dreams, ever since midday. Wine enjoys only a conventional popularity with serious drinkers. There is, in fact, in the matter of inebriety, white magic and black magic; wine is only white magic. Grantaire was a daring drinker of dreams. The blackness of a terrible fit of drunkenness yawning before him, far from arresting him, attracted him. He had abandoned the bottle and taken to the beerglass. The beer-glass is the abyss. Having neither opium nor hashish on hand, and being desirous of filling his brain with twilight, he had had recourse to that fearful mixture of brandy, stout, absinthe, which produces the most terrible of lethargies. It is of these three vapors, beer, brandy, and absinthe, that the lead of the soul is composed. They are three grooms; the celestial butterfly is drowned in them; and there are formed there in a membranous smoke, vaguely condensed into the wing of the bat, three mute furies, Nightmare, Night, and Death, which hover about the slumbering Psyche.

Grantaire had not yet reached that lamentable phase; far from it. He was tremendously gay, and Bossuet and Joly retorted. They clinked glasses. Grantaire added to the eccentric accentuation of words and ideas, a peculiarity of gesture; he rested his left fist on his knee with dignity, his arm forming a right angle, and, with cravat untied, seated astride a stool, his full glass in his right hand, he hurled solemn words at the big maid-servant Matelote:—

"Let the doors of the palace be thrown open! Let every one be a member of the French Academy and have the right to embrace Madame Hucheloup. Let us drink."

And turning to Madame Hucheloup, he added:—

"Woman ancient and consecrated by use, draw near that I may contemplate thee!"

And Joly exclaimed:—

"Matelote and Gibelotte, dod't gib Grantaire anything more to drink. He has already devoured, since this bording, in wild prodigality, two francs and ninety-five centibes."

And Grantaire began again:—

"Who has been unhooking the stars without my permission, and putting them on the table in the guise of candles?"

Bossuet, though very drunk, preserved his equanimity.

He was seated on the sill of the open window, wetting his back in the falling rain, and gazing at his two friends.

All at once, he heard a tumult behind him, hurried footsteps, cries of "To arms!" He turned round and saw in the Rue Saint-Denis, at the end of the Rue de la Chanvrerie, Enjolras passing, gun in hand, and Gavroche with his pistol, Feuilly with his sword, Courfeyrac with his sword, and Jean Prouvaire with his blunderbuss, Combeferre with his gun, Bahorel with his gun, and the whole armed and stormy rabble which was following them.

The Rue de la Chanvrerie was not more than a gunshot long. Bossuet improvised a speaking-trumpet from his two hands placed around his mouth, and shouted:—

"Courfeyrac! Courfeyrac! Hohée!"

Courfeyrac heard the shout, caught sight of Bossuet, and advanced a few paces into the Rue de la Chanvrerie, shouting: "What do you want?" which crossed a "Where are you going?"

"To make a barricade," replied Courfeyrac.

"Well, here! This is a good place! Make it here!"

"That's true, Aigle," said Courfeyrac.

And at a signal from Courfeyrac, the mob flung themselves into the Rue de la Chanvrerie.

III

Night Begins to Descend Upon Grantaire

The spot was, in fact, admirably adapted, the entrance to the street widened out, the other extremity narrowed together into a pocket without exit. Corinthe created an obstacle, the Rue Mondétour was easily barricaded on the right and the left, no attack was possible except from the Rue Saint-Denis, that is to say, in front, and in full sight. Bossuet had the comprehensive glance of a fasting Hannibal.

Terror had seized on the whole street at the irruption of the mob. There was not a passer-by who did not get out of sight. In the space of a flash of lightning, in the rear, to right and left, shops, stables, area-doors, windows, blinds, attic skylights, shutters of every description were closed, from the ground floor to the roof. A terrified old woman fixed a mattress in front of her window on two clothes-poles for drying linen, in order to deaden the effect of musketry. The wine-shop alone remained open; and that for a very good reason, that the mob had rushed into it.—"Ah my God! Ah my God!" sighed Mame Hucheloup.

Bossuet had gone down to meet Courfeyrac.

Joly, who had placed himself at the window, exclaimed:—

"Courfeyrac, you ought to have brought an umbrella. You will gatch gold."

In the meantime, in the space of a few minutes, twenty iron bars had been wrenched from the grated front of the wine-shop, ten fathoms of street had been unpaved; Gavroche and Bahorel had seized in its passage, and overturned, the dray of a lime-dealer named Anceau; this dray contained three barrels of lime, which they placed beneath the piles of paving-stones: Enjolras raised the cellar trap, and all the widow Hucheloup's empty casks were used to flank the barrels of lime; Feuilly, with his fingers skilled in painting the delicate sticks of fans, had backed up the barrels and the dray with two massive heaps of blocks of rough stone. Blocks which were improvised like the rest and procured no one knows where. The beams which served as props were torn from the neighboring house-fronts and laid on the casks. When

Bossuet and Courfeyrac turned round, half the street was already barred with a rampart higher than a man. There is nothing like the hand of the populace for building everything that is built by demolishing.

Matelote and Gibelotte had mingled with the workers. Gibelotte went and came loaded with rubbish. Her lassitude helped on the barricade. She served the barricade as she would have served wine, with a sleepy air.

An omnibus with two white horses passed the end of the street.

Bossuet strode over the paving-stones, ran to it, stopped the driver, made the passengers alight, offered his hand to "the ladies," dismissed the conductor, and returned, leading the vehicle and the horses by the bridle.

"Omnibuses," said he, "do not pass the Corinthe. *Non licet omnibus adire Corinthum.*"

An instant later, the horses were unharnessed and went off at their will, through the Rue Mondétour, and the omnibus lying on its side completed the bar across the street.

Mame Hucheloup, quite upset, had taken refuge in the first story.

Her eyes were vague, and stared without seeing anything, and she cried in a low tone. Her terrified shrieks did not dare to emerge from her throat.

"The end of the world has come," she muttered.

Joly deposited a kiss on Mame Hucheloup's fat, red, wrinkled neck, and said to Grantaire: "My dear fellow, I have always regarded a woman's neck as an infinitely delicate thing."

But Grantaire attained to the highest regions of dithryamb. Matelote had mounted to the first floor once more, Grantaire seized her round her waist, and gave vent to long bursts of laughter at the window.

"Matelote is homely!" he cried: "Matelote is of a dream of ugliness! Matelote is a chimæra. This is the secret of her birth: a Gothic Pygmalion, who was making gargoyles for cathedrals, fell in love with one of them, the most horrible, one fine morning. He besought Love to give it life, and this produced Matelote. Look at her, citizens! She has chromate-of-lead-colored hair, like Titian's mistress, and she is a good girl. I guarantee that she will fight well. Every good girl contains a hero. As for Mother Hucheloup, she's an old warrior. Look at her moustaches! She inherited them from her husband. A hussar indeed! She will fight too. These two alone will strike terror to the heart of the banlieue. Comrades, we shall overthrow the government as true as there are fifteen intermediary acids between margaric acid and formic acid; however, that is a matter of perfect indifference to me. Gentlemen, my father always detested me because I could not understand mathematics. I understand only love and liberty. I am Grantaire, the good fellow. Having never had any money, I never acquired the habit of it, and the result is that I have never lacked it; but, if I had been rich, there would have been no more poor people! You would have seen! Oh, if the kind hearts only had fat purses, how much better things would go! I picture myself Jesus Christ with Rothschild's fortune! How much good he would do! Matelote, embrace me! You are voluptuous and timid! You have cheeks which invite the kiss of a sister, and lips which claim the kiss of a lover."

"Hold your tongue, you cask!" said Courfeyrac.

Grantaire retorted:—

"I am the capitoul and the master of the floral games!"

Enjolras, who was standing on the crest of the barricade, gun in hand, raised his beautiful, austere face. Enjolras, as the reader knows, had something of the Spartan and of the Puritan in his composition. He would have perished at Thermopylæ with Leonidas, and burned at Drogheda with Cromwell.

"Grantaire," he shouted, "go get rid of the fumes of your wine somewhere else than here. This is the place for enthusiasm, not for drunkenness. Don't disgrace the barricade!"

This angry speech produced a singular effect on Grantaire. One would have said that he had had a glass of cold water flung in his face. He seemed to be rendered suddenly sober.

He sat down, put his elbows on a table near the window, looked at Enjolras with indescribable gentleness, and said to him:—

"Let me sleep here."

"Go and sleep somewhere else," cried Enjolras.

But Grantaire, still keeping his tender and troubled eyes fixed on him, replied:—

"Let me sleep here,—until I die."

Enjolras regarded him with disdainful eyes:—

"Grantaire, you are incapable of believing, of thinking, of willing, of living, and of dying."

Grantaire replied in a grave tone:—

"You will see."

He stammered a few more unintelligible words, then his head fell heavily on the table, and, as is the usual effect of the second period of inebriety, into which Enjolras had roughly and abruptly thrust him, an instant later he had fallen asleep.

IV

An Attempt to Console the Widow Hucheloup

Bahorel, in ecstasies over the barricade, shouted:—

"Here's the street in its low-necked dress! How well it looks!"

Courfeyrac, as he demolished the wine-shop to some extent, sought to console the widowed proprietress.

"Mother Hucheloup, weren't you complaining the other day because you had had a notice served on you for infringing the law, because Gibelotte shook a counterpane out of your window?"

"Yes, my good Monsieur Courfeyrac. Ah! good Heavens, are you going to put that table of mine in your horror, too? And it was for the counterpane, and also for a pot of flowers which fell from the attic window into the street, that the government collected a fine of a hundred francs. If that isn't an abomination, what is!"

"Well, Mother Hucheloup, we are avenging you."

Mother Hucheloup did not appear to understand very clearly the benefit which she was to derive from these reprisals made on her account. She was satisfied after the manner of that Arab woman, who, having received a box on the ear from her husband, went to complain to her father, and cried for vengeance, saying: "Father, you owe my husband affront for affront." The father asked: "On which cheek did you receive the blow?" "On the left cheek." The father slapped her right cheek and said: "Now you are satisfied. Go tell your husband that he boxed my daughter's ears, and that I have accordingly boxed his wife's."

The rain had ceased. Recruits had arrived. Workmen had brought under their blouses a barrel of powder, a basket containing bottles of vitriol, two or three carnival torches, and a basket filled with fire-pots, "left over from the King's festival." This festival was very recent, having taken place on the 1st of May. It was said that these munitions came from a grocer in the Faubourg Saint-Antoine named Pépin. They smashed the only street lantern in the Rue de la Chanvrerie, the lantern corresponding to one in the Rue Saint-Denis, and all the lanterns in the surrounding streets, de Mondétour, du Cygne, des Prêcheurs, and de la Grande and de la Petite-Truanderie.

Enjolras, Combeferre, and Courfeyrac directed everything. Two barricades were now in process of construction at once, both of them resting on the Corinthe house and forming a right angle; the larger shut off the Rue de la Chanvrerie, the other closed the Rue Mondétour, on the side of the Rue de Cygne. This last barricade, which was very narrow, was constructed only of casks and paving-stones. There were about fifty workers on it; thirty were armed with guns; for, on their way, they had effected a wholesale loan from an armorer's shop.

Nothing could be more bizarre and at the same time more motley than this troop. One had a round-jacket, a cavalry sabre, and two holster-pistols, another was in his shirt-sleeves, with a round hat, and a powder-horn slung at his side, a third wore a plastron of nine sheets of gray paper and was armed with a saddler's awl. There was one who was shouting: "Let us exterminate them to the last man and die at the point of our bayonet." This man had no bayonet. Another spread out over his coat the cross-belt and cartridge-box of a National Guardsman, the cover of the cartridge-box being ornamented with this inscription in red worsted: *Public Order*. There were a great many guns bearing the numbers of the legions, few hats, no cravats, many bare arms, some pikes. Add to this, all ages, all sorts of faces, small, pale young men, and bronzed longshoremen. All were in haste; and as they helped each other, they discussed the possible chances. That they would receive succor about three o'clock in the morning—that they were sure of one regiment, that Paris would rise. Terrible sayings with which was mingled a sort of cordial joviality. One would have pronounced them brothers, but they did not know each other's names. Great perils have this fine characteristic, that they bring to light the fraternity of strangers. A fire had been lighted in the kitchen, and there they were engaged in moulding into bullets, pewter mugs, spoons, forks, and all the brass table-ware of the establishment. In the midst of it all, they drank. Caps and buckshot were mixed pell-mell on the tables with glasses of wine. In the billiard-hall, Mame Hucheloup, Matelote, and Gibelotte, variously modified by terror, which had stupefied one, rendered another breathless, and roused the third, were tearing up old dish-cloths and making lint; three insurgents were assisting them, three bushy-haired, jolly blades with beards and moustaches, who plucked away at the linen with the fingers of seamstresses and who made them tremble.

The man of lofty stature whom Courfeyrac, Combeferre, and Enjolras had observed at the moment when he joined the mob at the corner of the Rue des Billettes, was at work on the smaller barricade and was making himself useful there. Gavroche was working on the larger one. As for the young man who had been waiting for Courfeyrac at his lodgings, and who had inquired for M. Marius, he had disappeared at about the time when the omnibus had been overturned.

Gavroche, completely carried away and radiant, had undertaken to get everything in readiness. He went, came, mounted, descended, re-mounted, whistled, and sparkled. He seemed to be there for the encouragement of all. Had he any incentive? Yes, certainly, his poverty; had he wings? yes, certainly, his joy. Gavroche was a whirlwind. He was constantly visible, he was incessantly audible. He filled the air, as he was everywhere at once. He was a sort of almost irritating ubiquity; no halt was possible with him. The enormous barricade felt him on its haunches. He troubled the loungers, he excited the idle, he reanimated the weary, he grew impatient over the thoughtful, he inspired gayety in some, and breath in others, wrath in others, movement in all, now pricking a student, now biting an artisan; he alighted, paused, flew off again, hovered over the tumult, and the effort, sprang from one party to another, murmuring and humming, and harassed the whole company; a fly on the immense revolutionary coach.

Perpetual motion was in his little arms and perpetual clamor in his little lungs.

"Courage! more paving-stones! more casks! more machines! Where are you now? A hod of plaster for me to stop this hole with! Your barricade is very small. It must be carried up. Put everything on it, fling everything there, stick it all in. Break down the house. A barricade is Mother Gibou's tea. Hullo, here's a glass door."

This elicited an exclamation from the workers.

"A glass door? what do you expect us to do with a glass door, tubercle?"

"Hercules yourselves!" retorted Gavroche. "A glass door is an excellent thing in a barricade. It does not prevent an attack, but it prevents the enemy taking it. So you've never prigged apples over a wall where there were broken bottles? A glass door cuts the corns of the National Guard when they try to mount on the barricade. Pardi! glass is a treacherous thing. Well, you haven't a very wildly lively imagination, comrades."

However, he was furious over his triggerless pistol. He went from one to another, demanding: "A gun, I want a gun! Why don't you give me a gun?"

"Give you a gun!" said Combeferre.

"Come now!" said Gavroche, "why not? I had one in 1830 when we had a dispute with Charles X."

Enjolras shrugged his shoulders.

"When there are enough for the men, we will give some to the children."

Gavroche wheeled round haughtily, and answered:—

"If you are killed before me, I shall take yours."

"Gamin!" said Enjolras.

"Greenhorn!" said Gavroche.

A dandy who had lost his way and who lounged past the end of the street created a diversion! Gavroche shouted to him:—

"Come with us, young fellow! well now, don't we do anything for this old country of ours?"

The dandy fled.

V

Preparations

The journals of the day which said that that *nearly impregnable structure*, of the barricade of the Rue de la Chanvrerie, as they call it, reached to the level of the first floor, were mistaken. The fact is, that it did not exceed an average height of six or seven feet. It was built in such a manner that the combatants could, at their will, either disappear behind it or dominate the barrier and even scale its crest by means of a quadruple row of paving-stones placed on top of each other and arranged as steps in the interior. On the outside, the front of the barricade, composed of piles of paving-stones and casks bound together by beams and planks, which were entangled in the wheels of Anceau's dray and of the overturned omnibus, had a bristling and inextricable aspect.

An aperture large enough to allow a man to pass through had been made between the wall of the houses and the extremity of the barricade which was furthest from the wine-shop, so that an exit was possible at this point. The pole of the omnibus was placed upright and held up with ropes, and a red flag, fastened to this pole, floated over the barricade.

The little Mondétour barricade, hidden behind the wine-shop building, was not visible. The two barricades united formed a veritable redoubt. Enjolras and Courfeyrac had not thought fit to barricade the other fragment of the Rue Mondétour which opens through the Rue des Prêcheurs an issue into the Halles, wishing, no doubt, to preserve a possible communication with the outside, and not entertaining much fear of an attack through the dangerous and difficult street of the Rue des Prêcheurs.

With the exception of this issue which was left free, and which constituted what Folard in his strategical style would have termed a branch and taking into account, also, the narrow cutting arranged on the Rue de la Chanvrerie, the interior of the barricade, where the wine-shop formed a salient angle, presented an irregular square, closed on all sides. There existed an interval of twenty paces between the grand barrier and the lofty houses which formed the background of the street, so that one might say that the barricade rested on these houses, all inhabited, but closed from top to bottom.

All this work was performed without any hindrance, in less than an hour, and without this handful of bold men seeing a single bear-skin cap or a single bayonet make their appearance. The very bourgeois who still ventured at this hour of riot to enter the Rue Saint-Denis cast a glance at the Rue de la Chanvrerie, caught sight of the barricade, and redoubled their pace.

The two barricades being finished, and the flag run up, a table was dragged out of the wine-shop; and Courfeyrac mounted on the table. Enjolras brought the square coffer, and Courfeyrac opened it. This coffer was filled with cartridges. When the mob saw the cartridges, a tremor ran through the bravest, and a momentary silence ensued.

Courfeyrac distributed them with a smile.

Each one received thirty cartridges. Many had powder, and set about making others with the bullets which they had run. As for the barrel of powder, it stood on a table on one side, near the door, and was held in reserve.

The alarm beat which ran through all Paris, did not cease, but it had finally come to be nothing more than a monotonous noise to which they no longer paid any attention. This noise retreated at times, and again drew near, with melancholy undulations.

They loaded the guns and carbines, all together, without haste, with solemn gravity. Enjolras went and stationed three sentinels outside the barricades, one in the Rue de la Chanvrerie, the second in the Rue des Prêcheurs, the third at the corner of the Rue de la Petite Truanderie.

Then, the barricades having been built, the posts assigned, the guns loaded, the sentinels stationed, they waited, alone in those redoubtable streets through which no one passed any longer, surrounded by those dumb houses which seemed dead and in which no human movement palpitated, enveloped in the deepening shades of twilight which was drawing on, in the midst of that silence through which something could be felt advancing, and which had about it something tragic and terrifying, isolated, armed, determined, and tranquil.

VI

WAITING

During those hours of waiting, what did they do?

We must needs tell, since this is a matter of history.

While the men made bullets and the women lint, while a large saucepan of melted brass and lead, destined to the bullet-mould smoked over a glowing brazier, while the sentinels watched, weapon in hand, on the barricade, while Enjolras, whom it was impossible to divert, kept an eye on the sentinels, Combeferre, Courfeyrac, Jean Prouvaire, Feuilly, Bossuet, Joly, Bahorel, and some others, sought each other out and united as in the most peaceful days of their conversations in their student life, and, in one corner of this wine-shop which had been converted into a casement, a couple of paces distant from the redoubt which they had built, with their carbines loaded and primed resting against the backs of their chairs, these fine young fellows, so close to a supreme hour, began to recite love verses.

What verses? These:—

> *Vous rappelez-vous notre douce vie,*
> *Lorsque nous étions si jeunes tous deux,*
> *Et que nous n'avions au cœur d'autre envie*
> *Que d'être bien mis et d'être amoureux,*
>
> *Lorsqu'en ajoutant votre âge à mon âge,*
> *Nous ne comptions pas à deux quarante ans,*
> *Et que, dans notre humble et petit ménage,*
> *Tout, même l'hiver, nous était printemps?*
>
> *Beaux jours! Manuel était fier et sage,*
> *Paris s'asseyait à de saints banquets,*
> *Foy lançait la foudre, et votre corsage*
> *Avait une épingle où je me piquais.*
>
> *Tout vous contemplait. Avocat sans causes,*
> *Quand je vous menais au Prado dîner,*

VICTOR HUGO

Vous étiez jolie au point que les roses
Me faisaient l'effet de se retourner.

Je les entendais dire: Est elle belle!
Comme elle sent bon! Quels cheveux à flots!
Sous son mantelet elle cache une aile,
Son bonnet charmant est à peine éclos.

J'errais avec toi, pressant ton bras souple.
Les passants croyaient que l'amour charmé
Avait marié, dans notre heureux couple,
Le doux mois d'avril au beau mois de mai.

Nous vivions cachés, contents, porte close,
Dévorant l'amour, bon fruit défendu,
Ma bouche n'avait pas dit une chose
Que déjà ton cœur avait répondu.

La Sorbonne était l'endroit bucolique
Où je t'adorais du soir au matin.
C'est ainsi qu'une âme amoureuse applique
La carte du Tendre au pays Latin.

O place Maubert! O place Dauphine!
Quand, dans le taudis frais et printanier,
Tu tirais ton bas sur ta jambe fine,
Je voyais un astre au fond du grenier.

J'ai fort lu Platon, mais rien ne m'en reste;
Mieux que Malebranche et que Lamennais,
Tu me démontrais la bonté céleste
Avec une fleur que tu me donnais.

Je t'obéissais, tu m'étais soumise;
O grenier doré! te lacer! te voir
Aller et venir dès l'aube en chemise,
Mirant ton jeune front à ton vieux miroir.

Et qui donc pourrait perdre la mémoire
De ces temps d'aurore et de firmament,
De rubans, de fleurs, de gaze et de moire,
Où l'amour bégaye un argot charmant?

Nos jardins étaient un pot de tulipe;
Tu masquais la vitre avec un jupon;
Je prenais le bol de terre de pipe,
Et je te donnais le tasse en japon.

Et ces grands malheurs qui nous faisaient rire!
Ton manchon brûlé, ton boa perdu!
Et ce cher portrait du divin Shakespeare
Qu'un soir pour souper nons avons vendu!

J'étais mendiant et toi charitable.
Je baisais au vol tes bras frais et ronds.
Dante in folio nous servait de table
Pour manger gaîment un cent de marrons.

La première fois qu'en mon joyeux bouge
Je pris un baiser à ta lèvre en feu,
Quand tu t'en allais décoiffée et rouge,
Je restai tout pâle et je crus en Dieu!

Te rappelles-tu nos bonheurs sans nombre,
Et tous ces fichus changés en chiffons?
Oh que de soupirs, de nos cœurs pleins d'ombre,
Se sont envolés dans les cieux profonds!

The hour, the spot, these souvenirs of youth recalled, a few stars which began to twinkle in the sky, the funeral repose of those deserted streets, the imminence of the inexorable adventure, which was in preparation, gave a pathetic charm to these verses murmured in a low tone in the dusk by Jean Prouvaire, who, as we have said, was a gentle poet.

In the meantime, a lamp had been lighted in the small barricade, and in the large one, one of those wax torches such as are to be met with on Shrove-Tuesday in front of vehicles loaded with masks, on their way to la Courtille. These torches, as the reader has seen, came from the Faubourg Saint-Antoine.

The torch had been placed in a sort of cage of paving-stones closed on three sides to shelter it from the wind, and disposed in such a fashion that all the light fell on the flag. The street and the barricade remained sunk in gloom, and nothing was to be seen except the red flag formidably illuminated as by an enormous dark-lantern.

This light enhanced the scarlet of the flag, with an indescribable and terrible purple.

VII

THE MAN RECRUITED IN THE RUE DES BILLETTES

Night was fully come, nothing made its appearance. All that they heard was confused noises, and at intervals, fusillades; but these were rare, badly sustained and distant. This respite, which was thus prolonged, was a sign that the Government was taking its time, and collecting its forces. These fifty men were waiting for sixty thousand.

Enjolras felt attacked by that impatience which seizes on strong souls on the threshold of redoubtable events. He went in search of Gavroche, who had set to making cartridges in the tap-room, by the dubious light of two candles placed on the counter by way of precaution, on account of the powder which was scattered on the tables. These two candles cast no gleam outside. The insurgents had, moreover, taken pains not to have any light in the upper stories.

Gavroche was deeply preoccupied at that moment, but not precisely with his cartridges. The man of the Rue des Billettes had just entered the tap-room and had seated himself at the table which was the least lighted. A musket of large model had fallen to his share, and he held it between his legs. Gavroche, who had been, up to that moment, distracted by a hundred "amusing" things, had not even seen this man.

When he entered, Gavroche followed him mechanically with his eyes, admiring his gun; then, all at once, when the man was seated, the street urchin sprang to his feet. Any one who had spied upon that man up to that moment, would have seen that he was observing everything in the barricade and in the band of insurgents, with singular attention; but, from the moment when he had entered this room, he had fallen into a sort of brown study, and no longer seemed to see anything that was going on. The gamin approached this pensive personage, and began to step around him on tiptoe, as one walks in the vicinity of a person whom one is afraid of waking. At the same time, over his childish countenance which was, at once so impudent and so serious, so giddy and so profound, so gay and so heart-breaking, passed all those grimaces of an old man which signify: Ah bah! impossible! My sight is bad! I am dreaming! can this be? no, it is not! but yes! why, no! etc. Gavroche balanced on his heels, clenched both fists in his pockets, moved his neck around like a bird, expended in a gigantic pout all the sagacity of his lower lip. He was astounded, uncertain, incredulous, convinced, dazzled. He had the mien of the chief of the eunuchs in the slave mart, discovering a Venus among the blowsy females, and the air of an amateur recognizing a Raphael in a heap of daubs. His whole being was at work, the instinct which scents out, and the intelligence which combines. It was evident that a great event had happened in Gavroche's life.

It was at the most intense point of this preoccupation that Enjolras accosted him.

"You are small," said Enjolras, "you will not be seen. Go out of the barricade, slip along close to the houses, skirmish about a bit in the streets, and come back and tell me what is going on."

Gavroche raised himself on his haunches.

"So the little chaps are good for something! that's very lucky! I'll go! In the meanwhile, trust to the little fellows, and distrust the big ones." And Gavroche, raising his head and lowering his voice, added, as he indicated the man of the Rue des Billettes: "Do you see that big fellow there?"

"Well?"

"He's a police spy."

"Are you sure of it?"

"It isn't two weeks since he pulled me off the cornice of the Port Royal, where I was taking the air, by my ear."

Enjolras hastily quitted the urchin and murmured a few words in a very low tone to a longshoreman from the winedocks who chanced to be at hand. The man left the room, and returned almost immediately, accompanied by three others. The four men, four porters with broad shoulders, went and placed themselves without doing anything to attract his attention, behind the table on which the man of the Rue des Billettes was leaning with his elbows. They were evidently ready to hurl themselves upon him.

Then Enjolras approached the man and demanded of him:—

"Who are you?"

At this abrupt query, the man started. He plunged his gaze deep into Enjolras' clear eyes and appeared to grasp the latter's meaning. He smiled with a smile than which nothing more disdainful, more energetic, and more resolute could be seen in the world, and replied with haughty gravity:—

"I see what it is. Well, yes!"

"You are a police spy?"

"I am an agent of the authorities."

"And your name?"

"Javert."

Enjolras made a sign to the four men. In the twinkling of an eye, before Javert had time to turn round, he was collared, thrown down, pinioned and searched.

They found on him a little round card pasted between two pieces of glass, and bearing on one side the arms of France, engraved, and with this motto: *Supervision and vigilance*, and on the other this note: "JAVERT, inspector of police, aged fifty-two," and the signature of the Prefect of Police of that day, M. Gisquet.

Besides this, he had his watch and his purse, which contained several gold pieces. They left him his purse and his watch. Under the watch, at the bottom of his fob, they felt and seized a paper in an envelope, which Enjolras unfolded, and on which he read these five lines, written in the very hand of the Prefect of Police:—

"As soon as his political mission is accomplished, Inspector Javert will make sure, by special supervision, whether it is true that the malefactors have instituted intrigues on the right bank of the Seine, near the Jena bridge."

The search ended, they lifted Javert to his feet, bound his arms behind his back, and fastened him to that celebrated post in the middle of the room which had formerly given the wine-shop its name.

Gavroche, who had looked on at the whole of this scene and had approved of everything with a silent toss of his head, stepped up to Javert and said to him:—

"It's the mouse who has caught the cat."

All this was so rapidly executed, that it was all over when those about the wine-shop noticed it.

Javert had not uttered a single cry.

At the sight of Javert bound to the post, Courfeyrac, Bossuet, Joly, Combeferre, and the men scattered over the two barricades came running up.

Javert, with his back to the post, and so surrounded with ropes that he could not make a movement, raised his head with the intrepid serenity of the man who has never lied.

"He is a police spy," said Enjolras.

And turning to Javert: "You will be shot ten minutes before the barricade is taken."

Javert replied in his most imperious tone:—

"Why not at once?"

"We are saving our powder."

"Then finish the business with a blow from a knife."

"Spy," said the handsome Enjolras, "we are judges and not assassins."

Then he called Gavroche:—

"Here you! go about your business! Do what I told you!"

"I'm going!" cried Gavroche.

And halting as he was on the point of setting out:—

"By the way, you will give me his gun!" and he added: "I leave you the musician, but I want the clarinet."

The gamin made the military salute and passed gayly through the opening in the large barricade.

VIII

Many Interrogation Points with Regard to a Certain Le Cabuc Whose Name May Not Have Been Le Cabuc

The tragic picture which we have undertaken would not be complete, the reader would not see those grand moments of social birth-pangs in a revolutionary birth, which contain convulsion mingled with effort, in their exact and real relief, were we to omit, in the sketch here outlined, an incident full of epic and savage horror which occurred almost immediately after Gavroche's departure.

Mobs, as the reader knows, are like a snowball, and collect as they roll along, a throng of tumultuous men. These men do not ask each other whence they come. Among the passers-by who had joined the rabble led by Enjolras, Combeferre, and Courfeyrac, there had been a person wearing the jacket of a street porter, which was very threadbare on the shoulders, who gesticulated and vociferated, and who had the look of a drunken savage. This man, whose name or nickname was Le Cabuc, and who was, moreover, an utter stranger to those who pretended to know him, was very drunk, or assumed the appearance of being so, and had seated himself with several others at a table which they had dragged outside of the wine-shop. This Cabuc, while making those who vied with him drunk seemed to be examining with a thoughtful air the large house at the extremity of the barricade, whose five stories commanded the whole street and faced the Rue Saint-Denis. All at once he exclaimed:—

"Do you know, comrades, it is from that house yonder that we must fire. When we are at the windows, the deuce is in it if any one can advance into the street!"

"Yes, but the house is closed," said one of the drinkers.

"Let us knock!"

"They will not open."

"Let us break in the door!"

Le Cabuc runs to the door, which had a very massive knocker, and knocks. The door opens not. He strikes a second blow. No one answers. A third stroke. The same silence.

"Is there any one here?" shouts Cabuc.

Nothing stirs.

Then he seizes a gun and begins to batter the door with the butt end.

It was an ancient alley door, low, vaulted, narrow, solid, entirely of oak, lined on the inside with a sheet of iron and iron stays, a genuine prison postern. The blows from the butt end of the gun made the house tremble, but did not shake the door.

Nevertheless, it is probable that the inhabitants were disturbed, for a tiny, square window was finally seen to open on the third story, and at this aperture appeared the reverend and terrified face of a gray-haired old man, who was the porter, and who held a candle.

The man who was knocking paused.

"Gentlemen," said the porter, "what do you want?"

"Open!" said Cabuc.

"That cannot be, gentlemen."

"Open, nevertheless."

"Impossible, gentlemen."

Le Cabuc took his gun and aimed at the porter; but as he was below, and as it was very dark, the porter did not see him.

"Will you open, yes or no?"

"No, gentlemen."

"Do you say no?"

"I say no, my goo—"

The porter did not finish. The shot was fired; the ball entered under his chin and came out at the nape of his neck, after traversing the jugular vein.

The old man fell back without a sigh. The candle fell and was extinguished, and nothing more was to be seen except a motionless head lying on the sill of the small window, and a little whitish smoke which floated off towards the roof.

"There!" said Le Cabuc, dropping the butt end of his gun to the pavement.

He had hardly uttered this word, when he felt a hand laid on his shoulder with the weight of an eagle's talon, and he heard a voice saying to him:—

"On your knees."

The murderer turned round and saw before him Enjolras' cold, white face.

Enjolras held a pistol in his hand.

He had hastened up at the sound of the discharge.

He had seized Cabuc's collar, blouse, shirt, and suspender with his left hand.

"On your knees!" he repeated.

And, with an imperious motion, the frail young man of twenty years bent the thickset and sturdy porter like a reed, and brought him to his knees in the mire.

Le Cabuc attempted to resist, but he seemed to have been seized by a superhuman hand.

Enjolras, pale, with bare neck and dishevelled hair, and his woman's face, had about him at that moment something of the antique Themis. His dilated nostrils, his downcast eyes, gave to his implacable Greek profile that expression of wrath and that expression of Chastity which, as the ancient world viewed the matter, befit Justice.

The whole barricade hastened up, then all ranged themselves in a circle at a distance, feeling that it was impossible to utter a word in the presence of the thing which they were about to behold.

Le Cabuc, vanquished, no longer tried to struggle, and trembled in every limb.

Enjolras released him and drew out his watch.

"Collect yourself," said he. "Think or pray. You have one minute."

"Mercy!" murmured the murderer; then he dropped his head and stammered a few inarticulate oaths.

Enjolras never took his eyes off of him: he allowed a minute to pass, then he replaced his watch in his fob. That done, he grasped Le Cabuc by the hair, as the latter coiled himself into a ball at his knees and shrieked, and placed the muzzle of the pistol to his ear. Many of those intrepid men, who had so tranquilly entered upon the most terrible of adventures, turned aside their heads.

An explosion was heard, the assassin fell to the pavement face downwards.

Enjolras straightened himself up, and cast a convinced and severe glance around him. Then he spurned the corpse with his foot and said:—

"Throw that outside."

Three men raised the body of the unhappy wretch, which was still agitated by the last mechanical convulsions of the life that had fled, and flung it over the little barricade into the Rue Mondétour.

Enjolras was thoughtful. It is impossible to say what grandiose shadows slowly spread over his redoubtable serenity. All at once he raised his voice.

A silence fell upon them.

"Citizens," said Enjolras, "what that man did is frightful, what I have done is horrible. He killed, therefore I killed him. I had to do it, because insurrection must have its discipline. Assassination is even more of a crime here than elsewhere; we are under the eyes of the Revolution, we are the priests of the Republic, we are the victims of duty, and must not be possible to slander our combat. I have, therefore, tried that man, and condemned him to death. As for myself, constrained as I am to do what I have done, and yet abhorring it, I have judged myself also, and you shall soon see to what I have condemned myself."

Those who listened to him shuddered.

"We will share thy fate," cried Combeferre.

"So be it," replied Enjolras. "One word more. In executing this man, I have obeyed necessity; but necessity is a monster of the old world, necessity's name is Fatality. Now, the law of progress is, that monsters shall disappear before the angels, and that Fatality shall vanish before Fraternity. It is a bad moment to pronounce the word love. No matter, I do pronounce it. And I glorify it. Love, the future is thine. Death, I make use of thee, but I hate thee. Citizens, in the future there will be neither darkness nor thunderbolts; neither ferocious ignorance, nor bloody retaliation. As there will be no more Satan, there will be no more Michael. In the future no one will kill any one else, the earth will beam with radiance, the human race will love. The day will come, citizens, when all will be concord, harmony, light, joy and life; it will come, and it is in order that it may come that we are about to die."

Enjolras ceased. His virgin lips closed; and he remained for some time standing on the spot where he had shed blood, in marble immobility. His staring eye caused those about him to speak in low tones.

Jean Prouvaire and Combeferre pressed each other's hands silently, and, leaning against each other in an angle of the barricade, they watched with an admiration in which there was some compassion, that grave young man, executioner and priest, composed of light, like crystal, and also of rock.

Let us say at once that later on, after the action, when the bodies were taken to the morgue and searched, a police agent's card was found on Le Cabuc. The author of this book had in his hands, in 1848, the special report on this subject made to the Prefect of Police in 1832.

We will add, that if we are to believe a tradition of the police, which is strange but probably well founded, Le Cabuc was Claquesous. The fact is, that dating from the death of Le Cabuc, there was no longer any question of Claquesous. Claquesous had nowhere left any trace of his disappearance; he would seem to have amalgamated himself with the invisible. His life had been all shadows, his end was night.

The whole insurgent group was still under the influence of the emotion of that tragic case which had been so quickly tried and so quickly terminated, when Courfeyrac again beheld on the barricade, the small young man who had inquired of him that morning for Marius.

This lad, who had a bold and reckless air, had come by night to join the insurgents.

BOOK THIRTEENTH
MARIUS ENTERS THE SHADOW

I

From the Rue Plumet to the Quartier Saint-Denis

The voice which had summoned Marius through the twilight to the barricade of the Rue de la Chanvrerie, had produced on him the effect of the voice of destiny. He wished to die; the opportunity presented itself; he knocked at the door of the tomb, a hand in the darkness offered him the key. These melancholy openings which take place in the gloom before despair, are tempting. Marius thrust aside the bar which had so often allowed him to pass, emerged from the garden, and said: "I will go."

Mad with grief, no longer conscious of anything fixed or solid in his brain, incapable of accepting anything thenceforth of fate after those two months passed in the intoxication of youth and love, overwhelmed at once by all the reveries of despair, he had but one desire remaining, to make a speedy end of all.

He set out at rapid pace. He found himself most opportunely armed, as he had Javert's pistols with him.

The young man of whom he thought that he had caught a glimpse, had vanished from his sight in the street.

Marius, who had emerged from the Rue Plumet by the boulevard, traversed the Esplanade and the bridge of the Invalides, the Champs-Élysées, the Place Louis XV, and reached the Rue de Rivoli. The shops were open there, the gas was burning under the arcades, women were making their purchases in the stalls, people were eating ices in the Café Laiter, and nibbling small cakes at the English pastry-cook's shop. Only a few posting-chaises were setting out at a gallop from the Hôtel des Princes and the Hôtel Meurice.

Marius entered the Rue Saint-Honoré through the Passage Delorme. There the shops were closed, the merchants were chatting in front of their half-open doors, people were walking about, the street lanterns were lighted, beginning with the first floor, all the windows were lighted as usual. There was cavalry on the Place du Palais-Royal.

Marius followed the Rue Saint-Honoré. In proportion as he left the Palais-Royal behind him, there were fewer lighted windows, the shops were fast shut, no one was chatting on the thresholds, the street grew sombre, and, at the same time, the crowd increased in density. For the passers-by now amounted to a crowd. No one could be seen to speak in this throng, and yet there arose from it a dull, deep murmur.

Near the fountain of the Arbre-Sec, there were "assemblages", motionless and gloomy groups which were to those who went and came as stones in the midst of running water.

At the entrance to the Rue des Prouvaires, the crowd no longer walked. It formed a resisting, massive, solid, compact, almost impenetrable block of people who were huddled together, and conversing in low tones. There were hardly any black coats or round hats now, but smock frocks, blouses, caps, and bristling and cadaverous heads. This multitude undulated confusedly in the nocturnal gloom. Its whisperings had the hoarse accent of a vibration. Although not one of them was walking, a dull trampling was audible in the mire. Beyond this dense portion of the throng, in the Rue du Roule, in the Rue des Prouvaires, and in the extension of the Rue Saint-Honoré, there was no longer a single window in which a candle was burning. Only the solitary and diminishing rows of lanterns could be seen vanishing into the street in the distance. The lanterns of that date resembled large red stars, hanging to ropes, and shed upon the pavement a shadow which had the form of a huge spider. These streets were not deserted. There could be descried piles of guns, moving bayonets, and troops bivouacking. No curious observer passed that limit. There circulation ceased. There the rabble ended and the army began.

Marius willed with the will of a man who hopes no more. He had been summoned, he must go. He found a means to traverse the throng and to pass the bivouac of the troops, he shunned the patrols, he avoided the sentinels. He made a circuit, reached the Rue de Béthisy, and directed his course towards the Halles. At the corner of the Rue des Bourdonnais, there were no longer any lanterns.

After having passed the zone of the crowd, he had passed the limits of the troops; he found himself in something startling. There was no longer a passer-by, no longer a soldier, no longer a light, there was no one; solitude, silence, night, I know not what chill which seized hold upon one. Entering a street was like entering a cellar.

He continued to advance.

He took a few steps. Some one passed close to him at a run. Was it a man? Or a woman? Were there many of them? he could not have told. It had passed and vanished.

Proceeding from circuit to circuit, he reached a lane which he judged to be the Rue de la Poterie; near the middle of this street, he came in contact with an obstacle. He extended his hands. It was an overturned wagon; his foot recognized pools of water, gullies, and paving-stones scattered and piled up. A barricade had been begun there and abandoned. He climbed over the stones and found himself on the other side of the barrier. He walked very near the street-posts, and guided himself along the walls of the houses. A little beyond the barricade, it seemed to him that he could make out something white in front of him. He approached, it took on a form. It was two white horses; the horses of the omnibus harnessed by Bossuet in the morning, who had been straying at random all day from street to street, and had finally halted there, with the weary patience of brutes who no more understand the actions of men, than man understands the actions of Providence.

Marius left the horses behind him. As he was approaching a street which seemed to him to be the Rue du Contrat-Social, a shot coming no one knows whence, and traversing the darkness at random, whistled close by him, and the bullet pierced a brass shaving-dish suspended above his head over a hairdresser's shop. This pierced shaving-dish was still to be seen in 1848, in the Rue du Contrat-Social, at the corner of the pillars of the market.

This shot still betokened life. From that instant forth he encountered nothing more.

The whole of this itinerary resembled a descent of black steps.

Nevertheless, Marius pressed forward.

II

An Owl's View of Paris

A being who could have hovered over Paris that night with the wing of the bat or the owl would have had beneath his eyes a gloomy spectacle.

All that old quarter of the Halles, which is like a city within a city, through which run the Rues Saint-Denis and Saint-Martin, where a thousand lanes cross, and of which the insurgents had made their redoubt and their stronghold, would have appeared to him like a dark and enormous cavity hollowed out in the centre of Paris. There the glance fell into an abyss. Thanks to the broken lanterns, thanks to the closed windows, there all radiance, all life, all sound, all movement ceased. The invisible police of the insurrection were on the watch everywhere, and maintained order, that is to say, night. The necessary tactics of insurrection are to drown small numbers in a vast obscurity, to multiply every combatant by the possibilities which that obscurity contains. At dusk, every window where a candle was burning received a shot. The light was extinguished, sometimes the inhabitant was killed. Hence nothing was stirring. There was nothing but fright, mourning, stupor in the houses; and in the streets, a sort of sacred horror. Not even the long rows of windows and stores, the indentations of the chimneys, and the roofs, and the vague reflections which are cast back by the wet and muddy pavements, were visible. An eye cast upward at that mass of shadows might, perhaps, have caught a glimpse here and there, at intervals, of indistinct gleams which brought out broken and eccentric lines, and profiles of singular buildings, something like the lights which go and come in ruins; it was at such points that the barricades were situated. The rest was a lake of obscurity, foggy, heavy, and funereal, above which, in motionless and melancholy outlines, rose the tower of Saint-Jacques, the church of Saint-Merry, and two or three more of those grand edifices of which man makes giants and the night makes phantoms.

All around this deserted and disquieting labyrinth, in the quarters where the Parisian circulation had not been annihilated, and where a few street lanterns still burned, the aerial observer might have distinguished the metallic gleam of swords and bayonets, the dull rumble of artillery, and the swarming of silent battalions whose ranks were swelling from minute to minute; a formidable girdle which was slowly drawing in and around the insurrection.

The invested quarter was no longer anything more than a monstrous cavern; everything there appeared to be asleep or motionless, and, as we have just seen, any street which one might come to offered nothing but darkness.

A wild darkness, full of traps, full of unseen and formidable shocks, into which it was alarming to penetrate, and in which it was terrible to remain, where those who entered shivered before those whom they awaited, where those who waited shuddered before those who were coming. Invisible combatants were entrenched at every corner of the street; snares of the sepulchre concealed in the density of night. All was over. No more light was to be hoped for, henceforth, except the lightning of guns, no further encounter except the abrupt and rapid apparition of death. Where? How? When? No one knew, but it was certain and inevitable. In this place which had been marked out for the struggle, the Government and the insurrection, the National Guard, and popular societies, the bourgeois and the uprising, groping their way, were about to come into contact. The necessity was the same for both. The only possible issue thenceforth was to emerge thence killed or conquerors. A situation so extreme, an obscurity so powerful, that the most timid felt themselves seized with resolution, and the most daring with terror.

Moreover, on both sides, the fury, the rage, and the determination were equal. For the one party, to advance meant death, and no one dreamed of retreating; for the other, to remain meant death, and no one dreamed of flight.

It was indispensable that all should be ended on the following day, that triumph should rest either here or there, that the insurrection should prove itself a revolution or a skirmish. The Government understood this as well as the parties; the most insignificant bourgeois felt it. Hence a thought of anguish which mingled with the impenetrable gloom of this quarter where all was at the point of being decided; hence a redoubled anxiety around that silence whence a catastrophe was on the point of emerging. Here only one sound was audible, a sound as heart-rending as the death rattle, as menacing as a malediction, the tocsin of Saint-Merry. Nothing could be more blood-curdling than the clamor of that wild and desperate bell, wailing amid the shadows.

As it often happens, nature seemed to have fallen into accord with what men were about to do. Nothing disturbed the harmony of the whole effect. The stars had disappeared, heavy clouds filled the horizon with their melancholy folds. A black sky rested on these dead streets, as though an immense winding-sheet were being outspread over this immense tomb.

While a battle that was still wholly political was in preparation in the same locality which had already witnessed so many revolutionary events, while youth, the secret associations, the schools, in the name of principles, and the middle classes, in the name of interests, were approaching preparatory to dashing themselves together, clasping and throwing each other, while each one hastened and invited the last and decisive hour of the crisis, far away and quite outside of this fatal quarter, in the most profound depths of the unfathomable cavities of that wretched old Paris which disappears under the splendor of happy and opulent Paris, the sombre voice of the people could be heard giving utterance to a dull roar.

A fearful and sacred voice which is composed of the roar of the brute and of the word of God, which terrifies the weak and which warns the wise, which comes both from below like the voice of the lion, and from on high like the voice of the thunder.

III

The Extreme Edge

Marius had reached the Halles.

There everything was still calmer, more obscure and more motionless than in the neighboring streets. One would have said that the glacial peace of the sepulchre had sprung forth from the earth and had spread over the heavens.

Nevertheless, a red glow brought out against this black background the lofty roofs of the houses which barred the Rue de la Chanvrerie on the Saint-Eustache side. It was the reflection of the torch which was burning in the Corinthe barricade. Marius directed his steps towards that red light. It had drawn him to the Marché-aux-Poirées, and he caught a glimpse of the dark mouth of the Rue des Prêcheurs. He entered it. The insurgents' sentinel, who was guarding the other end, did not see him. He felt that he was very close to that which he had come in search of, and he walked on tiptoe. In this manner he reached the elbow of that short section of the Rue Mondétour which was, as the reader will remember, the only communication which Enjolras had preserved with the outside world. At the corner of the last house, on his left, he thrust his head forward, and looked into the fragment of the Rue Mondétour.

A little beyond the angle of the lane and the Rue de la Chanvrerie which cast a broad curtain of shadow, in which he was himself engulfed, he perceived some light on the pavement, a bit of the wine-shop, and beyond, a flickering lamp within a sort of shapeless wall, and men crouching down with guns on their knees. All this was ten fathoms distant from him. It was the interior of the barricade.

The houses which bordered the lane on the right concealed the rest of the wine-shop, the large barricade, and the flag from him.

Marius had but a step more to take.

Then the unhappy young man seated himself on a post, folded his arms, and fell to thinking about his father.

He thought of that heroic Colonel Pontmercy, who had been so proud a soldier, who had guarded the frontier of France under the Republic, and had touched the frontier of Asia under Napoleon, who had beheld

Genoa, Alexandria, Milan, Turin, Madrid, Vienna, Dresden, Berlin, Moscow, who had left on all the victorious battle-fields of Europe drops of that same blood, which he, Marius, had in his veins, who had grown gray before his time in discipline and command, who had lived with his sword-belt buckled, his epaulets falling on his breast, his cockade blackened with powder, his brow furrowed with his helmet, in barracks, in camp, in the bivouac, in ambulances, and who, at the expiration of twenty years, had returned from the great wars with a scarred cheek, a smiling countenance, tranquil, admirable, pure as a child, having done everything for France and nothing against her.

He said to himself that his day had also come now, that his hour had struck, that following his father, he too was about to show himself brave, intrepid, bold, to run to meet the bullets, to offer his breast to bayonets, to shed his blood, to seek the enemy, to seek death, that he was about to wage war in his turn and descend to the field of battle, and that the field of battle upon which he was to descend was the street, and that the war in which he was about to engage was civil war!

He beheld civil war laid open like a gulf before him, and into this he was about to fall. Then he shuddered.

He thought of his father's sword, which his grandfather had sold to a second-hand dealer, and which he had so mournfully regretted. He said to himself that that chaste and valiant sword had done well to escape from him, and to depart in wrath into the gloom; that if it had thus fled, it was because it was intelligent and because it had foreseen the future; that it had had a presentiment of this rebellion, the war of the gutters, the war of the pavements, fusillades through cellar-windows, blows given and received in the rear; it was because, coming from Marengo and Friedland, it did not wish to go to the Rue de la Chanvrerie; it was because, after what it had done with the father, it did not wish to do this for the son! He told himself that if that sword were there, if after taking possession of it at his father's pillow, he had dared to take it and carry it off for this combat of darkness between Frenchmen in the streets, it would assuredly have scorched his hands and burst out aflame before his eyes, like the sword of the angel! He told himself that it was fortunate that it was not there and that it had disappeared, that that was well, that that was just, that his grandfather had been the true guardian of his father's glory, and that it was far better that the colonel's sword should be sold at auction, sold to the old-clothes man, thrown among the old junk, than that it should, to-day, wound the side of his country.

And then he fell to weeping bitterly.

This was horrible. But what was he to do? Live without Cosette he could not. Since she was gone, he must needs die. Had he not given her his word of honor that he would die? She had gone knowing that; this meant that it pleased her that Marius should die. And then, it was clear that she no longer loved him, since she had departed thus without warning, without a word, without a letter, although she knew his address! What was the good of living, and why should he live now? And then, what! should he retreat after going so far? should he flee from danger after having approached it? should he slip away after having come and peeped into the barricade? slip away, all in a tremble, saying: "After all, I have had enough of it as it is. I have seen it, that suffices, this is civil war, and I shall take my leave!" Should he abandon his friends who were expecting him? Who were in need of him possibly! who were a mere handful against an army! Should he be untrue at once to his love, to country, to his word? Should he give to his cowardice the pretext of patriotism? But this was impossible, and if the phantom of his father was there in the gloom, and beheld him retreating, he would beat him on the loins with the flat of his sword, and shout to him: "March on, you poltroon!"

Thus a prey to the conflicting movements of his thoughts, he dropped his head.

All at once he raised it. A sort of splendid rectification had just been effected in his mind. There is a widening of the sphere of thought which is peculiar to the vicinity of the grave; it makes one see clearly to be near death. The vision of the action into which he felt that he was, perhaps, on the point of entering, appeared to him no more as lamentable, but as superb. The war of the street was suddenly transfigured by some unfathomable inward working of his soul, before the eye of his thought. All the tumultuous interrogation points of reverie recurred to him in throngs, but without troubling him. He left none of them unanswered.

Let us see, why should his father be indignant? Are there not cases where insurrection rises to the dignity of duty? What was there that was degrading for the son of Colonel Pontmercy in the combat which was about to begin? It is no longer Montmirail nor Champaubert; it is something quite different. The question is no longer one of sacred territory,—but of a holy idea. The country wails, that may be, but humanity applauds. But is it true that the country does wail? France bleeds, but liberty smiles; and in the presence of liberty's smile, France forgets her wound. And then if we look at things from a still more lofty point of view, why do we speak of civil war?

Civil war—what does that mean? Is there a foreign war? Is not all war between men, war between brothers? War is qualified only by its object. There is no such thing as foreign or civil war; there is only just and unjust war. Until that day when the grand human agreement is concluded, war, that at least which is the effort of the future, which is hastening on against the past, which is lagging in the rear, may be necessary. What have we to reproach that war with? War does not become a disgrace, the sword does not become a disgrace, except when it is used for assassinating the right, progress, reason, civilization, truth. Then war, whether foreign or civil, is iniquitous; it is called crime. Outside the pale of that holy thing, justice, by what right does one form of man despise another? By what right should the sword of Washington disown the pike of Camille Desmoulins? Leonidas against the stranger, Timoleon against the tyrant, which is the greater? the one is the defender, the other the liberator. Shall we brand every appeal to arms within a city's limits without taking the object into a consideration? Then note the infamy of Brutus, Marcel, Arnould von Blankenheim, Coligny, Hedgerow war? War of the streets? Why not? That was the war of Ambiorix, of Artevelde, of Marnix, of Pelagius. But Ambiorix fought against Rome, Artevelde against France, Marnix against Spain, Pelagius against the Moors; all against the foreigner. Well, the monarchy is a foreigner; oppression is a stranger; the right divine is a stranger. Despotism violates the moral frontier, an invasion violates the geographical frontier. Driving out the tyrant or driving out the English, in both cases, regaining possession of one's own territory. There comes an hour when protestation no longer suffices; after philosophy, action is required; live force finishes what the idea has sketched out; Prometheus chained begins, Arostogeiton ends; the encyclopedia enlightens souls, the 10th of August electrifies them. After Æschylus, Thrasybulus; after Diderot, Danton. Multitudes have a tendency to accept the master. Their mass bears witness to apathy. A crowd is easily led as a whole to obedience. Men must be stirred up, pushed on, treated roughly by the very benefit of their deliverance, their eyes must be wounded by the true, light must be hurled at them in terrible handfuls. They must be a little thunderstruck themselves at their own well-being; this dazzling awakens them. Hence the necessity of tocsins and wars. Great combatants must rise, must enlighten nations with audacity, and shake up that sad humanity which is covered with gloom by the right divine, Cæsarian glory, force, fanaticism, irresponsible power, and absolute majesty; a rabble stupidly occupied in the contemplation, in their twilight splendor, of these sombre triumphs of the night. Down with the tyrant! Of whom are you speaking? Do you call Louis Philippe the tyrant? No; no more than Louis XVI. Both of them are what history is in the habit of calling good kings; but principles are not to be parcelled out, the logic of the true is rectilinear, the peculiarity of truth is that it lacks complaisance; no concessions, then; all encroachments on man should be repressed. There is a divine right in Louis XVI, there is *because a Bourbon* in Louis Philippe; both represent in a certain measure the confiscation of right, and, in order to clear away universal insurrection, they must be combated; it must be done, France being always the one to begin. When the master falls in France, he falls everywhere. In short, what cause is more just, and consequently, what war is greater, than that which re-establishes social truth, restores her throne to liberty, restores the people to the people, restores sovereignty to man, replaces the purple on the head of France, restores equity and reason in their plenitude, suppresses every germ of antagonism by restoring each one to himself, annihilates the obstacle which royalty presents to the whole immense universal concord, and places the human race once more on a level with the right? These wars build up peace. An enormous fortress of prejudices, privileges, superstitions, lies, exactions, abuses, violences, iniquities, and darkness still stands erect in this world, with its towers of hatred. It must be cast down. This monstrous mass must be made to crumble. To conquer at Austerlitz is grand; to take the Bastille is immense.

There is no one who has not noticed it in his own case—the soul,—and therein lies the marvel of its unity complicated with ubiquity, has a strange aptitude for reasoning almost coldly in the most violent extremities, and it often happens that heartbroken passion and profound despair in the very agony of their blackest monologues, treat subjects and discuss theses. Logic is mingled with convulsion, and the thread of the syllogism floats, without breaking, in the mournful storm of thought. This was the situation of Marius' mind.

As he meditated thus, dejected but resolute, hesitating in every direction, and, in short, shuddering at what he was about to do, his glance strayed to the interior of the barricade. The insurgents were here conversing in a low voice, without moving, and there was perceptible that quasi-silence which marks the last stage of expectation. Overhead, at the small window in the third story Marius descried a sort of spectator who appeared to him to be singularly attentive. This was the porter who had been killed by Le Cabuc. Below, by the lights of the torch, which was thrust between the paving-stones, this head could be vaguely distinguished. Nothing could be stranger, in that sombre and uncertain gleam, than that livid, motionless, astonished face, with its bristling hair, its eyes fixed and staring, and its yawning mouth, bent over the street in an attitude of curiosity. One would have said that the man who was dead was surveying those who were about to die. A long trail of blood which had flowed from that head, descended in reddish threads from the window to the height of the first floor, where it stopped.

BOOK FOURTEENTH
THE GRANDEURS OF DESPAIR

I

The Flag: Act First

As yet, nothing had come. Ten o'clock had sounded from Saint-Merry. Enjolras and Combeferre had gone and seated themselves, carbines in hand, near the outlet of the grand barricade. They no longer addressed each other, they listened, seeking to catch even the faintest and most distant sound of marching.

Suddenly, in the midst of the dismal calm, a clear, gay, young voice, which seemed to come from the Rue Saint-Denis, rose and began to sing distinctly, to the old popular air of "By the Light of the Moon," this bit of poetry, terminated by a cry like the crow of a cock:—

> *Mon nez est en larmes,*
> *Mon ami Bugeaud,*
> *Prête moi tes gendarmes*
> *Pour leur dire un mot.*

> *En capote bleue,*
> *La poule au shako,*
> *Voici la banlieue!*
> *Co-cocorico!*

They pressed each other's hands.

"That is Gavroche," said Enjolras.

"He is warning us," said Combeferre.

A hasty rush troubled the deserted street; they beheld a being more agile than a clown climb over the omnibus, and Gavroche bounded into the barricade, all breathless, saying:—

"My gun! Here they are!"

An electric quiver shot through the whole barricade, and the sound of hands seeking their guns became audible.

"Would you like my carbine?" said Enjolras to the lad.

"I want a big gun," replied Gavroche.

And he seized Javert's gun.

Two sentinels had fallen back, and had come in almost at the same moment as Gavroche. They were the sentinels from the end of the street, and the vidette of the Rue de la Petite-Truanderie. The vidette of the Lane des Prêcheurs had remained at his post, which indicated that nothing was approaching from the direction of the bridges and Halles.

The Rue de la Chanvrerie, of which a few paving-stones alone were dimly visible in the reflection of the light projected on the flag, offered to the insurgents the aspect of a vast black door vaguely opened into a smoke.

Each man had taken up his position for the conflict.

Forty-three insurgents, among whom were Enjolras, Combeferre, Courfeyrac, Bossuet, Joly, Bahorel, and Gavroche, were kneeling inside the large barricade, with their heads on a level with the crest of the barrier, the barrels of their guns and carbines aimed on the stones as though at loop-holes, attentive, mute, ready to fire. Six, commanded by Feuilly, had installed themselves, with their guns levelled at their shoulders, at the windows of the two stories of Corinthe.

Several minutes passed thus, then a sound of footsteps, measured, heavy, and numerous, became distinctly audible in the direction of Saint-Leu. This sound, faint at first, then precise, then heavy and sonorous, approached slowly, without halt, without intermission, with a tranquil and terrible continuity. Nothing was to be heard but this. It was that combined silence and sound, of the statue of the commander, but this stony step had something indescribably enormous and multiple about it which awakened the idea of a throng, and, at the same time, the idea of a spectre. One thought one heard the terrible statue Legion marching onward. This tread drew near; it drew still nearer, and stopped. It seemed as though the breathing of many men could be heard at the end of the street. Nothing was to be seen, however, but at the bottom of that dense obscurity there could be distinguished a multitude of metallic threads, as fine as needles and almost imperceptible, which moved about like those indescribable phosphoric networks which one sees beneath one's closed eyelids, in the first mists of slumber at the moment when one is dropping off to sleep. These were bayonets and gun-barrels confusedly illuminated by the distant reflection of the torch.

A pause ensued, as though both sides were waiting. All at once, from the depths of this darkness, a voice, which was all the more sinister, since no one was visible, and which appeared to be the gloom itself speaking, shouted:—

"Who goes there?"

At the same time, the click of guns, as they were lowered into position, was heard.

Enjolras replied in a haughty and vibrating tone:—

"The French Revolution!"

"Fire!" shouted the voice.

A flash empurpled all the façades in the street as though the door of a furnace had been flung open, and hastily closed again.

A fearful detonation burst forth on the barricade. The red flag fell. The discharge had been so violent and so dense that it had cut the staff, that is to say, the very tip of the omnibus pole.

Bullets which had rebounded from the cornices of the houses penetrated the barricade and wounded several men.

The impression produced by this first discharge was freezing. The attack had been rough, and of a nature to inspire reflection in the boldest. It was evident that they had to deal with an entire regiment at the very least.

"Comrades!" shouted Courfeyrac, "let us not waste our powder. Let us wait until they are in the street before replying."

"And, above all," said Enjolras, "let us raise the flag again."

He picked up the flag, which had fallen precisely at his feet.

Outside, the clatter of the ramrods in the guns could be heard; the troops were re-loading their arms.

Enjolras went on:—

"Who is there here with a bold heart? Who will plant the flag on the barricade again?"

Not a man responded. To mount on the barricade at the very moment when, without any doubt, it was again the object of their aim, was simply death. The bravest hesitated to pronounce his own condemnation. Enjolras himself felt a thrill. He repeated:—

"Does no one volunteer?"

II

The Flag: Act Second

Since they had arrived at Corinthe, and had begun the construction of the barricade, no attention had been paid to Father Mabeuf. M. Mabeuf had not quitted the mob, however; he had entered the ground floor of the wine-shop and had seated himself behind the counter. There he had, so to speak, retreated into himself. He no longer seemed to look or to think. Courfeyrac and others had accosted him two or three times, warning him of his peril, beseeching him to withdraw, but he did not hear them. When they were not speaking to him, his mouth moved as though he were replying to some one, and as soon as he was addressed, his lips became motionless and his eyes no longer had the appearance of being alive.

Several hours before the barricade was attacked, he had assumed an attitude which he did not afterwards abandon, with both fists planted on his knees and his head thrust forward as though he were gazing over a precipice. Nothing had been able to move him from this attitude; it did not seem as though his mind were in the barricade. When each had gone to take up his position for the combat, there remained in the tap-room where Javert was bound to the post, only a single insurgent with a naked sword, watching over Javert, and himself, Mabeuf. At the moment of the attack, at the detonation, the physical shock had reached him and had, as it were, awakened him; he started up abruptly, crossed the room, and at the instant when Enjolras repeated his appeal: "Does no one volunteer?" the old man was seen to make his appearance on the threshold of the wine-shop. His presence produced a sort of commotion in the different groups. A shout went up:—

"It is the voter! It is the member of the Convention! It is the representative of the people!"

It is probable that he did not hear them.

He strode straight up to Enjolras, the insurgents withdrawing before him with a religious fear; he tore the flag from Enjolras, who recoiled in amazement and then, since no one dared to stop or to assist him, this old man of eighty, with shaking head but firm foot, began slowly to ascend the staircase of paving-stones arranged in the barricade. This was so melancholy and so grand that all around him cried: "Off with your hats!" At every step that he mounted, it was a frightful spectacle; his white locks, his decrepit face, his lofty, bald, and wrinkled brow, his amazed and open mouth, his aged arm upholding the red banner, rose through the gloom and were enlarged in the bloody light of the torch, and the bystanders thought that they beheld the spectre of '93 emerging from the earth, with the flag of terror in his hand.

When he had reached the last step, when this trembling and terrible phantom, erect on that pile of rubbish in the presence of twelve hundred invisible guns, drew himself up in the face of death and as though he were more powerful than it, the whole barricade assumed amid the darkness, a supernatural and colossal form.

There ensued one of those silences which occur only in the presence of prodigies. In the midst of this silence, the old man waved the red flag and shouted:—

"Long live the Revolution! Long live the Republic! Fraternity! Equality! and Death!"

Those in the barricade heard a low and rapid whisper, like the murmur of a priest who is despatching a prayer in haste. It was probably the commissary of police who was making the legal summons at the other end of the street.

Then the same piercing voice which had shouted: "Who goes there?" shouted:—

"Retire!"

M. Mabeuf, pale, haggard, his eyes lighted up with the mournful flame of aberration, raised the flag above his head and repeated:—

"Long live the Republic!"

"Fire!" said the voice.

A second discharge, similar to the first, rained down upon the barricade.

The old man fell on his knees, then rose again, dropped the flag and fell backwards on the pavement, like a log, at full length, with outstretched arms.

Rivulets of blood flowed beneath him. His aged head, pale and sad, seemed to be gazing at the sky.

One of those emotions which are superior to man, which make him forget even to defend himself, seized upon the insurgents, and they approached the body with respectful awe.

"What men these regicides were!" said Enjolras.

Courfeyrac bent down to Enjolras' ear:—

"This is for yourself alone, I do not wish to dampen the enthusiasm. But this man was anything rather than a regicide. I knew him. His name was Father Mabeuf. I do not know what was the matter with him to-day. But he was a brave blockhead. Just look at his head."

"The head of a blockhead and the heart of a Brutus," replied Enjolras.

Then he raised his voice:—

"Citizens! This is the example which the old give to the young. We hesitated, he came! We were drawing back, he advanced! This is what those who are trembling with age teach to those who tremble with fear! This aged man is august in the eyes of his country. He has had a long life and a magnificent death! Now, let us place the body under cover, that each one of us may defend this old man dead as he would his father living, and may his presence in our midst render the barricade impregnable!"

A murmur of gloomy and energetic assent followed these words.

Enjolras bent down, raised the old man's head, and fierce as he was, he kissed him on the brow, then, throwing wide his arms, and handling this dead man with tender precaution, as though he feared to hurt it, he removed his coat, showed the bloody holes in it to all, and said:—

"This is our flag now."

III

GAVROCHE WOULD HAVE DONE BETTER TO ACCEPT ENJOLRAS' CARBINE

They threw a long black shawl of Widow Hucheloup's over Father Mabeuf. Six men made a litter of their guns; on this they laid the body, and bore it, with bared heads, with solemn slowness, to the large table in the tap-room.

These men, wholly absorbed in the grave and sacred task in which they were engaged, thought no more of the perilous situation in which they stood.

When the corpse passed near Javert, who was still impassive, Enjolras said to the spy:—

"It will be your turn presently!"

During all this time, Little Gavroche, who alone had not quitted his post, but had remained on guard, thought he espied some men stealthily approaching the barricade. All at once he shouted:—

"Look out!"

Courfeyrac, Enjolras, Jean Prouvaire, Combeferre, Joly, Bahorel, Bossuet, and all the rest ran tumultuously from the wine-shop. It was almost too late. They saw a glistening density of bayonets undulating above the barricade. Municipal guards of lofty stature were making their way in, some striding over the omnibus, others through the cut, thrusting before them the urchin, who retreated, but did not flee.

The moment was critical. It was that first, redoubtable moment of inundation, when the stream rises to the level of the levee and when the water begins to filter through the fissures of dike. A second more and the barricade would have been taken.

Bahorel dashed upon the first municipal guard who was entering, and killed him on the spot with a blow from his gun; the second killed Bahorel with a blow from his bayonet. Another had already overthrown Courfeyrac, who was shouting: "Follow me!" The largest of all, a sort of colossus, marched on Gavroche with his bayonet fixed. The urchin took in his arms Javert's immense gun, levelled it resolutely at the giant, and fired. No discharge followed. Javert's gun was not loaded. The municipal guard burst into a laugh and raised his bayonet at the child.

Before the bayonet had touched Gavroche, the gun slipped from the soldier's grasp, a bullet had struck the municipal guardsman in the centre of the forehead, and he fell over on his back. A second bullet struck the other guard, who had assaulted Courfeyrac in the breast, and laid him low on the pavement.

This was the work of Marius, who had just entered the barricade.

IV

The Barrel of Powder

Marius, still concealed in the turn of the Rue Mondétour, had witnessed, shuddering and irresolute, the first phase of the combat. But he had not long been able to resist that mysterious and sovereign vertigo which may be designated as the call of the abyss. In the presence of the imminence of the peril, in the presence of the death of M. Mabeuf, that melancholy enigma, in the presence of Bahorel killed, and Courfeyrac shouting: "Follow me!" of that child threatened, of his friends to succor or to avenge, all hesitation had vanished, and he had flung himself into the conflict, his two pistols in hand. With his first shot he had saved Gavroche, and with the second delivered Courfeyrac.

Amid the sound of the shots, amid the cries of the assaulted guards, the assailants had climbed the entrenchment, on whose summit Municipal Guards, soldiers of the line and National Guards from the suburbs could now be seen, gun in hand, rearing themselves to more than half the height of their bodies.

They already covered more than two-thirds of the barrier, but they did not leap into the enclosure, as though wavering in the fear of some trap. They gazed into the dark barricade as one would gaze into a lion's den. The light of the torch illuminated only their bayonets, their bear-skin caps, and the upper part of their uneasy and angry faces.

Marius had no longer any weapons; he had flung away his discharged pistols after firing them; but he had caught sight of the barrel of powder in the tap-room, near the door.

As he turned half round, gazing in that direction, a soldier took aim at him. At the moment when the soldier was sighting Marius, a hand was laid on the muzzle of the gun and obstructed it. This was done by some one who had darted forward,—the young workman in velvet trousers. The shot sped, traversed the hand and possibly, also, the workman, since he fell, but the ball did not strike Marius. All this, which was rather to be apprehended than seen through the smoke, Marius, who was entering the tap-room, hardly noticed. Still, he had, in a confused way, perceived that gun-barrel aimed at him, and the hand which had blocked it, and he had heard the discharge. But in moments like this, the things which one sees vacillate and are precipitated, and one pauses for nothing. One feels obscurely impelled towards more darkness still, and all is cloud.

The insurgents, surprised but not terrified, had rallied. Enjolras had shouted: "Wait! Don't fire at random!" In the first confusion, they might, in fact, wound each other. The majority of them had ascended to the window on the first story and to the attic windows, whence they commanded the assailants.

The most determined, with Enjolras, Courfeyrac, Jean Prouvaire, and Combeferre, had proudly placed themselves with their backs against the houses at the rear, unsheltered and facing the ranks of soldiers and guards who crowned the barricade.

All this was accomplished without haste, with that strange and threatening gravity which precedes engagements. They took aim, point blank, on both sides: they were so close that they could talk together without raising their voices.

When they had reached this point where the spark is on the brink of darting forth, an officer in a gorget extended his sword and said:—

"Lay down your arms!"

"Fire!" replied Enjolras.

The two discharges took place at the same moment, and all disappeared in smoke.

An acrid and stifling smoke in which dying and wounded lay with weak, dull groans. When the smoke cleared away, the combatants on both sides could be seen to be thinned out, but still in the same positions, reloading in silence. All at once, a thundering voice was heard, shouting:—

"Be off with you, or I'll blow up the barricade!"

All turned in the direction whence the voice proceeded.

Marius had entered the tap-room, and had seized the barrel of powder, then he had taken advantage of the smoke, and the sort of obscure mist which filled the entrenched enclosure, to glide along the barricade as far as that cage of paving-stones where the torch was fixed. To tear it from the torch, to replace it by the barrel of powder, to thrust the pile of stones under the barrel, which was instantly staved in, with a sort of horrible obedience,—all this had cost Marius but the time necessary to stoop and rise again; and now all, National Guards, Municipal Guards, officers, soldiers, huddled at the other extremity of the barricade, gazed stupidly at him, as he stood with his foot on the stones, his torch in his hand, his haughty face illuminated by a fatal resolution, drooping the flame of the torch towards that redoubtable pile where they could make out the broken barrel of powder, and giving vent to that startling cry:—

"Be off with you, or I'll blow up the barricade!"

Marius on that barricade after the octogenarian was the vision of the young revolution after the apparition of the old.

"Blow up the barricade!" said a sergeant, "and yourself with it!"

Marius retorted: "And myself also."

And he dropped the torch towards the barrel of powder.

But there was no longer any one on the barrier. The assailants, abandoning their dead and wounded, flowed back pell-mell and in disorder towards the extremity of the street, and there were again lost in the night. It was a headlong flight.

The barricade was free.

V

END OF THE VERSES OF JEAN PROUVAIRE

All flocked around Marius. Courfeyrac flung himself on his neck.

"Here you are!"

"What luck!" said Combeferre.

"You came in opportunely!" ejaculated Bossuet.

"If it had not been for you, I should have been dead!" began Courfeyrac again.

"If it had not been for you, I should have been gobbled up!" added Gavroche.

Marius asked:—

"Where is the chief?"

"You are he!" said Enjolras.

Marius had had a furnace in his brain all day long; now it was a whirlwind. This whirlwind which was within him, produced on him the effect of being outside of him and of bearing him away. It seemed to him that he was already at an immense distance from life. His two luminous months of joy and love, ending abruptly at that frightful precipice, Cosette lost to him, that barricade, M. Mabeuf getting himself killed for the Republic, himself the leader of the insurgents,—all these things appeared to him like a tremendous nightmare. He was obliged to make a mental effort to recall the fact that all that surrounded him was real. Marius had already seen too much of life not to know that nothing is more imminent than the impossible, and that what it is always necessary to foresee is the unforeseen. He had looked on at his own drama as a piece which one does not understand.

In the mists which enveloped his thoughts, he did not recognize Javert, who, bound to his post, had not so much as moved his head during the whole of the attack on the barricade, and who had gazed on the revolt seething around him with the resignation of a martyr and the majesty of a judge. Marius had not even seen him.

In the meanwhile, the assailants did not stir, they could be heard marching and swarming through at the end of the street but they did not venture into it, either because they were awaiting orders or because they were awaiting reinforcements before hurling themselves afresh

VICTOR HUGO

on this impregnable redoubt. The insurgents had posted sentinels, and some of them, who were medical students, set about caring for the wounded.

They had thrown the tables out of the wine-shop, with the exception of the two tables reserved for lint and cartridges, and of the one on which lay Father Mabeuf; they had added them to the barricade, and had replaced them in the tap-room with mattresses from the bed of the widow Hucheloup and her servants. On these mattresses they had laid the wounded. As for the three poor creatures who inhabited Corinthe, no one knew what had become of them. They were finally found, however, hidden in the cellar.

A poignant emotion clouded the joy of the disencumbered barricade.

The roll was called. One of the insurgents was missing. And who was it? One of the dearest. One of the most valiant. Jean Prouvaire. He was sought among the wounded, he was not there. He was sought among the dead, he was not there. He was evidently a prisoner. Combeferre said to Enjolras:—

"They have our friend; we have their agent. Are you set on the death of that spy?"

"Yes," replied Enjolras; "but less so than on the life of Jean Prouvaire."

This took place in the tap-room near Javert's post.

"Well," resumed Combeferre, "I am going to fasten my handkerchief to my cane, and go as a flag of truce, to offer to exchange our man for theirs."

"Listen," said Enjolras, laying his hand on Combeferre's arm.

At the end of the street there was a significant clash of arms.

They heard a manly voice shout:—

"Vive la France! Long live France! Long live the future!"

They recognized the voice of Prouvaire.

A flash passed, a report rang out.

Silence fell again.

"They have killed him," exclaimed Combeferre.

Enjolras glanced at Javert, and said to him:—

"Your friends have just shot you."

VI

The Agony of Death After the Agony of Life

A peculiarity of this species of war is, that the attack of the barricades is almost always made from the front, and that the assailants generally abstain from turning the position, either because they fear ambushes, or because they are afraid of getting entangled in the tortuous streets. The insurgents' whole attention had been directed, therefore, to the grand barricade, which was, evidently, the spot always menaced, and there the struggle would infallibly recommence. But Marius thought of the little barricade, and went thither. It was deserted and guarded only by the fire-pot which trembled between the paving-stones. Moreover, the Mondétour alley, and the branches of the Rue de la Petite Truanderie and the Rue du Cygne were profoundly calm.

As Marius was withdrawing, after concluding his inspection, he heard his name pronounced feebly in the darkness.

"Monsieur Marius!"

He started, for he recognized the voice which had called to him two hours before through the gate in the Rue Plumet.

Only, the voice now seemed to be nothing more than a breath.

He looked about him, but saw no one.

Marius thought he had been mistaken, that it was an illusion added by his mind to the extraordinary realities which were clashing around him. He advanced a step, in order to quit the distant recess where the barricade lay.

"Monsieur Marius!" repeated the voice.

This time he could not doubt that he had heard it distinctly; he looked and saw nothing.

"At your feet," said the voice.

He bent down, and saw in the darkness a form which was dragging itself towards him.

It was crawling along the pavement. It was this that had spoken to him.

The fire-pot allowed him to distinguish a blouse, torn trousers of coarse velvet, bare feet, and something which resembled a pool of blood.

Marius indistinctly made out a pale head which was lifted towards him and which was saying to him:—

"You do not recognize me?"

"No."

"Éponine."

Marius bent hastily down. It was, in fact, that unhappy child. She was dressed in men's clothes.

"How come you here? What are you doing here?"

"I am dying," said she.

There are words and incidents which arouse dejected beings. Marius cried out with a start:—

"You are wounded! Wait, I will carry you into the room! They will attend to you there. Is it serious? How must I take hold of you in order not to hurt you? Where do you suffer? Help! My God! But why did you come hither?"

And he tried to pass his arm under her, in order to raise her.

She uttered a feeble cry.

"Have I hurt you?" asked Marius.

"A little."

"But I only touched your hand."

She raised her hand to Marius, and in the middle of that hand Marius saw a black hole.

"What is the matter with your hand?" said he.

"It is pierced."

"Pierced?"

"Yes."

"What with?"

"A bullet."

"How?"

"Did you see a gun aimed at you?"

"Yes, and a hand stopping it."

"It was mine."

Marius was seized with a shudder.

"What madness! Poor child! But so much the better, if that is all, it is nothing, let me carry you to a bed. They will dress your wound; one does not die of a pierced hand."

She murmured:—

"The bullet traversed my hand, but it came out through my back. It is useless to remove me from this spot. I will tell you how you can care for me better than any surgeon. Sit down near me on this stone."

He obeyed; she laid her head on Marius' knees, and, without looking at him, she said:—

"Oh! How good this is! How comfortable this is! There; I no longer suffer."

She remained silent for a moment, then she turned her face with an effort, and looked at Marius.

"Do you know what, Monsieur Marius? It puzzled me because you entered that garden; it was stupid, because it was I who showed you that house; and then, I ought to have said to myself that a young man like you—"

She paused, and overstepping the sombre transitions that undoubtedly existed in her mind, she resumed with a heartrending smile:—

"You thought me ugly, didn't you?"

She continued:—

"You see, you are lost! Now, no one can get out of the barricade. It was I who led you here, by the way! You are going to die, I count upon that. And yet, when I saw them taking aim at you, I put my hand on the muzzle of the gun. How queer it is! But it was because I wanted to die before you. When I received that bullet, I dragged myself here, no one saw me, no one picked me up, I was waiting for you, I said: 'So he is not coming!' Oh, if you only knew. I bit my blouse, I suffered so! Now I am well. Do you remember the day I entered your chamber and when I looked at myself in your mirror, and the day when I came to you on the boulevard near the washerwomen? How the birds sang! That was a long time ago. You gave me a hundred sous, and I said to you: 'I don't want your money.' I hope you picked up your coin? You are not rich. I did not think to tell you to pick it up. The sun was shining bright, and it was not cold. Do you remember, Monsieur Marius? Oh! How happy I am! Every one is going to die."

She had a mad, grave, and heart-breaking air. Her torn blouse disclosed her bare throat.

As she talked, she pressed her pierced hand to her breast, where there was another hole, and whence there spurted from moment to moment a stream of blood, like a jet of wine from an open bung-hole.

Marius gazed at this unfortunate creature with profound compassion.

"Oh!" she resumed, "it is coming again, I am stifling!"

She caught up her blouse and bit it, and her limbs stiffened on the pavement.

VICTOR HUGO

At that moment the young cock's crow executed by little Gavroche resounded through the barricade.

The child had mounted a table to load his gun, and was singing gayly the song then so popular:—

"En voyant Lafayette,
Le gendarme répète:—
Sauvons nous! sauvons nous!
sauvons nous!"

"On beholding Lafayette,
The gendarme repeats:—
Let us flee! let us flee!
let us flee!

Éponine raised herself and listened; then she murmured:—

"It is he."

And turning to Marius:—

"My brother is here. He must not see me. He would scold me."

"Your brother?" inquired Marius, who was meditating in the most bitter and sorrowful depths of his heart on the duties to the Thénardiers which his father had bequeathed to him; "who is your brother?"

"That little fellow."

"The one who is singing?"

"Yes."

Marius made a movement.

"Oh! don't go away," said she, "it will not be long now."

She was sitting almost upright, but her voice was very low and broken by hiccoughs.

At intervals, the death rattle interrupted her. She put her face as near that of Marius as possible. She added with a strange expression:—

"Listen, I do not wish to play you a trick. I have a letter in my pocket for you. I was told to put it in the post. I kept it. I did not want to have it reach you. But perhaps you will be angry with me for it when we meet again presently? Take your letter."

She grasped Marius' hand convulsively with her pierced hand, but she no longer seemed to feel her sufferings. She put Marius' hand in the pocket of her blouse. There, in fact, Marius felt a paper.

"Take it," said she.

Marius took the letter.

She made a sign of satisfaction and contentment.

"Now, for my trouble, promise me—"

And she stopped.

"What?" asked Marius.

"Promise me!"

"I promise."

"Promise to give me a kiss on my brow when I am dead.—I shall feel it."

She dropped her head again on Marius' knees, and her eyelids closed. He thought the poor soul had departed. Éponine remained motionless. All at once, at the very moment when Marius fancied her asleep forever, she slowly opened her eyes in which appeared the sombre profundity of death, and said to him in a tone whose sweetness seemed already to proceed from another world:—

"And by the way, Monsieur Marius, I believe that I was a little bit in love with you."

She tried to smile once more and expired.

VII

Gavroche as a Profound Calculator of Distances

Marius kept his promise. He dropped a kiss on that livid brow, where the icy perspiration stood in beads.

This was no infidelity to Cosette; it was a gentle and pensive farewell to an unhappy soul.

It was not without a tremor that he had taken the letter which Éponine had given him. He had immediately felt that it was an event of weight. He was impatient to read it. The heart of man is so constituted that the unhappy child had hardly closed her eyes when Marius began to think of unfolding this paper.

He laid her gently on the ground, and went away. Something told him that he could not peruse that letter in the presence of that body.

He drew near to a candle in the tap-room. It was a small note, folded and sealed with a woman's elegant care. The address was in a woman's hand and ran:—

"To Monsieur, Monsieur Marius Pontmercy, at
M. Courfeyrac's, Rue de la Verrerie, No. 16."

He broke the seal and read:—

My dearest, alas! my father insists on our setting out immediately.
We shall be this evening in the Rue de l'Homme Armé, No. 7.
In a week we shall be in England.

Cosette
June 4th

Such was the innocence of their love that Marius was not even acquainted with Cosette's handwriting.

What had taken place may be related in a few words. Éponine had been the cause of everything. After the evening of the 3d of June she had cherished a double idea, to defeat the projects of her father and the ruffians on the house of the Rue Plumet, and to separate Marius and Cosette. She had exchanged rags with the first young scamp she came across who had thought it amusing to dress like a woman, while Éponine disguised herself like a man. It was she who had conveyed to Jean Valjean in the Champ de Mars the expressive warning: "Leave your house." Jean Valjean had, in fact, returned home, and had said to Cosette: "We set out this evening and we go to the Rue de l'Homme Armé with Toussaint. Next week, we shall be in London." Cosette, utterly overwhelmed by this unexpected blow, had hastily penned a couple of lines to Marius. But how was she to get the letter to the post? She never went out alone, and Toussaint, surprised at such a commission, would certainly show the letter to M. Fauchelevent. In this dilemma, Cosette had caught sight through the fence of Éponine in man's clothes, who now prowled incessantly around the garden. Cosette had called to "this young workman" and had handed him five francs and the letter, saying: "Carry this letter immediately to its address." Éponine had put the letter in her pocket. The next day, on the 5th of June, she went to Courfeyrac's quarters to inquire for Marius, not for the purpose of delivering the letter, but,—a thing which every jealous and loving soul will comprehend,—"to see." There she had waited for Marius, or at least for Courfeyrac, still for the purpose of *seeing*. When Courfeyrac had told her: "We are going to the barricades," an idea flashed through her mind, to fling herself into that death, as she would have done into any other, and to thrust Marius into it also. She had followed Courfeyrac, had made sure of the locality where the barricade was in process of construction; and, quite certain, since Marius had received no warning, and since she had intercepted the letter, that he would go at dusk to his trysting place for every evening, she had betaken herself to the Rue Plumet, had there awaited Marius, and had sent him, in the name of his friends, the appeal which would, she thought, lead him to the barricade. She reckoned on Marius' despair when he should fail to find Cosette; she was not mistaken. She had returned to the Rue de la Chanvrerie herself. What she did there the reader has just seen. She died with the tragic joy of jealous hearts who drag the beloved being into their own death, and who say: "No one shall have him!"

Marius covered Cosette's letter with kisses. So she loved him! For one moment the idea occurred to him that he ought not to die now.

Then he said to himself: "She is going away. Her father is taking her to England, and my grandfather refuses his consent to the marriage. Nothing is changed in our fates." Dreamers like Marius are subject to supreme attacks of dejection, and desperate resolves are the result. The fatigue of living is insupportable; death is sooner over with. Then he reflected that he had still two duties to fulfil: to inform Cosette of his death and send her a final farewell, and to save from the impending catastrophe which was in preparation, that poor child, Éponine's brother and Thénardier's son.

He had a pocket-book about him; the same one which had contained the note-book in which he had inscribed so many thoughts of love for Cosette. He tore out a leaf and wrote on it a few lines in pencil:—

"Our marriage was impossible. I asked my grandfather, he refused; I have no fortune, neither hast thou. I hastened to thee, thou wert no longer there. Thou knowest the promise that I gave thee, I shall keep it. I die. I love thee. When thou readest this, my soul will be near thee, and thou wilt smile."

Having nothing wherewith to seal this letter, he contented himself with folding the paper in four, and added the address:—

"To Mademoiselle Cosette Fauchelevent, at M. Fauchelevent's, Rue de l'Homme Armé, No. 7."

Having folded the letter, he stood in thought for a moment, drew out his pocket-book again, opened it, and wrote, with the same pencil, these four lines on the first page:—

"My name is Marius Pontmercy. Carry my body to my grandfather, M. Gillenormand, Rue des Filles-du-Calvaire, No. 6, in the Marais."

He put his pocketbook back in his pocket, then he called Gavroche.

The gamin, at the sound of Marius' voice, ran up to him with his merry and devoted air.

"Will you do something for me?"

"Anything," said Gavroche. "Good God! if it had not been for you, I should have been done for."

"Do you see this letter?"

"Yes."

"Take it. Leave the barricade instantly" (Gavroche began to scratch his ear uneasily) "and to-morrow morning, you will deliver it at its address to Mademoiselle Cosette, at M. Fauchelevent's, Rue de l'Homme Armé, No. 7."

The heroic child replied

"Well, but! in the meanwhile the barricade will be taken, and I shall not be there."

"The barricade will not be attacked until daybreak, according to all appearances, and will not be taken before to-morrow noon."

The fresh respite which the assailants were granting to the barricade had, in fact, been prolonged. It was one of those intermissions which frequently occur in nocturnal combats, which are always followed by an increase of rage.

"Well," said Gavroche, "what if I were to go and carry your letter to-morrow?"

"It will be too late. The barricade will probably be blockaded, all the streets will be guarded, and you will not be able to get out. Go at once."

Gavroche could think of no reply to this, and stood there in indecision, scratching his ear sadly.

All at once, he took the letter with one of those birdlike movements which were common with him.

"All right," said he.

And he started off at a run through Mondétour lane.

An idea had occurred to Gavroche which had brought him to a decision, but he had not mentioned it for fear that Marius might offer some objection to it.

This was the idea:—

"It is barely midnight, the Rue de l'Homme Armé is not far off; I will go and deliver the letter at once, and I shall get back in time."

BOOK FIFTEENTH
THE RUE DE L'HOMME ARMÉ

I

A Drinker is a Babbler

What are the convulsions of a city in comparison with the insurrections of the soul? Man is a depth still greater than the people. Jean Valjean at that very moment was the prey of a terrible upheaval. Every sort of gulf had opened again within him. He also was trembling, like Paris, on the brink of an obscure and formidable revolution. A few hours had sufficed to bring this about. His destiny and his conscience had suddenly been covered with gloom. Of him also, as well as of Paris, it might have been said: "Two principles are face to face. The white angel and the black angel are about to seize each other on the bridge of the abyss. Which of the two will hurl the other over? Who will carry the day?"

On the evening preceding this same 5th of June, Jean Valjean, accompanied by Cosette and Toussaint had installed himself in the Rue de l'Homme Armé. A change awaited him there.

Cosette had not quitted the Rue Plumet without making an effort at resistance. For the first time since they had lived side by side, Cosette's will and the will of Jean Valjean had proved to be distinct, and had been in opposition, at least, if they had not clashed. There had been objections on one side and inflexibility on the other. The abrupt advice: "Leave your house," hurled at Jean Valjean by a stranger, had alarmed him to the extent of rendering him peremptory. He thought that he had been traced and followed. Cosette had been obliged to give way.

Both had arrived in the Rue de l'Homme Armé without opening their lips, and without uttering a word, each being absorbed in his own personal preoccupation; Jean Valjean so uneasy that he did not notice Cosette's sadness, Cosette so sad that she did not notice Jean Valjean's uneasiness.

Jean Valjean had taken Toussaint with him, a thing which he had never done in his previous absences. He perceived the possibility of not returning to the Rue Plumet, and he could neither leave Toussaint behind nor confide his secret to her. Besides, he felt that she was devoted and trustworthy. Treachery between master and servant begins in curiosity. Now Toussaint, as though she had been destined to be Jean

Valjean's servant, was not curious. She stammered in her peasant dialect of Barneville: "I am made so; I do my work; the rest is no affair of mine."

In this departure from the Rue Plumet, which had been almost a flight, Jean Valjean had carried away nothing but the little embalmed valise, baptized by Cosette "the inseparable." Full trunks would have required porters, and porters are witnesses. A fiacre had been summoned to the door on the Rue de Babylone, and they had taken their departure.

It was with difficulty that Toussaint had obtained permission to pack up a little linen and clothes and a few toilet articles. Cosette had taken only her portfolio and her blotting-book.

Jean Valjean, with a view to augmenting the solitude and the mystery of this departure, had arranged to quit the pavilion of the Rue Plumet only at dusk, which had allowed Cosette time to write her note to Marius. They had arrived in the Rue de l'Homme Armé after night had fully fallen.

They had gone to bed in silence.

The lodgings in the Rue de l'Homme Armé were situated on a back court, on the second floor, and were composed of two sleeping-rooms, a dining-room and a kitchen adjoining the dining-room, with a garret where there was a folding-bed, and which fell to Toussaint's share. The dining-room was an antechamber as well, and separated the two bedrooms. The apartment was provided with all necessary utensils.

People re-acquire confidence as foolishly as they lose it; human nature is so constituted. Hardly had Jean Valjean reached the Rue de l'Homme Armé when his anxiety was lightened and by degrees dissipated. There are soothing spots which act in some sort mechanically on the mind. An obscure street, peaceable inhabitants. Jean Valjean experienced an indescribable contagion of tranquillity in that alley of ancient Paris, which is so narrow that it is barred against carriages by a transverse beam placed on two posts, which is deaf and dumb in the midst of the clamorous city, dimly lighted at midday, and is, so to speak, incapable of emotions between two rows of lofty houses centuries old, which hold their peace like ancients as they are. There was a touch of stagnant oblivion in that street. Jean Valjean drew his breath once more there. How could he be found there?

His first care was to place *the inseparable* beside him.

He slept well. Night brings wisdom; we may add, night soothes. On the following morning he awoke in a mood that was almost gay. He thought the dining-room charming, though it was hideous, furnished with an old round table, a long sideboard surmounted by a slanting mirror, a dilapidated armchair, and several plain chairs which were encumbered with Toussaint's packages. In one of these packages Jean Valjean's uniform of a National Guard was visible through a rent.

As for Cosette, she had had Toussaint take some broth to her room, and did not make her appearance until evening.

About five o'clock, Toussaint, who was going and coming and busying herself with the tiny establishment, set on the table a cold chicken, which Cosette, out of deference to her father, consented to glance at.

That done, Cosette, under the pretext of an obstinate sick headache, had bade Jean Valjean good night and had shut herself up in her chamber. Jean Valjean had eaten a wing of the chicken with a good appetite, and with his elbows on the table, having gradually recovered his serenity, had regained possession of his sense of security.

While he was discussing this modest dinner, he had, twice or thrice, noticed in a confused way, Toussaint's stammering words as she said to him: "Monsieur, there is something going on, they are fighting in Paris." But absorbed in a throng of inward calculations, he had paid no heed to it. To tell the truth, he had not heard her. He rose and began to pace from the door to the window and from the window to the door, growing ever more serene.

With this calm, Cosette, his sole anxiety, recurred to his thoughts. Not that he was troubled by this headache, a little nervous crisis, a young girl's fit of sulks, the cloud of a moment, there would be nothing left of it in a day or two; but he meditated on the future, and, as was his habit, he thought of it with pleasure. After all, he saw no obstacle to their happy life resuming its course. At certain hours, everything seems impossible, at others everything appears easy; Jean Valjean was in the midst of one of these good hours. They generally succeed the bad ones, as day follows night, by virtue of that law of succession and of contrast which lies at the very foundation of nature, and which superficial minds call antithesis. In this peaceful street where he had taken refuge, Jean Valjean got rid of all that had been troubling him for some time past. This very fact, that he had seen many shadows, made him begin to perceive a little azure. To have quitted the Rue Plumet without complications or incidents was one good step already accomplished. Perhaps it would be wise to go abroad, if only for a few months, and to set out for London. Well, they would go. What difference did it make to him whether he was in France or in England, provided he had Cosette beside him? Cosette was his nation. Cosette sufficed for his happiness; the idea that he, perhaps, did not suffice for Cosette's happiness, that idea which had formerly been the cause of his fever and sleeplessness, did not even present itself to his mind. He was in a state of collapse from all his past sufferings, and he was fully entered on optimism. Cosette was by his side, she seemed to be his; an optical illusion which every one has experienced. He arranged in his own mind, with all sorts of felicitous devices, his departure for England with Cosette, and he beheld his felicity reconstituted wherever he pleased, in the perspective of his reverie.

As he paced to and fro with long strides, his glance suddenly encountered something strange.

In the inclined mirror facing him which surmounted the sideboard, he saw the four lines which follow:—

My dearest, alas! my father insists on our setting out immediately. We shall be this evening in the Rue de l'Homme Armé, No. 7. In a week we shall be in England.

Cosette
June 4th

Jean Valjean halted, perfectly haggard.

Cosette on her arrival had placed her blotting-book on the sideboard in front of the mirror, and, utterly absorbed in her agony of grief, had forgotten it and left it there, without even observing that she had left it wide open, and open at precisely the page on which she had laid to dry the four lines which she had penned, and which she had given in charge of the young workman in the Rue Plumet. The writing had been printed off on the blotter.

The mirror reflected the writing.

The result was, what is called in geometry, *the symmetrical image*; so that the writing, reversed on the blotter, was righted in the mirror and presented its natural appearance; and Jean Valjean had beneath his eyes the letter written by Cosette to Marius on the preceding evening.

It was simple and withering.

Jean Valjean stepped up to the mirror. He read the four lines again, but he did not believe them. They produced on him the effect of appearing in a flash of lightning. It was a hallucination, it was impossible. It was not so.

Little by little, his perceptions became more precise; he looked at Cosette's blotting-book, and the consciousness of the reality returned to him. He caught up the blotter and said: "It comes from there." He feverishly examined the four lines imprinted on the blotter, the reversal of the letters converted into an odd scrawl, and he saw no sense in it. Then he said to himself: "But this signifies nothing; there is nothing written here." And he drew a long breath with inexpressible relief. Who has not experienced those foolish joys in horrible instants? The soul does not surrender to despair until it has exhausted all illusions.

He held the blotter in his hand and contemplated it in stupid delight, almost ready to laugh at the hallucination of which he had been the dupe. All at once his eyes fell upon the mirror again, and again he beheld the vision. There were the four lines outlined with inexorable clearness. This time it was no mirage. The recurrence of a vision is a reality; it was palpable, it was the writing restored in the mirror. He understood.

Jean Valjean tottered, dropped the blotter, and fell into the old armchair beside the buffet, with drooping head, and glassy eyes, in utter bewilderment. He told himself that it was plain, that the light of the world had been eclipsed forever, and that Cosette had written that to some one. Then he heard his soul, which had become terrible once more, give vent to a dull roar in the gloom. Try then the effect of taking from the lion the dog which he has in his cage!

Strange and sad to say, at that very moment, Marius had not yet received Cosette's letter; chance had treacherously carried it to Jean Valjean before delivering it to Marius. Up to that day, Jean Valjean had not been vanquished by trial. He had been subjected to fearful proofs; no violence of bad fortune had been spared him; the ferocity of fate, armed with all vindictiveness and all social scorn, had taken him for her prey and had raged against him. He had accepted every extremity when it had been necessary; he had sacrificed his inviolability as a reformed man, had yielded up his liberty, risked his head, lost everything, suffered everything, and he had remained disinterested and stoical to such a point that he might have been thought to be absent from himself like a martyr. His conscience inured to every assault of destiny, might have appeared to be forever impregnable. Well, any one who had beheld his spiritual self would have been obliged to concede that it weakened at that moment. It was because, of all the tortures which he had undergone in the course of this long inquisition to which destiny had doomed him, this was the most terrible. Never had such pincers seized him hitherto. He felt the mysterious stirring of all his latent sensibilities. He felt the plucking at the strange chord. Alas! the supreme trial, let us say rather, the only trial, is the loss of the beloved being.

Poor old Jean Valjean certainly did not love Cosette otherwise than as a father; but we have already remarked, above, that into this paternity the widowhood of his life had introduced all the shades of love; he loved Cosette as his daughter, and he loved her as his mother, and he loved her as his sister; and, as he had never had either a woman to love or a wife, as nature is a creditor who accepts no protest, that sentiment also, the most impossible to lose, was mingled with the rest, vague, ignorant, pure with the purity of blindness, unconscious, celestial, angelic, divine; less like a sentiment than like an instinct, less like an instinct than like an imperceptible and invisible but real attraction; and love, properly speaking, was, in his immense tenderness for Cosette, like the thread of gold in the mountain, concealed and virgin.

Let the reader recall the situation of heart which we have already indicated. No marriage was possible between them; not even that of souls; and yet, it is certain that their destinies were wedded. With the exception of Cosette, that is to say, with the exception of a childhood, Jean Valjean had never, in the whole of his long life, known anything of that which may be loved. The passions and loves which succeed each other had not produced in him those successive green growths, tender green or dark green, which can be seen in foliage which passes through the winter and in men who pass fifty. In short, and we have insisted on it more than once, all this interior fusion, all this whole, of which the sum total was a lofty virtue, ended in rendering Jean Valjean a father to Cosette. A strange father, forged from the grandfather, the son, the brother, and the husband, that existed in Jean Valjean; a father in whom there was included even a mother; a father who loved Cosette and adored her, and who held that child as his light, his home, his family, his country, his paradise.

Thus when he saw that the end had absolutely come, that she was escaping from him, that she was slipping from his hands, that she was gliding from him, like a cloud, like water, when he had before his eyes this crushing proof: "another is the goal of her heart, another is the wish of her life; there is a dearest one, I am no longer anything but her father, I no longer exist"; when he could no longer doubt, when he said to himself: "She is going away from me!" the grief which he felt surpassed the bounds of possibility. To have done all that he had done for the purpose of ending like this! And the very idea of being nothing! Then, as we have just said, a quiver of revolt ran through him from head to foot. He felt, even in the very roots of his hair, the immense reawakening of egotism, and the *I* in this man's abyss howled.

There is such a thing as the sudden giving way of the inward subsoil. A despairing certainty does not make its way into a man without thrusting aside and breaking certain profound elements which, in some cases, are the very man himself. Grief, when it attains this shape, is a headlong flight of all the forces of the conscience. These are fatal crises. Few among us emerge from them still like ourselves and firm in duty. When the limit of endurance is overstepped, the most imperturbable virtue is disconcerted. Jean Valjean took the blotter again, and convinced himself afresh; he remained bowed and as though petrified and with staring eyes, over those four unobjectionable lines; and there arose within him such a cloud that one might have thought that everything in this soul was crumbling away.

He examined this revelation, athwart the exaggerations of reverie, with an apparent and terrifying calmness, for it is a fearful thing when a man's calmness reaches the coldness of the statue.

He measured the terrible step which his destiny had taken without his having a suspicion of the fact; he recalled his fears of the preceding summer, so foolishly dissipated; he recognized the precipice, it was still the same; only, Jean Valjean was no longer on the brink, he was at the bottom of it.

The unprecedented and heart-rending thing about it was that he had fallen without perceiving it. All the light of his life had departed, while he still fancied that he beheld the sun.

His instinct did not hesitate. He put together certain circumstances, certain dates, certain blushes and certain pallors on Cosette's part, and he said to himself: "It is he."

The divination of despair is a sort of mysterious bow which never misses its aim. He struck Marius with his first conjecture. He did not know the name, but he found the man instantly. He distinctly perceived, in the background of the implacable conjuration of his memories, the unknown prowler of the Luxembourg, that wretched seeker of love adventures, that idler of romance, that idiot, that coward, for it is cowardly to come and make eyes at young girls who have beside them a father who loves them.

After he had thoroughly verified the fact that this young man was at the bottom of this situation, and that everything proceeded from that quarter, he, Jean Valjean, the regenerated man, the man who had so labored over his soul, the man who had made so many efforts to resolve all life, all misery, and all unhappiness into love, looked into his own breast and there beheld a spectre, Hate.

Great griefs contain something of dejection. They discourage one with existence. The man into whom they enter feels something within him withdraw from him. In his youth, their visits are lugubrious; later on they are sinister. Alas, if despair is a fearful thing when the blood is hot, when the hair is black, when the head is erect on the body like the flame on the torch, when the roll of destiny still retains its full thickness, when the heart, full of desirable love, still possesses beats which can be returned to it, when one has time for redress, when all women and all smiles and all the future and all the horizon are before one, when the force of life is complete, what is it in old age, when the years hasten on, growing ever paler, to that twilight hour when one begins to behold the stars of the tomb?

While he was meditating, Toussaint entered. Jean Valjean rose and asked her:—

"In what quarter is it? Do you know?"

Toussaint was struck dumb, and could only answer him:—

"What is it, sir?"

Jean Valjean began again: "Did you not tell me that just now that there is fighting going on?"

"Ah! yes, sir," replied Toussaint. "It is in the direction of Saint-Merry."

There is a mechanical movement which comes to us, unconsciously, from the most profound depths of our thought. It was, no doubt, under the impulse of a movement of this sort, and of which he was hardly conscious, that Jean Valjean, five minutes later, found himself in the street.

Bareheaded, he sat upon the stone post at the door of his house. He seemed to be listening.

Night had come.

II

The Street Urchin an Enemy of Light

How long did he remain thus? What was the ebb and flow of this tragic meditation? Did he straighten up? Did he remain bowed? Had he been bent to breaking? Could he still rise and regain his footing in his conscience upon something solid? He probably would not have been able to tell himself.

The street was deserted. A few uneasy bourgeois, who were rapidly returning home, hardly saw him. Each one for himself in times of peril. The lamp-lighter came as usual to light the lantern which was situated precisely opposite the door of No. 7, and then went away. Jean Valjean would not have appeared like a living man to any one who had examined him in that shadow. He sat there on the post of his door, motionless as a form of ice. There is congealment in despair. The alarm bells and a vague and stormy uproar were audible. In the midst of all these convulsions of the bell mingled with the revolt, the clock of Saint-Paul struck eleven, gravely and without haste; for the tocsin is man; the hour is God. The passage of the hour produced no effect on Jean Valjean; Jean Valjean did not stir. Still, at about that moment, a brusque report burst forth in the direction of the Halles, a second yet more violent followed; it was probably that attack on the barricade in the Rue de la Chanvrerie which we have just seen repulsed by Marius. At this double discharge, whose fury seemed augmented by the stupor of the night, Jean Valjean started; he rose, turning towards the quarter whence the noise proceeded; then he fell back upon the post again, folded his arms, and his head slowly sank on his bosom again.

He resumed his gloomy dialogue with himself.

All at once, he raised his eyes; some one was walking in the street, he heard steps near him. He looked, and by the light of the lanterns, in the direction of the street which ran into the Rue-aux-Archives, he perceived a young, livid, and beaming face.

Gavroche had just arrived in the Rue de l'Homme Armé.

Gavroche was staring into the air, apparently in search of something. He saw Jean Valjean perfectly well but he took no notice of him.

Gavroche after staring into the air, stared below; he raised himself on tiptoe, and felt of the doors and windows of the ground floor; they were all shut, bolted, and padlocked. After having authenticated the fronts of five or six barricaded houses in this manner, the urchin shrugged his shoulders, and took himself to task in these terms:—

"Pardi!"

Then he began to stare into the air again.

Jean Valjean, who, an instant previously, in his then state of mind, would not have spoken to or even answered any one, felt irresistibly impelled to accost that child.

"What is the matter with you, my little fellow?" he said.

"The matter with me is that I am hungry," replied Gavroche frankly. And he added: "Little fellow yourself."

Jean Valjean fumbled in his fob and pulled out a five-franc piece.

But Gavroche, who was of the wagtail species, and who skipped vivaciously from one gesture to another, had just picked up a stone. He had caught sight of the lantern.

"See here," said he, "you still have your lanterns here. You are disobeying the regulations, my friend. This is disorderly. Smash that for me."

And he flung the stone at the lantern, whose broken glass fell with such a clatter that the bourgeois in hiding behind their curtains in the opposite house cried: "There is 'Ninety-three' come again."

The lantern oscillated violently, and went out. The street had suddenly become black.

"That's right, old street," ejaculated Gavroche, "put on your night-cap."

And turning to Jean Valjean:—

"What do you call that gigantic monument that you have there at the end of the street? It's the Archives, isn't it? I must crumble up those big stupids of pillars a bit and make a nice barricade out of them."

Jean Valjean stepped up to Gavroche.

"Poor creature," he said in a low tone, and speaking to himself, "he is hungry."

And he laid the hundred-sou piece in his hand.

Gavroche raised his face, astonished at the size of this sou; he stared at it in the darkness, and the whiteness of the big sou dazzled him. He knew five-franc pieces by hearsay; their reputation was agreeable to him; he was delighted to see one close to. He said:—

"Let us contemplate the tiger."

He gazed at it for several minutes in ecstasy; then, turning to Jean Valjean, he held out the coin to him, and said majestically to him:—

"Bourgeois, I prefer to smash lanterns. Take back your ferocious beast. You can't bribe me. That has got five claws; but it doesn't scratch me."

"Have you a mother?" asked Jean Valjean.

Gavroche replied:—

"More than you have, perhaps."

"Well," returned Jean Valjean, "keep the money for your mother!"

Gavroche was touched. Moreover, he had just noticed that the man who was addressing him had no hat, and this inspired him with confidence.

"Truly," said he, "so it wasn't to keep me from breaking the lanterns?"

"Break whatever you please."

"You're a fine man," said Gavroche.

And he put the five-franc piece into one of his pockets.

His confidence having increased, he added:—

"Do you belong in this street?"

"Yes, why?"

"Can you tell me where No. 7 is?"

"What do you want with No. 7?"

Here the child paused, he feared that he had said too much; he thrust his nails energetically into his hair and contented himself with replying:—

"Ah! Here it is."

An idea flashed through Jean Valjean's mind. Anguish does have these gleams. He said to the lad:—

"Are you the person who is bringing a letter that I am expecting?"

"You?" said Gavroche. "You are not a woman."

"The letter is for Mademoiselle Cosette, is it not?"

"Cosette," muttered Gavroche. "Yes, I believe that is the queer name."

"Well," resumed Jean Valjean, "I am the person to whom you are to deliver the letter. Give it here."

"In that case, you must know that I was sent from the barricade."

"Of course," said Jean Valjean.

Gavroche engulfed his hand in another of his pockets and drew out a paper folded in four.

Then he made the military salute.

"Respect for despatches," said he. "It comes from the Provisional Government."

"Give it to me," said Jean Valjean.

Gavroche held the paper elevated above his head.

"Don't go and fancy it's a love letter. It is for a woman, but it's for the people. We men fight and we respect the fair sex. We are not as they are in fine society, where there are lions who send chickens to camels."

"Give it to me."

"After all," continued Gavroche, "you have the air of an honest man."

"Give it to me quick."

"Catch hold of it."

And he handed the paper to Jean Valjean.

"And make haste, Monsieur What's-your-name, for Mamselle Cosette is waiting."

Gavroche was satisfied with himself for having produced this remark.

Jean Valjean began again:—

"Is it to Saint-Merry that the answer is to be sent?"

"There you are making some of those bits of pastry vulgarly called *brioches* (blunders). This letter comes from the barricade of the Rue de la Chanvrerie, and I'm going back there. Good evening, citizen."

That said, Gavroche took himself off, or, to describe it more exactly, fluttered away in the direction whence he had come with a flight like that of an escaped bird. He plunged back into the gloom as though he made a hole in it, with the rigid rapidity of a projectile; the alley of l'Homme Armé became silent and solitary once more; in a twinkling, that strange child, who had about him something of the shadow and of the dream, had buried himself in the mists of the rows of black houses, and was lost there, like smoke in the dark; and one might have thought that he had dissipated and vanished, had there not taken place, a few minutes after his disappearance, a startling shiver of glass, and had not the magnificent crash of a lantern rattling down on the pavement once more abruptly awakened the indignant bourgeois. It was Gavroche upon his way through the Rue du Chaume.

III

WHILE COSETTE AND TOUSSAINT ARE ASLEEP

J ean Valjean went into the house with Marius' letter.

He groped his way up the stairs, as pleased with the darkness as an owl who grips his prey, opened and shut his door softly, listened to see whether he could hear any noise,—made sure that, to all appearances, Cosette and Toussaint were asleep, and plunged three or four matches into the bottle of the Fumade lighter before he could evoke a spark, so greatly did his hand tremble. What he had just done smacked of theft. At last the candle was lighted; he leaned his elbows on the table, unfolded the paper, and read.

In violent emotions, one does not read, one flings to the earth, so to speak, the paper which one holds, one clutches it like a victim, one crushes it, one digs into it the nails of one's wrath, or of one's joy; one hastens to the end, one leaps to the beginning; attention is at fever heat; it takes up in the gross, as it were, the essential points; it seizes on one point, and the rest disappears. In Marius' note to Cosette, Jean Valjean saw only these words:—

"I die. When thou readest this, my soul will be near thee."

In the presence of these two lines, he was horribly dazzled; he remained for a moment, crushed, as it were, by the change of emotion which was taking place within him, he stared at Marius' note with a sort of intoxicated amazement, he had before his eyes that splendor, the death of a hated individual.

He uttered a frightful cry of inward joy. So it was all over. The catastrophe had arrived sooner than he had dared to hope. The being who obstructed his destiny was disappearing. That man had taken himself off of his own accord, freely, willingly. This man was going to his death, and he, Jean Valjean, had had no hand in the matter, and it was through no fault of his. Perhaps, even, he is already dead. Here his fever entered into calculations. No, he is not dead yet. The letter had evidently been intended for Cosette to read on the following morning; after the two discharges that were heard between eleven o'clock and midnight, nothing more has taken place; the barricade will not be attacked seriously until daybreak; but that makes no difference, from the moment when "that man" is concerned in this war, he is lost; he is caught in the gearing. Jean Valjean felt himself delivered. So he was about to find himself alone with Cosette once more. The rivalry would cease; the future was beginning again. He had but to keep this note in his pocket. Cosette would never know what had become of that man. All that there requires to be done is to let things take their own course. This man cannot escape. If he is not already dead, it is certain that he is about to die. What good fortune!

Having said all this to himself, he became gloomy.

Then he went downstairs and woke up the porter.

About an hour later, Jean Valjean went out in the complete costume of a National Guard, and with his arms. The porter had easily found in the neighborhood the wherewithal to complete his equipment. He had a loaded gun and a cartridge-box filled with cartridges.

He strode off in the direction of the markets.

IV

GAVROCHE'S EXCESS OF ZEAL

In the meantime, Gavroche had had an adventure.

Gavroche, after having conscientiously stoned the lantern in the Rue du Chaume, entered the Rue des Vieilles-Haudriettes, and not seeing "even a cat" there, he thought the opportunity a good one to strike up all the song of which he was capable. His march, far from being retarded by his singing, was accelerated by it. He began to sow along the sleeping or terrified houses these incendiary couplets:—

> "L'oiseau médit dans les charmilles,
> Et prétend qu'hier Atala
> Avec un Russe s'en alla.
> Où vont les belles filles,
> Lon la.

> "Mon ami Pierrot, tu babilles,
> Parce que l'autre jour Mila
> Cogna sa vitre et m'appela,
> Où vont les belles filles,
> Lon la.

> "Les drôlesses sont fort gentilles,
> Leur poison qui m'ensorcela
> Griserait Monsieur Orfila.
> Où vont les belles filles,
> Lon la.

> "J'aime l'amour et les bisbilles,
> J'aime Agnès, j'aime Paméla,
> Lise en m'allumant se brûla.
> Où vont les belles filles,
> Lon la.

"Jadis, quand je vis les mantilles
De Suzette et de Zéila,
Mon âme à leurs plis se mêla,
Où vont les belles filles,
Lon la.

"Amour, quand dans l'ombre où tu brilles,
Tu coiffes de roses Lola,
Je me damnerais pour cela.
Où vont les belles filles,
Lon la.

"Jeanne à ton miroir tu t'habilles!
Mon cœur un beau jour s'envola.
Je crois que c'est Jeanne qui l'a.
Où vont les belles filles,
Lon la.

"Le soir, en sortant des quadrilles,
Je montre aux étoiles Stella,
Et je leur dis: 'Regardez-la.'
Où vont les belles filles,
Lon la."

Gavroche, as he sang, was lavish of his pantomime. Gesture is the strong point of the refrain. His face, an inexhaustible repertory of masks, produced grimaces more convulsing and more fantastic than the rents of a cloth torn in a high gale. Unfortunately, as he was alone, and as it was night, this was neither seen nor even visible. Such wastes of riches do occur.

All at once, he stopped short.

"Let us interrupt the romance," said he.

His feline eye had just descried, in the recess of a carriage door, what is called in painting, an *ensemble*, that is to say, a person and a thing; the thing was a hand-cart, the person was a man from Auvergene who was sleeping therein.

The shafts of the cart rested on the pavement, and the Auvergnat's head was supported against the front of the cart. His body was coiled up on this inclined plane and his feet touched the ground.

Gavroche, with his experience of the things of this world, recognized a drunken man. He was some corner errand-man who had drunk too much and was sleeping too much.

"There now," thought Gavroche, "that's what the summer nights are good for. We'll take the cart for the Republic, and leave the Auvergnat for the Monarchy."

His mind had just been illuminated by this flash of light:—

"How bully that cart would look on our barricade!"

The Auvergnat was snoring.

Gavroche gently tugged at the cart from behind, and at the Auvergnat from the front, that is to say, by the feet, and at the expiration of another minute the imperturbable Auvergnat was reposing flat on the pavement.

The cart was free.

Gavroche, habituated to facing the unexpected in all quarters, had everything about him. He fumbled in one of his pockets, and pulled from it a scrap of paper and a bit of red pencil filched from some carpenter.

He wrote:—

> "*French Republic.*"
> "Received thy cart."
> And he signed it: "GAVROCHE."

That done, he put the paper in the pocket of the still snoring Auvergnat's velvet vest, seized the cart shafts in both hands, and set off in the direction of the Halles, pushing the cart before him at a hard gallop with a glorious and triumphant uproar.

This was perilous. There was a post at the Royal Printing Establishment. Gavroche did not think of this. This post was occupied by the National Guards of the suburbs. The squad began to wake up, and heads were raised from camp beds. Two street lanterns broken in succession, that ditty sung at the top of the lungs. This was a great deal for those cowardly streets, which desire to go to sleep at sunset, and which put the extinguisher on their candles at such an early hour. For the last hour, that boy had been creating an uproar in that peaceable arrondissement, the uproar of a fly in a bottle. The sergeant of the banlieue lent an ear. He waited. He was a prudent man.

The mad rattle of the cart, filled to overflowing the possible measure of waiting, and decided the sergeant to make a reconnaisance.

"There's a whole band of them there!" said he, "let us proceed gently."

It was clear that the hydra of anarchy had emerged from its box and that it was stalking abroad through the quarter.

And the sergeant ventured out of the post with cautious tread.

All at once, Gavroche, pushing his cart in front of him, and at the very moment when he was about to turn into the Rue des Vieilles-Haudriettes, found himself face to face with a uniform, a shako, a plume, and a gun.

For the second time, he stopped short.

"Hullo," said he, "it's him. Good day, public order."

Gavroche's amazement was always brief and speedily thawed.

"Where are you going, you rascal?" shouted the sergeant.

"Citizen," retorted Gavroche, "I haven't called you 'bourgeois' yet. Why do you insult me?"

"Where are you going, you rogue?"

"Monsieur," retorted Gavroche, "perhaps you were a man of wit yesterday, but you have degenerated this morning."

"I ask you where are you going, you villain?"

Gavroche replied:—

"You speak prettily. Really, no one would suppose you as old as you are. You ought to sell all your hair at a hundred francs apiece. That would yield you five hundred francs."

"Where are you going? Where are you going? Where are you going, bandit?"

Gavroche retorted again:—

"What villainous words! You must wipe your mouth better the first time that they give you suck."

The sergeant lowered his bayonet.

"Will you tell me where you are going, you wretch?"

"General," said Gavroche "I'm on my way to look for a doctor for my wife who is in labor."

"To arms!" shouted the sergeant.

The master-stroke of strong men consists in saving themselves by the very means that have ruined them; Gavroche took in the whole situation at a glance. It was the cart which had told against him, it was the cart's place to protect him.

At the moment when the sergeant was on the point of making his descent on Gavroche, the cart, converted into a projectile and launched with all the latter's might, rolled down upon him furiously, and the sergeant, struck full in the stomach, tumbled over backwards into the gutter while his gun went off in the air.

The men of the post had rushed out pell-mell at the sergeant's shout; the shot brought on a general random discharge, after which they reloaded their weapons and began again.

This blind-man's-buff musketry lasted for a quarter of an hour and killed several panes of glass.

In the meanwhile, Gavroche, who had retraced his steps at full speed, halted five or six streets distant and seated himself, panting, on the stone post which forms the corner of the Enfants-Rouges.

He listened.

After panting for a few minutes, he turned in the direction where the fusillade was raging, lifted his left hand to a level with his nose and thrust it forward three times, as he slapped the back of his head with his right hand; an imperious gesture in which Parisian street-urchindom has condensed French irony, and which is evidently efficacious, since it has already lasted half a century.

This gayety was troubled by one bitter reflection.

"Yes," said he, "I'm splitting with laughter, I'm twisting with delight, I abound in joy, but I'm losing my way, I shall have to take a roundabout way. If I only reach the barricade in season!"

Thereupon he set out again on a run.

And as he ran:—

"Ah, by the way, where was I?" said he.

And he resumed his ditty, as he plunged rapidly through the streets, and this is what died away in the gloom:—

> *"Mais il reste encore des bastilles,*
> *Et je vais mettre le holà*
> *Dans l'ordre public que voilà.*
> *Où vont les belles filles,*
> *Lon la.*

> *"Quelqu'un veut-il jouer aux quilles?*
> *Tout l'ancien monde s'écroula*
> *Quand la grosse boule roula.*
> *Où vont les belles filles,*
> *Lon la.*

"Vieux bon peuple, à coups de béquilles,
Cassons ce Louvre où s'étala
La monarchie en falbala.
Où vont les belles filles,
Lon la.

"Nous en avons forcé les grilles,
Le roi Charles-Dix ce jour-là,
Tenait mal et se décolla.
Où vont les belles filles,
Lon la."

The post's recourse to arms was not without result. The cart was conquered, the drunken man was taken prisoner. The first was put in the pound, the second was later on somewhat harassed before the councils of war as an accomplice. The public ministry of the day proved its indefatigable zeal in the defence of society, in this instance.

Gavroche's adventure, which has lingered as a tradition in the quarters of the Temple, is one of the most terrible souvenirs of the elderly bourgeois of the Marais, and is entitled in their memories: "The nocturnal attack by the post of the Royal Printing Establishment."

VICTOR HUGO

A Note About the Author

Victor Hugo (1802–1885) was a French writer and prominent figure during Europe's Romantic movement. As a child, he traveled across the continent due to his father's position in the Napoleonic army. As a young man, he studied law although his passion was always literature. In 1819, Hugo created *Conservateur Littéraire*, a periodical that featured works from up-and-coming writers. A few years later he published a collection of poems *Odes et Poésies Diverses* followed by the novel *Han d'Islande* in 1825. Hugo has an extensive catalog, yet he's best known for the classics *The Hunchback of Notre-Dame* (1831) and *Les Misérables* (1862).

A Note from the Publisher

Spanning many genres, from non-fiction essays to literature classics to children's books and lyric poetry, Mint Edition books showcase the master works of our time in a modern new package. The text is freshly typeset, is clean and easy to read, and features a new note about the author in each volume. Many books also include exclusive new introductory material. Every book boasts a striking new cover, which makes it as appropriate for collecting as it is for gift giving. Mint Edition books are only printed when a reader orders them, so natural resources are not wasted. We're proud that our books are never manufactured in excess and exist only in the exact quantity they need to be read and enjoyed.

bookfinity™

Discover more of your favorite classics with Bookfinity™.

- Track your reading with custom book lists.
- Get great book recommendations for your personalized Reader Type.
- Add reviews for your favorite books.
- AND MUCH MORE!

Visit **bookfinity.com** and take the fun Reader Type quiz to get started.

Enjoy our classic and modern companion pairings!